For a free Ebook or Kindle Book visit JoelJenkins.net.

Portions of Coming of Crow have been previously published.

Against the Gathering Darkness was first published in Dark Worlds © Summer 2010.

Wyrm Over Diablo was first published in How the West was Weird © 2010.

The Five Disciples was first published in Low Noon © 2012.

Long Night in Little China was first published in Six Guns Straight from Hell © 2010.

The Shadow Walkers was first published in Showdown at Midnight © 2011.

The Vanishing City was first published in Science Fiction Trails #9 © 2012.

Old Mother Hennessy was first published in Gunslingers and Ghost Stories © 2012.

The Steam Devil was first published in How the West was Weird 3 © 2014.

The Eye of Ulutoth was first published in Strange Trails © 2013.

The Coming of Crow is published by PulpWork Press.
Copyright © 2014 by Joel Jenkins.
ISBN-13: 978-0692225271
ISBN: 0692225277

THE COMING OF CROW

JOEL JENKINS

The Coming of Crow

Table of Contents:

Against the Gathering Darkness

Wyatt Earp slapped the flat of the crowbar into his open palm as he gazed at the solitary Indian that stood in front of him in the shadows of the Alaska Commercial Company's St Michael's warehouse. Being a bit of a character himself, he was a keen judge of character—but savages were always a bit of an enigma to him.

"Well, your papers seem square, Lone Crow—but what do I know? It's not often that I have an institution of higher learning pony-express a letter to me via Indian mail, but if this Miskatonic University wants to pay me five hundred cartwheels to put the licks in to Lake Bennett and look for this missing archaeologist then I'm up for some fresh air. Running the tavern here keeps me in sinkers and gravy, but I've been feeling a bit cooped. Besides, we've got a shipment that needs to go up to the mining camp at Lake Bennett."

Lone Crow threw the heavy bag of twenty-dollar silver coins on a barrel head. "I'm pleased that you accept their offer. What are you shipping?"

"They don't tell me," said Wyatt. "Let's find out. I like to go through the crates just to see if there's something I might need." He jammed the crowbar in at the edge of the lid and pried away the top of the crate with the angry screech of bending nails. Inside neat rows of red explosive cylinders were stacked and packed in sawdust, each trailing a long fuse."

"Hmmph,"said the former lawmen. "I'm glad we didn't light up a match to get a better view. You think they'd mark these crates better."

Lone Crow's face was somber. "How do we reach Lake Bennett?"

"We'll have to float up to Skagway, and then it's a two or three days riding a shank's mare or one day on horseback. You'll need to keep a sharp eye in Skagway or Soapy Smith will bilk you for everything you're worth."

"A friend of yours?" asked Lone Crow, and because of Lone Crow's somber expression Wyatt couldn't tell if the Indian was getting a dig in.

"A second hand acquaintance," explained Wyatt. "Through Bat Masterson. I've never had the pleasure of meeting Soapy in person."

Lone Crow nodded as if he understood. "I've met Bat once myself. When can we leave for Skagway?"

"The tramp steamer Queen will depart tomorrow. I suggest you do your drinking here. A bottle of brew runs a cartwheel in my tavern, and two and a half in Skagway, and I hear tell that Soapy likes to water the drinks in his establishments."

Lone Crow shook his head, his long, black hair falling over his shoulders. "I've sworn off the white man's firewater; it brings nothing but tragedy."

"Do you gamble? I've got a roulette wheel and a few California prayer books."

"I've seen many a man gunned down over a card game."

Wyatt cocked an eyebrow and the waxed end of his handlebar mustache dipped. "What's your point?"

"I don't have much use for gambling, either."

"Huh, I've never heard of a Mormon redskin, but suit yourself. There's a room over the tavern you can use tonight. The heat rises, so you'll keep nice and toasty. I'll have the cook get you some fixings to warm your belly"

"Much obliged," said Lone Crow, with an incongruous and studied drawl that would have made most think he was a gentleman banker, had they not seen his savage demeanor.

"So what in tarnation is an archaeologist doing up near Lake Bennett?"

"He claimed to have discovered remnants of a pre-Tlinget civilization.

His early letters were very promising, but the later letters were more confused and even paranoid. Then they ceased coming altogether."

"There's more than a few claim jumpers in them parts. It's very possible one of them thought he was digging a rich vein, not pottery shards. How many did he have in his party?"

"It was Professor Powell, his daughter, Abigail, and two students from Miskatonic. His letters tell that he hired three Tlingets as guides and diggers, but apparently they became frightened by some of his discoveries and decided to find employment elsewhere."

"Those savages are a suspicious lot," Wyatt glanced up and abruptly recalled who he was talking to. "Present company excepted, of course…"

"Of course," answered Lone Crow.

****

When Wyatt and Lone Crow disembarked down the peeling gang plank of the tramp steamer, Queen, the spring air was brisk and a chill wind blew in off the cold blue waters of the Pacific. Skagway was nestled at the base of Alaska's coastal mountain range, the peaks of which were perpetually glazed in a frosty white.

The town itself was an array of tents and ramshackle buildings thrown up along a muddy trek. Gold fever had hit and the town had swollen from a single dock and a handful of residents to a thriving metropolis chock full of every vice one could imagine. Fancy ladies leaned against the rails of garish saloons calling to the miners passing by, and gambling dens, some little more than canvas tents, were open to all comers that had a few coins or dollars to lose. Supply houses offered provisions for the miners, and guides stood on every corner selling their services at highly inflated prices.

Wyatt took a deep breath. "I smell opportunity in the air, perhaps I'll throw down a few cards before we move on to Lake Bennett."

"No time to waste," said Lone Crow. "Let's find some horses and a guide and get moving."

A man with a lazy eye, and wearing a preacher's collar nosed through the meandering crowd. "Excuse me, but I couldn't help but overhear you talking. My name's Father Browning, and I know where you can find some good horses for a reasonable price. One of my parishioners has a few horses that he lends."

"Father Browning," said Wyatt, and he shot a sly glance at Lone Crow. "My savage friend and I have been having a debate, and a sin-buster like yourself is just the man we need to settle our feud. He claims that the book of Job is in the Old Testament, and I maintain that it is in the New Testament—and since the both of us have neglected to bring our Bible prospecting, you can see our predicament."

"Indeed," said Father Browning. "It's a simple matter to settle—the book of Job is in the New Testament. Now about those horses…"

"The book of Job is in the Old Testament," interrupted Lone Crow. "At least in my Bible it is."

"Indeed, I believe you are right," said Wyatt. "Why Father Browning is no preacher at all, but a two-bit grifter dressed up like a priest to help relieve us of our money. What was the game, Father Browning? Perhaps you intended to sell us two dried up nags on the verge of death, or perhaps you intended to delay us in town a few days while you figured a way to rob us? Go tell Soapy Smith that Wyatt Earp is in town and he don't play that game."

Father Browning shrugged and swore in a most unholy fashion when he realized his disguise had been pierced. "I don't reckon your reputation means much around here. I ain't never heard of you…"

Wyatt scowled. "Soapy has and he knows better than to stick me in the neck. Tell him I want him to round me up a cart and a pair of good horses and at a reasonable price. We'll be at the Gold Dust Saloon quenching our thirst in the meantime."

"And who is that traveling with you? Soapy will want to know."

"Lone Crow," answered Wyatt.

The counterfeit priest's eyebrows raised up and his mouth hung open for the briefest of moments. "You the Lone Crow that took down the Sundance Kid and the Hole in the Wall Gang?"

"I had some help," answered Lone Crow.

"I'm sure Soapy will want to cooperate with you fellows," said Browning. "I'll find you later in the Gold Dust. Tell the bartender that the drinks are on Soapy." The counterfeit priest disappeared into the throng of disembarking miners and hustling stevedores anxious to unload the steamer.

"I'll be tarred and feathered," said Wyatt. "That fellow heard of you and not me. Were you really the one that gutted Sundance?"

"I used to hunt criminals for bounties," said Lone Crow. "I hear you've still got a warrant for killing a man in Arizona."

"Stillwell? That skeesick shot down my brother while he was leaning over a pool table," said Wyatt and his hand drifted toward the butt of his pistol. "Are you nosing for trouble?"

Lone Crow chuckled, the first time that Wyatt had seen the Indian smile since he had met him. "I've got no quarrel with you, Mr. Earp. As far as I'm concerned you were well within your rights. I just wanted to see how far you could be pushed before you got your ire up. You've got a reputation for being a dependable man in a pinch, but I wanted to see just how far someone would have to push before you stood your ground."

"I don't like people pulling my tail, Crow. Now I figure you owe me some straight up talk about yourself and our venture. What makes a professor so important that a respectable University is willing to pay me twenty-five silver slugs to find him, and why would they send you? Again, no offense intended, but an Indian doesn't tend to get much cooperation or respect—whether they killed the Sundance Kid or not."

"That's exactly why they requested that I look you up," said Lone Crow. "A white man is bound to get more cooperation from the locals, and especially a white man with a reputation like yours—not withstanding the Preacher's ignorance. And your skill with a gun may also prove of value, should our worst fears be realized."

"Claim jumpers, again," mused Wyatt. "These mountains are full of them." He spied the swinging sign for the Gold Dust Saloon far down Skagway's muck-mired main street and began to slog that direction.

"Or worse…" added Lone Crow.

"So what makes Professor Powell and his daughter worth five hundred dollars—plus whatever they are paying you?"

"Miskatonic University has some wealthy benefactors who put a high price on certain ancient artifacts that Professor Powell has proved proficient at obtaining. He happened to have mentioned a particularly coveted artifact in one of his letters—a gold encrusted hunk of jade called the Eye of Ulutoth, a particularly fine representation of the pre-Tlinget culture and one that is also rumored to have some occult value."

"So these benefactors don't really give a flying hoot about Professor Powell or his daughter Abigail."

"That's according to Hoyle," replied Lone Crow. "They charged me with bringing back the Eye of Ulutoth, but I told them I was a man hunter not a thing hunter, and that if they wanted my services they'd have to pay me to find the Professor and his daughter, and that if it were reasonably possible I'd bring them back the Eye of Ulutoth at the same time."

By the time they reached the Gold Dust Saloon a thick mist had rolled in from the mountain glens and a gloom had set upon Skagway. A dark feeling descended upon the unlikely companions and strangers eyed them warily, even with dread and fear. They kicked the mud off their boots against the sill of the saloon door and entered beneath the squeaking sign that continued to waver even though the chill wind had settled, and a thick fog descended.

Saloon patrons scattered when they saw Earp and Crow approach, and many raised their eyes from drink or nourishment to see the strange pair. A sallow-skinned saloon girl, bosom barely contained in a low cut blouse of red frills, approached them as they took a table in the corner of the saloon, both with backs to the wall. "What can I get'ya?"

"A Brigham Young cocktail and some eats," said Earp. "Soapy says that it's on him."

"I'll have some grub," said Lone Crow. "Whatever you've got."

The saloon girl cast a side-long glance at the Indian and spoke to Earp. "We don't serve no Tlingets here. There's a hog trough down the road for his type."

"This man ain't no Tlinget. Crow's my friend, so get him some grub before I wake snakes and have a word with a proprietor."

The saloon girl gave him a sullen stare. "You'd best hope that Soapy really did offer you drinks on the dead, because he has a way with dealing with people that cross him." She left with her nose in the air and an unseemly sway in her hips, but soon came back with a shot of whiskey for Wyatt and a plate of stew for Lone Crow.

Lone Crow nodded to Wyatt. "Thanks for putting in a word for me, but it wasn't necessary."

"Of course it was," said Wyatt. "My friends get the ace-high, not disrespected by some saloon wench."

Lone Crow ate in silence, the stew was more than palatable to a hungry man, and soon Wyatt was nursing a beer and working at his own plate of stew. "Tell me," said Earp. "How does an Indian learn to speak English like a city dude?"

"I was ten years old when the Comanches wiped out my tribe. Some settlers in South Colorado were kind enough to take me in and raise me."

"So you've got white step-parents in Colorado?"

"Horse thieves killed them while I was away hunting venison. Finding their killers was my first taste of manhunting. I do have a brother in Colorado, and a sister in California."

"Do you have those photographs of the Professor and his daughter handy?" asked Earp.

Crow removed a waxed envelope from the inside of his buckskin jacket and handed it to his cohort, and Earp sauntered up to the bar, greasing a conversation with the balding barkeep, who stood barely chest high behind the Gold Dust's bar, with a five dollar coin that he pushed across the greasy surface of the counter top.

"I'm working for a Massachusetts University that's had one of its professors gone missing in the Lake Bennett area."

"You might want to start by checking the miner's camp at Lake Bennett," said the barkeep while he polished a glass. "It's a rough place—a lot can happen to a man, especially a greenhorn mucking about in things he shouldn't."

"So you have heard of him?" asked Earp, he showed the barkeep the photographs in his hand. One depicted a respectable looking fellow in a tweed jacket and a bowtie, a clean-shaven face tending toward the long side, and wearing a somber expression. The other showed a younger woman with wild hair that curled around the oval of her finely-featured face, and fell in a thick profusion around her shoulders.

"He came through here about six months back. Thousands of prospectors come through hoping to strike it rich and I wouldn't have remembered him—except his daughter is a fine piece of calico, easy on the eyes and not easy to forget. Not too many women of that caliber passing through Skagway."

"And you haven't seen him—or her—since?"

"No ... I've heard stories, that's all and then there's those gunslingers that were looking for him. A week ago they came riding into Skagway, stinking like a rotting carcass, and asking questions about the Professor. Seems that he has something that they want."

"His daughter?"

The barkeep shook his bald head. "Something called the eye of Yewlishoth, or some such thing."

Lone Crow had crept up near the bar to better listen to the conversation, but hadn't yet interjected as some folks didn't much care to carry on a conversation with an Indian. "Ulutoth," he said now. "Professor Powell is said to be in the possession of such a thing."

The bartender gave Lone Crow a keen glance and spoke to Earp. "Ulutoth sounds right, but it's all gibberish to me."

"Perhaps Miskatonic University isn't the only institution of higher learning that wants this artifact," said Wyatt. "It looks like we'd better get a move on. If they've got a week start on us they may have already laid their mitts on this artifact, and I don't wager that the Professor and Abigail will have fared too well at the hands of some hired guns."

"Well that's the thing," hissed the bartender, who leaned close. "The gunslingers didn't go to Lake Bennett right off. They said something about the way being prepared, and they would wait here to deal with the heretics who would soon be arriving."

"So these gunslingers are still in town?" asked Wyatt.

The barkeep nodded. "They've got a couple of rooms down at the Shaky Horse. I know William, the proprietor there, and he says that they don't do much sleeping. They pace their rooms all night long, disturbing the other guests with their footsteps—that and their infernal stench. Their smell is driving out the other customers, but William is to skeered to kick them loose, and they paid up front in gold dust."

"Thank you," said Wyatt. "You've been very helpful."

"The funny thing is that they weren't the only ones inquiring about the Professor. We had some nancy-boy city slickers in town not two weeks ago asking about him and if we might have seen anything he dug up from that claim of his by Lake Bennett. They were offering a wad of Lincoln skins to anyone that had any information."

Wyatt had the good grace not to ask the barkeep just how many Lincoln skins he had procured from the nancy-boy city slickers. He and Lone Crow returned to their table, and the handlebar-mustached gunfighter speared a piece of stew meat with his fork. "The sooner Soapy can line us up with a pair of horses, the better. There's no point in looking for trouble here in Skagway when the job is up North at Lake Powell."

"I agree," said Lone Crow.

They lapsed into a silence while they devoured their stew, but an uneasy feeling hung in the air and both Earp and Crow noted the hostile and suspicious looks thrown their directions by the locals in the tavern.

Between mouthfuls of gristle-laden beef, Wyatt spoke out of the side of his mouth. "Doesn't seem as though we're welcome here."

"Get used to it," said Lone Crow. "You're breaking bread with an Indian."

"No, it's more than that," said Wyatt. "I've got a horrible feeling, and I just can't seem to shake it."

"My tribe used to call it shakpar; it roughly translates into a premonition of something bad."

The saloon doors swung open and in from the mist four gunslingers in tattered, earth-soiled clothing strode into the Gold Dust with an uneven, tottering gait. Their skin was pallid, their long hair matted and unkempt, and the stench of a long journey, or something worse, followed them.

The leader was a big man with a bristling beard and small mouth into which was thrust a smoldering cigar. He brushed back his stained overcoat, disturbing a few flies that rested on the hem of his pocket flap. He wore a tarnished shooting iron on his hip, and rested the heel of his hand upon the curve of the pistol grip. His cold, dead eyes roved the tavern. They lingered for a moment upon the strange pair eating stew, and both Wyatt and Lone Crow dropped their forks and let their hands fall to the hog legs belted to their waist, but then the bearded man turned to the bar and bellowed at the tavernkeeper.

"A bottle of rotgut for me and my men! We've ridden from the gates of hell and have worked up an unquenchable thirst." He laid down a moldering bag of gold dust, which the balding barkeep scooped up and locked away in his cash box before producing an unopened bottle of whiskey from behind the bar.

The bearded man and his three accomplices took bar stools while the barkeep filled their shotglasses, but many times they cast their glassy gazes over the shoulders of their damp riding coats, and stared long at Wyatt and Lone Crow, their purpled lips twisted into sneers or scowls.

"They're spoiling for a fight," said Wyatt.

"We'll give it to them if we must," said Lone Crow. "But first I finish my dinner. No one rushes my dinner."

Despite the pervading stench that threatened to ruin their appetites, Wyatt and Lone Crow finished scraping clean their plates, and mopping up the gravy with their crusty whole wheat bread. Only when they had finished their repast did they stand and move toward the door.

"Where are you going?" bellowed the bearded gunslinger. "We've got business with you heretics."

"You've got long overdue business with a bathtub," said Lone Crow, his hand already at the butt of his Colt. "Your business with us can wait."

Wyatt flashed an icy grin, but his hand was also warming the handle of his six-shooter. They sidled through the swinging doors of the saloon, and onto the boardwalk as the Bearded gunslinger and his companions came to their feet, their stools toppling to the floor. The doors swung shut and Wyatt leaped from the boardwalk and into the muddy street, the thick mist clinging and swirling about his limbs as if trying to slow their sudden movement. He took up position behind a full water barrel, while Lone Crow swung to the side of the doorway, with pistol in his hand.

It was only a moment before the Bearded gunslinger lurched through the door, gun in his fist, with his tattered cohorts right behind him. He caught sight of Wyatt behind the barrel and fired even as he lowered his aim. The bullet punched through Wyatt's hat and parted his hair. The lawman returned fire, putting two pieces of .45 caliber lead into the gunslinger's beefy body in the vicinity of his heart.

Gunsmoke lingered in the air and the Bearded gunslinger staggered forward, but to Wyatt's amazement he did not fall. Instead he let out a roar and fixed his black, black eyes on the target of his hatred. The rust-flecked pistol belched hot flame and the barrel tremored as streams of water spontaneously began to spill out where the bullets punched through the staves. Wyatt returned fire, peppering the Bearded gunslinger's torso with four more rounds, until his firing pin was falling on empty chambers. Dark, viscous puss leaked from the wounds, but the Bearded gunslinger still rocked forward with heavy boot falls, pausing only when his own pistol was empty, to let the smoking casings shells tumble to the ground and to replace them with fresh cartridges from his bandolier.

As the other gunslingers began to squeeze through the door, Lone Crow came from around the corner of the door frame and fired at point blank. His Eagle-Butt Peacemaker .45 barked four times, and each of the three gunslingers squeezing through the door reeled to the rough-hewn planks of the Gold Dust Saloon, one firing the hair-trigger of his double-action twice, and cracking a mirror on the wall, and another bullet holing a spittoon—the bullet creating an infernal racket as it ricocheted inside.

Lone Crow wheeled, his coat flapping like the dark wings of his namesake, and he put his last two bullets into the back of the Bearded gunslinger—mere distractions, that did nothing but slow the reloading time of the burly man, buying Earp a couple of seconds.

"Shoot for the eye!" shouted Crow.

Though Wyatt's pistol was just as empty as the Bearded gunslinger's he had the advantage of the hold out pistol tucked into the rear of his waistband. It was an all metal Colt First Model that held one .41 caliber bullet—excellent for discreetly resolving gambling disputes. With practiced speed and precision he whipped out this gun and aimed. Most practiced gunfighters realized that it was foolish to try any fancy shooting when engaged in a gun battle; shoot for the torso, the biggest and easiest part of the target to hit—it was that maxim that kept men alive. But Wyatt had already put six bullets into the burly chest of this enraged gunslinger and he seemed none the worse for the wear, so with each fraction of a second counting against life or death he took a moment to sight down the square barrel of his Colt and pulled the trigger, shooting the bearded gunslinger through his left eye.

With a groan, the bearded gunslinger crumpled to his knees, his half-loaded pistol falling onto the boardwalk, before he pitched face first alongside it. The stench was thick in Wyatt's nostrils as he climbed the steps to meet Crow and survey their grim handiwork.

"Three out of four shots you hit the gunslingers in the eye," mused Earp. "Not too shabby."

"Most of the shots were made from less than two feet away," replied Crow.

"Who are these men that don't fall when you shoot them?"

"Some call them demons, and some texts call them abominations," said Lone Crow. "They're dead men who have been given a semblance of life by evil many eons old; evil that existed before this earth was created, before Satan was thrown laughing from the heavens with his host of demonic angels."

Earp scowled. "That's not exactly what I was hoping to hear."

Most of the taverns patrons were leaving through the back door, not anxious to be a part of the gunfight's aftermath, and Wyatt watched them go. "So, how did you know that they could be killed by shooting them in the eye?"

"If thine eye be evil, the whole body shall be full of darkness," quoted Crow. "Destroy the eye and the darkness cannot stay."[1]

One of the gunslingers stirred, moaning as he tried to push himself into a sitting position. He failed and fell down to one elbow, black ooze streaming from the socket of his right eye. He fixed his one good eye on Earp and Crow as if memorizing their faces. "The way is being prepared," he rasped. "Ulutoth comes to make a prey of human kind. There's nothing you can do to stop i..."

The gunslinger convulsed and fell in a wretched, stinking heap.

"What in the infernal tarnation was that all about?" asked Earp.

Crow frowned. "It's becoming readily apparent that we're dealing with powers beyond our limited human comprehension. I should have known it when Miskatonic sought me out to find the Professor and his artifact. Perhaps the Tlingets will be able to shed some light on what is happening here."

Wyatt kicked at one of the putrid corpses and then spit as if to rid his palate of the taste of evil befouling it. "So why would the University hire

---

1 *Matthew 6:23*

you on to deal with this sort of thing? Are you some sort of shaman or something?"

Crow frowned. "No, but it seems I have an uncanny knack for running into strange things."

The barkeep came alongside Wyatt, his head coming to the lawman's chest. "Dad-blast-it. Their bodies seem to be decaying before my eyes, like they've been in the grave for three months already."

A loud voice interrupted the barkeep's horror laden reverie, and they looked to find the false preacher, no longer wearing his preacher's garb, had halted near a body. "Soapy warned me not to leave you boys alone for long or that you'd find yourself some trouble."

"It looks like Soapy was right," said Wyatt. "Did he come through for us with some horses and a cart?"

"They're waiting around the corner," said Preacher. "I'm to escort you to Lake Powell and serve as guide and bodyguard."

"How much?" growled Earp.

"Only fifty dollars," said Preacher. "With the Gold Rush on, that's half the going rate for a cart and guide to Lake Powell. Since the two of you are acquaintances, out of the goodness of his heart Soapy is absorbing the rest of his expenses."

"The goodness of his heart?" cracked Wyatt. "That's out and out highway robbery."

Preacher shrugged. "If you don't require my services I'll just leave you to hire another horse and cart. Might I suggest the teamsters down the…"

"That won't be necessary," said Lone Crow. "We'll pay your fee on arrival at Lake Powell."

Wyatt stepped over the festering body of one of the gunslingers Crow had slain. "Let's get down to the dock and load up the crates. I've got a shipment to deliver for the Alaska Trading Company."

"Yes, sirree," said Preacher, a sly smile playing at the corners of his lips.

****

White Pass was a rutted toll road littered with the bones and crow-pecked carcasses of dead horses that hadn't survived the brutal cold of the trek during the harsh winter, before spring had brought warmer winds. The going was slow over the rough roadways, and they were but one of many in the stream of prospectors with gold fever that had heard the rumors of wealth lurking near the shores of Lake Bennett, or more likely down the Yukon River in Dawson City.

It was a three day journey and Preacher kept up a non-stop prattling which Lone Crow found particularly tiring, but Earp took the opportunity to pump the con-man for information about Soapy Smith and his operations. It appeared to Crow that Earp admired the clever methods by which Soapy bilked the prospectors that poured through Skagway, but Crow found it irritating that one human being would go to so much effort to make a dishonest dollar.

"The funny thing about the telegraph office," said Preacher, "is that the wires run only as far as the walls of the building. The telegraph operator just pretends to tap out a telegram for the sourdoughs and the message goes nowhere. Soapy brings in a hundred dollars a day from that venture." He cast a glance at Lone Crow's impassive features. "I don't suppose you Indians use the telegraph, though."

"Just smoke signals," answered Crow in a dry tone. "When the signals don't get passed on we scalp the operator."

Preacher opened his mouth, but then shut it abruptly. Wyatt burst into laughter at his discomfort. "Why I believe that's the first time you've shut your bazoo since we started this journey."

Preacher frowned. "So what is this thing exactly that you and Crow are looking for in Lake Bennett?"

Crow glanced at Wyatt and he shook his head.

"We're looking for people," said Crow. "A Professor Powell and his daughter Abigail."

"They must be important people if a University sent you all the way across a continent to find them," said Preacher. The cart rounded a steep corner, and the vista opened up before them—a sea of tents edging upon the shores of the mountain-hemmed lake of crystal blue which reflected the glowering gray of the clouds overhead. At the lake's edge hundreds of boats were being constructed from lumber hewn from the surrounding forests and the sound of saw and axe carried in the crisp air. As they rolled into town, the steel-rimmed cart wheels throwing up thick clots of mud and the horses straining through the mire, a half dozen men rushed toward the cart. Both Wyatt and Crow's hands fell to the butts of their pistols, but before they drew they realized that the men intended nothing more than a verbal assault, calling forth sales pitches for boats, guides, taverns and tents warmed by camp strumpets.

"All we need," said Wyatt, "is directions to the Alaska Trading Company post."

Disappointed, a large-eared man with patchy whiskers pointed out a fenced area alongside the lake, behind which stood a rough-hewn cabin and skids full of freight. "That's it yonder, but if ye need a belly full of whiskey after ye drop your cargo, visit the Lakeside tavern. It's the tent with the flaps painted yeller."

"We'll do that," said Wyatt, and Preacher urged the horses onward.

Drunken fist-fights roared around them as they proceeded through the town, and hard-faced women called to them from dingy tents before they came to the gates of the Alaskan Trading Company's Lake Bennett outpost. Wyatt gratefully dismounted from the buckboard and stretched his legs while calling over the gate and rapping on it with the butt of his pistol.

In a few moments the door of the cabin pushed open on its leather hinges and a wolf hound bolted out the door, barking and growling as it hurled itself against the gate. Wyatt pulled back his gun hand to avoid the snapping jaws of the hound, and thumbed back the lever of his Colt in the case that the dog broke through the gate. Then a stolid man wearing a leather apron and a ten-gallon hat pulled down over his ears called from the shelter of the doorway.

"Ease up, Killer. You folks have some business with Allen Adlin or the Alaskan Trading Company?"

"I reckon so," replied Earp. "I've got four crates of dynamite in this here wagon, which need to be ferried up the Yukon."

Adlin came to the gate and took hold of Killer's collar and unhooked the hasp with his other hand. "Good, it'll bring a pretty penny up North. Get your injun to load them onto the sledge over there."

"He's not my injun," said Earp. "And I've personally seen him put a bullet through the eye of three different men, so if I were you I'd ask his help very respectful-like."

Adlin started, noted the large Peacemaker at Crow's side, then thought better of asking for any help at all. "That's okay. I'll tie my dog and unload the crates myself."

Crow jumped out of the cart and began to unload the first crate. "I've no objection to helping tote these crates, but perhaps you can help us on another matter."

"Why certainly, sir," said Adlin to Crow. "I'd be happy to help you and Mr…"

"Mr. Wyatt Earp," said the gunfighter, and Adlin blanched, his formerly ruddy face losing whatever color it still had left.

Crow set down the first crate within the fence and handed Adlin a picture of Professor Powell and his daughter. "We're looking for this man and woman. Have you seen them pass through?"

"Why, that's Abigail Powell. She's the washwoman that lives right down the street. Half the men in town are wishing they could court her, but she won't have nothing to do with none of them."

"And the man?"

"That's the Professor, but we haven't seen hide nor hair or him for nigh on five months. He claimed to have found pottery or some such thing from some ancient city in a played out mine on the east side of the lake. He had a couple of students working with him, and a handful of Tlingets digging for him, but they got spooked by something and went back to the tribe. Then one day Abigail wandered back into town, acting like she seen the devil hisself. She wouldn't say nothing about what happened to her father or his students, but started taking in laundry for the prospectors, and spends most of the day in front of a washtub down by the lake's edge."

****

Preacher tagged along, and they did indeed find Abigail Powell underneath an overcast sky and by the lakeside, the sleeves of her dress rolled to her shoulders as she worked grimy trousers over a washboard protruding from a suds-filled tub that had once been part of a whiskey cask. Her hair was a mass of dark red curls that was tied back at the nape of her neck. She barely favored the mismatched trio with a glance as they approached. "Set your laundry on the crate, and I'll have it cleaned and dried for you by tomorrow morning."

"You're Miss Abigail Powell?" asked Lone Crow.

She nodded. "That I am, but I'm afraid I have no time for polite conversation." She gestured to the crate and the tottering tower of unpleasant smelling clothing. "As you can see I'm quite busy."

"My name is Lone Crow and this is my associate Wyatt Earp. We're on commission from Miskatonic University to find you and your father and return you to Massachusetts."

Abigail ceased her scrubbing. Crow could see tears forming at the corners of her dark lashes, and she finally responded in a soft, tremulous voice. "I didn't think you'd ever come; I thought I'd be stuck here forever, trying to earn enough for passage back down the coast."

"And what of your father?" asked Earp. "Has he come to an ill end in the mine?"

She turned now, fully facing them and shook the suds from her pale arms. "You might say that. He found something in that mine that changed him—obsessed him. Oh, he's always been obsessive about his books and about knowledge, but this was something more—something that twisted his entire personality and slowly drove him insane."

"Was this thing the Eye of Ulutoth that he wrote to the administrators at Miskatonic of?" asked Crow.

Abigail began drying her arms with a rag. "That was what he called it. It was really a hideous-looking thing—a piece of jagged jade with specks of gold melted into its surface, and carved with obscene inscriptions."

"There were pictures?" asked Wyatt curiously.

"They weren't pictures, they were just runes," explained Abigail, her skin flushing with embarrassment. "But the translation my father made makes me shudder to even think of it, and the eye feels evil; just being in its presence fills you with despair and hopelessness."

"The townsfolk say that the Tlingets abandoned you," said Crow. "What happened to the students your father brought with you?"

"Mr. Penrose and Mr. Gifford," said Abigail, and she shook her head. "They just disappeared one day. I'd overheard talk in their tent of their growing dissatisfaction with my father and his questionable sanity—and I'm sure my father overheard it, too. The next morning their tent was gone, and all of their belongings, as well. I was angry that they didn't think to take me with them; I thought they'd be back at Miskatonic by now..."

"It's a long journey," said Lone Crow. "Perhaps our paths crossed somewhere along the way, but they had yet to return when I left Massachusetts six weeks ago."

Abigail began wringing her hands. "I do hope they've arrived safely."

Wyatt put his arm around the shoulders of the girl. "I'm sure they have. Travel from the Western coast isn't without its unavoidable delays."

She shifted uncomfortably, and slipped away from Earp to put on a shawl. She looked to the overhanging clouds with full gray bellies. "We've a stiff rain on the horizon. When can we depart for home?"

"First we need to take a look at the mine to see if I can find your father," said Crow.

Her face tightened in anguish. "It pains me to say this, Mr. Crow, but the father I know no longer exists. I stayed with him as long as I could, but his mind is gone. When he started rambling about shedding his own blood to release Ulutoth from his imprisonment I couldn't bear to stay any longer and witness his self-inflicted death. You'll probably find him dead at his own hand."

"We understand if you don't want to return to the mine," said Wyatt. "Perhaps you can suggest someone to guide us to the encampment."

"Al'ooni and Woosaani are in town offering to guide prospectors up the river."

"A loon eye?" asked Wyatt.

"Al'ooni and Woosaani are Tlingets that helped with the dig until the Eye of Ulutoth was uncovered."

"You think they'd have the guts to take us up there?" asked Wyatt.

"You'll have to ask them. You can probably find them out front of the Prospector's Saloon. I've got a cot in the woodshed out back of the saloon, and it's not far from here."

"A pretty girl like you shouldn't be sleeping in a wood shed," said Wyatt. "I'll rent a room for you, and you can sleep in a warm bed until we leave for Skagway."

"That won't be necessary. The shed is a lean-to against the stove wall of the saloon and it gets plenty warm—warm enough for me to hang and dry my laundry. Now if you'll excuse me I've got prospectors depending upon me for fresh clothing. If I don't have these ready tomorrow, there'll be some prospectors walking around in their unmentionables; not a pretty sight."

As they returned into the heart of Bennett's makeshift city, Preacher, who had been uncharacteristically silent, thrust his thumbs into his belt and laughed at Earp. "That purty piece of calico sure shot you down. Oh, it may not have been with bullets but she gave you the mitten, alright."

Earp's face tightened. "I was just being gentlemanly, nothing more."

"Oh, sure you was," said Preacher. "Listen, I've been a roper for long enough to know a come-on when I hear one. Maybe I'll telegram your woman in Nome, and she can decide whether or not it was an honest offer."

Earp's hand dropped to his gun and he turned with murder in his eyes. "You talk a good game. Can you back that with bullets?"

Preacher raised his hands in front of him. "Hey, I was just funnin' with you. No harm intended. You know that the telegraph in Skagway is bunco."

"I'd best not hear another word of this," said Earp. "From you or from anyone else. If I do I'll come looking for you."

Preacher pressed his fingers together, imitating a closed mouth. "Hey, I'll keep it dry. Not a word from my lips."

As they approached the split rail of the boardwalk in front of the Prospector's Saloon, they made out two Tlingets lingering nearby, wearing feathered caps of wicker, and colorful shawls threaded with ornate designs.

"You take the lead," said Wyatt to Crow. "I'm sure they'll be more friendly to a fellow Indian."

Crow snorted. "The Indian tribes spent thousands of years slaughtering each other before white man showed his pale face. I'm just as likely to be considered an enemy as you."

"I didn't mean..."

Crow raised a dark hand. "No offense taken, and I'll talk to them. You keep an eye on Preacher and see that he doesn't go stirring up trouble by cheating prospectors of their gold."

Al'ooni and Woosaani were both anxious for work, but Al'ooni balked when Crow explained where they needed to go.

"That mine is an evil place," said Al'ooni. "There are magics in this land much more ancient than the Tlinget, and much more powerful than the Tlinget magic. Professor Powell—he is not Professor Powell anymore, he is lookanaa."

"What is lookanaa?" asked Crow.

Al'ooni looked at his companion, and then Woosana attempted to explain. "There is a dark evil that dwells deep within these mountains. It has always existed, but the Tlinget have learned to dwell in harmony with it because we do not remind it of our existence, but the white men do not know how to dwell in harmony. White man uses his axe and gun to subdue nature, because they do not realize that it can never truly be tamed."

"And how does this relate to Professor Powell?" asked Crow.

Al'ooni smiled and tapped his head. "The Professor is a smart man, but not a wise one. He wants more and more knowledge to fill up his head, but doesn't have the wisdom to know that some knowledge is best left buried."

Woosana frowned. "We thought he was looking for gold, and then he discovered the Eye of Ulutoth and we knew he had deceived us. From that moment the dead began to walk, and Ulutoth began to corrupt the Professor's mind, slowly bending him to its will until he might willingly open up the gates that hold Ulutoth within the earth and seas."

"There are gates on the mine?" asked Crow.

Woosana laughed. "You have the skin of an Indian, but you think like a white man. The gates are not made by man, but are mystical forces that bind Ulutoth's servants within the earth."

"So what is it that Professor Powell has to do to open them?"

"Some act of evil," shrugged Al'ooni. "We do not know what exactly."

"Shedding his own blood," murmured Crow, remembering what Abigail Powell had said. "We must find him and stop him before the Eye of Ulutoth takes over his mind so completely that he kills himself and opens the gate."

"If you are correct," said Woosana, "then Ulutoth will not let you approach unhindered. Ulutoth has power to bring the wicked dead to life to perform its will."

"Then Ulutoth has already realized that we are a threat," said Lone Crow. "In Skagway, Earp and I fought men who were not wholly dead nor wholly alive."

Woosana and Al'ooni began to speak in their own tongue, making animated gestures and pointing at Crow and Earp as they spoke. Finally they came to some sort of conclusion and turned again to the Indian who waited patiently for them to finish their discussion.

"Pay us fifty dollars in white man's coin and we will take you there," said Woosana.

"That reminds me," interjected Preacher as he approached from behind. "I believe you and Earp owe me some Lincoln skins."

****

It was nearing ten o' clock when Abigail Powell finished hanging the laundry in the wood shed. Every bit of space not consumed by the stacked cord wood was taken by the criss-crossing lines slung with damp clothing, each piece wrung with her strong hands. The heat from the wood-fired stove brought a sheen of sweat to her face, so with her daily chores done, she stripped down to her worn petticoat and knelt in the wood chips by her cot to say her nightly prayers.

"Though I walk through the valley of the shadow of death, please preserve me and those you have sent to bring me home…"

Beyond the tinkling ivories of the saloon's piano she heard heavy footsteps outside the shed, guttural voices, and then the door shuddered, the slats snapping and breaking as a shadowed form forced its way through the splintered wreckage and into the wavering lantern light.

Abigail screamed as her eyes fell upon the rotting features of the fiend that stood within her humble abode, but her cry was muted by a thin wall and fell upon ears deafened by drink and raucous song.

****

As Al'ooni dipped a paddle in the cold waters of Lake Bennett and pushed the canoe across the dark depths, Wyatt crouched low on his seat and murmured to Lone Crow. "Ironic, don't you think, that they'd be so concerned about white man living out of harmony with nature, yet be so willing to take the white man's coin?"

"White man is full of hypocrisy," said Crow. "Why should the red man be any different?"

In the rear of the canoe, Preacher spun the full cylinder of his pistol, and then snapped it shut. He slipped it back into its leather holster and watched the orange moon slip from behind full bellied clouds that had yet to disgorge their fierce rains upon the earth. "When I told Soapy that I'd see that Wyatt didn't come to any harm, I didn't realize I'd be exploring played out gold mines in the dead of the night."

"I told you that it wasn't necessary for you to come along," said Wyatt.

"You've never met Soapy in person, have you?" said the Preacher. "When he gives an order he expects it to be carried out to the letter. See, if he found out that I didn't come with you, my career in Soapy's gang would be over very quickly. What do you think Powell found in that there mine of his that's got so many people interested?"

Earp frowned beneath his massive handlebar mustache, his face shrouded in shadow as he lifted his oar. "It's hard to say, but here's hoping that we find Powell alive, and can drag the addle-headed dandy across Lake Bennett by sunrise."

Preacher rolled a cigarette while the other four paddled. "You don't really buy all this bosh about evil forces within the earth and dead men rising, do you?"

"I don't know," said Earp. "Those men we fought in Skagway weren't normal men. I shot one six times at close range and he didn't even flinch."

Preacher struck a match and the flare of the flame illuminated the harsh lines of his face as he sucked his cigarette into a slow burn. The scent of smoldering tobacco drifted across the lake. "What about you, Crow?

You believe it?"

"I believe it," said Crow. "But for your own peace of mind, find a way to rationalize or deny it. Once you go down this road there's no going back."

Preacher laughed off Crow's warning, but his chuckle sounded strained as it echoed from the lake's glimmering surface. As they reached the shadowing trees of the far shore, a light breeze rippled the surface of the lake and the scent of impending rain hung in the air. They leaped onto the rocky shore and Earp hoisted a burlap rucksack over his shoulder.

"What have you got in there?" asked Preacher. "Some magic Indian trinkets?"

"You might call them magic trinkets," said Earp. "Just a little something I borrowed from the Alaskan Trading Company."

"There's another canoe pulled into the shrubs over here," said Al'ooni.

"Another prospector?" asked Earp.

"Possibly," answered the Tlinget, but behind the masking scent of Preacher's tobacco smoke Crow could smell a lingering stench.

A narrow trail climbed between a screen of thrusting branches and Crow climbed into the shrouding darkness, his keen eyes using the faint illumination of the moon to guide his feet. Twenty feet up the trail, he found a scrap of torn white cloth clinging to a branch. He plucked it away and felt the texture of the cloth between his thumb and forefinger.

Earp came up alongside of him and instantly identified the piece of cloth. "It looks like a piece of petticoat to me."

An impression thrust itself upon Crow's mind, and he again remembered Abigail Powell's words, but now he fully understood what she had not. "Al'ooni, lead the way. We must hurry."

As Al'ooni pushed his way to the front of the line, they heard a horrible cry from the lake where Preacher had lingered to enjoy the last of his cigarette, and then a moment later they saw him burst through the screen of foliage at the head of the trail, his eyes wild and his mouth agape. "The lake! They're coming out of the lake!"

Crow stepped higher on the trail, and through a hole in the foliage he had a clear view of the wind-rippled waters that lapped and slurped against the rocky shore. Thrusting from the cold, caliginous depths were dead rotting things, sloshing and trudging to the shore, eyes glowing with an evil light—the wicked dead brought to life by the lingering powers of the waiting Ulutoth.

"It's time for those magic trinkets," said Crow.

Earp dropped to one knee and opened the mouth of the rucksack. He produced a three stick bundle of dynamite with the fuses twisted together, and handed the bundle to Crow. "Courtesy of the Alaskan Trading Company."

Preacher wheeled and began firing wildly into the dark, the flame of his gun flashing in the night, and the sound of the shots echoing across the lake. A couple of his bullets fired true, and smacked into rotting flesh, but the undead things lurched forward, as if they were unaware that they had been struck.

Lone Crow held the dynamite in front of him as Earp fired a match on a nearby rock and ignited the fuse. Crow waited a moment as the fuses began to burn down and then he hurled the bundle, sparking through the air so that it fell in the canoe as a host of reeling dead emerged dripping around it.

The earth rumbled and shook as the canoe burst into jagged shards of wooden shrapnel that sliced and sundered the wicked dead, the roiling flame lighting the night as if it were day and hurling torn limb and torso, so that a gory rain of pallid flesh fell upon the canopy of the forest and back into the depths of the lake.

Earp laughed out loud. "How's that for some magic, Preacher!"

But Preacher was in no mood for humor, and staggered up the trail, hands covering his ringing ears and his face spattered with dark gore.

"Quick," said Woosana. "Up to the caves before Ulutoth gathers his strength and sends more of the dead against us."

So, drunk on fear, they reeled through the darkness, climbing high above Lake Bennett, casting dread glances over their shoulders and into the tar-like shadows that painted the thick forest around them.

****

As Orrin Powell tied his horror-stricken daughter to the mining cart, he no longer resembled the respected professor of archeology that he once was. His broken spectacles lay somewhere within the mine shaft, and his face was thick with beard. His subservience to the Eye of Ulutoth had come at a cost and he looked twenty years older than when he had first began excavations at the old cavern; brown hair had turned a frosty white, thick lines had formed in his brow and jowl, his brilliant mind was broken, and his eyes shone with insanity.

Abigail, partially recovered from the sheer terror of her nighttime abduction by some rotting denizen of the deep, struggled against the ropes that bound her, calling out.

"Father, Father! It's me, Abigail! Why are you doing this to me?"

Professor Powell did not respond, but he clutched at the Eye of Ulutoth and fondled its cold, jade surface and the voice rumbled again in his mind, commanding him to do evil. "You must die," he croaked. "I must shed my own blood to free Ulutoth from his imprisonment." His right hand closed around the wood handle of a miner's pick, so that he could obey the edict of Ulutoth, but then the voice rumbled again in his brain—a warning of others coming to interrupt the sacrifice.

****

When the sound of Abigail Powell's voice filtered through the dense brush, they renewed their frenetic climb up the dark, treacherous path, jagged branches tearing and slapping at them. Woosana led the way, nimbly negotiating the path he had traveled many times before, and spurred on by a glimpse of Abigail's pale and struggling form tied to the mining cart. The skin of her wrists was chafed and bloodied as she tried to tear free of her bonds.

Abigail heard the rustle of brush and saw the Tlinget guide emerge from the undergrowth, recognized his features in the moonlight as his wicker hat caught on a branch and tumbled away, and called out a warning. "Woosana, watch out!"

Woosana cast a glance to his side and saw a flicker of movement as Professor Powell swung a miner's pick. Abigail's warning saved him from having his skull punctured by the sharp point, but he was not able to move quickly enough to altogether avoid the blow. The pick buried in the flesh of his shoulder, the bloody point standing out the other side of his arm, and he fell with a horrible scream of pain.

The Professor did not relinquish his grip upon the pick, and wrenched it from the wound in a bloody spray while Woosana writhed upon the ground. He raised it high, ready to finish the howling Tlinget but, at that moment, Lone Crow emerged from the brush and he fired the eagle-butted Peacemaker in his hand. Flame and smoke burst twice from the muzzle, and the Professor stumbled, a pair of crimson blossoms forming on his vest. He staggered backward toward the cart on which his straining daughter was tied, the pick falling from his hands, and the jade and golden Eye of Ulutoth tumbling from the loosened pouch at his waist as he pitched over. But before the last vestiges of life left him, he performed one last evil act. As he dropped to the ground, he grabbed hold of the brake handle on the cart and wrenched it loose, so that the cart began to roll down the track and into the beckoning darkness of the cave mouth.

"I shed my own blood," he croaked. "That the servitor of Ulutoth may come forth…" The Professor's eyes rolled back into his skull and he lay across the tracks as the screeching cart picked up speed and Abigail's screams were swallowed up in the depths of the cavern.

Lone Crow moved quickly, chasing the cart into the blackness of the cave mouth where the moonlight could not penetrate and his eyes could not pierce the veil of inky shadows. He heard the distant screech of the cart's wheels echo up to him, but then all was silence. Rather than blindly pursue the cart and tumble down an open mine shaft, Crow returned to the mouth of the cavern and used a flint to ignite an oil lamp.

He could see Al'ooni crouched down by Woosana, trying to ease his pain, even while Preacher searched the tall grasses by the light of the moon. Earp stood over the dead body of Orrin Powell. "Looks like the Professor will be returning to Massachusetts in a coffin. Is the girl healthy?"

"I couldn't see well enough to find out," said Crow. "I'm going back in for her."

Al'ooni looked up from the sufferings of his brother and called to Crow. "Miss Abigail is as good as dead now. The lookanaa will devour her, and it will eat you, too, if you go into the cave to find her."

At one point in his life Lone Crow might have ignored Al'ooni's warnings as foolish ramblings, but he had seen too much to dismiss them out of hand. "Can I borrow your rucksack?" he asked Wyatt.

Earp nodded and let the rucksack slide off his shoulder until he held the strap in his hand. He extended it to Crow who accepted it, but kept it well clear of the lantern in his other hand.

"I'm going with you," said Earp.

Crow did not answer, because out of the corner of his eye he saw Preacher lift something from the grass and tuck it into his pocket, then without saying a word the con-man from Soapy's gang slipped back into the forest.

"Preacher has the Eye of Ulutoth," said Crow.

Earp glanced over his shoulder and saw Preacher's dark form disappearing into the brush. "I'm going after him. You tend to the girl."

The wind gusted and in the black heavens, the clouds finally opened up their swollen bellies and began dumping torrential rains upon the earth. Crow watched Earp disappear into the forest, pistol in hand and then Crow entered the shelter of the mine shaft, the wind moaning behind him, and his lantern a wild, flickering flame as he descended along the rail line.

The black walls of the cavern closed around him, pick-gouged walls painted with the creosote of torch flame, and other walls scrawled with the pictographs of an unknown race. This shaft had been ancient before the ancestors of the Tlingets and Chilkoots had found this land, and only more recently had prospectors discovered a vein of gold, mined it and abandoned it, while spreading the rumors of the cave-paintings that had eventually reached the ears of Professor Powell and piqued his interest.

A shriek echoed up the shaft and, encouraged that Abigail Powell was still alive, Crow redoubled his speed, ignoring a number of diverging passages and plunging deeper into the cavern. As he surged forward, his booted foot struck upon something loose and flapping like a tarp, but when he halted and played the lantern light upon the thing, he shrank back in horror. It was no tarp, but the clothing and skin of a man that hung loosely over a framework of bone, as if the flesh had been sucked away from the poor fellow, leaving it an empty, sagging envelope.

Thankfully, Crow had no time to ponder the man's horrific fate, but only another hundred yards down the shaft he encountered another such empty shell next to a pile of moldering valises and the rotting canvas of a tent—then he recalled Professor Powell's two assistants who had disappeared one night after arguing with the Professor. Their journey had been much shorter than Abigail had presumed.

In the hazy light of the lantern, Crow caught a glimmer of pale flesh and white petticoat atop the mining cart, which rested haphazardly against a pile of mining rubble. Abigail twisted and heaved, vainly attempting to wrench her bleeding wrists away from the sturdy knots that her deranged father had tied. She convulsed and attempted to sob or to scream, Crow could not be sure which, but her tongue could find no voice in the utter abysses of her fear.

Then, Crow caught a glimpse of a keeling shape that loomed, nearly filling the shaft of the mine in the far rays of the feeble illumination cast by his lantern. It moved forward with unsteady gait on four-toed feet that bristled with chitin, its spindly legs supporting a twisted, bulbous travesty of form. Its head was massive, with great black eyes deep as the cold outer wastes of the cosmos, and great horns—hollow at the tips and stained with gore—that thrust forth from the knotted flesh. For a moment, confronted with this mind-blasting abomination, a perversion of nature and all its laws, Crow was frozen to the spot, unable to move his limbs, or even blink.

He had thought himself inured against such horrors, having before encountered strange and unseemly creatures whose existence lurked only at the edges of the wildest human imaginings, but complete despair engulfed him in a dark ocean of hopelessness which threatened to overwhelm and drown him. Though his lips could not move to utter the words, he prayed to the Great Spirit as his people referred to the Supreme Being—the Heavenly Father of which his foster parents had taught him—and he begged for release.

****

Preacher had a long head start and it wasn't until they reached the rocky shore of Lake Powell that Earp caught him dragging the hidden canoe, which Al'ooni had spotted earlier, into the water among the still-smoldering shards of the other. Earp paused at the mouth of the trail and drew a bead on Preacher.

"Stop there, Preacher—and throw down the Eye of Ulutoth."

Preacher paused, holding onto the canoe, his legs still in the icy water, heavy rain pocking the surface of the lake, and dripping from the brim of his hat. "So you do know about the Eye, after all. No more pretending that you don't know nothing about what the Professor dug up in that cave, eh?"

"It was none of your business," said Earp, "And it still isn't, so drag that canoe back to shore or I'll shoot you where you stand."

"I'm sorry, Earp," replied the Preacher, as he tried to suppress a sly smile. "But I've got a much better offer waiting for me if I get this pretty trinket back to Skagway. See some queer fish showed up a couple of weeks before you and the redskin aired your ugly faces there, and they offered a thousand dollar bounty for this here jade and gold eye."

"You won't be able to collect your bounty in hell," growled Earp as he tightened his finger on the trigger.

Instead of quavering in fear, Preacher laughed and hopped into the bark canoe. "You'll be there sooner than I, Earp."

Even as Preacher clambered into his canoe, Earp heard a rustling in the brush behind him—some long dead thing imbued with the infernal powers of Ulutoth and shambling through the trees, a tomahawk in its hand and rotting scraps of clothing hanging from its sunken frame. Its eyes glowed with unholy light as it raised its axe. Earp fired twice, putting two bullets through its right eye, the sounds of the shots swallowed up in the roar of the deluge. The thing staggered forward and fell at Earp's feet, a foul mound of rotting, wormy flesh.

Earp whirled, returning his attention to Preacher lest the con-man put a bullet in his back. Instead, he found that Preacher had used his brief respite to paddle far out onto the choppy waters of the rain-swept lake, and he bellowed a mocking laugh at the former lawman stuck on the shore, while he raised a small jade object in his hand.

"Is this what you wanted, Earp? Come and get it. I'll wait for you while you swim out."

Earp grunted and raised his pistol. It was dark, a long shot, the weather was bad, and the choppy waters made Preacher an erratic target. For the briefest of moments the bead of his gun sight rested just below Preacher's sternum and Earp squeezed the trigger. The canoe rocked, temporarily swallowed in a trough, and the bullet went high, taking off Preacher's index finger and sending the Eye of Ulutoth spinning into the deeps of Lake Bennett.

Preacher cried out and reached out as if to catch the lost artifact, but lost his balance in the shifting canoe, and toppled into the heaving waters, capsizing the canoe so that it rapidly filled and foundered.

Earp raised an eyebrow, amazed at the results of his shot. "Lucky shot," he mumbled to himself. But when he called out to the drowning man there was more bravado in his voice. "Who's swimming now, Preacher?"

****

No sooner had Crow recited the words of prayer in his mind than he was given the strength to break free from the horrible bonds of fear that had held him as surely as chains on the limbs of a slave. And though complete revulsion and fear still washed through him as the abomination tottered forward, he found the will to reach into Earp's rucksack and pluck forth a stick of dynamite. He thrust the fuse into the flame of the oil lamp and pulled it away as the wick began to spark and coruscate. As the fuse began to burn down, he ran toward the abomination and hurled the sputtering stick, so that it whirled down the dark corridor and bounced to the creature's feet.

For a moment the servitor of Ulutoth cast malign eyes at the burning dynamite, and Lone Crow took the opportunity to cut Abigail loose from the cart, his hunting knife gleaming a dull yellow as he severed the ropes. She tried to speak as he pulled her off the cart, but fear had taken hold of her tongue and Crow pushed her down behind the pile of rubble.

"Cover your ears!" ordered Crow, and he followed suit just before a deafening explosion rocked the mine shaft, and the world became a rush of hot wind and pelting rubble. The force of the explosion picked up one end of the cart and tumbled it backward, so that the open side fell over the top of them, and they were plunged into darkness for a brief moment before the cart was whirled away and splintered against the far bend in the cavern wall.

As the tumult died, Crow stood and pulled Abigail to her feet, her red hair a wild halo about her pale face and crimson lips. The Indian glanced back and saw the misshapen form of the servitor still standing, the dark eyes vacant as if perhaps the explosive concussion had temporarily stunned him. But servitor of Ulutoth was evil incarnate, birthed in the cold, alien voids of the universe and its physical form could not be so easily harmed.

When Crow saw that the dynamite had only momentarily shaken the horned abomination, he began to drag Abigail up the mine shaft, until her lost circulation was restored and her own limbs would support her. When the Indian saw that she could walk on her own he halted.

"Get to the top of the shaft as quickly as you can," said Crow. "Whatever you do, don't look back."

"What about you?" stammered Abigail.

"I've got some business to take care of," said Crow. "If I don't make it out, Wyatt Earp or the Tlinget guides will get you back to Bennett."

"Al'ooni and Woosaani?"

"That's right," said Crow. "Now get moving."

Numb from the recent events, the disheveled Abigail staggered toward the mine's entrance in her torn and dirt-stained petticoat. Crow fished a roll of fuse out of Earp's rucksack and stacked a pile of the remaining dynamite. He wrapped these together in three-stick bundles, and twisted together the fuses with a longer length of fuse that he reeled out behind him. Each time he came to a support beam he wedged one of these bundles into it. As he lit the fuses one by one, he saw dark shadows gathering as the servitor came reeling after the Indian, palpable evil preceding him—chilling the very marrow of Crow's bones.

Rising in a haze of smoke, Crow took to his heels for the mouth of the cavern. Behind him, the sputtering fuses raced toward the wedged dynamite, and the malign servitor of Ulutoth reeled after him. Unused to such resistance from mortal nourishment, it sent a mental blast of hatred and despair which pushed through Crow's mind like a tidal wave, obliterating all thought and reason, and burying them in unhinged oblivion.

Crow clutched at his head, and his hat tumbled off as he careened to the floor, screaming the agony that cavorted and careened inside his skull. The servitor reeled nearer, and lowered its great hollowed horns, so to suck out the innards of its writhing prey. Then, far down the mine shaft, the first bundle of explosives went off, sending a super-heated wave of rubble and flame billowing upward, even as a portion of the mine collapsed in upon itself.

Though untouched and unharmed, the servitor of Ulutoth was momentarily distracted by the great rumbling within the earth and, in that brief moment, Crow's thinking cleared and he scrambled away as the alien thing looked aside. Using every bit of speed he could muster, he jarred bone and muscle, negotiating the uneven floor of the dark cavern, and then he hurled himself out the opening of the cave mouth even as the other bundles of dynamite exploded, one after another, in an earth-rending cacophony. Rubble spattered and stung against Lone Crow's exposed skin, and flame singed his dark hair. The mine shaft crumbled inward, tons of crushing rock filling the void as the support pillars were blown to splinters.

Choking dust billowed into the air, and Crow fought his way free of the cloud to find the injured Woosana waiting for him on a log at the edge of the clearing, blood soaking the bandage his brother had tied around his arm, and cradling his battered rifle. Woosana managed a feeble smile when he saw Lone Crow emerge, like a specter, from the rolling clouds of gray dust.

"Once again the lookanaa is trapped within the earth," said Woosana.

"Is Al'ooni with the Powell girl?" asked Crow.

Woosana nodded. "They went on ahead. I was too weak to go with them. I said I'd wait here to shoot the lookanaa should he devour you and emerge from the cavern."

"I doubt if I would have been enough nourishment," said Crow. "It seems that the servitor of Ulutoth was held in that cavern by some force that it could only overcome if someone willingly sacrificed his own kin."

"But the jade eye?" grunted Woosana. "It must be destroyed. It corrupted the Professor, made him an evil man. Given time, it could call forth Ulutoth, itself."

"Perhaps," said Crow as he cast a glance over his shoulder at the collapsed mine, the rain still beating down the roiling gray dust.

****

At the shores of Lake Powell they found Abigail Powell huddled beneath the shelter of a sturdy tree, bundled in Earp's duster while the former lawman and the Tlinget, A'looni, stood guard—weapons drawn, and peering with dread into the shifting shadows among the rain-lashed foliage. Lightning flashed and Crow eased the burden of Woosana to the earth, beneath the tree. In that brief moment of flickering illumination he saw the prow of the last canoe sinking beneath the frothy waves.

"It looks like we'll be taking the long way around the lake, come morning," said Crow. "Where is Preacher?"

"Sunk, along with the canoe, and the Eye of Ulutoth," said Earp, his mouth a dark shape in the shadows of his massive handlebar mustache. "It looks as though Miskatonic University will have to be satisfied with you bringing back just a third of what they hoped."

Crow's raven hair gusted behind him and rolling thunder drowned his reply.

"It seems," continued Earp, "that Miskatonic wasn't the only one looking for that blasted jade eye. Someone had offered Preacher a pretty penny for it."

"I'm not surprised," said Crow. "Preacher talks a lot, and he let a few hints slip that there might be others looking for the eye."

Rain streamed off the brim of Earp's hat as he tilted his head forward. "I wouldn't trust the intentions of anyone who wants that eye—even the associates of Miskatonic that hired you to find it."

Crow grinned and another flash of lightning illumined his craggy features. "As far as I'm concerned, the eye is irretrievably lost. I'm not diving for it. It can stay at the bottom of the lake and keep company with the fish."

"Ain't that the truth," said Earp, and he slapped the pocket that contained a deck of cards. "And since you buried Ulutoth under a hundred ton of rock, it looks like we've got time for a couple rounds of poker."

Crow's eyes narrowed. "I told you before, Wyatt. I'm not a gambler."

"Not a gambler?" said Earp. "What do you call a man who stays in a mineshaft with a rabid beast and lights enough dynamite to level a mountain?"

Wyrm over Diablo

Carina Crawley leaned forward over the table in the eastward bound diner car of the Pacific Railroad Company. She spoke words of power—hypnotic suggestion enforced with ancient incantations and the blood charms that incongruously adorned her wrists; words like the chains that bound Cerberus to the gates of Hades; words falling from slender lips on perfumed tongue; words like the serpent that enthralled and enticed Eve to partake of the forbidden fruit.

"You will give me the Eye of Ulutoth, and you will give it to me now."

A pure-blooded Indian sat in the seat across from her, hair the color of raven's wings falling in disarray about the shoulders of his weathered duster. His cowboy hat sat on the table next to him, and his right hand fell to the Eagle-butted Colt Peacemaker that he wore habitually at his side, a holy relic capable of killing that which is already dead—for though the woman was slender and of no menace to the casual eye, Lone Crow knew that he was in every bit of danger as if he were standing amidst a hail of bullets. He squirmed as her words ate into his brain, but he resisted because he had been endued with the rights to call upon another higher power.

Lone Crow's dark eyes observed his opponent. Her waist was tightly-corsetted and her maroon dress pinned at the neck and wrists. A few strands of hair the color of freshly-turned New Mexico tilth escaped the bun at the nape of her neck, and were plastered to her forehead beneath her Parisian hat. Dusk was falling and the sky was a wide panoply of orange and reds arrayed over the parched Arizona prairies and thirsty sagebrush.

"I've heard of you Miss Crawley—you're a member of Blavatsky's Aryans, an offshoot of the less than benign Theosophic Society. What errand of mischief are you on, and what could you possibly want with the Eye of Ulutoth?"

Crawley licked her forefinger and raised it in the air. "Score one point for the ignorant savage, but you're not unknown to me, Mr. Crow. I know about the work you've been doing for Miskatonic University, and some of the significant items that you've recovered for them."

Lone Crow shrugged in a self-effacing manner. "Most everyone's heard some tall tales about me. It's only for the reason of my somewhat exaggerated reputation that the white man even tolerates my presence on this train."

"Well, who would want to tell a reputed gunfighter that he can't buy a train ticket?" mused Carina Crawley. "How many men did you kill in Brantsville when they tried to lynch you for killing that woman?"

"It wasn't me that killed her," said Crow. "Now if you'll excuse me, I've a matter which needs my attention." The Indian began to stand, but Crawley's hand shot out and gripped him around his left wrist. Several passengers noticed the action and the lips of ladies dressed in finery began to flutter even while they fanned themselves for a respite from the heat.

"If by 'matter' you're referring to a certain Abigail Powell, then I can assure you that she is already being attended to by a colleague of mine."

Crow's dark eyes narrowed. "What are you saying?"

"Do you have an inkling how tongues wag when a white woman is seen traveling in the company of a savage? Why the gossip is unseemly and even if I didn't have the ability of location I could have found you by the trail of dead bodies—some blown into very small pieces. Do you carry a crate of dynamite with you wherever you go?"

"You might be surprised what I consider essential travel gear."

"And you might be surprised at the rumors I've heard. Why, did you know that some people refer to you as Abigail Powell's savage lover?"

"I'm not concerned with what people think, Miss Crawley. Now unhand me before I give the gossips on this train something real to talk about."

"My, my..." clucked the earth-haired witch. "It seems I've touched a nerve. You're in love with Miss Powell aren't you? But you don't dare express your feelings for her because you fear you're nothing but a savage in her eyes." Crawley's eyes glittered as she leaned forward, delving into the dark places of Crow's mind. "Why don't you just take what you want? You've got the power and might makes right. There's nothing wrong with indulging your secret desires. The Theosophic Society has a place for men like you, men not afraid to take their rightful place among the great and powerful—and those men can have any woman they want, no matter the color of their skin."

Crow wrenched his arm away from the witch, the sensation of her touch still crawling on his skin and the nausea of her intrusion still worming in his mind. "Stay out of my head, woman—or so help me I'll shoot you where you sit."

"You'd shoot a helpless woman aboard a train? You'd become a hunted man—just like all the criminals you've hunted down, captured or killed. But I like this side of you, it shows a ruthlessness that I find admirable. However, if you don't want Abigail Powell to come to a painful end by the hands of my associate then I suggest you be more cooperative. Mr. Shima has Miss Powell in custody in her private apartment, but he has thirsty knives and a penchant for using them."

"I'm afraid that your efforts are wasted," said Crow. "The Eye of Ulutoth has never been in my possession, and it is resting at the bottom of a lake in Alaska. May it stay lost forever."

Carina Crawley cursed in a very unlady like manner. "You have no clue what that artifact means."

"Unfortunately, I have some idea," said Crow.

"No you don't!" snapped Crawley. "You think that the artifact is inextricably linked to Ulutoth, but it is not. It is a device that allows passage at will between the physical plane and the outer dimensions where the dark powers reside. The trigger is the shedding of innocent blood."

Crow glowered, buying time while he figured the best course of action—one that might save Abigail from the knife-happy Mr. Shima. "You've no qualms about shedding innocent blood to bring forth some evil?"

"Qualms?" laughed Crawley. "I've bathed in the blood of innocents, listened to their screams while the flames of their burning huts licked into the midnight sky. I revel in the power that their fleeting lives bring me in their sacrifice."

Though Crow hesitated to leave such a creature as Carina Crawley free to perpetrate further evil upon mankind, his first concern was Abigail Powell. "Now that you see I don't have the item that you're looking for, I should think you would have no problem asking Mr. Shima to release my acquaintance and let us be on our separate ways."

Carina Crawley's eyes were dead of emotion. "It's not so easy as that, Lone Crow. I thought that perhaps our encounter here on this train, on this day, at this very hour was a grand convergence of dark design arranged by the Wyrm Orribillus, but now I see it is merely unfortunate coincidence and that you, Abigail Powell and everyone else upon this train will serve as nourishment for Orribillus when she rises from the ashes at the bottom of Diablo Gulch."

"What are you talking about?" demanded Crow.

"I'm talking about resurrection, about destroying the old patriarchal order and remaking the world under the matriarchal power of the Wyrm."

"And just how is the Wyrm Orribillus being brought forth?" asked Crow.

"Eons ago she was vanquished from the mortal plains by her brother wyrms, but the Aryan Society—a select group of like-minded women and men drawn from the membership of the Theosophic Society—has long planned for her return. Tell me, Crow, are you familiar with the concept of ley lines?"

"I've encountered the idea. It seems that the supernatural thrives along these supposed borders that run across the terrain."

"There is nothing supposed about them. They are lines of mystical energy that criss-cross the earth, and at their convergence points their power is the strongest. Stonehenge and the pyramids are built at such convergences."

Lone Crow glanced out at the burnt umber of the desert plains, which still glowered hotly beneath the orange sky. "Are we headed toward a convergence now?"

Carina Crawley's face radiated fervent passion. "Not only a convergence of the ley lines which cross at the bottom of Diablo Gulch, but a convergence of the planets and of time itself. The dark dimension is pregnant with energy and ready to rebirth the Wyrm Orribillus in her physical form."

"But such a physical manifestation requires sustenance to maintain its existence," said Crow.

"I was so sure that you carried the Eye of Ulutoth, but I've glimpsed into your mind and I see that you tell me the truth. You understand, the Eye is capable of opening a conduit into the dark dimensions through which the Great She-Wyrm could draw indefinite energy to sustain her. However, all is not lost; she can sustain herself by feeding."

Crawley's eyes smoldered with something hateful and so evil that Crow found that he could not stand her loathsome gaze. "The ley lines are enough to draw the Wyrm forth?"

"Not exactly," replied the witch. "Certain members of the Aryan Group are wealthy investors in the rail lines—wealthy enough to influence the course upon which this train track was laid. The iron rails serve as a conduit, drawing rampant energies from multiple ley lines and funneling them to Diablo. The Coming Forth of the She-Wyrm has been planned for many decades and today it comes to fruition!"

Indeed, as the rail cars jostled down the tracks the wheels seemed to crackle with an unexplainable energy, and as Crow surveyed the interior of the dining car he saw that time itself had ceased to function—for all but he and Carina Crawley existed in a dreamy torpor, their movements slowed to a slug-like pace, each footfall like a feather sinking through water, even while the train hurtled on to oblivion.

It became obvious to Lone Crow that little else was to be gained in verbal jousting with Crawley. It was true that Crawley had threatened Abigail Powell's life should he leave his seat, but now it was apparent that everyone aboard the train was in dire jeopardy—and inaction would only guarantee their deaths. He leaped from his seat, ducking past the smartly-uniformed conductor that meandered down the aisle, and toward the rear door of the dining car.

Carina Crawley lurched to her feet when she saw that Lone Crow hadn't succumbed to her spell and she spat a curse laced with lacerating shards of the darkest magic festering in her black heart, but the rail car was unsteady as it roared toward Diablo Gulch and the dark shards, called forth by forbidden words spoken in tongues ancient before the world was formed, went awry, striking the conductor so that his heart burst within his ribcage. The conductor's knees slowly buckled, and he fell in prolonged agony, swaying toward the bucking floor of the train, eyes cinched down and hands clawing at his chest.

As Crow leaped into the vestibule of the car he drew his Peacemaker and fired. Flame spurted forth in great gouts, but as soon as the bullets left the blessed barrel they became subject to Carina's spell, their flight retarded to a snail's pace, crawling through the air. Carina swatted aside the lead as if they were slow-moving gnats and Crow grabbed up a stout length of wood that leaned against the wall of the vestibule. This was the brakeman's club, and Crow jammed it into the brake wheel and used it as leverage to tighten the brake shoes against the spinning wheels of the car.

The dining car lurched and vibrated, the locked wheels howling as they vainly attempted to halt the forward momentum of the train. Each car had its own braking mechanism, which would need to be triggered if the train were to be stopped before it reached Diablo Gulch and the great bridge that crossed its jagged teeth.

Either the locomotive was not under Carina Crawley's spell or the deadman's brake had been activated because the locomotive was no longer straining down the track. Still, unless Crow was able to activate enough of the braking mechanisms the train had more than enough momentum to reach and even cross Diablo Gulch—if some obscene entity weren't lying in wait to devour the train and every living soul aboard.

Still clutching his pistol in his right hand, Crow withdrew the brakeman's club from the wheel brake. He saw Carina Crawley bracing herself in the door of the vestibule, standing over the slowly writhing body of the conductor. She'd lost her hat, and earth-colored hair spilled in waves across her glowering visage and the shoulders of her high-necked dress. Forbidden words fell from her lips, wrenching and rocking the very foundation of existence by the obscene blasphemies that she called upon.

Black smoke twisted from her forked tongue and snaked through the vestibule, dark roots of poison that twisted and entwined everything in their path. Crow staggered out onto the open porch of the dining car and slammed shut the door not a moment before those mystical roots began threading through it, eating away its substance. Through the cracking window laced with dark webs, Crow could see Carina Crawley's face—radiating dark evil, palpable and thick as the night within that thrice-cursed New Orleans mausoleum that Crow had explored so many years ago—that night he'd lost his beloved to the wyrds within.

Crow turned and fled through the connected smoking car, dodging thick clouds of tobacco fog while pipes surreally flared and kindled in prolonged moments, and conversations were carried on in lengthened tones that sounded odd and alien to his ears. He spun around a woman who was in the sluggish process of scandalously accepting a lit cigarette from a bearded and bespectacled lawyer and then entered the vestibule at the rear of the car where he spun the wheel brake with his club. The smoking car wobbled as the emergency brake pads squeezed the train's wheels.

The Indian caught sight of Carina Crawley parting the smoke as she strode down the aisle of the smoking car. There was a glint of something sharp in her hand, and the woman with the cigarette lurched to one side, her neck split open, and blood leaking in slow rivulets that stained her linen dress.

"Quit running," shouted Crawley, her voice husky and her breathing heavy—excited even. "Quit running or I'll kill them all!"

Crow knew that every man, woman and child aboard the train was already as good as dead so Crawley's threat did nothing to dissuade him, and he pushed through the door into the sleeping car. Narrow berths, mostly empty, were veiled by heavy curtains. He caught a glimpse of a woman sleeping with a baby swaddled and clasped to her breast, and then he came to the narrow cabins, tracking the numbers painted on the doors as he moved down the aisle.

He threw open the door to cabin number five, and dodged as a knife whirled slowly by his head and imbedded itself, quivering, in the door frame. Crow aimed his Colt at the Asian man that stood behind Abigail Powell with one hand full of her flaming red hair as he stretched her neck back, the pale skin exposed and nicked with crimson where the razor touch of his blade had already marked her.

By magic, or more likely sleight of hand, another blade appeared in Mr. Shima's hand. A dark scowl crossed his otherwise oddly slack features. "It seems that Miss Crawley's been disturbing the natural flow of time and reality... again. Knives are meant to be thrown in the natural momentum of the mortal plane. Now, not a step further, savage—unless you want to see a woman's throat slit."

"I'm sorry," said Abigail through gritted teeth. "He surprised me while I was resting."

Mr. Shima grinned and brandished a lady's one-shot derringer. "I plucked this right from her lap. Not that a mere bullet could have laid one low that has undergone the ancient rites of baptism in the blood of murdered innocents. My body swallows up the bullets and casts them out in the draught. Knife wounds close up as if a doctor were stitching them with thread and needle."

Crow wondered if Mr. Shima might be exaggerating for intimidation's sake, but he slipped his Colt back into its leather, realizing that a bullet would be as useless as a thrown knife while the train was still under the effects of Carina Crawley's spell. He undid the loop of his Bowie knife and gripped the haft. "Let her go or I'll test your knife work against my own."

Again Mr. Shima's crooked smile split his sallow face. "I've studied with knife masters on three different continents, and that is a challenge I'd gladly take up, if, alas, I only had more time. You see, the Wyrm Orribillus is waiting her nourishment and I have little time for such amusements. Now stand back or I'll cut the woman's throat, and we'll have a chance to play at knives after all."

Lone Crow saw little choice in the matter and he backed against the wall of the small cabin. Mr. Shima pressed his small blade directly against Abigail's jugular. Crow's eyes looked into Abigail's for just a moment, and in those green depths he saw fear and despair… and a plea for rescue.

"I'll be coming for you," said Crow.

Her long lashes fluttered and a single tear rolled down her lightly freckled cheek, then she was gone—dragged down the hall by Mr. Shima, who was scarcely larger than she. In the front vestibule of the train they met Carina Crawley who waved dismissively at Crow as he peered from the doorway of the cabin.

"There's nothing you can do to stop the inevitable," she cried. "Beg me for mercy and perhaps I'll spare the life of you and your woman—or continue your futile resistance and become meat for the Wyrm. I care not one way or the other."

Crow met the offer with a stony silence and ducked back into the cabin as Mr. Shima prodded Abigail to climb the ladder to the top of the rail car. He knelt beside the bunk and pulled out Abigail's traveling trunk from beneath, then reached behind and found the canvas rucksack that Wyatt Earp had given him as he and Abigail had left the Alaskan Trading Company outpost in St. Michael's Alaska. He slung the sack over his shoulder and exited the sleeping chamber into the corridor in time to see Carina Crawley's slender ankle disappear up the ladder.

Instead of following he turned and ran to the vestibule at the other end of the car where he cranked the brake lock tight. Then he slipped across the narrow walk to the caboose, and found the caboose attendant staring dreamily from the window while adjusting his greasy cap in an enchanted torpor. Crow passed by him and engaged the wheel brake, and then amidst the cacophony of squealing wheels and a spray of sparks he hurled himself from the rear of the train. He landed hard on his shoulder and then rolled up to his feet with a grunt of pain as the train slid away from him, and toward the trestle at Diablo Gulch.

Beyond the train, a spiral of black dust swirled against the umber sky, protruding from the floor of the gulch and engulfing the trestle in a twisting shape that danced and cavorted against the painted sky. Though the shape shifted and moved, Crow could see that it was gathering energies from the rails and was coalescing into the form of a great worm, which threatened to blot out the heavens and shadow the earth beneath its bloated manifestation.

Such a magnificent and horrible power, Crow knew, was far beyond his abilities to face, and should he try he expected his life would be snuffed out by the merest effort of the Wyrm Orribillus. To the Wyrm he would be nothing more than a gnat, a miniscule piece of living energy to be absorbed—to help satiate, in the tiniest degree, its ravenous and unending appetite.

There was one hope and, as the whispers of the forming Wyrm carried across the plains blasphemous words spoken in a voice that sounded like the belly of a snake over a washboard, Crow knelt alongside the tracks and offered up a prayer in his heart even as he untied the mouth of his rucksack and viewed the remnants of what Wyatt Earp had loaned him upon his leave from Alaska.

Inside, among a coil of cordite fuse rested five sticks of dynamite which Earp had removed from a crate being shipped to the miners traveling up from Skagway and down the Yukon River to Dawson City. Crow took two of these sticks and shoved one under each rail of the track. He spliced the fuses side by side and twisted them together before striking a match on the rough head of a railroad spike.

The match flared in his cupped hand and then the fuse caught, sputtering and hissing as it worked its way toward the red-paper cylinders packed with stabilized nitroglycerin. Crow turned and fled toward the train which continued its indefatigable momentum toward the spinning black column billowing from Diablo Gulch. He counted each step and sprinted twenty footfalls before hurling himself forward on his face, covering his ears and head with his arms. Three more counts left his lips and a wave of scorching heat rolled over him as the very earth shook beneath. Clots of ground rained down, and the deafening explosion hurtled shards of railroad tie into the air. A chunk of rail spun in a deadly arc over Crow's head, and tumbled down the railroad track, while the second rail peeled away into a curl of malformed iron. Rampant energy gathered from thousands of miles of ley lines, coruscated upon the broken rail and dispersed into the air.

The Wyrm Orribillus groaned and rocked as a portion of her sustenance was severed, and that great groan caused Crow to shudder—the very
marrow of his bones freezing within him. The Indian staggered to his feet
and stared into the swirling black chaos of the Wyrm and saw that she
continued to gather her physical form. It came more slowly now that the
rail had been blown, but still it gathered and Crow muttered to himself.

"The Wyrm must be collecting energies from the rails at the other side
of the gulch." It was clear to him what he must do and, as the train finally
ran out of momentum and screeched to a halt midway on the great iron
trestle that crossed Diablo Gulch, he ran to it, leaping from rail tie to rail
tie as the great chasm grew beneath him. There was nothing but his own
innate balance to keep him from falling into the rocky gulch below, and the
slightest of missteps would cause his foot to slip between the ties. Past those
creosote-soaked pieces of lumber there was nothing to halt his fall—except
for maybe the great metal latticeworks of the trestle, which would cut him
to pieces as he plummeted.

He dared a glance through the window of the smoking car as he passed
and saw panicked passengers rising so slowly that their screams seemed to
be perpetually painted upon their lips. Time continued to move at a slowed
pace within, while outside the train it continued its accustomed rhythm.

Black gusts of foul grit buffeted Crow as he passed the steaming vents
of the locomotive, and they threatened to dislodge him from his precarious perch. As they rocked him he fell forward onto his knees and blindly
pulled himself forward through the maelstrom of evil. Blackness descended
upon his soul, depravity and abject desolation so deep that it threatened to
destroy him—ravaging his sanity and rending his flesh.

Finally, as he emerged upon the other side of the trestle, the insubstantial took form, and the black winds created a towering black column of
segmented, sinuous flesh that glistened slime and writhed with a million
cilia. Above and below were massive maws lined with thousands of teeth
to gnash and grind, but still the Wyrm Orribillus tottered and wavered,
gathering strength from the energies funneled by the rails that ran along
the mystical ley lines.

Momentarily free from the overwhelming darkness and currently beneath the notice of the horror that lurched and waved above, Crow scrabbled in the earth and planted another stick of dynamite beneath each rail. He twisted the cordite fuses together and tried to light a match, but the evil winds extinguished its embryonic spark before it could blossom into life.

He tried again and again, striking his matches against the rail spikes until all but one of them lay smoldering and smoking. The Wyrm turned its attention to the freight train, hovering over it as if considering how best to ingest the metal carcass and the tiny lives inside, and Crow saw the smallest of chances.

With the dark sands having taken the form of the Wyrm Orribillus, Crow could move more freely on the trestle, and even though foul winds continued to gust up from the chasm he was able to leap from tie to tie, so that he was able to cross, unnoticed, past the dripping black trunk of Orribillus and reach the locomotive. Bathed in the swirling steam, and one hand still unreeling cordite fuse, Crow climbed the mechanical monstrosity and swung into the cabin. The engineer stood in almost frozen awe, jaw agape as he craned his neck into the sky, but the Indian continued past him and into the boiler room where sweat-bathed men stood with coal-laden shovels, about to plunge them into the licking flames of the furnace.

Crow tossed the remainder of his coiled fuse into the furnace instead, and it sparked and flared among the flames before igniting a coruscating trail of sparks that ate its way across the windswept rails and through the foul miasma that oozed from the great Wyrm. Orribillus swayed and opened wide its great jagged mouth to swallow up the train, but as it undulated forward a great explosion buffeted the gargantuan Wyrm, severing the Diablo Gulch bridge from its southward moorings. Jagged shards of railroad ties, some as long as three feet, peppered the body of the Wyrm and hot flame bathed its viscous black body.

Orribillus groaned as she was separated from the life-giving energy of the ley lines and the very earth seemed to groan with her. Then she spat anger and hurt, frothing trails of foam flying from her great maw as she howled in unleashed rage. The energies required to keep her substantive upon the mortal coil were no longer available to her, but while she lingered she would make her presence known.

Her fetid stench swept across the locomotive and Crow lit his last stick of dynamite as the Wyrm lurched forward, jaw gaping like the mouth of hell. He ran through the vestibule and leaped up the ladder into the coal car, and then Orribillus was upon them, rending and tearing the locomotive with sword-like incisors that chomped through the thick metal walls, crushing and mangling the engine and all those unfortunate enough to still be trapped inside. The Wyrm snapped her head to one side and tore the locomotive loose from its coupling to the coal car. The entire train reeled forward, the coal car upon which Crow stood coming off the track so that it pitched at a steep angle, held in place only by the railroad ties of the trestle.

Coal rolled across Crow's booted feet and he scrambled to keep his balance even as he hurled the sparking stick of dynamite into the black abyss of the Wyrm's maw, so that it sparkled for a moment as it spun alongside the mangled locomotive and then disappeared into the fiend's endless gullet. Then came a rush of flame and splitting of flesh and skin reminiscent of a ripe melon being dropped, and the Wyrm Orribillus ruptured, spraying dark viscous innards over the dry stones of Diablo Gulch.

The Wyrm collapsed under its unsupported weight, drawing the locomotive down to the bottom of the gulch, where its sinuous trunk rent asunder, and the bedrock of Diablo Gulch quaked as the death cries of Orribillus bombarded its stony ramparts. Crow suspected that had not the Wyrm been cut off from the energies that fed her, that a stick of dynamite—or even a crate of dynamite—would not have slain the horror and sent her back to the dark realms from which she had sprung.

Crow crawled through the bin, emerging black and dusty as he made the treacherous transition to the dining car, which was, by the miraculous hand of God, still resting on its rails. He heard a horrible scream echo across the gulch, and he glanced through the window of the dining car's vestibule to find the passengers moving about in a panic, darting from one side to the other, peering through the grimy glass to see what might have befallen them. They had been released from the magicks under which they had been influenced and, as Crow mounted the ladder of the dining car, Carina Crawley came into view—or rather a madwoman that resembled her, for she was upon her knees, gnashing her teeth and tearing clumps of hair from her head as she cried and frothed with the anguish of the damned, bewailing the loss of her vanquished god.

Over her stood Abigail Powell, her petticoat and blazing red hair ruffled by the wretched wind that gusted up from Diablo Gulch. She reached down and grabbed Carina Crawley by the scruff and waist of her high-collared dress and heaved her off the side of the train car. Bone snapped when she struck alongside the track, near the mouth of the broken bridge, and Carina Crawley lay still in a pitiful mewling heap.

Now the passengers of the train were pouring out onto the still hot plains, wondering at how they had come to such a pass. The sun was barely visible over the distant horizon, and the sky a bloody red with the wisps of a few cerulean clouds hanging high in the atmosphere.

Lone Crow climbed atop the dining car and when Abigail saw him she rushed to him and he took her in his arms. "I thought you were dead," she murmured.

"Nearly so," he admitted. "But it was you that I was worried about."

A few in the crowd gasped as they saw the scandalous sight of a savage embracing a white woman—she wearing little else than a petticoat, no less, and they covered the eyes of their children.

"Where did Mr. Shima get off to?" asked Crow.

"He went looking for you when you dynamited the rear tracks," said Abigail. "I…

Crow released Abigail and spun around as he heard soft footfalls on the roof of the dining car behind him. Mr. Shima came running across the tin-plated rooftop as light and agile as a cat, but he was counting on his stealth to surprise his quarry and was already committed to his attack when Crow whirled, drawing and slashing with his Bowie knife in the same movement.

The Bowie cut deep through the shoulder of Mr. Shima's suit, slicing to the bone so that rivulets of hot blood sprayed out. Mr. Shima's face contorted in pain, but before Lone Crow's amazed eyes the wound begin to knit, and the Asian took a knife fighting stance which Crow had never before seen.

"A lucky blow," said Mr. Shima through gritted teeth. "But I am the master of three different knife arts, each centuries old. You'll feel the bite of my blade-work momentarily."

"Words are empty," said Crow. "But perhaps they are all you have."

Mr. Shima spun his knife in a kata of patterned movement intended to confuse, but Crow lashed out with his Bowie hacking away three fingers and Shima's blade clattered against the dining car and spun over the side, dropping into Diablo Gulch.

Shima went down to one knee, clutching at his maimed hand in disbelief. "Impossible..."

Crow pulled up a sleeve and exhibited a series of scars on his arm. "I may not have learned three different knife arts, but I have learned by hard experience."

"So I see," said Mr. Shima. "I submit to your mercy. Clearly you are the superior warrior this day."

Abigail stood a safe distance behind her dark-haired champion. "Don't let him fool you, Crow. He's not as helpless as you think. Finish him before he— "

Mr. Shima's dark eyes glinted dangerously. "I can see that I've underestimated your intelligence, Miss Powell. I can also see that I should have slit your lovely throat long ago. Perhaps this will make up for my lack of foresight!" So saying, he palmed a knife blade from his left sleeve and drew back to throw with his good hand.

Before Mr. Shima could release the throwing knife Lone Crow's Peacemaker barked twice and a pair of bullets spewed from the gun blessed by a prophet on the dusty salt plains of Utah when men not wholly alive nor dead closed about them. Mr. Shima spun at the impact and slipped over the side of the dining car, striking the rail ties of the bridge, and then his body rebounded and flailed, bouncing and breaking against the stone walls of the jagged gulch.

Abigail came to Lone Crow's side and pried the gun from his still twitching fingers. She gently slid it back into its leather holster at the Indian's waist. "So ends the reign of the Wyrm Orribillus and the ambitions of her servants."

"It seems so," said Crow, but his words held no conviction. "At least, perhaps, we can return to Massachusetts without being hounded every step of the way by Blavatsky and her misguided Aryans."

"Noble ones," said Abigail. "That's what they called themselves."

Crow glanced at the flame-haired girl, a question in his eyes.

"Once Mr. Shima had a blade at my throat he couldn't keep his tongue from wagging. It seems Blavatsky and her associates have a friend at Miskatonic University that's been providing them with information."

The Indian shrugged out of his coal-smudged duster and draped it around Abigail's pale shoulders. "We'll take care of that when we return."

Abigail gathered the duster tightly around her as a foul stench gusted up from Diablo Gulch. "My father was a student of Blavatsky. The halls of Miskatonic are riddled with them. Perhaps we'd be safer not to return."

"Where would I take you?" asked Crow.

She shrugged, her green eyes looked into Crow's. "There's a lot of places in the U.S. Territories where a husband and a wife could carve out a humble existence and raise a family."

A slow smile spread across Crow's habitually somber features. "Why Miss Powell, I don't believe I've ever received a more attractive proposition."

The Trail of the Twisted Tail

The lobby of the New York Chapter of the Plato Society was strangely barren, a solitary desk guarding a pair of ornately carved cherry wood doors. Behind the desk sat a dark-haired woman, a pair of reading glasses perched on her well-formed nose. She was so engrossed in the book that was before her that she failed to notice the approach of the dark-skinned savage.

"Twelve Demons: *Une Histoire Complet de Cultes Antédiluvien*," read Lone Crow from the inscription at the top of the page.

The receptionist jumped at the sound of his voice. She adjusted the glasses on her nose as if to more completely view her surprise visitor, but if she was further alarmed to see an Indian standing in the lobby next to her desk she did not let on. He was dressed in the fashion of a cowboy with broad-brimmed hat and a split tail duster that had seen years of harsh weather—not at all attire that was commonplace here on the East Coast of the States.

She glanced down at her schedule and spoke in accented tones. "Mr. Lone Crow, do you speak French?"

"I read just enough to know that the book you're reading is considered dangerous material by certain professors at Miskatonic University."

The receptionist dismissed his warning with a wave of her slender hand. An ornate circlet rested upon her ring finger. An ancient Greek coin lay on the desk near her, the face of which was stamped with a large chisel stamp. "We have quite an extensive library here at the Plato Society. If your application is accepted you'll have complete access." She smoothed the pages of the ancient tome with her other hand. "This is one of the lighter reads."

"Well, Mrs—"

"Miss Amandine Fonteneau," she introduced. "I see you have an appointment with the board of admission."

"That is correct. I have a most horrific tale to tell them."

"Indeed? I should like to hear that tale."

"I don't suppose the board of application will allow you to sit in on my interview?"

"Nothing of the sort," she said. "A woman's place is not in the drawing room. I serve a strictly decorative purpose here at the Plato Society."

"I suspect there is more to you than meets the eye," he replied.

"Why, Mister Crow. In France we might suspect such dialog as being flirtatious."

Crow removed his hat, revealing dark hair that was unbraided and fell across his broad shoulders. "I meant no disrespect, Miss Fonteneau."

"I took it as a compliment, Mr. Crow." She stood and ushered Lone Crow toward the door. She was dressed in a Japanese kimono which was odd attire for a French woman. The hem drifted scandalously high, exposing her well-turned ankles and the zoris she wore upon her feet. Crow thought he saw a bit of leather protruding from beneath the hem—something strapped to her calf.

Miss Fonteneau opened the double doors, revealing a hallway that was lined with ancient artifacts and curios. The floor was adorned with a carpet woven in Uzbekistan. "Take the first hallway to your right and through the third door on the left you will find the board of admission awaiting your arrival.

"Thank you, Miss Fonteneau."

"Mr. Crow—your gun." She indicated the Eagle-butted Colt revolver that was peering from beneath the folds of his jacket.

"What of it?" grunted Crow.

"It is the policy of the Plato Society that all visitors remove their weapons before entering the inner sanctum."

Crow tensed.

"However, I'm sure that you can be trusted to only use it in cases of severe extremity."

Crow nodded, his saturnine expression relaxing into something resembling gratitude. "I hope that you'll continue to give me the benefit of the doubt."

"The clock is ticking, Mr. Crow. We don't want to keep the board of admissions waiting."

The draped and padded corridor seemed muted in comparison to the vast and echo-laden lobby. Niches displayed ancient Hyborian masks of polished wood; the scrolls of Acheron said there were six of these in existence and that they gave the wearer great powers—and also drove them utterly mad. Crow could see fragments of charred flesh that clung to the edges of the scorched mask. He was sure that there was an interesting tale behind that.

Hanging high on the wall, out of his reach, were spears and blowguns inscribed with powerful sigils that blessed and cursed the weapons. Crow's own pistol had been blessed by a prophet. He passed by the collection of bolas and boomerangs, some still stained a rusty brown, and down the hallway to the third door on the left.

Here was a drawing room that reeked of cigar smoke and moldering paper, a fire blazed in the great hearth at the back of the room, casting wavering fingers of light across the book cases and overstuffed chairs. Three men rose when he entered—a thing that Crow found most peculiar because very few men showed such respect, even reluctantly, to a red man. The only time that a man got on his feet when Crow entered an establishment was when they were slapping their gun leather—so Crow nearly went for his own pistol, jerking his hand toward the eagle-handled Colt beneath his jacket. He refrained at the last moment, when he saw that none of the three were going for their weapons. In fact, they appeared to be unarmed.

The first wore muttonchops and a tailored suit the likes of which Crow had never seen out West. His eyes were beady, and a sheen of sweat shone upon his brow. "I'm Jonathan Harkness, director of the Plato Society Board of Admissions." He motioned to the painfully thin fellow to his right. "This is Lord Baldwin, Head Barrister for the law firm of Baldwin, Congers, and Devonshald."

Crow noted Baldwin's sallow skin and tubercular appearance. "Lord?"

Baldwin stifled a series of racking coughs and appeared somewhat apologetic. "It's an ancestral title—doesn't mean much in the states, but I'm actually thirty-second in line for the throne of England. Not that it will ever come to that of course, but my partners in law—Congers and Devonshald—feel that it lends some cache to our firm and perhaps attracts some of the upper-crust clientelle, so to speak, to our firm.

Crow nodded. "I see. I myself am chief of my tribe. Of course, I am the only surviving member so that, I expect, puts me in a place of somewhat less importance than the thirty-second in line for the throne of England."

Baldwin chuckled at Crow's self effacing comments. "It's surely a tragedy, though, that you are the last of your people. It must be lonely..."

"You have no idea," said Crow.

The last of the three nodded brusquely and resumed his former position in the overstuffed leather armchair. He was amply-padded, himself, and his jowls seemed like the dewlaps of a great dog. Though graying and grizzled, by the steel in his eyes, Crow could see that the man was a warrior and should not be underestimated.

"I've chased the likes of you across plain and through mountain passes. If it were up to me you would not be sitting here—but the rules of admission to the Plato Society are singularly lenient if you have had an experience of momentous horror which can be succinctly defined."

Harkness spoke. "You'll have to excuse General Burns demeanor, but admittedly he speaks for many of our membership who are unlikely to welcome the presence of a savage in our midst—even one as well spoken as you seem to be."

Crow ignored the insult. "I don't expect your love or even your friendship—just your respect."

"You have the respect of many men," grunted General Burns. "Wasn't it you that eviscerated Butch Cassidy and hung his guts from a tree in Nicaragua?"

"It wasn't quite so colorful as that," said Crow. "And it was Costa Rica."

"Hmphh," said General Burns. "I stand corrected, but the fact remains that your exploits are noised far and wide. You are a renowned gunman and if it weren't for Plato Society bylaws which require all weapons to be left at the front desk, we would not risk our lives by being in your presence."

"Let me clarify the requirement for admission," said Harkness."This event of singular horror that you have experienced—it must not be of a common nature that thousands or even hundreds have experienced."

"Such as the horror of war," grunted General Burns. "It is a mind-blasting experience but it is entirely expainable in terms of human greed and lust for power. Your experience must be of a more, dare I say, unexplainable nature—something beyond human fathoming."

"It is most definitely beyond humanity," said Crow. "Once I relate my tale I think that at least two of you will find it beyond fathoming."

"It takes just two of us—a majority—to vote you into the society," said Lord Baldwin. "Though we generally find that applications are unanimously rejected. Only a small portion of applicants are actually granted membership to the Plato Society.

Harkness frowned. "The very nature of the required experience makes this, by necessity, a club of rare exclusivity."

"Perhaps," said Lord Baldwin, "now that we have more clearly elucidated the requirements of membership, would you like to withdraw your application and depart the Plato Society?"

Crow would not be chased away so easily. "I would rather tell my story. As I said before, I am sure that at least two you will find it a worthy entry in the annals of the Plato Society."

Harkness scratched at his muttonchops. "Then by all means, proceed. I do warn you that if we find your tale mundane, in the least, we will terminate this interview and eject you from the premises."

"Fair enough," said Crow. "I've had more than just one unfathomable experience, but let me confine myself to the one that interests me most.

"Once I was not a lonely man, and for three years I was married to a beautiful red-haired white woman, the daughter of a Professor Powell, and made a homestead in the Oklahoma Territories. I was content to abandon my wanderlust and live off the land, enjoying the company of my wife and hoping that children would someday grace our family."

"Where did Professor Powell teach?" interjected General Burns.

"Archaeology at Miskatonic University."

"And your wife's name?"

"Abigail Powell—or rather it…"

"She was a white woman and she shacked up with a savage?"

"We were married by a justice of the peace," said Crow, a hard edge to his voice. "She became Abigail Crow."

"So you gave up gunfighting for a couple of years because of the love of a good woman," said General Burns. "I don't see anything of interest in this story."

"One night," said Crow, "we were woken from our sleep by a tremor in the earth. Though I had never experienced an earthquake this far to the East I had experienced one while I was in Costa Rica. This tremor was short-lived and so when I had ascertained that the livestock had calmed and no serious damage had been done to the house we retired again to bed."

"Earthquakes, I am afraid, fall into the category of the mundane experience," said Lord Baldwin. "I vote that we save Mr. Crow any further embarrassment and close this interview."

"Not so fast," grunted General Burns. "I sense something of interest coming up."

Lord Baldwin dabbed at his ear with his handkerchief and blew his nose. "Really, General Burns, we both know this is a fruitless exercise. The man is a savage and his natural superstitions make him unfit for differentiating a truly supernatural event from say, the wind shifting due to natural weather patterns and bringing in clouds after a rain dance."

Crow didn't wait for permission to continue his story. "I can't tell you much about rain-dances, but when Abigail awoke she went down to the lake to fetch water as she usually does in the morning. When she came back she was different. Her skin had taken on a yellowish cast and her eyes were strange to me, dull and glazed. Naturally, I thought she was sick."

Lord Baldwin yawned. "And I'm sure that she was—end of story."

"Actually, there's more. She began to behave strangely and talked incessantly of parasites and metamorphosis. Then sometimes I would catch her doing things that she would later claim she had no memory of—and when in this state she would speak in a language that I have never heard the likes of."

The General shrugged. "How many languages do you know? There must be thousands of different languages and dialects. Your wife may have been exposed to something you're unfamiliar with when she traveled with her archaeologist father."

"I've traveled extensively," said Crow." I've encountered people from all over the world. It was a language that was completely alien to me."

Lord Baldwin frowned. "Everything that you've described could be the result of an illness or something as common as a fever. Those in the depths of fever will speak on nonsensical subjects and perhaps even speak snatches of foreign dialogue that they have picked up during their travels. She was probably asking where the bathroom was in Czech."

"She began to waste away," continued Crow. "She was a robust woman and she became as thin as a skeleton, suffering from coughing fits and ruptures of bilious yellow fluid from her ear canal."

"An unfortunate illness," muttered Lord Baldwin. "Nothing but an unfortunate illness."

Harkness again scratched at his bristling mutton chop. "So it appears, Mr. Crow. We're sorry to have taken your time."

"When she died, something viscous and slug-like crawled from her ear. It was about two feet long and it moved on hundreds of tendrils that were covered in gray. You see, this thing had inserted itself into my wife's minds and sent out these shoots, like roots, that anchored in Abigail's brain. As they grew deeper they took more and more control of her actions—but this parasite also sapped the life from her as surely as it is sapping the life from you, Lord Baldwin."

"What are you talking about?" snapped Baldwin.

Crow reached over and snatched up the handkerchief that Baldwin had set on the book table beside his stuffed leather seat. "When I saw the thing that had inhabited my wife I grabbed up an axe from the fireplace. The thing scrabbled through a crack in the floorboards, but I managed to cut off its tail as it fled."

Deliberately, Crow slipped his hand beneath his jacket and pulled a sealed jar from beneath. Within it writhed a slimy yellow thing. It was a barbed tail with numerous strands which squiggled and squirmed. "The curious thing is that the tail never completely died—and always the spade upon the tail twisted and turned in the direction of the body it was once attached to."

Now, the Indian had the rapt attention of the three board members. "I followed the parasite from beneath my house, and pursued its trail into the woods. I followed it into Mobeetie where it inhabited the body of a lady of the evening, who immediately came under its influence and boarded a coach for the East Coast. I followed its trail from victim to victim and now it has come here to New York City; here to the Plato Society; here to this room."

General Burns and Harkness leaned forward to examine the twitching tail. "The spade does point toward Lord Baldwin," observed Harkness.

"This is ludicrous," coughed Lord Baldwin. "You're going to believe this savage's preposterous tale that I've got something eating my brain?"

Crow opened up the handkerchief that he had stolen from Lord Baldwin's book table. A bilious yellow stain spread at its center. "This is from your ear. The hemorrhaging is already starting. You don't have much time left, Lord Baldwin."

The startled expression on Baldwin's face changed into a vicious and triumphant grin. "Foolish mortal, do you think that you've gained some sort of victory by tracking me here? My trail was not exactly subtle, and furthermore you've reunited me with my missing tail."

Harkness and Burns began to slide away from Lord Baldwin, gazing at him in horror.

"Lone Crow," spat Lord Baldwin's form. "That's a fitting appellation for an outcast who is shunned even by the people he so desperately attempts to fit in with. You lived alone and you'll die alone—and finally the full measure of my vengeance shall be performed."

"Vengeance?" asked Crow.

"You think it an accident that my craft plunged through frigid dimensions and voids to land near your desolate habitation?"

Crow started in his chair. A chill creeping up his spine. "It was no coincidence?"

"How many times have you blindly destroyed what you did not understand? Did you think that those depradations would go unanswered—that we would blithely ignore your murders and let you live a life of peaceful harmony, despite the bloody deeds of your past?"

"Abigail?"

"Yes, she died because of you—a retribution for your past offenses."

"And why not me?" said Crow. "Later, when you were controlling her actions you could have killed me in my sleep."

"We could have, but we wanted to you to suffer for longer."

General Burns leaped for the fireplace and grabbed up the poker. He swung hard and caved in the side of Lord Baldwin's skull. A high-pitched scream emitted from between Baldwin's teeth—a wailing cry of a tone and tenure that human vocal cords could not create nor sustain. Harkness clutched at his ears and staggered back against the shelves.

Despite the crushing blow, the thing that was Lord Baldwin rose to his feet, uttering obscene blasphemies in a language that was not Czech or, for that matter, any other earthly tongue.

Baldwin lashed out with inhuman strength, striking General Burns and throwing him back into the fireplace, where his clothes caught fire and he went up in a ball of flame. The scent of burning flesh rose into the air, but the General did not scream. Baldwin's blow had shattered his spine, killing him instantly.

Crow's hand darted beneath the flaps of his duster and found his Colt pistol. He fired three times as he threw himself backward and out of the path of Baldwin's flailing attacks.

The bullets punctured Baldwin's chest and he fell backward. Baldwin's body began to cave. The bones collapsed inward, and then there was a great squelching sound as the alien fiend departed its host's body, exiting through the ear.

It had grown since Crow had first encountered it and now it was full three feet long and a foot wide, a viscous yellow glob that oozed through the ear canal and then reformed, flailing cilia propelling it at amazing speed, so that before Crow could recover from his amazement it had climbed Harkness's legs and crawled in through his gaping mouth.

Crow knew that it was too late for Harkness and fired his pistol directly at the fiend, so that it punctured the putrescent yellow skin, passed through the creature, and came out the back of Harkness's head. Harkness slumped, reaching out and collapsing a shelf of books that tumbled over his fallen form.

The viscous creature flailed and writhed and Crow emptied the last two bullets from his pistol into the alien monstrosity.

It continued to twitch as Crow reloaded and then fired all six cartridges into the creature. Finally, the shrilling parasite became still.

Crow dragged General Burns' flaming corpse from the fire and beat out the flame with a tapestry. That's when Miss Fonteneau entered the room.

She glanced around, giving the room a cursory examination. "I trust you have finished what you came to accomplish?"

"You knew about this?" asked Crow. He gestured to the bilious alien form that soiled the carpet.

"I suspected," admitted Miss Fonteneau, "but I did not know which of the Plato Society members had been infected."

Crow took up the poker and pushed the corpse of the alien fiend into the fireplace where it went up in a smoky blaze. When he was satisfied that it would burn completely he threw the twitching tail into the fire. The jar shattered and the tail burned.

"It's a shame about the General and Mr. Harkness," said Miss Fonteneau.

"They were good men," said Crow.

"Despite their prejudices?"

"I'll not hold it against them," said Crow. "I've got other larger concerns."

"You'd best leave the premises," said Miss Fonteneau. "I've altered the records to show they were holding an interview with a Mr. Luciano Redgrave. With some luck I may be able to keep your name clear of this incident."

"Why are you helping me?"

Miss Fonteneau narrowed her left eye and arched her right brow in an expression that indicated she would not tolerate any further questions. "The clock is ticking, Mr. Crow."

The Wolves of Five Points

Amandine Fontenau led the way into the sixth ward with a sureness of foot that inspired her companion, who strode just a fraction of a pace behind her, to believe that she had visited this downtrodden and dangerous portion of New York City just a few times before. They passed through the swamp land north of city hall and as they neared the intersection of Five Points the clamor of rude jests and drunken singing rose up into the new night sky, which exhibited a waning, but still nearly full, moon which was already fringed by a few pale stars.

Five Points, so named because it was the intersection of Mulberry, Anthony, Cross, Orange, and Little Water Street was notorious for its wickedness, and indeed the basement doors of the rundown tenements were thrown open even at this early hour to welcome visitors into their subterranean rum cellars, card dens, and moldy dance halls—many of which were thinly disguised covers for less reputable activities.

A number of the buildings in the vicinity tilted at precarious angles as the swamps began to reclaim the landfill upon which they had been built. Clothes lines were being reeled into the starch houses which had hung laundry to dry earlier in the day, and gangs of ruffians were already prowling the streets looking for the weak to prey upon.

As they caught sight of Miss Fonteneau in her close fitting bodice and crinolette they began to whistle and catcall. Her companion who was dressed in a buckskin jacket with a broad-brimmed cowboy's hat shadowing his face looked up, revealing long black hair that framed the dark skin and brooding features of a Native American Indian. His brown eyes narrowed and he scowled as he took in the aspect of the dozen ruffians clad in stovepipe hats, vests, and trousers of black, the latter of which were tucked into high-heeled calfskin boots. To offset the black they each wore crimson shirts and all carried brick bats—pieces of masonry or stone in a sock or gunnysack, nonchalantly cast over their shoulders.

"They are a remnant of the Bowery Boys gang—out of their territory and looking for trouble," hissed Fonteneau, her voice tinged with a heavy French accent that her companion found both fascinating and difficult to understand. "Don't look them in the eye and keep on walking."

Lone Crow ignored Miss Fontenau's advice and found the eyes of their leader. He brushed back his jacket and put his hand on the eagle-carved butt of his Colt .45 revolver. The oily light of the overhead lanterns gleamed from the bandolier of ammunition that he wore across his chest. Crow didn't say a word, but his actions spoke eloquently enough—and their leader, swept off his hat, revealing a mop of oil slicked hair, and bowed low as the walked past.

"A pleasure to make your acquaintance Madame and Sir. Please do enjoy your visit to Five Points."

"Well," commented Fontenau as they drew a safe distance away. "That was certainly a welcome change from the aspersions they were casting upon my character a few moments before."

"They just required the proper incentive to remember their manners," said Crow.

"I do apologize for my earlier comment. For a moment I forgot that my escort is the same man that defeated Butch Cassidy, impaled him upon a tree and let the vultures eat his flesh."

"That's not quite how it happened," said Crow.

"Well, it makes for an interesting conversation starter at cocktail parties, does it not?"

"I don't believe that I've ever been to a cocktail party."

"Vraiment? They are dreadfully banal—or boring, I should say. You are not missing much, but I'm sure that your presence would liven up the evening immeasurably."

Hucksters called at them from either side of the street, beckoning them to enter the mouths of dark caverns for entertainments of various natures.

"The locals call those underground taverns oyster bars," said Fonteneau.

"Why is that?" asked Crow.

"Because they are always open and they lure you in with something shiny—like the promise of winning big in a game of cards, or plentiful rum bought cheaply, or a promiscuous woman…"

"And then when you are inside the oyster shell closes," said Crow, who was seeing where the analogy was headed. "Much like the taverns in San Francisco where they put drug in your drink and rob you."

"Exactly," said Miss Fonteneau. "Have you had personal experience with this?"

"Drinking is not one of my vices," said Crow. "And that has saved me from a number of misfortunes, I am sure."

"And what are your vices, Monsieur Crow?"

"Unless I submit to them they are merely temptations," said Crow who saw that it would be wise to change the subject. "I've followed you because you said that you needed my help, but I would like to know just where we are headed."

"Haven't I gained just a little bit of your trust?" she asked, her smile bordering on the coquettish.

Crow regarded the pale oval face, crimson lips, and dark hair of his companion. "You have, but I don't like to go into situations blind. I find that it helps to be prepared."

"Monsieur Crow, you have been prepared for this moment since the day of your birth. Don't you believe in predestination?"

He shook his head. "Every man has been endowed with his own free will by the Creator. Perhaps I have been foreordained to do certain things, but my choices determine by own destiny."

Fonteneau seemed impressed. "Very good! However, you will find many philosophers that will disagree with your assessment. They will find your declarations to be foolish, illiterate and uninformed."

"The wisdom of this world is foolishness with God," said Crow as they turned down Orange Street. "I don't much care what men think of me."

"We're here," said Fonteneau. They halted in front of a brick dwelling that was a little better kept up than the buildings around it. It stood three stories high and its windows were deep set and barred with iron grills. "This one's built on bedrock—the swamp won't reclaim it for some time yet."

Crow compared the structure to the others around it. "It would make a good fortress. I even see a few loopholes disguised in the stonework."

"Sharp eye," commented Fonteneau and she climbed the stoop, removing a coin from her handbag as she rapped on the heavy oak door.

An eye level hatch slipped open and Fonteneau held up the old Greek coin and Crow saw that the casting had been defaced by a chisel stamp.

"What say you?" requested a voice from beyond the door and Crow thought he detected a quavering in the words.

Fonteneau leaned forward and spoke a few words in a conspiratorial tone. Despite the bludgeoning of years of gunfire, Crow's ears were sharp enough to hear what she said.

"Socrates is mad."

"What is it we're doing here?" asked Crow again.

Fonteneau cast a glance over her shoulder and her lips turned in an enigmatic quirk. "I've a club that I'd like you to join."

"I've had enough of clubs, thank you," replied Crow.

"At least hear me out," said Fonteneau. "You owe me that much."

Crow made no reply, but since he didn't turn and walk away Fonteneau figured that the Indian had acquiesced to her request.

Large bolts clanked and then the door opened. Crow slipped through the gap after Fonteneau and into an antechamber that was illuminated with a ruddy light cast by a trio of overhead lanterns which hung in the arch of the ceiling. A cloying odor lingered thick in the air.

Fonteneau's nose wrinkled. "What is that scent?"

A skinny white man wearing a suit of Italian manufacture slammed the door shut and quickly began to replace a series of heavy bolts. "A guest is burning incense. A great deal of it, I'd judge."

Fonteneau frowned. "We're here to see Monsieur Grenier."

"That may be difficult," stammered the doorman.

Fonteneau seemed irritated. "I've gone to a lot of trouble to bring Monsieur Crow here. I think that the least Monsieur Grenier can do is show some common civility and take a few minutes to speak with our guest."

"You can see Monsieur Grenier," said the doorman, "but I'm afraid that he won't be able to see you."

Fonteneau lifted a katana from a rack of weaponry just beyond the lobby and slung it over her shoulder as the doorman escorted them up a narrow flight of twisting stairs that brought them to the third floor.

"Do you know how to use that sword?" asked Crow.

Fonteneau nodded. "I spent my childhood in Japan and learned Kenjutsu. I am considered a hanshi."

"What is a hanshi?"

"A title that means master," said Fonteneau. "Do you know anything about the art of the sword?"

Crow shook his head. "I'm considered a gunman, Miss Fonteneau. I hope you didn't bring me here because you thought I knew the sword."

"Nothing of the sort. It's just that I heard some rumors."

"I do know my way around the bow and the tomahawk."

"Perhaps that was it," said Fonteneau, but she failed to elucidate any futher.

The doorman paused a few feet away from an open door. Lantern light danced across the burnished wood floors and Crow could smell the all too familiar scent of death in the air.

"I found him like this," said the doorman.

They peered into the room and found Mr. Grenier sprawled upon the floor in a pool of sticky blood, his throat and his entrails ripped out. Careful not to tread in the crimson blood, Crow approached and crouched next to the body. "I've seen the bodies of those who have been made meals by wild animals. This man was killed by a beast. There are marks of the fang upon his body."

"But there are no beasts within the sanctum," said Fonteneau.

Crow gestured toward bloody paw marks on the carpet. "These prints suggest otherwise."

"But how could it have gotten in?" mused Fonteneau.

Crow went to the open window and tested the iron bars. He found them firmly entrenched in the mortar and stone. "Nothing came through this window."

"Villichuck?" called the French woman.

The doorman still stood at the doorway of the room, his face as pale as a freshly-starched sheet. "Yes, Mademoiselle Fonteneau?"

"Does the sanctum have any other tenants this evening?"

"Five, Mademoiselle Fonteneau. A cossack, Valerii Onopko, a gentleman and gentlewoman, Jack Scarlet and his wife Maura Scarlet, a Welshman, Vychan Gough, and a man of the cloth—one Father Gibbons."

Fonteneau mused on this. "Both Gibbons and Grenier were involved in an altercation with the Swordsmen of Xeniades a year past. I wonder if

Grenier had some information for us about the Swordsmen. Perhaps that is why he has been killed. Villichuck, have you checked all the windows and doors of the sanctum?"

"All are secure," said Villichuck. "No one beside the two of you has entered or left for the past three hours."

"Grenier hasn't been dead for more than twenty minutes," said Crow, "or the blood would have already clotted. The footprints end just outside the door. Did any of your visitors bring an animal with them?"

Villichuck scowled. "The Russian, Onopko, brought a great hound with him, but I told him he must lock it in a cage in the basement. He insisted that it would sleep at the foot of his bed."

"And you relented?" asked Fonteneau.

Villichuck swallowed hard. "He is a very persuasive man."

"Of these five visitors all of them presented proper identification?"

"They all presented the currency of Diogenes and spoke the password. I must assume they are members of the Diogenes Club."

"Then we have a traitor in our midst," said Fonteneau.

"What is the Diogenes Club?" asked Crow.

"It's a very select association," said Fonteneau, "but we must make haste if we hope to catch the fiend that killed Monsieur Grenier."

"Perhaps I should fetch the constable," said Villichuck. "And let him handle the matter."

Fonteneau shrugged with practiced nonchalance. "Crow and I encountered a dozen Bowery Boys on the way to the sanctum. They were only deterred by a show of force, but perhaps you think that you can be as intimidating as Monsieur Crow?"

Villichuck regarded the somber demeanor of Crow's visage—a face that he considered wild and savage. "Perhaps I should stick close to the two of you… in case you should require my help."

"That's a most excellent idea," said Fonteneau with the slightest of smiles. "Besides, you well know that the Diogenes Club prefers to tend to its own affairs—without any outside interference."

"Yes, mademoiselle."

"Tres bon! Now show us to Monsieur Onopko's room. I'd like to take a look at this dog of his."

Onopko's room was on the second floor, the door to his room next to a plinth that contained the sculpture of a wild hound. Villichuck knocked on the door and then apprehensively backed away.

"Why are you disturbing my rest?" roared a voice from within.

"Sir, Mademoiselle Fonteneau would like to speak with you."

"The woman I saw passing through the lobby earlier this evening?"

"Yes, sir," replied Villichuck. "The one you inquired about."

Fonteneau did not change her expression in the least at this revelation.

"Well why didn't you say so?" replied Onopko and he threw open the door. He had a great beard which grew to the bottom of his chest and his long brown hair was wavy and oiled into ringlets. He wore a ruffled shirt with braided epaulets of gold that matched at least two of his teeth.

"Ah, Mademoiselle Fontenau. You are still as lovely as the first time I glimpsed you."

"That's so gratifying to know that you approve of my appearance, Monsieur Onopko. I trust that you find your accomodations suitable for you and your hound?"

Onopko frowned. "You are not here to tell me that I must turn out Sasha, are you?"

"I leave matters of housekeeping and animal husbandry to others," she said, and glanced at Villichuck. "However, I am most interested in making the acquaintance of Sasha."

"You are a dog lover, eh? There is no more noble an animal and no better friend than a dog."

"So I am told," said Fonteneau, "but I have yet to be convinced."

Onopko snapped his fingers and Sasha trotted from an unseen corner of the room. The wolf hound stood three feet high at the shoulder, its hair falling in glossy waves. It was an impressive animal but its narrow nose and teeth were unblooded. "Sasha, she is a fine beast and more loyal than most men or women."

Fonteneau thrust her fingers through the dog's fur as if petting it, but in actuality she was seeing if the hair had recently been cleaned. However there was no sign of dampness. "What business brings you to New York?"

"The business of Diogenes," rumbled Onopko. "I'm to contact a certain privateer and arrange for him to stage a raid upon an enclave that opposes our goals."

"What enclave is that?"

"It's a tightly held secret, which even I do not yet know. I'm meeting with Grenier tomorrow morning to discuss the details."

"That may present some difficulties," said Fontenau.

Onopko arched a bushy brow. "How so?"

Crow carefully examined the Russian wolf hound. "The jaw of this hound is too narrow to be the beast we're looking for."

"Are you matching tooth marks? I hardly think that boot Sasha got a hold of merits this sort of…"

"That was a fifty dollar pair of boots imported from France," said Villichuck, his face tight.

"Then you shouldn't have been so careless to leave it out," shrugged Onopko. "Apparently, the Diogenes Club can afford to pay its manservants much better than it pays its agents if you can afford to import your boots from France."

"The boots were in my chamber, tucked beneath my bed. I hardly think that qualifies as carelessness."

"Well, it does if there are animals in the house," grunted Onopko.

"The rules specifically state that no animals should be allowed within the sanctum," replied Villichuck. "Some enemies of Diogenes, such as the Disciples of Plato, have been known to use beasts as spies."

"Are you suggesting that my Sasha is familiar to a Disciple of Plato?" said Onopko with great umbrage.

"Not unless that Disciple of Plato has a particular predilection for footwear," said Villichuck.

"We're wasting time here," said Crow. "If Mr. Onopko won't take responsibility for the actions of his hound, I'll buy you a new pair of boots."

"What?" cried Onopko. "You let some savage into the sanctum to insult me and suggest I am unable to pay for my own obligations?"

Fonteneau smiled archly. "So you will pay Villichuck for his ruined boot, then. C'est bon! Now we must make haste. Who is next on our list?"

"That would be Mr. and Mrs. Scarlet. They also have taken a room upon this level."

"Wait, what is this all about?" asked Onopko. "I sense that this concerns something more than a chewed boot."

Fonteneau hurried down the hall after the brisk stride of Villichuck. "A little late to the game, Monsieur Onopko."

Onopko trailed Crow down the corridor, Sasha at his side. "You said that my meeting with Grenier might present some difficulties. Has he been slain?" He waved a finger in the air as he struck upon the point that he had been missing. "He has been slain by a beast. You have found tooth marks upon him!"

"You are catching up quickly," said Fonteneau.

Onopko came up alongside of Crow and sneered at him. "If this savage will stand aside I will aid in the investigation." The Indian remained expressionless, not reacting to Onopko's insults, but neither did he move aside as they negotiated the circuitous corridors of the sanctum. The intervals between lanterns were quite large and so there were stretches where they traveled in shadow, barely able to discern their surroundings. Finally, Villichuck took down a lantern and held it in front of him as they proceeded past rows of doors with dusty brass handles and heavy locks. Some archways appeared to have been bricked up entirely, forever sealing the room beyond.

Fonteneau noticed Crow's curious glances at these long unopened chambers and bricked in portals. "The Diogenes Club has many secrets and enemies. Some are best forgotten."

A marrow-freezing growl, followed by a howl stopped Villichuck dead in his tracks. His eyes widened. "That growl seemed to come from Mr. and Mrs. Scarlet's room!"

"Stand aside," bellowed Onopko. He hurled himself at the door, but rebounded from the thick, brass bound planks.

"Stay out!" warned a deep voice from within the room. "It's not safe for you!"

"How convenient that he should be concerned about our safety," said Onopko and he again threw all of his considerable weight against the door. The frame splintered, but the door did not come open.

"I'm warning you," said the voice. "If you break into the room I may not be able to control her."

Villichuck stood a wary distance behind the rest of the group. "That door has three deadbolts on it, Mr. Onopko."

"I hit it enough times and it will give," snarled Onopko. He was about to rush a third time at the portal when Fonteneau put a hand on his chest.

"Let me try a different tack," said Fonteneau, and then she called through the door. "Monsieur Scarlet, we have a problem that requires immediate attention. Monsieur Grenier has been killed by a great hound and we need to find the killer."

"Give me a moment and I'll open the door," replied Scarlet. "But make no sudden moves. We don't want to alarm her."

"Who is 'her?'" questioned Fonteneau.

There was no response, but a few moments later the dead bolts were slid back one by one and the door opened about a foot wide. A dark-haired man with stubbled chin and startling green eyes—the right one which was curiously notched like a keyhole—appeared in the gap. "I'm sorry, but my wife has a peculiar condition which she has not yet learned to control. When the disease rests heavy upon her, others must be most careful not to alarm her."

"Tres interessant," said Fonteneau. "This disease wouldn't happen to be lycanthropy, now would it?"

Scarlet blinked. "You know of lycanthropy?"

"I once chased a maurauding werewolf through Paris," said Fonteneau, "but the closest I got was the devoured corpses it left behind, and the sight of a great lupine form bounding across the rooftops."

Jack Scarlet slowly pushed the door open just a bit further, affording them a view of a furry form that was not wholly man nor wolf. It was chained to the brass bedpost, though none of them expected that the bedpost could restrain the beast if she threw herself against her shackle.

"I've calmed her," said Scarlet. "If you make no threatening gestures she may transform back into her human form."

Indeed, before their eyes the great canine began to transform into a human female. Scarlet turned and threw a blanket over his wife to conceal her nakedness. "Is that close enough to a werewolf for you?"

"I don't believe I'd like to come any closer," muttered Villichuck, whose back was pressed against the far wall, his limbs galvanized to propel him down the hall at top speed, should the change suddenly reverse itself.

Onopko muttered a curse in Russian, but Crow's expression remained inscrutable until finally his words revealed his thoughts. "The Navajo call them skinwalkers."

Mrs. Scarlet gathered the blanket around her, blond hair spilling in long waves around her shoulders and down her back. She blinked, momentarily concealing her copper-colored eyes. "What happened, Jack? I... I... I didn't hurt anybody, did I?"

"No," said Jack. "I was right here in the room with you for the whole transformation."

"I don't see any blood on her," said Crow. "If she had been the one who ate Grenier she would be covered in blood."

Fonteneau muttered an imprecation. "Well, if it wasn't Madame Scarlet then who was it?" Her face turned fierce. "Monsieur Scarlet, tell me how it was that Diogenes rebutted Plato's argument that a human was but a featherless biped."

"I don't see the significance," said Mr. Scarlet.

"Of course you don't," said Fonteneau. "A true member of the Diogenes Club would know the answer to that question."

"He brought in a plucked chicken and told Plato that he had brought him a man," said Mrs. Scarlet. "I remember reading the story."

"My point is," said Fonteneau, "that neither of you are members of the Diogenes Club. You are infiltrators."

"It is true," said Mr. Scarlet. "I learned the password when I came across a murder taking place in a New Orleans alley. The murderer was a lycanthrope like my wife, and he was extracting the name of his victim and the method for entering sanctums of the Diogenes Club. I had never heard of the Diogenes Club, but the murderer seemed to know of it."

"And what happened to this murderer?" asked Fonteneau.

"Unfortunately, he escaped me. He's the reason that Maura and I are here."

"Please excuse me for a moment," said Mrs. Scarlet. She passed behind a dressing screen of stained glass, threw the blanket over the screen and began to remove the tatters of her dress and change into more modest attire.

"You know this murderer?"

"Earl Graymorton—a traitor to his wolf pack and all lycanthropes. He has thrown his lot in with the Swordsmen of Xeniade."

"Earl Graymorton!" gasped Fontenau. "I met him in Paris. I should have known that his mocking platitudes were a screen for something more. He was the werewolf that I was chasing—and all that time in front of my very nose!"

"He doesn't go by Graymorton anymore," said Scarlet. "He has taken the identity of the man he murdered—one Vychan Gough. I believe he is in the Five Points region. I've picked up his scent, though it was somewhat masked by incense, so I don't know just how long ago he was here. I was hoping that perhaps he would return."

"He's more than been here," said Villichuck. "He's a guest here right now!"

"And apparently he's on a mission of vengeance," said Onopko. "If he's killed Grenier already then Father Gibbons has got to be next on his list."

Fonteneau glared at Jack Scarlet and his wife. "You two stay here. I'll deal with you later!"

"The Diogenes Club does not look kindly upon imposters," said Onopko with a leer scarcely concealed behind his thick beard.

Mrs. Scarlet perched herself, now fully dressed, upon the edge of her bed. Her shackle hung loosely around her leg. She breathed slowly, methodically, as if attempting to exert control over her rebelling body. "I can feel the moon working upon my blood. If I am agitated I may turn again."

"Fortunately, we have locks on the outside of all our doors as well as the insides," said Villichuck.

"Wait," said Jack Scarlet. "Let me go with you. The reason I'm here is to track down Graymorton and stop him before he reveals the location of the wolf clans to the Swordsmen of Xianades. Let me help."

"What do you care about the survival of a bunch of half-wolf abominations?" spat Onopko. The wolf-hound at his side seemed to have recovered from her initial terror at seeing a much larger canine and now she barked and growled at Jack and Maura Scarlet.

Fonteneau shook her head. "His wife is one of them, Monseur Onopko. Now, no more foolish questions." She turned her attention away from the Russian. "What of your wife, Monsieur Scarlet? If we bring her will she be able to control her urges?"

"No, I must stay!" cried Mrs. Scarlet. "Lock the door from the outside and I will do my best to maintain my shape."

"And a nice shape it is," muttered Onopko as he patted Sasha. "Too bad there's a lunatic wolf inside of it."

Jack Scarlet gave Onopko a sharp glance, and the Russian wondered how the gentleman's ears had discerned the words spoken beneath his breath.

"You heard the mademoiselle," said Fonteneau to Villichuck. "Lock the door and lock it well."

Villichuck came forward and with a deferential glance to Jack Scarlet closed the door and began to bolt it shut.

"I hear something," said Jack Scarlet. He began to run down the hall and though none of the rest of them had sensed anything besides Sasha's growling, they followed him.

Scarlet halted at an intersection of four corridors and peered into the gloomy pennant-draped halls. He lifted his nose and his nostrils quivered for just a moment and then he plunged down the corridor to the right. Villichuck came running down the corridor after Fonteneau, Crow, and Onopko and his wolf-hound. "Wait for me…" he huffed.

Fonteneau paused just a moment. "Is Scarlet headed toward—"

"Yes," nodded Villichuck vigorously. "He's headed toward Father Gibbon's chambers."

Sasha caught wind of something. She broke loose from Onopko's grip upon her diamond-studded collar and raced after Scarlet as if she were on the hunt.

"Come back here, you fool hound," shouted Onopko, but Sasha was far enough down the hall now that she pretended not to hear.

Scarlet arrived at Father Gibbon's chambers just a moment or two before Sasha caught up with him. The door was broken asunder, the thick slats lay shattered on the carpeted floor. Father Gibbons was strung up from the rafters, hanging by his own entrails. Graymorton was doing more than gaining vengeance on the Diogenes Club, he was leaving a warning of what would happen to anyone else that might interfere with him or the Swordsmen of Xianades.

Sasha began to bark at Scarlet, her tail slung low but Jack Scarlet let a deep growl rumble from the bottom of his throat. Immediately, Sasha began to whimper and offered up her paw in a sign of submission.

"That's better, girl," said Scarlet. "I'm the pack leader, here, and don't you forget it."

There were large and bloody pawprints upon the floor, and these exited the room and continued down the corridor. Crow had taken the lead of the rest and when he arrived he immediately spotted the pawprints marking the Venetian carpet that unfurled down the hallway. He didn't pause as he rushed past the room and saw the still quivering wreckage of Father Gibbons body, instead he continued down the hall and followed the fading blood prints around the corner and down a narrow flight of stairs which descended to the first floor, then deeper into the cellar.

Though Crow was moving at reckless speed, his pistol in hand, Scarlet bounded down the stairs after him with amazing alacrity.

"Fall back behind me," warned Scarlet. "Lycanthropes aren't affected by bullets the same way as an uninfected human."

They paused at a closed door at the bottom of the stair. Crow worked the handle and pushed it open revealing a dank chamber that was stacked with crates, over which loomed the statue of the blood-vomiting jaguar which was patron god of the Mayans. "Where did they get that idol?" grunted Crow.

"The Diogenes Club delves into strange things," said Scarlet. "I know little else about them—now stay back. Graymorton has got to be inside somewhere. Your bullets will do nothing but make him angry—unless you happen to have silver bullets loaded into that pistol."

Crow gazed at Scarlet with inscrutable brown eyes. "There is more to this pistol than you understand."

"Seriously, your gun has no chance of hurting…" Scarlet reached out to pluck the gun out of Crow's grip, but when he touched the barrel Scarlet hissed and jerked his hand back. For an instant, Crow saw a brand seared across Scarlet's hand, but the burn began to heal the moment the grip was relinquished.

"Your wife isn't the only skinwalker in your family," said Crow.

"It seems that there is more to your pistol than meets the eye, after all," replied Scarlet without confirming or denying Crow's accusation.

"Whose side do you fall on?" asked Crow. "Are you for or against this Graymorton?"

"Against," spat Scarlet. "He's responsible for the deaths of many of my kind."

"Then swear to do me no harm," said Crow.

"For as long as you are no danger to me or mine," said Scarlet.

"Can you smell out Graymorton?"

Scarlet shook his head. "Graymorton's bathed himself in the smoke of incense to mask his scent. He's here, though."

Crow nodded and motioned for Scarlet to take the east side of the room while he went to the west, creeping through the shadowed paths between tottering piles of artifacts. Just as they began to fan out Fonteneau entered the room. She set a lantern on the crate next to the door and her katana rasped from its sheath, gleaming dully in the wavering light.

At that moment Sasha burst past Fonteneau, barking wildly. She skittered to a stop on the cobbled floor at the center of the room and began spinning in circles, nose in the air as she tried to locate Graymorton. It was then that a great roar reverberated through the cellar and a tower of crates toppled as a hairy creature leaped from the umbra. Great fangs descended upon Sasha's skull and splintered it. The beast roared and shook Sasha's body like a terrier with a rat before flinging it across the room with a jerk of its corded neck.

Graymorton was in full werewolf form and he turned his baleful yellow eyes upon Fonteneau who stood in the center aisle—sword raised in the jodan position and weight evenly distributed over both feet in the koshimi stance. With a bloodthirsty howl Graymorton leaped upon Fonteneau. She moved swiftly, her katana lopping off one clawed paw, before the werewolf batted her to the cobblestones. The force of the impact sent her katana careening across the cobblestones.

That would have been the end of Fonteneau's life right there if Crow hadn't begun firing from atop a teetering pile of crates where he had climbed the moment he heard the werewolf's howl. The pile of crates was not stable and Crow rode the falling stack to the earth, firing four of his six bullets down the spine of the beast before crashing to the earth and rolling across the ground.

Graymorton reared up, roaring in pain—and anger. He would have ended Fonteneau's life with a slash of his paw had not Scarlet made a superhuman leap that carried him onto Graymorton's back. Scarlet wrapped an arm around the beast's throat and wrenched the head backward, but Graymorton was not so easily subdued. With a bestial cry he shook off Scarlet and sent him tumbling into a wall of crates, which crashed down upon him—crushing him beneath.

Then Graymorton turned tail and disappeared behind a screen of crates draped with blood-stained and moth-eaten banners that once waved at the forefront of some ancient crusade. Crow darted after the fleeing Graymorton and found a narrow tunnel hidden behind the crates. The tunnel led into the unlit recesses of the earth. Crow sent his last two bullets winging after the shadowy shape as it retreated into the blackness, but couldn't be satisfied that either of them connected with their target.

He took a moment to push out the hot brass from his smoking pistol and reload the cylinder with fresh cartridges from the bandolier beneath his buckskin jacket. Crow heard raging cries of grief from Onopko as the Russian entered the room and found the body of his wolf hound.

"I'll kill that mangy lycanthrope if it is the last thing I do," he bellowed with shaking fist. "Where did he go?"

Fonteneau emerged around the corner of the crate wall where the secret passage was hidden and found Crow reloading his eagle-butted pistol. She was smudged with dirt and her dress was torn, but she appeared to be otherwise intact. She hurled a hairy paw at Crow's feet.

"Graymorton may have knocked me for a loop, but he didn't get away unscathed."

Before Crow's very eyes the great hairy paw began to shrink and in a few moments it resumed the form of a severed human hand.

Scarlet loomed up behind Fonteneau. "Is there silver in that blade?"

Fonteneau nodded. "Mais oui, just enough to allow me to wound a werewolf without ruining the strength of the alloy."

"He's severely wounded," said Crow. "That should slow him. If we give pursuit we may be able to overtake him."

"The hand will grow back," said Scarlet. "The silver may retard the healing, but given time it will regenerate."

Fonteneau muttered an imprecation about lycanthropes. "What if we cut off Graymorton's head? That won't grow back, will it?"

Scarlet shook his head. "No, that would do the trick."

"Any idea where this tunnel leads?" asked Crow.

"I heard a rumor that there was a tunnel that connected with the old brewery and came out near the swamps," said Fonteneau, "but that was a closely guarded secret even among the Diogenes elite. I don't know how Graymorton would have known about it."

"He seemed to know exactly where to find the tunnel," commented Scarlet.

"Indeed," said Fonteneau.

"Where is that wolf!" cried Onopko, who rose bloody from the corpse of his slain hound. "I'll pull out his guts with my bare hands!" He found the trio at the mouth of the secret tunnel and jabbed a finger at Scarlet. "Your wife is one of them! I'll make her pay, too—and you, you sick, twisted—"

"We don't have time for pointless threats," interrupted Fonteneau. "Monsieur Onopko, you come with me through the tunnel. Scarlet and Crow will head toward the swamps and we'll see if we can't pin Graymorton between us."

Onopko opened his mouth in outrage. "We can't trust them! Neither of them are members of Diogenes and one of them is nothing but a mindless savage!"

"Then you and I had best hurry if we plan to catch up with Graymorton," said Fonteneau.

Onopko reached for a heavy-handled five shot Beaumont Adams .50 caliber pistol that was thrust into his waist. He snarled at Scarlet. "You and I aren't done yet, wolf lover."

Then Onopko disappeared into the tunnel following after the curvaceous form of Amandine Fonteneau.

"Thanks for not telling him my secret," said Scarlet as soon as the Russian left.

Lone Crow shrugged. "He'll figure it out soon enough, when he remembers that unlikely leap you made onto the back of the werewolf."

"Are you coming with me?"

"Right behind you, skinwalker," said Crow and he leaped up the stairs after Scarlet who was rapidly gaining the lead by bounding up six and seven steps at a time—a feat which Crow could not hope to duplicate.

There was no sign of Villichuck as they ran out the lobby and onto the streets of Five Points. As they sprinted toward the swamps they left Orange Street and the sights and sounds of the city assailed them. Harlots and drunkards cried out to them, hucksters from rum cellars and gaming dens shouted for their business, but these flashed by in a pounding of footsteps and the harsh rasp of their pumping lungs. Crow couldn't keep up with Scarlet, who disappeared into the gloaming of the hanging street lamps. Just a few blocks past the brewery, now a leaning tenement that was slowly being reclaimed by the swamp, a cordon of Bowery boys closed in around him—a forest of stove-pipe hats with trunks of calf-skin boots. They had gathered reinforcements since Crow's previous encounter with them.

Crow noticed a livid scar tracing the cheekbone of the leader as the Bowery Boy sauntered forward a pace or two, flanked by a dozen of his thugs. Another dozen of the Bowery Boys moved up from behind Crow, making escape impossible. He saw that in addition to the brickbats and hatchets they had carried earlier, that at least three of them had managed to scare up pepperbox pistols. They were four-barreled gambling guns with a poor range and holding one bullet per barrel. They were small caliber and meant for close up gunwork, so Crow resolved not to let that trio of gun-man get any closer.

"What happened to that nice-looking lady friend of yours?" asked the gang leader. "I have something that I want to show her."

"She's currently attending to business," said Crow. "Now if you'll let me pass, I also have business to attend to."

"I don't think so, injun. You and me, we've got a score to settle." That's when the gangleader jerked his pepperbox pistol from his belt, signalling the henchman on his left and right to do the same. Crow's hand moved as quick as lightning and his Peacemaker began to belch fiery death. Though the gangleader had begun the draw before Crow, the Indian gunslinger was the first to fire.

His bullet split the flesh along the gangleader's forearm and lodged between the ribs beneath the Bowery Boy's armpit. The gangleader jerked back the trigger of his pepperbox, but his aim had been thrown awry by the bullet and a cluster of four bullets scathed past Crow and peppered one of the Bowery Boys that was creeping up behind with a raised brickbat.

Crow's second shot was less hurried and better aimed. It took the hench-man on the gangleader's right, in the heart, and the henchman dropped like a burlap bag of wheat onto the cobbles. The third shot from Crow's gun took the last gunman through the belly and his pepperbox fired, blowing fragments of cobblestone from the street where the quartet of bullets struck and ricocheted away.

One of the bullets spat between Crow's legs and he heard a Bowery Boy cry out as it struck him. Then the mob converged upon the Indian gunslinger with raised chunks of brick or swinging socks that contained stones. Crow fired three more times, taking down three more of the Bowery Boys and then the pummeling began. He took a number of blows on his body. A brickbat struck a glancing blow against his skull and he went reeling to his knees.

He lashed out with his elbow, trying to clear some space around him, and heard the snap of a Bowery's boy knee. The same Bowery Boy pitched backward and dropped his hatchet. Crow snatched it from amid the storm of stomping and kicking feet, even as he took a number of crushing blows upon his back. The sheer numbers of his enemy had overwhelmed him and he didn't even have room to swing the hatchet upon which he had laid his hands.

Just when Crow thought the next blow would finish him he heard the gangleader cry out. "It's a giant wolf!"

For a moment the beating stopped and the crowd parted just enough so that Crow could see the injured gangleader resting on the pavement, finishing the reloading of his pepperbox. He followed the gangleader's eyes and then he saw Graymorton, in skinwalker form, emerging from an alley that ran toward the swamp. For a moment the Bowery Boys were frozen into inaction as the great werewolf stalked through the shadows, turning his baleful yellow glare upon the gathered hosts of the stove-piped ruffians.

Probably, Graymorton would have limped past them and into the shadows of the next road or alley, but the gangleader raised the gun with both hands—experiencing some difficulty because of his injured right arm and the bullet between his ribs—and fired his pepperbox. The bullets that struck Graymorton were not enough to seriously injure, but they stung enough to enrage him. With a great roar that was accompanied by a fetid exhalation, the werewolf leaped into the midst of the Bowery Boys, batting to the left and right with swings of his powerful paw.

Stove pipe hats and Bowery Boy heads rolled down the cobblestones and bodies were hurled through the air. Crow took this moment of distraction to rise from his crouch and his hair flailed wildly as he struck out with the edge of his hatchet. He took out two Bowery Boys with his first blow and the second blow firmly lodged the axe in the skull of another.

That was enough for the Bowery Boys. Anyone capable of fleeing scattered from the area as fast as their legs would carry them. This left a number of corpses scattered upon the street, and the Bowery Boys gangleader cried out futilely as his companions deserted him. He staggered to his feet, but didn't take more than a dozen steps before Graymorton pounced on him and tore out his throat with those great fangs.

Crow was too bruised and beaten to do anything else but stand his ground. He dumped out the empty brass from his pistol and began to reload. Graymorton turned and fixed that glowing yellow glare upon him, but Crow was already resigned to death and he returned the glare with his dark, somber eyes. All the while, his fingers nimbly shoved fresh cartridges into his pistol.

It was unlikely that Crow would have enough time to reload his pistol and fire before Graymorton pounced on him, but that was when Fonteneau and Onopko emerged from the alley, mud-stained and bedraggled.

Onopko began cursing the lycanthrope and drew his five shot pistol. "Come on you mangy dog! I've got a gift for you."

"Don't even bother," said Fonteneau. "Not unless you're loaded with silver bullets."

"These are .50 caliber rounds," said Onopko. "I've taken down a charging elephant with these, I'm sure I can take down a flea-bitten mutt."

Onopko strode forward, pausing to fire between each step. Indeed, the .50 caliber rounds seemed to enrage Graymorton even more than the storm of lead fired from the Bowery Boys' pepperboxes, and they even appeared to slow him down a bit, but Graymorton absorbed each round and for every step that Onopko took forward so did the werewolf. It was only moments before Onopko and Graymorton met, and Crow opted to close the cylinder of his pistol before he had loaded the last round into place—in the hopes that he could forestall Onopko's impending demise.

With his last bullet ineffectually fired, Onopko found himself face to face with the great beast and Graymorton opened his bloody maw to finish the unfortunate Russian. Then, like a thunderbolt through the shadows, a furry form streaked down the street and plowed into Graymorton. The two lupine forms tumbled across the cobblestones in a flurry of slashing paws and rending teeth. Fur flew in the air and for a moment it seemed that the two foes were evenly matched.

However, Graymorton had been weakened by three bullets into the spine from Crow's blessed gun, and one paw had been sliced clean off by Fonteneau's blade—and finally the second werewolf lunged and took hold of Graymorton's throat. The sharp fangs tore through the fur and the jugular spurted crimson as it was ripped wide open. In a frenzy of blood lust the victor shook his dying opponent until the last vestiges of life had left Graymorton, and then it cast aside the body in a manner that suggested contempt.

The blood lust was still upon the surviving werewolf, and with a growl it turned upon the motley trio that had witnessed his victory.

"Does anyone happen to have some .50 caliber silver bullets?" asked Onopko feebly.

"I'm fresh out," said Crow, his impassive face not betraying the sarcasm that had left his lips.

"That thing must have eaten Scarlet," said Onopko. "Serves the wolf lover right."

"That thing is Scarlet," said Fonteneau. Crow nodded in concurrence.

"You knew this, also?" hissed Onopko. "Why didn't I know?"

The werewolf that was Jack Scarlet gained control of his rage and he turned away from the trio, slinking into the shadows and disappearing into the dangerous back alleys that surrounded Five Points—and which, for the moment, were no longer safe for the cutpurses, roughnecks, and cutthroats that made them their haven.

"I suppose we'd better dispose of the giant wolf carcass, before too many questions get asked," said Onopko.

"No need," said Fonteneau. Before their eyes the canine form began to shrink and the hirsute characteristics withdrew until a wiry and sallow man with bulging eyes and prominent teeth lay naked upon the cobbles. "Let Graymorton lie. The residents of Five Points will think him just another victim of the Bowery Boys."

"They might even wonder how such a scrawny weakling managed to kill so many of them," laughed Onopko.

"Let's get back to the sanctum on Orange Street," said Fonteneau. "I expect that once Scarlet is able to change that he'll be back for his wife."

"And then I'll have a few words with him," said Onopko.

"They had better include the phrase 'thank you'," said Fonteneau as she started down the street. "He did save your life, after all. Or had you already forgotten that?"

"Don't remind me," growled Onopko. "The last thing I need is to be indebted to a werewolf."

"Something's been bothering me," said Crow.

"So the silent savage speaks," said Onopko. "Tell us what's been bothering you—because I'm oh so interested in hearing the thoughts of a mindless savage."

"Your dog chewed up Villichuck's boots which were imported from France. You said they cost more than you could afford."

"Don't you dare impugn Sasha…"

"Graymorton had remarkable knowledge of the Diogenes Club. He knew that Grenier and Father Gibbons were going to be staying there and he knew about the tunnel to the swamps. I think that Villichuck is on the payroll of this rival organization, The Swordsmen of Xianades, and that Villichuck gave them the information about the sanctum and its guests."

"Hmph," said Onopko. "Maybe you are not as stupid as you look. Villichuck did disappear about the time we found Graymorton in the cellar."

"Maybe it's you that lacks the intelligence, Valerii," said Fonteneau. "If you persist in your insults Crow may just split you wide open—or I may do it for him, considering his temperament is far too even."

"Wha…" choked Onopko. Then Crow and Fonteneau took off running for the sanctum, and still smarting from Fonteneau's words he took up chase after them.

*****

Maura Scarlet sat on the edge of her bed as Villichuck came skulking into her room bearing a five shot Smith and Wesson loaded with silver bullets. Her extraordinary senses had picked up his stealthy foot treads in the hallway and even his scent long before he had arrived.

"You've come to kill me for the Swordsmen of Xianades," she said, her beautiful features in calm repose.

"How… how did you know?" asked Villichuck.

"When I'm able to control the frenzy of the wolf I'm quite intuitive," she said. "How long have you been on their payroll?"

"Six months," said Villichuck as he leveled the pistol. "They aren't miserly sods, like the Diogenes Club. I've lived quite well since they started sending me monthly stipends."

"Aim for the heart or better yet the head," said Maura Scarlet. "That's the only guarantee of killing a werewolf instantly—and only if your bullets are cast from pure silver. It's like poison to us."

"Thanks for the tip," said Villichuck. He adjusted his aim to the center of the beautiful lycanthrop's skull and squeezed the trigger.

With inhuman speed Maura Scarlet jerked aside, the bullet plowing into the wall, and then she moved underneath Villichuck's aim, grabbed hold of his neck and slammed him against the door frame. The Smith and Wesson shook loose from his grasp. With immense strength that seemed impossible in such a delicate woman, she applied pressure to his windpipe.

"I thought you were chained," gasped Villichuck.

"Apparently you didn't see my husband slip me the key before he left," she responded with a whisper.

When Fonteneau, Crow and Onopko arrived, they found Maura Scarlet sitting demurely on her bed. Villichuck lay in the open door way, his neck snapped and twisted at an unnatural angle and a pistol loaded with silver bullets lying a few feet away.

"Have you seen my husband?" asked Maura Scarlet.

"He'll be along a little bit later," said Fonteneau. "Monsieur Graymorton, however, will not be paying us a return visit."

The Five Disciples

Lone Crow climbed Telegraph Hill, winding his way through clusters of tents and ramshackle wooden shelters of the Chileno encampment that clung to the slopes like barnacles on a ship's hull. Behind him San Francisco Bay sprawled out, the rays of the falling sun glistering against the waves, and shadowing the clusters of ships that jammed the harbor—ships abandoned by their crews, who had been infected with gold fever.

Brown eyes viewed him from parted tent flaps and voices called and hands beckoned. Crow looked neither to the left or the right until he reached a campfire around which three Chileno women gathered, stirring a pot of beans and frying a corn tortilla on a skillet.

"We're not working, gringo," said the tallest, with a quick motion of her upraised hand. "Go visit one of the tents."

Crow wore a buckskin jacket, a kerchief about his neck and a gun belt that was weighted on the right with a .45 Colt Peacemaker, the butt of which was engraved with the image of an eagle. He pushed back his hat and revealed his dark skin and long black hair, his features certainly not those of a white man.

"An Indian!" gasped the woman. "We don't do business with your kind. I thought you were a cowboy."

"I'm looking for Buena Holguin," said Crow.

The trio of harlots crossed themselves at the mentions of Buena's name, as if the mere mention might bring evil upon them.

"She might do business with an Indian," said the woman who was crouched next to the fire. She deftly flipped the tortilla so that it could fry on the opposite side. "But she has charmed that black fellow. Finds him useful."

"Buena's not doing business with anyone, anymore," snorted the hard-eyed woman who tended to the bubbling pot of beans. "She only does business when she's looking for a new papacita."

"Where can I find her?" persisted Crow.

"Take a right at the crest of the hill and it's the yellow tent with the ribbon tied to the post," replied the woman with the skillet. "But I'm warning you, her new papacita gives a lacing to anyone who used to be Buena's customers."

"Would this happen to be Buena's new boyfriend?" said Crow, and he unrolled a wanted poster that featured a photo of a fierce looking black man.

"Shotgun Ferguson? He's wanted for murder?" The woman extricated the cooked tortilla and placed it on a wooden plate beside her.

The tallest of the harlots blinked. "That's him all right. There's a three thousand dollar reward for his capture or death?"

"Are you a bounty hunter?" asked the woman stirring the beans.

"Well, I do aim to collect the reward," said Crow. He tipped his hat. "Thank you for your help, ladies."

"You come back and pay us a visit after you collect that reward," called the woman with the skillet, who apparently had reconsidered their policy against doing business with Indians.

Crow did not respond. Instead he climbed to the crest of the hill and strode along a footpath flanked by ragged tents that were mildewed and faded by alternating fogs and sunshine. He found the yellow tent with a ribbon tied to the pole. The ribbon, he'd been told, signified that Buena was engaged with a customer, but he suspected that customer was Shotgun Ferguson.

Throwing aside the flap of the tent, Crow strode inside, his pistol drawn. Buena was a sloe-eyed woman with a small mole on her left cheek and a wealth of dark hair that fell in lustrous waves about her shoulders. She was attired in a simple dress and lounging on a few crates that had been jetsam washed ashore. These were draped with a swatch of red velvet and a number of throw pillows.

Crates also served as a table that held a mostly empty bottle of rye and a deck of pasteboards that were laid out in a very specific order. The tent was partitioned by a hanging blanket, which slightly swayed, and Crow could see the toe of a bare foot protruding.

Buena smiled coyly at Crow and slipped the strap of her dress from her shoulder. "Are you looking for me, cowboy?"

She wore a cloying and heady perfume that was thick in Crow's nostrils and Crow could feel the tug of strange magics combining with the physical allure of the witch. Crow, however, understood full well that she was attempting to draw his attention. Instead he threw himself to one side. Barely had he accomplished this when the double-barreled blast of a shotgun roared inside the tent, tearing a gaping hole through the hanging blanket. Pellets of lead scathed the air where Crow had stood but a moment prior, and then peppered the flap of the tent.

Crow reached up and tore down the quivering blanket, revealing a black man so large that his head scraped the peak of the tent. He was breaking open his double-barreled shotgun in order to push in fresh cartridges when Crow pointed his revolver mid-chest.

"Drop the gun, Ferguson!"

Crow wondered just how many bullets it would take to stop a man that big, but thankfully Ferguson didn't appear anxious to put that question to the test. He dropped the shotgun and raised his hands to shoulder height. Keeping his pistol trained on Ferguson, Crow took a pair of steps backward to stay out range of those over-sized mitts, just in case Ferguson couldn't resist the temptation.

"Sit cross-legged on the floor," ordered Crow, "and put your hands behind your head."

Ferguson did as ordered.

"Why didn't you look at me?" demanded Buena. "Don't you like women?"

"I didn't want to end up dead," said Crow. "Now get down on the floor next to Mr. Ferguson."

"Or what? You'll shoot me, too? There's no bounty on my head. What do you want with me?"

Crow caught a closer glimpse of the pasteboards on the table and now he could see that they weren't a standard deck of cards. They were altered to include cryptic symbols, lewd drawings, and occult figures so that the pasteboards were converted into some sort of tarot deck. "I want nothing to do with you, witch. Now get on the floor."

She complied with a deliberate lack of urgency, baiting Crow.

"I got a good look at you," said Shotgun Ferguson. "All those white man clothes can't hide your red skin.

"And running all the way from South Carolina can't save you from justice," replied Crow. He holstered his gun and cinched Ferguson's wrists together with practiced movements. At that moment Buena glanced over her still-bared shoulder and saw that Crow had no weapon in his hand. She lunged, raking at him with her long nails. He avoided her initial attack and gave her a shove that sent her tumbling.

In that brief moment, Ferguson untangled his crossed legs and lurched to his feet. Before he could find his balance Crow gave him the heel of his boot and the big man staggered into a divan made from old sea crates. They splintered beneath his weight and Ferguson found himself sitting among the broken slats, his hands still bound behind him.

"Justice?" spat Ferguson. "I'm a black man, there's no justice for me and if you think you can fool the white men into giving you justice because you wear their clothes, then you're fooling yourself. You're an Indian and you'll always be one."

"You're wanted for three murders," said Crow.

"And they send their lapdog to execute justice?" Ferguson's laugh was bitter.

"Come along without a fuss and I won't have to do any executing," said Crow. "I'll take you to the law, and you'll be sent back to South Carolina to face trial."

"A lynching, you mean. I killed those three men, all right—but they were white and I'm not. It doesn't matter what they did to my sister."

Buena began to mutter incantations underneath her breath.

"Save your curses, witch," said Crow. "I'm immune to your magics."

"You may be immune to my charms, Indian, but other men are not."

Crow frowned and spoke to Ferguson. "What did they do to your sister?"

Ferguson struggled upright. "They forced her, then killed her so that she wouldn't tell nobody. I happened into the barn where they did the deed. They were trying to hide her body beneath the straw. I took away a shotgun and turned it on its owner. Two barrels at close range—it cut him in half."

"No kidding," said Crow, who recalled how close he had been to suffering the same demise.

"The other two men I killed with my bare hands." Ferguson shuddered as he relived the incident.

"I understand you killed Philips and Morganstern when they tracked you down in Kansas City."

"The bounty hunters?" said Ferguson. "They didn't count on me taking my shotgun to the outhouse with me."

"Are you going to hold that against him?" cried Buena. "He was just defending his life."

"But is he telling the truth?" asked Crow.

She raised her chin in proud defiance. "He's under my charms. He can't tell a lie, and he is completely under my control. All it takes is one visit and I can make any man my slave… except for you, it seems." She raised a beckoning hand toward him. "But given some time, perhaps…"

"Enough," said Crow, who felt temptation as keenly as any man.

"Are you scared of the passion that I might unleash?"

"I've met Philips and Morganstern," said Crow, who abruptly changed the subject. "The righteous of the world won't mourn their loss."

"Where are the other four of you?" questioned Buena.

"What are you talking about?" said Crow, who wondered if Buena was again using some sort of ploy to pull away his attention.

Buena shook her finger. Her hands were covered with rings and arcane amulets dangled between her breasts. "I read the cards. They said that five were on the way. That's how Shotgun knew to be ready for you."

"Five what?" asked Crow.

"Five followers or acolytes," said Buena. "The cards were unclear, but they are men of great power. I sensed a power about you, so I mistook you as one of them. But you, you possess a different sort of power. It shrivels my guts…"

Crow hissed between his teeth. "I'm not the only one in San Francisco that's looking for Shotgun Ferguson. Five Chinese bounty hunters rode into town two nights ago. They've been asking about Shotgun. It's hard to hide a black man your size—even in a place as big as San Francisco."

Buena furrowed her brow. "What did these bounty hunters call themselves?"

"I don't know how they refer to themselves, but I've heard others refer to them as The Disciples. Disciples of what, I'm not sure."

"The Disciples of the Immortals," spat Buena. "What a fool I was to charm a man with such a large bounty on his head. I should have known it would bring doom upon me."

"It doesn't much matter how I meet my death," said Shotgun Ferguson, "but I'd prefer to do it with a gun in my hand, spitting in the face of the Devil instead of swinging from a tree."

"They're coming now," moaned Buena. Her long lashes flickered and her eyes darted, alternating between a glassy stare and the whites of her eyes. "I can feel them. The Immortals have imbued the Disciples with a fraction of their power so that they might go forth and bring fear and terror into the world."

Buena's vision regained focus. "Let me go!" she shrieked. "I beg of you. Let me go!"

"Fine," said Crow.

Without waiting for any further elaboration Buena cast one glance at her tied paramour. "Ha sido divertido, Shotgun." She lurched across the tent, her hand diving beneath a cushion and she produced a Colt Pocket Dragoon pistol, a five shot .31 caliber gun with a stagecoach raid engraved on the cylinder. Crow nearly fired a shot through Buena, but instead of targeting the Indian bounty hunter the witch reeled through the tent flap and into the falling dusk.

The intoxicating scent of the perfume still lingered after Buena's departure, but when she opened the flap a breeze passed into the tent clearing much of the air.

Ferguson breathed a heavy sigh. "Where am I, and why am I tied up?"

"I'm Lone Crow, here to collect you and the bounty on your head."

Shotgun Ferguson tested his bonds and Crow could hear the fiber of the new ropes creaking under the forces exerted by those muscular arms. "The last thing I remember is coming inside of the tent of a Chileno harlot. I didn't mean to, I was just passing through."

"It's safer to stand in holy places," said Lone Crow. "Telegraph Hill is not the place for the likes of you or me."

"I'm a wanted murderer," said Shotgun. "Does it matter which other of the ten commandments I break?"

"Your killings were done in the name of justice and the defense of your own life," said Crow. He plucked an eighteen-inch knife out of the sheath tied to his leg.

"What are you doing?" asked Ferguson.

"I'll make it quick," said Crow. He brought the knife across the strands of the rope that bound Ferguson's wrists. The rope unraveled and Ferguson rubbed at the grooves in his flesh.

"The harlot had you bewitched," said Crow. "You're free now."

"Except for the fact that you plan to bring me in for that bounty," said Ferguson. "I'm telling you now, that I'm not going to let that happen. I'd rather die than go back to South Carolina."

A wind whipped through the tents and shanties of Telegraph Hill, shaking the tent in which they stood. "Load your shotgun," said Crow. "They'll be here, shortly."

Ferguson found his open shotgun lying on the dirt floor. He pulled out the spent shells and pushed a pair of new ones into the breach of the barrels. "This is still warm. It's been fired recently."

"You fired it," said Crow. "Nearly cut me in half."

Ferguson locked the barrels into firing position. "So it's just you and me now, red man. Are we taking this out into the streets for a showdown? Is that your plan—to give me a fighting chance?"

"We'll fight," said Crow, "but I don't know if we'll have a chance. I can sense their presence. They are already here."

Ferguson seemed perplexed. "I can feel something, too. What is it?"

"They are called The Disciples, Chinese warriors trained by members of the Immortals—or so Buena informed me."

"The only immortal I know of is Jesus Christ," said Ferguson.

"There are others," said Crow, "but none so holy."

The drum of hoofbeats rang from the trail winding up the side of Telegraph Hill, and then the sound of footsteps preceding them came to Crow's ears. A piercing shriek rose above the howl of the rising winds and Buena staggered back into the tent, more unsteady than when she had departed.

She tried to speak, but blood bubbled on her lips and she pitched forward. Buena fell on her face and three wounds were visible on her back. Two shurikens had been thrown hard and were so deep in the flesh that they were invisible, except for the wound they had caused. One sharp point of the third throwing star still protruded and this told the cause of Buena's demise.

A sonorous voice that possessed more than a hint of Chinese accent, spoke from beyond the flap of the tent. "I am Kong Tien, the voice of the wind, and I am here to slay Shotgun Ferguson. Send him forth that he may meet his fate like a man."

"Meet my shotgun!" shouted Ferguson, and he unleashed a double barreled blast through the flap of the tent.

Crow cut a slit through the back of the tent and exited onto the steep slope of Telegraph Hill. Standing on the roof of a shanty, built just below Buena's tent was a Chinese man dressed in a pien-fu, a long tunic that fell to the knee of his underlying trousers. He wore a leather cap that was decorated with pheasant feathers and he carried an unsheathed broadsword.

"Did I not say that I am the voice of the wind? I merely threw my voice to the front of your abode, but stood here awaiting the inevitable exit of a coward. Now stand aside and give me the man known as Shotgun Ferguson or…" Kong Tien nodded toward his sword to indicate just what fate he intended for Crow, should he interfere.

Crow wasn't the fastest draw in the West, but he had bested many who thought that they were. He slapped leather and the blessed steel of his eagle-butted Colt Pistol appeared in his hand. He thumbed back the hammer and squeezed off a pair of shots, but a wind arose even as he pulled the trigger. The wind tore at his hat and sent it tumbling away, his black hair whipping behind him, but the gust also pushed his gun hand so that the two shots went awry, and the booming echoes of the firing pistol were lost in the howling winds and carried into the darkling skies.

Kong Tien laughed. "I have been schooled in the secrets of the Celestials, learned at the feet of the Immortals. The very winds are mine to command." Even as he spoke the wind rose at his back, billowing his pien-fu and carrying him through the air toward Crow. A second wind blasted from the roiling clouds above, striking Crow like a hammer and driving him to his knees. So strong was the blast that Crow could not bring his pistol to bear upon Kong Tien as the Chinese warrior drew closer with lifted sword.

Shotgun Ferguson plucked Buena's Colt Pocket Dragoon from her stiffening fingers and stumbled out of the tent through the slit in the back, the still smoking shotgun in his other hand and his trouser pockets full of shells. The winds whipped at his clothing, but the full force of the gusts were not directed at him. When he saw Kong Tien hurtling closer, borne aloft by the very elements, he began firing the Pocket Dragoon.

Ferguson was no marksman, hence his penchant for the shotgun which blasted a wide swath and required less in the way of aiming, so he fired wildly into the wind. The short-barreled gun bucked and twisted in his hand, but in a few moments he emptied an erratic five-shot volley into the winds. One of the bullets was plucked up by the wind and struck Kong Tien just over the left ear, entering the disciple's brain and killing him almost instantly.

The strength of the winds decreased immediately and Kong Tien's body was dropped unceremoniously onto the slope, where it tumbled down and finally came to a rest against the wall of the shanty.

"Nice shooting," said Crow as he lifted himself from the ground.

"Thanks," said Ferguson, who stared at his gun, surprised that he had actually been able hit something let alone kill his foe.

To the south of them, among a tangle of half-flattened tents and shacks, a pug-faced Chinese man with a broad-brimmed hat and a bright crimson cloak paused to pick up Crow's hat. He plucked a single hair from within and laid it on his cloak. Instantly, he flickered from Crow's sight.

"Did you see that?" asked Crow.

"If you mean that plug-ugly warrior with the huge straw hat, he just jumped between those two tents."

"He didn't disappear?" asked Crow.

"Well, he ran real fast, if that's what you mean," said Shotgun Ferguson.

"That's not what I mean," said Crow. "Let's skedaddle. If Buena was reading her witch cards right, there are three more disciples besides that one."

Crow started down the slope but Ferguson paused next to an oversized tent stake to pry the empty shells out of his shotgun and replace them with a pair of fresh cartridges. Crow glanced up the slope and saw a glimmer of movement, perhaps just a shifting of shadows, in the tent behind Ferguson.

"Behind you!" cried Crow.

Ferguson snapped the barrel of his shotgun closed and whirled. Before he could complete the turn, a pug-faced warrior reached out and plucked a curly black hair from his head and laid it on his crimson cloak. For an instant Ferguson saw the warrior and then, as soon as the hair touched the cloak, the warrior's form disappeared from view. This didn't stop Ferguson from unleashing both barrels of the shotgun at the last position he had seen the warrior.

The belching flame of the shotgun lit up the tent for just a moment and black gunsmoke rose thick into the air. No voice raised a cry of pain and no blood spattered upon the dirt floor of the tent as a result of the double-barreled shotgun blast.

"Get down!" cried Crow. From his vantage point down the slope he could see a shape moving among the fog of gunsmoke, whereas Ferguson, who was amidst the black smoke could not discern the form of his enemy or the sword blade that was rising to behead him.

This time Ferguson listened to Crow and he hurled himself backward, tumbling head over heels down the slope. An invisible sword blade descended and cut clean through the tent stake next to which Ferguson had stood a moment before. For a brief instant a void in the gunsmoke clearly delineated the form of the invisible warrior and Crow lifted his Eagle-butted .45 Peacemaker and fired three times.

This time there was a cry of pain and the tent wall caved inward as a heavy weight, invisible to the naked eye, fell upon it. Then a crimson stain spread upon the concavity of the tent's canvas, a pool of blood collecting.

Ferguson came to his feet a few yards from Crow. He was covered in dirt and grass, and bleeding from a couple of gashes caused by sharp stones on his way down the slope. "Did you get him!"

"Keep moving," said Crow. "If we let the three of them catch up to us at the same time we won't stand a chance."

"Three?" cried Ferguson. "So you did get that invisible son of a gun!"

They hurtled down the slopes as fast as their legs could safely take them, running between shanties made from sticks and boards, cracks filled with mud and grass, and through seas of tents. They leaped smoldering fires and past perplexed residents. Ferguson lost his balance and took a misstep that carried him right through a tent, leveling it and leaving its grappling occupants to cry out curses and grope their way out.

Crow hazarded a glance over his shoulder and his fears were realized. Pursuing them from behind came a Chinese woman who leaped as graceful as a gazelle from the sod roofs of shacks to the pinnacles of soot-stained tents. Her steps seemed nearly weightless, as she scarcely left an impression upon the canvas beneath her footfalls. Her hair flowed raven behind her and her hairpins caught the dying light, glittering as ferociously as the pair of swords that she bore.

To their right, pursuing a parallel course, was a handsome Chinese man that sprinted down the trail with such speed that he would easily outpace those he pursued. As the handsome warrior caught sight of Crow and Ferguson he pulled a badger skin cloak over his shoulders and instantly his visage was tranformed into a hideous mask that was caught between human and animal. The smooth skin of his body became mottled and leathery and then he altered his course inward to intercept the fleeing Indian and black man.

Crow cast about for the last of The Disciples, wondering where the third surviving warrior would manifest himself. Then he saw this last warrior standing ahead, riding a great stallion which trampled tents and sent Chileno harlots and their patrons scrambling away. His sword glittered and he cut them down as they ran. A harsh laugh redounded from the hideous wooden mask that concealed his true features.

"We're between the bull and the barbed wire," said Crow. He slowed his pace but he didn't cease running, even as he opened the cylinder to his pistol and began levering out spent shells.

Ferguson did the same, cracking open his shotgun and shaking out the remnants of the paper cartridges. He slipped two more into place, but the female warrior was gaining fast upon him, leaping over the heads of terrified ladies of the line, from sod roof to sod roof. A gambler reeled out of one tent and sent a hail of bullets in the warrior's direction. She whirled, changing directions in mid-air, defying momentum and the laws of physics. Bullets spattered from her sword blades, and she alit next to the gambler. There was a blur of movement as one of her swords whipped forward, and then the gambler's head went rolling in the dirt—even while his body crumpled.

A terrified mauk went shrieking to her knees and the warrior's narrow eyes appraised her with glittering intensity. Then, apparently deciding that she was no danger, she leaped back into the air, and onto the pinnacle of the nearest tent. This distraction, which came at the cost of a gambler's life, gave Shotgun Ferguson and Lone Crow a few extra moments, but the fact was that they were boxed in on all sides, and that box was closing in upon them.

Crow and Ferguson whirled as a great yowl rose from their right. The warrior who had transformed when he had pulled tight his badger's cloak came charging at them, his broadsword raised. Ferguson loosed one barrel from his shotgun and even though he was mid-stride the scathing hail of lead pellets struck the warrior's torso.

Normally, this would have been a devastating blast—enough to bring the toughest man to his knees, with a belly full of hot lead. But the lead pellets ricocheted from the thickened hide of the hideous badger warrior, doing little more than slowing his pace just half a stride.

That half a stride was enough for Crow to slap the cylinder of his pistol shut and fire a pair of .45 rounds. Unlike the shotgun pellets these two bullets burned right through the thick hide on the badger-warrior's chest. Still, the badger-warrior's momentum kept him running forward and Crow feared that upraised sword might be able to cleave either he or Ferguson in twain.

Crow fired two more bullets into the badger-warrior's chest, and the badger-warrior's knees buckled and he pitched forward onto his face— broadsword still clutched in his spasming fingers.

"Why did your bullets hurt him, and not my shotgun?" complained Ferguson.

"My pistol has been blessed by a prophet," said Crow. With an uncharacteristic flourish, he spun the .45 Peacemaker and dropped into his gunleather. "Has your shotgun been blessed by a prophet?"

"No," growled Ferguson, "but my fist has blessed a few people in the face."

Crow put a boot on the wrist of the badger-warrior and pried the broadsword loose from his fingers. He handed it to Ferguson. "Wrap your fist around this. It might be the only thing that can cut through the mystical defenses of the others."

Again, they were off and running. This time they followed the trail of destruction that the badger-warrior had left behind him. Ribboned tents, severed limbs, and dead bodies lay in a bloody wake, but this allowed Crow and Ferguson to escape the box. The duo of remaining Disciples shifted their courses to chase down or intercept the Indian and the black man. The fugitives managed to reach the path which Crow had used to ascend Telegraph Hill, but that was when the female warrior caught up with them. She ascended to the trail, her long black hair trailing like wings and her broadwords crossed in front of her. She was a stunning beauty and, given any other situation, Ferguson and even Crow might have been inclined just to admire her graceful form and beautiful features.

"The Immortals have named me Qi Zhuo," she said. "Lay down your weapons and submit to your fate."

"What exactly is our fate?" huffed Ferguson.

"You have killed the lover of Qi Zhuo. There can only be one penalty for destroying love—the one true gift of the Celestials."

"We've killed three," said Ferguson. "Which one was your lover?"

Crow slipped one more bullet into the cylinder of his Peacemaker. That gave him three loaded rounds. He thought about trying for a fourth, but the masked horseman appeared on the trail, blocking their retreat.

"Each in his own time," replied Qi Zhuo. "I have lived for a century—my life extended by the power of the Immortals—and my love, like a river's flow, cannot be confined by any bounds."

"Ain't that swell," said Ferguson. He fired the last remaining barrel of his shotgun.

Qi Zhuo's blades rasped as they parted, and the flats of the blade caught and deflected much of the concentrated blast. Still, not even her supernal martial prowess could shunt away all of the pellets. A few slipped past the shield of her sword blades, and pocked her silky skin with blossoms of crimson.

She cried out in anger—and perhaps even pain—as the hot pellets violated her immortalized flesh. Qi Zhuo spun forward, her blades forming a whirling scythe that descended upon Shotgun Ferguson. Ferguson had never held a sword blade before this evening and he realized that not even the most skilled swordsmen would have a chance of defeating this storm of swords. In a desperate effort he threw the broadsword into the maelstrom of steel.

It was easily deflected and tossed a dozen feet away. At that moment Crow ascertained the trouble that Ferguson was in and he turned, firing past the black man. The first round snapped one of Qi Zhou's blades in two and the fragment went spinning through the air, severing a half dozen tent lines and collapsing a pair of tents before imbedding in the earth.

Crow's second shot struck the hilt of Qi Zhuo's left-handed blade and deflected, shattering her hand. Qi Zhuo cried out and spun to a halt, a dervish in the midst of a dust storm. She abandoned her broken and mangled swords and clutched at her hand. "You'll both pay for this—an eternity of torture. This I vow!"

Crow was about to fire his third and final round at Qi Zhuo when the pounding of horse's hooves reminded him of the masked warrior that had blocked their retreat. He spun and took careful aim as the spotted horse bearing the Chinese swordsman bore down upon him. Crow seemed heedless to the fact that in a few moments he would be pulped beneath those great beating hooves. He had just one bullet to spend and he didn't want to let it go to waste with an ill-aimed shot.

He expelled the breath he'd been holding in the caverns of his chest and squeezed the trigger. The Peacemaker rocked in his fist and the final bullet slammed through the forehead of the enchanted mask. The horseman tumbled from his spotted steed and Crow and Ferguson threw themselves aside just a moment too late to avoid being crushed by the great equine.

To their surprise the horse faded into nothingness, passing them like the rush of wind and leaving them unharmed. The body of the fallen horseman crumbled into black ash, which swirled away on the eddying wind, leaving nothing but the hideously-painted mask with a bullet hole in the center of its forehead.

Ferguson turned and found Qi Zhuo still clutching her shattered hand. In turn, she fixed Ferguson and Crow in her baleful gaze. "I'll remember your faces, mortals. The fickle finger of fortune will not be so kind to you next time we meet."

After this dire pronouncement, Qi Zhuo smiled sweetly. "Sweet dreams, mortals." Then she turned to smoke and was was whisked into the air by the strange winds that swept up Telegraph Hill from the frothing bay.

In the tumultuous waters of the bay, abandoned ships jostled against each other, the prow of a steamship stoving in the side of a clipper. For awhile Crow and Ferguson watched the clipper as it reeled, foundered, and then slowly was swallowed up by the waves.

"Where did this storm come from?" said Ferguson, finally.

"It came with the Five Disciples," said Crow. "They bring dark magics in their wake."

"Why would such powerful beings, like the Disciples, waste their time on collecting a bounty of three thousand dollars?" asked Ferguson. "Don't they have more important things to do?"

Crow slowly plucked the spent shells out of his revolver and tossed them into the ashes. "Their kind of immortality is not like that of our Savior's. They are still caught up in the desires and lusts of the natural man. They desire wealth and power, enjoy inflicting misery and pain upon those weaker themselves."

Ferguson laughed. "I guess we turned the table on them, didn't we red man?"

"Call me Crow," said the Indian.

"I've been thinking, Crow. Why don't you go ahead and take me in—collect that reward that everyone seems so fired up about collecting."

Crow shook his head. "You're not the cold-blooded murderer that you're made out to be. I'll move on and leave you to your own devices. If you take my advice, you'll stay clear of Telegraph Hill—and all of San Francisco, for that matter."

Ferguson rolled his broad shoulders. "There ain't a cell made that can hold me. I'll break out and find you. Then you'll split that reward with me. Half for me and half for you."

"That doesn't quite seem honest," said Crow. "To turn you in and then help you break out."

"I'm not asking for you to help break me out," said Ferguson. "I can do that myself. The men who offered that three thousand dollar reward know what really went down. They figure they can cover the truth by blaming it on a black man. They even accused me of killing my own sister!"

"You were the one that was afraid that they might lynch you without a fair trial," said Crow. "What if you aren't able to escape? I don't want innocent blood on my concience."

Ferguson clapped his hand on Crow's back—a blow strong enough to stagger the Indian. "I never said any of that. You worry too much, Crow. We're not immortals, we need to put bread on our tables."

"I'm not convinced," said Crow.

"Not yet," said Ferguson. "Now why don't you go buy us a few brews so we can celebrate our victory over these dad-burned Disciples."

"I don't drink," said Crow. He started down the trail, his booted foot crushing the mystical mask. "And you'd be well advised to stay away from the taverns and dancehalls of San Francisco. They are nothing but dens of iniquity. They'll put knock-out drops in your beer if you're lucky, or bludgeon you over the head with a club, if you're not so lucky, and strip you of everything that you own. San Francisco has more thieves than it has rats—and it has a lot of rats."

Ferguson shoved new cartridges into his shotgun. "This shotgun is the only thing that I own."

"Then you'd best hang onto it," said Crow. "With both hands."

Long Night in Little China

Lone Crow knew better than to draw upon one Tong hatchetman, let alone three. Yet there he was, standing in the streets of Little China, hand resting on his eagle-butted Colt revolver, facing down three fighting men of the Hop Sing Tong.

They wore low broad-brimmed hats of black, the braided tails of their hair snaking over their shoulders and down their backs. The long silken belts they wore were thrust through with hatchets and knives, but the center Tong fighter cast aside the long-haired Chinese girl who was struggling in his grip and Crow could see the pistol grips of a pair of Colt Navy .36's jutting forward.

Crow had seen one other gunfighter wear his gun butts forward and he was fast enough to rack up a string of kills and an impressive reputation, but in Crow's opinion he would have been even faster if he would have wore his gun handles back. Still, Crow had been in enough gunfights to know that winning was more about the accuracy of the shooter than the speed of the shooter. Those that had accuracy were deadly and those that had both were nigh on unstoppable.

"Leave the woman and I'll let you live!" shouted Crow, but he knew that the boo how doy fighting men of the Tongs would not be so easily cowed, even by a redman with the demeanor of a savage.

"She belongs to Hop Sing," said the Chinese gunman, and to emphasize the fact he booted the girl in the belly and sent her sprawling in the mud. "She is the Tong's to use or abuse. No white man or Indian slave has claim to her."

The girl pushed herself to her hands and knees, the oval of her sublime face framed by curtains of dark hair, and her lips again formed a desperate plea for help. Crow was aware that the Tongs brought in young girls by the boatload, for gold fever wasn't the only lust that afflicted the forty-niners. In China, girls could be purchased from hungry families for twenty dollars and they would fetch ten times that in San Francisco or be put immediately to work in the stalls or parlor houses of Jackson and Washington Streets.

"I'm making claim," said Crow and he knew that he needed to make an ultimatum. "I'm counting to three and if any of you are still in my sight I'm going to start shooting."

Before Crow had reached the count of two a pair of hatchetmen were charging upon him from either flank. He hadn't seen any gun holsters on either of these Tong killers, but it was possible that they had a hold-out hidden in their belt or among their loose blouses. Most of the boo how doy preferred to fight with hatchet or knife, but that didn't mean that they weren't, perhaps, even more dangerous than the Chinese gunfighter who stood his ground at the center and began to draw his pair of Navy Colts.

Each step of the sprinting Tong warriors carried them closer, clots of earth spewing from their feet, and hatchets raising in their hands. Crow burst into action and his Eagle-butted Colt .45, blessed by a prophet in the salty wastes on a night the dead came reeling from the grave, leaped into his hand as if by its own volition. He moved to his left so that, if the Chinese gunfighter's draw was fast, his aim would be hindered by the body of his sprinting ally.

Crow ducked and a hatchet went whirling by his shoulder, then Crow fired two shots into the chest of the hatchetman, and he fell stone dead, face first in the muck at Crow's feet. Before the dead hatchetman had settled in the mud, Crow turned his aim to the second fighter, who had delayed the throw of his axe while his companion was standing in the way.

Flame belched from the barrel of Crow's .45 and a bullet caught the second hatchetman at the bridge of his nose. He toppled like a burlap bag of corn from the shoulder of a tired farmer. A bullet tugged at Crow's hat and pulled it from his head. Long hair that had been tucked beneath spilled out like the unfurling wings of a raven. If Crow had not been in a crouch, that bullet would have caught him in the throat or chest.

The Tong gunman held a pistol in each hand and began firing with more enthusiasm than accuracy. The road spit gouts of mud as bullets spattered about Crow. The Indian wheeled about, took careful aim, and sent his last three bullets winging toward the Tong gunman. The first ricocheted from the head of a hatchet concealed beneath his blouse, the second pierced just beneath the ribs and the final bullet caught in the gunman's lung. The Chinese fighter reeled and then went to his knees, his guns sagging in his grip.

His enemy was still conscious and holding a pair of pistols, and Crow was out of ammunition. He could reload, but in those precious seconds his enemy might gather enough moxy to shoot him down. Crow caught sight of a hatchet jutting from the belt of the dead Tong fighter at his feet and he plucked it out of the sash. Crow was no stranger to the hatchet, though he preferred the balance of a tomahawk which he had been trained with since his youth. Still, he plucked it up, and threw it, whirling, over the head of the Chinese girl. It missed her by scant inches, then the axe caught the Tong gunman full in the face, splitting his skull to the teeth, and then he fell backward into the muck of the street.

Before Crow took another step he opened his pistol and shook the empty shells onto the street. He methodically reloaded his pistol, scanning the street with sharp eyes lest more trouble appear. The buildings were a mixture of tents and rude wooden structures packed together in an interminable hodgepodge that possessed no discernable rhyme or reason. There were a number of spectators, standing on the stoop of a Chinese laundry and others who had poked their heads out of their tents when they heard the sound of gunfire. Word would get back to the Tongs quickly, figured Crow, and it wouldn't be hard for the Tongs to identify an indian wearing a duster and a cowboy hat.

Crow retrieved his hat, shook off the mud and placed it on his head. He trudged over to the woman and helped her to her feet. She couldn't have been more than eighteen or nineteen years of age. Despite her disheveled robes and mud-flecked hair she possessed a supernal beauty radiating beyond the dirt and the mire staining her clothing. Her features were fine, her teeth even and white, and in her presence Crow had a difficult time remembering the faces of any of the beautiful women he had known—even his childhood crush, Sky Raven, whose face had continously haunted him since that day his tribe had been exterminated by their old tribal enemies and he had been cast, a lone child, into the wilderness to fend for himself.

She spoke a broken English, but for some reason Crow found it as easy to understand as if she had been speaking his own native language. "Thank you, stranger. I owe you my life." She bowed her head. "I am at your disposal."

"You know English?"

"My family lived by the great sea and I learned some from the visiting sailors," she said. "And I had many months to learn it when I was sold into slavery and cast into the hold of the English ship, Far Trader. Eventually I found myself in this strange land."

Crow began to walk, figuring it best to find his way out of Little China before word of his exploits spread. "Where were the hatchetmen taking you?"

"To be one of the wives of Hop Sing. They said that, at least, I would not be a common crib-girl. I'd rather die than fall to such a fate. It is said that when Hop Sing tires of his wives he sends them to the parlors or cribs."

"I can't imagine anyone tiring of you," said Crow. Still, he'd heard stories of Hop Sing—a brutal man with a reputation for having access to dark magics. He cast a long glance over his shoulder as they wound their way out of Little China, but San Francisco was a crime-ridden town and danger might also lurk in the colony of Chileno harlots and thieves that colonized the waterfront streets of Pacific and Broadway and the steeps of Telegraph Hill, or among the escaped convicts of Van Diemen's Land and Tasmania that gathered in Sydney Town to hatch their dastardly deeds. "I need to take you somewhere where you'll be safe. There's a Salvation Army Mission that takes in escaped girls of the line, or I know some Mormon families that might be willing to take you in."

The girl shook her head. "I've already imposed upon you more than I should have. If I stay at this Salvation Mission or with these families I should put them in great danger. I've heard tales that Hop Sing is a man who does not like to be crossed. He will consider the honor of his Tong violated and hurt anyone who dares shelter me."

Crow bit at his lower lip, but was silent. This was going to put a crimp in his plans. A rather lovely crimp, but he was visiting San Francisco on business and it was going to be difficult to carry out his commission if he was dragging a pretty piece of calico through the scrub. There were a lot of testy gold hunters in the hills and valleys who would just as soon shoot first and ask questions later if they thought someone was intruding on their claim.

She put her hand on his shoulder, her fingers were cool where they brushed past his collar and touched his neck, but the contact seemed ambrosia to his senses and he caught her gaze, suddenly enraptured by the dark deep pools of her eyes. "I don't mean to be any trouble. If you just let me stay with you I promise that you won't regret it."

The Indian shook himself free of her entrancing gaze. "I already regret it." Then he saw the hurt expression on her face and wished he hadn't spoken so quickly. "Don't misunderstand me. If time backed up ten minutes and I were presented with the same choice I would rescue you again. No woman deserves to be sold into such a fate. But the Hop Sing Tong is not to be trifled with. They'll send their boo how doy after me and this time they won't make the mistake of arming themselves only with hatchets and knives. They'll send their gunmen—all of them—after me. I've got to leave San Francisco and probably, even, California on a fast horse."

"Take me with you," she pleaded. "I am a respectful woman. I excel at cooking and cleaning and have the skill to make husband a happy man."

For a moment Crow found himself considering the proposition. The China girl possessed a transcendent loveliness and it was all he could do to tear his eyes away from her face and figure. Though her skin possessed the colorations of the Chinese the texture was of a soft snow and her demeanor was delicate and vulnerable. "I've known you for all of ten minutes. I don't even know your name. Don't you think you're being a bit hasty?"

"I am called Jing-Wei Hsein. Jing-Wei means small bird."

"And Hsein?"

"That name is not so easily translated," she said, an expression of consternation appearing on her face.

Crow rolled her name over his tongue. "Jing-Wei. It is a lovely name. Odd, isn't it, that we're both named after birds?"

"I am sure that it is not coincidence. Our lives were meant to intersect. It was fate."

"Perhaps, but what brought me to San Francisco was a missing man. I hadn't intended to entangle myself with the Tongs."

"Perhaps I can help you find this man," said Jing-Wei.

"Are you also a hunter of men?" asked Crow, a smile playing at the corner of his lips.

"No, but my father is a Taoist Sorcerer like Hop Sing. He is one who takes the left hand path—an evil man—and in his presence I learned some of the secrets of his magic. I can use these secrets for some good purpose just as well as he can use them for his evil purposes."

"A taoist sorcerer? You're full of surprises, Jing-Wei. Is it your sorcery that caused me to face down three Tong hatchetmen in the street? Is it your sorcery that convinces me to keep you at my side, despite my better judgment?"

"It is your innate goodness that caused you to face down those Tong killers," said Jing-Wei. "You're a good man—a holy man. I can sense it now, there is the power of God in you, but still you wrestle with your own desires. It is only you that can save me, Lonely Crow, and you needn't let the sadness, the loneliness consume you. Be my champion and let me ease the burden of your loneliness."

"Who said that I was lonely?" said Crow, but his defiance was merely show. He was the last of his tribe and though he had found some friends among the enclaves of the West, he dwelt with the constant dread that they would be plucked away just as were the white settlers that had adopted him after the massacre that had destroyed his tribe. So he preempted the impending loss and pushed away his friends and disappeared into the beckoning embrace of the wilderness, the solitude of which he both feared and sought.

"It's in your name," said Jing-Wei and she straightened the robe she wore. "There is much in a name—even secrets."

Crow paused, uncomfortable with the direction the conversation was heading. He gestured toward a narrow alley that wound between stained canvas tents and makeshift shacks. Wood smoke drifted on an errant breeze and curled around the Indian's limbs. "I've got a tent behind the Leaning Horseshoe Stable. The yard is fenced and the owner keeps a close eye on my things. The accomodations aren't much…"

"They'll be an improvement over the hold of the Far Trader," replied Jing-Wei. "And I'll be grateful for any place I can lay and rest my head."

He led Jing-Wei through the alley, wary for the possibility of sappers and hoodlums that might leap from the shadows between tents. Indeed, he spotted several suspicious figures lurking in hiding, but when they saw Crow, assessed his carriage and saw the pistol on his hip, they chose not to risk an encounter and sank back into hiding, waiting for easier prey.

Crow rapped on the gate of the Leaning Horseshoe and the proprietor, Jake Higgins, a man who covered his pock-marked face with a heavy beard, came through the door of his listing barn, cradling a shotgun in his arms.

"Aah, it's you, Crow. There's been some Sydney Ducks lurking about. I was worried that I might have some trouble."

"It's not the ducks I'm worried about, Jake" said Crow, as Higgins opened the gate and let the pair of them through. "I'm afraid I've crossed the Hop Sing Tong. We'll be leaving first thing in the morning. I don't want to draw their wrath in your direction."

"I'm sorry to hear that," said Higgins. "It's been good having you—" Higgins paused when he saw Jing-Wei. Whether it was surprise at seeing Crow arrive with a strange woman or whether it was her beauty that caused his tongue to seize, Crow didn't know.

"Who is this woman?"

"She's the reason for the tong's wrath," said Crow.

Wei-Jing extended her hand to Higgins and spoke in Chinese. Higgins only understood a few words of the language, which he'd picked up from his contact with the residents of Little China, but he seemed to comprehend her meaning.

"Pleasure to meet you, also, ma'am."

"This is Jing-Wei. Maybe you can find a bit of extra straw for her and give her a spot in the loft," suggested Crow.

Higgins scratched at his beard. "That shouldn't be a problem at all, and I'll have your horse ready to go in the morning. What of Reynolds? Have you picked up on his trail?"

"An outfitter remembers he and his party coming through town, but once he headed for the gold fields out south no one seems to have seen hide nor hair of him or his men."

"Good luck finding him. Men have a way of disappearing in the gold fields, never to be heard from again."

Once Higgins had retreated into the barn, Crow led Wei-Jing into the yard behind the stable. He fired some kindling and began to prepare a stew of venison and carrots. He raised a bunch of the long orange vegetables. "A dollar a carrot, can you believe it? Everything sells for a fortune in San Francisco."

Jing-Wei didn't respond. Instead she seemed lost in thought.

"Why didn't you speak English to Higgins?" asked Crow.

She regarded him from beneath long lashes, her skirts gathered about her ankles as she sat on a log in front of the tent. "He understood me well enough. It's been many ages since I've eaten a fresh vegetable. Is dinner about ready?"

"Just about," said Crow. He stirred the broth and let the savory aroma waft into the air. He scooped a serving into a tin bowl and she fell to the meal with a gusto that Crow had only seen in starving men. She consumed enough stew to satiate three famished men after a long day of sod-busting and Crow couldn't help but let an amused smile creep across his face.

Finally she set aside her tin with a sigh of delight. "That was heavenly. However, next time I must prepare a meal for you. I promise you, I can prepare a meal so tasty that you will decide you should immediately make me your wife."

Crow grinned. "Is that so? Well, I'm looking forward to tasting this meal. If it lives up to even a portion of its billing I'm sure it will be wonderful."

Jing-Wei sucked a bit of broth from her finger. "A woman should never underestimate the power of a good meal on a man's heart."

Her smile was intoxicating, but their light mood broke suddenly as a howl shattered the spreading dusk. It was a long guttural cry, more broken and bestial than that of a hound, and the sound of it froze Crow's marrow. Jing-Wei's smile turned to dismay. "They didn't dare!"

"They didn't dare what?" asked Crow.

Jing-Wei rose. "We must leave now, before the t'ien kou is upon us!"

"T'ien kou?" repeated Crow. "What are you talking about? What aren't you telling me?"

She gazed upon him with plaintive eyes. "I'm afraid that there is much I haven't told you. I thought that we would have more time. I didn't think that they would dare release the devil hound. He'll be able to smell us out wherever we go."

"There are ways of defeating hounds," said Crow. "There's any number of streams or even rivers we could cross on our way out of San Francisco to confuse their scent. Are these hounds that Hop Sing owns?"

Jing-Wei seemed frantic. "You don't understand, but it is not your fault. I have not been completely honest with you. This hound, it was kept with me in the hold of the Far Traveler. It is an ancient evil thing drawn from the voids of space and bound to earth by my father. It is a thing that is pure evil and it cannot be slain by earthly weapons. If it knows a man's scent, it can track that man across all the deserts and oceans of the earth. My father sold it, and me, to Hop Sing at a great price—for dark secrets can be pried from the jaws of the t'ien kou if certain incantations are uttered."

"Then we unbind it from earth," said Crow, who wasn't unfamiliar with the workings of the supernatural.

"Only a great sorcerer could accomplish that," said Wei-Jing. "The t'ien kou is the dark yin of the balance and, to bind him, my father tied him to a thing of great purity—something that the t'ien kou desires to violate and use for its own purposes."

Crow shook himself, frustrated. "Then is there nothing that we can do to stop this t'ien kou? If it's flesh, surely we can make it bleed…"

Jing-Wei shook her head mournfully. "I'm sorry to have brought this fate upon you. I didn't think that the Hop Sing would dare order its release."

"Why not?"

"The t'ien kou is not flesh and blood as we know it. Its skin and flesh is hardened, inured to the chill voids of the outer darknesses. It is an alien power—difficult to understand and command, even for a master of the Left Hand Way. It is ill omen incarnate and even to say its name has caused mortal men to lose their minds."

A cold chill descended upon Crow as he listened to Jing-Wei's words, but he pushed away the dread fear that they brought, and whispered a prayer seeking the Holy Spirit that was his right and privilege—finding that when the prayer was uttered, the unreasoning fear left him.

He stood and listened as the beast howled again, its ululating cry carrying a frost-brand of terror to every ear that heard it. Throughout San Francisco grown men shrieked, falling in the gutter and clapping their hands over their ears. Gamblers lost their nerve and cast away winning hands, while others dropped dice from numbed fingers. In brothels and bagnios through the city, harlots and their customers paused in their iniquity. Some ran naked and howling into the streets and other men went mad, murdering until they were brought down in a hail of gunfire or until they were wrested from their insanity by the light of the morning sun.

But the sun was many hours away and Crow looked upon Jing-Wei with clearer eyes that weren't befuddled by her celestial beauty. "There is much that you've neglected to tell me."

"I thought that there was more time," she repeated. "I hoped that first you would fall completely under the spell of my charms, and once you were in love with me I could reveal the sordid truths. For does not love overcome all?"

"Perhaps," mused Crow, "but not without the cost of blood. Tell me now, what is it that can defeat this fiend?"

Jing-Wei shook her lovely head, long lashes fluttering like the bird of her namesake, and her dark, dark tresses falling like black waters across her slender shoulders and spilling across the brocade

"You're letting the fear take hold," said Crow. "Think harder. Does the beast have any weakness at all that we might turn to our advantage?"

Again she regarded Crow with a sad smile. "It does not like the great waters. While in the hold of the Far Trader it howled like the damned souls of hell. The t'ien kou come from the far reaches of space where all moisture is ice. The vast seas are as alien to the t'ien kou as—"

"Can we drown the beast?" snapped Crow.

"It cannot die as you understand death. The t'ien kou is not mortal flesh."

"Fine, but at least water unnerves it. Even if that's all I can hope for, then we'll head to the bay."

"But it's coming from the bay!" objected Jing-Wei.

"Then we'll lead it on a chase. Are you going to come with me or are you going to wait here for the beast to come take you?"

At Crow's urging, she rose swiftly from the log where she had been perched. "I'm with you unto the death, my love!"

Before Crow and Jing-Wei fled the Leaning Horseshoe Stables, they warned Higgins that he should vacate the premises, interrupting him as he groomed a bay with a blaze on his snout.

"But I can't leave," he objected. "Thieves will break in and steal the horses if I leave them unattended."

"I'm sorry, but it appears that Jing-Wei has left a trail for the tong to follow. There will be more of them than you and I can handle with shotgun and rifle." Crow laid a heavy pouch on the table.

"What's that?" asked Higgins.

"It's my split of the money we got for bringing in Rotgut Anderson. If the tong does any damage, it will be enough to replace and rebuild the Leaning Horseshoe."

"I'm not taking your money," bristled Higgins. "If there's trouble I'll stand with you. You know I'm not a man of the gun, but I can hold my own when the fat is in the fire."

"If I were to lay odds I'll be dead before sunrise," said Crow. "Anyone with me will suffer the same fate. Keep the money. At least you'll be alive to use it."

"What about the China girl? You're not taking her with you…"

"It's Jing-Wei that they're after. The tong hatchetmen are running a hound that's got her scent."

Higgins shivered in spite of himself and the horses moved skittishly in their stalls. "Is that the unearthly howling I've been hearing? If so, I'll skedaddle just like you're telling me."

"May God go with you, Brother."

"See you on the other side, Crow."

****

The moonlight spread its orange light across the natural horseshoe of San Francisco Bay. In the mad rush of gold fever men had descended in droves upon the settlement of San Francisco and the site of Sutter's Mill, abandoning their ships and tearing the mill to the ground as they sought for speck and nugget of the yellow metal. Half a thousand ships lay abandoned in the harbor with no sailor to sail them, for all had tossed aside the ill-paying profession of seamen for the lure of easy money. It wasn't difficult for Crow and Jing-Wei to find an empty longboat pulled upon the shore. Crow threw his boots in the bottom of the boat and pushed it out into the chill waters. He leaped in alongside of Jing-Wei and again they heard the horrible howl that had been pursuing them through the maddened city streets. They looked and saw a great bear-like beast, with baleful eyes glowing purple, and mangy, scabrous flesh which grew patches of wiry fur. Its great jaw hung slack and foam trailed from its flaccid lips as its eight powerful limbs propelled it forward in great leaps.

The sorcerer, Hop Sing, did not follow the beast—for he commanded it from afar—but a dozen tong hatchetmen trailed the t'ien kou at respectful length. Even at this distance and in the dim light of the moon Crow could tell by their stride that they were unnerved by the supernatural fiend that accompanied them. Still, they came armed with pistol, curved knife, and hatchet.

Crow's strokes at the oars carried them into the shadow of an empty ship, and he heard Jing-Wei's breath coming in short gasps. "My fate is upon me."

Crow grunted, not willing to resign himself to defeat so quickly. He hoisted his Henry .44 rifle to his shoulder and let the boat drift into the umbra of an overshadowing hulk. He fired twice in quick succession at the t'ien kou, striking it on the breastbone and in the skull. Both bullets ricocheted away and the hound from the dark outer voids came snarling to the end of the wharf, unhurt.

"It is futile," said Jing-Wei. "Did not I tell you that no earthly weapon can harm it?"

The beast paused and gazed suspiciously at the calaginous waters that lapped against the barnacled pilings. It yelped plaintively and the cry stabbed like a cold knife into Crow's brain. He winced and shifted his aim, steadying his rifle against the oarlock and timing the swells. If he couldn't hurt the beast, perhaps he could thin out the ranks of boo how doy. At the moment, they approached in clear view of his rifle, confident that the astral hound would draw his fire. They seemed more concerned about staying away from the fangs of their own ally than they were about bullets being fired from an unsteady boat in the bay.

A swell sent Crow's first shot singing high and over the head of his target. His second shot was better timed and a tong fighter crumpled into the mud, a bullet rattling in his chest.

The boo how doy fighters had the long braids of their queues wrapped around their hats, always a tell-tale sign that they were on a mission of deadly intent. Seeing one of their number down, they wasted no time reaching for the pistols thrust through their sashes. As they descended the steep street to the bay, they sent a barrage of lead skipping across the water. A few shots struck the longboat and more than a few buried themselves in the strakes of the ship behind them. Crow and Jing-Wei were in the shadows beneath that ship and difficult to target; however there was so much lead in the air that a chance shot might easily strike either of them.

The t'ien kou continued to snarl and spit, hesitating to plunge into the bay to pursue its prey. A tong gunman made the mistake of stepping a bit too close and it leaped, venting its spleen on the hapless boo how doy, and rending him to bloody ribbons.

Crow glanced to Jing-Wei and noticed she sat upright on the bench of the longboat, not flinching as the bullets flew around her. "Get down," he shouted. "You'll be killed!"

"If only I should be so fortunate," she said, but she complied as Crow timed another shot and sent a tong gunfighter spinning to the ground.

The t'ien kou was frantic to reach its prey, but it was still loathe to plunge into the churning waters. It scrabbled down the wharf and leaped onto an empty barge that was listing to port. From there it leaped to a water-logged skiff, and then used its eight legs and prehensile tail to walk the mooring line of an empty steamboat. Crow saw that derelict ships were so thick upon the bay that by using this method the t'ien kou might reach them without ever having to touch the water.

The boo how doy scrambled after the fiend, following its lead, leaping across mist strewn chasms between forsaken watercraft and swarming up anchor and mooring lines. Crow might have picked off a few more of them, but he took hold of the oars and began drawing upon them as fast as he could, taking them deeper into the maze of empty crafts.

The fogs grew thicker and Crow and the fiend played cat and mouse among the towering shadows of the ship graveyard. Occasionally, the piercing cry of the t'ien kou would float through the spectral mists and, though the boo how doy moved mostly in silence, they hooted strange calls to each other as they split their forces, spreading their numbers among a few different vessels so that Crow and Jing-Wei wouldn't be able to double back to the safety of shore.

Crow caught glimpses of the dark shapes of tong hatchetmen lurking among the mists and several times he heard the clicking of long nails, like rain upon a canvas tent, as the t'ien kou's many legs propelled it across the bare decks of ships whose shadows they had just departed. More than once shots echoed among the maze of ships as they rowed themselves behind the safety of another hulk.

Through the sliding mists Crow read the name Euphemia on the side of a ship that was draped with rigging that trailed over the ship's sides. He called softly to Jing-Wei, "Catch hold. The tong fighters have us pinned down."

Crow abandoned his oars and the two of them clambered into the slick netting, and then the Indian shoved the longboat away with his foot, so that it sliced through the waters, empty of passengers—a drifting ghost ship to divert the attention of the boo how doy. Indeed, Crow's estimation was correct, for as soon as the boat drifted from its cover of ship and shadow, a volley of gunshots rang out, splintering oars and strakes. While this barrage of lead chewed at the longboat, Crow and Jing-Wei climbed over the edge of the brig.

Drawing a holdout .45 pistol from his waist, Crow shoved it into Jing-Wei's hands. "If a hatchetman gets to you, shoot him with this. There's only one shot, but I'll come running."

"And if the T'ien kou reaches me?"

"I'll see what I can do to prevent that," said Crow.

He expected Jing-Wei to ask him just how he was planning to accomplish this but, mercifully, the question was interrupted as they heard wailing and the gnashing of teeth resonating from the decks beneath their feet. For a moment, Crow thought that the ship was possessed for he had seen such things in his life, but then he remembered a conversation with Jake Higgins about the sheriff and his lack of room for prisoners.

"It's a prison ship," said Crow. "The prisoners are locked below. Whatever you do, don't let them persuade you to let them free. The worst of the worst are aboard this ship." With that, he glided to the mast and began mounting the tattered rigging that remained. From this vantage point he peered down through the coalescing fog. Feet firmly entrenched in the rigging, he leaned his Henry rifle against the mast and laid the bead on a shadow that moved across the deck of a nearby freighter. Crow's rifle spoke when the shadow moved into the opening.

A tong warrior cried out and fell to the deck. Crow shifted his aim and glimpsed a shadow detaching itself from the leaning mast of a ship to his right. It seemed that Crow hadn't been the only one with the idea of gaining the vantage point of height. Still, though the tong fighter in the mast of the adjacent craft had the drop on Crow, he wasn't equipped with a rifle. The range was long enough to be difficult with a rifle; with a pistol there was little chance of hitting and the bullets went awry—lost in the fog.

Crow levered another bullet into the chamber, ejecting the spent brass of his previous shot so that it spiraled and was lost in the darkness. He heard it tinkle against the deck below and he fired. The tong warrior pitched back, but his foot was tangled in the rigging, so he hung upside down, twisting as he bled to death.

Seeing no other available targets, Crow fished ammunition from the bandolier beneath his duster and replaced his spent rounds. Crow had accounted for a third of the tong fighters, but he had been very fortunate. The Henry rifle held ten cartridges plus one in the barrel and scarcely had Crow finished reloading, the scent of lingering cordite heavy in his nostrils, when he saw a dark bulk leap from a barnacled scow to the freighter. By its size and the way that it moved, Crow realized that it could only be the t'ien kou, and with an exclamation he slung the rifle over his shoulder and slid down the rigging, finally swinging to the deck.

He found Jing-Wei backed against the rail, a tong hatchetman in a slouch hat advancing upon her with a long curved knife in his hand. How Crow had missed seeing the tong fighter he didn't know, but it was possible he had been on the ship before he and Jing-Wei had even reached it. At the sound of Crow landing on the deck the hatchetman whirled. Crow reached for his rifle—a mistake, for the tong fighter was upon him with a speed he hadn't imagined possible. He barely managed to raise his rifle and deflect the descending blow of the hatchetman's knife with the barrel.

The tong fighter raised his knife again for a blow that would take off Crow's scalp, but a shot rang out and a crimson stain spread across his blouse. He crumpled to the deck and Jing-Wei stood behind him, gun smoke curling out of the barrel of the hold-out pistol. Crow had no time to thank her for saving his life. Instead, he snatched up the curved blade from the fallen tong fighter and rushed across the deck of the brig, the shouts and curses of the imprisoned calling to him from below.

He was not a moment too soon to reach the stern of the ship, for the t'ien kou came gliding across a mooring line, eight legs and tail moving in concert, so that he performed the task with a graceful ease that belied his hulking form. Just the appearance of such a beast had blasted the minds of lesser men and even Crow felt the icy fingers of fear clawing at his heart. But he steeled himself and moved forward, laying the tong blade to the mooring line and severing the thick hempen line that was drawn taut by the weight of the fiend. The strands parted like wheat beneath the reaver's scythe and the spitting fiend went tumbling into the waters where it thrashed and wailed.

For just an instant Crow had a hope that it might drown, but to his great chagrin he saw the legs begin to paddle and the thing moved through the lapping waters toward the Euphemia. Crow threw his Henry rifle to his shoulder and began to fire at the swimming beast. Bullets ricocheted off its sloped skull and it lurched out of the waters gripping the strakes of the brig with its clawed paws. It pulled itself up the side of the ship as surely as a spider on a wall, even while Crow poured a barrage of .44 bullets over the side.

When he fired the last bullet and expended the last empty brass cartridge Crow threw aside the rifle, fully convinced that Jing-Wei's words had been true—no mortal weapon could harm the t'ien kou. Still, he was no sorcerer, how could he combat a fiend that was untouchable by bullet or blade? He didn't have long to ponder the riddle for the t'ien kou leaped the last ten feet to the rail of the Euphemia and scrabbled over the edge and onto the deck.

The glowing violet eyes of the fiend caught Crow's and he found himself unable to act or even to think. Surely a moment more of inaction would have meant that he'd been helplessly rent to pieces beneath the beast's claws, but something in Crow's mind broke free from the t'ien kou's mesmerizing gaze and he struck with frantic strength, bringing the curved blade he'd taken from the tong fighter down between the fiend's glowing eyes. The tang of the blade snapped off and went spinning past Crow's head, and just before the t'ien kou rushed upon him he realized he was holding nothing but the hilt of the blade.

The fiend bowled Crow over and he was tossed and turned beneath the tread of the many feet of the t'ien kou, the claws ripping and tearing at him as it passed. For the t'ien kou had fixed its sights on Jing-Wei, who was standing next to the far rail. Apparently, the t'ien kou's lust for angelic beauty was greater than his hunger for the flesh of a holy man or gunfighter and it brushed Crow aside, as if he were inconsequential, as it rushed forward to savage the China girl.

Before the t'ien kou reached Jing-Wei, Crow rolled to his feet, his clothes hanging in bloody tatters, and he reached for his eagle-butted Colt pistol as he remembered the words that she had spoken to him in the Leaning Horseshoe Stable: "It is a thing that is pure evil and it cannot be slain by earthly weapons."

But what of an earthly weapon that was blessed by the celestial power of a living prophet? Jing-Wei pulled herself on top of the rail, clinging to the rigging, but ready to hurl herself into the water if it would buy her just a moment of respite from the t'ien kou. Her dark hair floated like a halo about her, but terror was written on her heavenly features.

Crow fired his blessed Colt and the .45 caliber slugs tore through the thick skin of the t'ien kou. Black blood spilled out and it howled, scrabbled to a halt, and then twisted around to focus its baleful glare upon the cause of its pain. Crow took a breath, held it and aimed. He squeezed the trigger twice and extinguished one of those great glaring orbs. It lurched toward Crow, fangs snapping, and then it fell and dark ichor washed across the Indian's bare feet.

The gun smoke drifted slowly and Crow passed through it, still holding the blessed weapon. All along he had possessed the means to defeat the demonic fiend. If only he had understood earlier, he might have escaped the scathing claws that had trampled him underfoot. He moved past the fallen t'ien kou and helped Jing-Wei down from her perch. As he did, she leaned forward and kissed him on the lips.

The sensation was akin to none that Crow had ever experienced before, but he had no time to ponder the kiss for her limbs seemed to dissolve beneath his grip, the flesh becoming insubstantial. He looked up and saw that she was fading into the night, becoming a ghost through which he could see the pale moon beyond.

"By slaying the t'ien kou you have freed me from the sorcereries binding me to it," said Jing Wei. She read the confused expression on Crow's face. "Surely, you knew that I was something more than merely mortal?"

"You knew my name before I gave it to you," said Crow. "But I didn't know if you were a lure sent by my enemies or if you possessed some powers beyond my understanding."

"I am of the hsien, the immortal race that sucks the wind and drinks the dew. I mount on clouds and vapor and rove beyond the seven seas. It was my purity that was bound to the evil of the t'ien kou and kept us both locked in mortal form and subject to its depradations and pains—though neither of us could be truly slain by a weapon that did not possess some supernal power."

"The hsien?" voiced Crow. "You said that was your surname…"

"The hsien are known as the feathered folk, young mortal."

"But you have no feathers." Then even as Crow spoke he saw great wings unfurling from between her shoulders, and her skin shone like the frost reflecting the morning sun's rays, her robe fluttered as pennants in the wind and she sailed into the sky.

"Farewell, Crow. Seek your hunted man among the mines of the far terraces; he is still alive but not well. And seek true love in Olympus, above the salty wastelands."

"And what of your professions of love?" called Crow.

"I thought to make the best of my mortal form," replied Jing-Wei, her words carried on the mists. "But now I am freed, and no earthbound man can claim a hsien as a mate. I go where the breeze and misty vapors take me. Look for me only in your dreams." Then she was gone from Crow's vision and hearing.

Stunned, he wandered past the horrible form of the slain t'ien kou and recovered his rifle. Mechanically, he began reloading the gun—counting out ten bullets, and another for the barrel. A shot exploded from a pistol in the mist, casting splinters from the great mast, and Crow sighed. By his estimation there were seven tong fighters left. It was going to be a long night.

The Pythagorean Hounds

It was nearing dusk when, for the last time, Professor Splinus rolled up the parchment he had painstakingly copied from manuscript 512, which was housed in the Biblioteca Naciaonal at Rio de Janeiro. They had spent weeks traveling into the interior of the Mato Grosso region of Brasil with a half dozen Bororo Indians serving as their porters and their headman as guide—and they had nearly reached their goal.

"How close are we, Professor?" asked Doctor Sylvia Spelling. Her brunette hair was drawn tightly behind her skull in a bun, and this over-emphasized the severity of her bookish beauty. She wore a pith helmet and a loose khaki shirt and shorts which wouldn't be considered lady-like among polite society, but were quite practical when traveling the depths of the Amazonian jungle.

Professor Splinus's fingers trembled as he tied the parchment shut, betraying his excitement. "If we but descend from this ridge we should be at the mouth of the Lost City of da Silva Guimarães."

"I wish we could catch a glimpse of it," said Doctor Spelling, "just to confirm that we haven't been on a wild goose chase."

Professor Splinus pushed aside the flap of the tent and exited onto the ridge. The Bororo were sitting around the campfire warming their naked flesh against the strange chill of the heavy fog which had arisen as they traveled. Their headman, Rapua, played a dirge-like song on the poari, his mouth closed around a reed which punctured a gourd decorated with parrot feathers.

"It possesses tones akin to a clarinet," commented the Doctor.

"Naturally," replied Professor Splinus, combing at his bushy white hair, momentarily distracted from his quest for the Lost City of da Silva Guimarães by Doctor Spelling's beauty. She seemed an ethereal goddess as she passed through the vestiges of the misty vapors which had halted their forward progress earlier that day. "The instrument is, after all, idioglottal in nature."

"I suppose we should be pleased that Rapua is playing the poari instead of singing. The shaman has a decent voice, but Rapua sounds like someone stepped on the tail of an alley ca… " Doctor Spelling halted in mid-word as she caught sight of strange structures growing out of the mist in the valley below.

"All these hours we were camped here and the Lost City was literally beneath our proboscises," muttered Professor Splinus.

This brought a faint smile to Doctor Spelling's lips, for she did enjoy word play, and she was relieved that their journey wasn't for naught. "I suppose we should have been able to smell the city out."

Professor Splinus was about to formulate an answering pun when he gave a start, for emerging out of the mist came a shadow in the form of a human, but with a great horn emerging at an angle perpendicular to its head. The Bororo Indians saw the figure too, and the Professor assumed that their resounding cries were of a superstitious nature, but then he realized that they were shouting out greetings.

The figure resolved itself from the mist as it drew nearer. It was a man dressed in the clothing of an American cowboy, complete with broad-brimmed hat and an Eagle-butted Peacemaker riding on his hip. The projection that the professor had mistaken as a horn of some sort was actually a Winchester short-barreled carbine slung over the man's shoulder. Beneath the brim of the hat the face was dark-skinned and impassive, and though he was definitely descended from natives, he was not indigenous to the Amazon or any of the South American tribes.

"Lone Crow," muttered Professor Splinus and his tone suggested that he was not pleased. "Where have you been?"

"Scouting ahead," answered the American Indian in a mid-west accent.

"I thought I told everyone to stay inside the camp until I gave the order to move on out."

"I might remind you," said Lone Crow, "that I don't answer to you."

"But you do answer to the directors at Miskatonic University," said Professor Splinus, who expanded his chest. "Let me remind you that I do have a certain amount of clout with the board of directors. Unless you want to go back to 'punching cattle', I suggest you do what I say."

Lone Crow's manner suggested that he didn't much care if the board of directors at Miskatonic cut him loose or continued to employ him. "Let the chips fall where they may."

Professor Splinus noticed a bemused expression on Doctor Spelling's face. "Is there something amusing of which I am not aware?"

"Perhaps you are not aware of this," replied Doctor Spelling, "but you are exhibiting classic alpha male behavior."

"In what respect?"

Doctor Spelling hesitated. "Well, the type of behavior that is engaged in by males competing for the attention of a potential mate."

"I fail to see the significance of—" The Professor broke off and turned back to face Lone Crow, an imposing man with a reputation that included many feats Professor Splinus considered to be of a rather dubious nature. "What did you find?"

Lone Crow motioned to towers that protruded above the blanket of fog. "I found your lost city and a handful of these." He extended a hand and dropped a silver coin into the palm of Professor Splinus, and another into the palm of Doctor Spelling.

Professor Splinus held up the spherical coin and found that it was minted from gold. On one side there was an image of a kneeling youth and on the other side a bow and arrow overlaying a crown. "These symbols appear Greek in origin. See the pyramidal form on the crown? That's the tetractys, a Pythagorean symbol. But how could Greek symbology have found its way into the inner tracts of the Brasilian wilderness?"

"There are a number of evidences that indicate outside cultural presence in Southern America," said Doctor Spelling. "As well as a number of theological records that attest so. I believe that Lone Crow can confirm that."

"How can one confirm religious balderdash?" replied the Professor. "I believe only the evidence of my five senses."

Now Rapua and his Bororo tribal mates gathered around the trio crying out acclamations. Lone Crow reached into his pouch and presented each of them with a gold coin he had found among the ruins of the Lost City. They examined these with great interest and a couple were held aloft so that they caught the last rays of the setting sun, scintillating in its golden light.

"Those coins belong to the university," said Professor Splinus. "Who authorized you to hand them out like they were cheap trinkets or shiny baubles?"

"The board of directors authorized me to make whatever arrangements necessary in order that we have reliable guides into the Mato Grosso. This area is taboo to the Bororo and it was only by promising them a share of what we found that they agreed to come. However, if you care to renegotiate the terms you should speak with Rapua."

Professor Splinus grumbled at this invitation. He knew full well that for some inexplicable reason the Bororo had taken a liking to his Native American bodyguard. They declined to negotiate with anyone but Lone Crow and they refused to take orders unless they were relayed through the mouth of Lone Crow. It was all a rather frustrating enigma to Splinus to understand why they had respect for a savage, but no respect for a white man who, by dint of his superior brain had climbed the pinnacle of European education. "Just how much of our gold and silver did you promise them?"

"One fifth," replied Lone Crow. "Which is a rather petty amount, considering that they might have been leading us into taboo wilderness for one-fifth of nothing."

"These Bororo tribesmembers have very low intellectual capabilities," judged the Professor. "Do you think that they actually comprehend the concept of one-fifth, or will they demand it all once the time comes?"

"I think that you underestimate them," said Crow.

"It was my intellect that uncovered the actual location of the Lost City," the Professor reminded the American Indian.

"I have never implied otherwise," said Lone Crow. "I do have a word of caution, however."

The Professor pretended to be engrossed in his examination of the coin. "What is it?"

"The city appears to be abandoned, but there may be other dangers."

"Other dangers? Such as hostile tribes or wild animals? Those are problems you are paid to deal with."

Lone Crow shrugged. "I am aware of that, but hostile tribes and wild animals aren't my main concern. The city has the feeling of evil upon it."

"You do understand," said Professor Splinus, "that this expedition is both educational and financial in nature? Miskatonic University needs funding if it is to support further investigational expeditions such as this one and it also needs the prestige that such a find as this will bring to it… and myself."

"What are you saying?"

"I'm saying that I'm not going to let the superstitions of some savage dissuade me from visiting that city. Do you really think that I'd write a scholarly paper without seeing the city with my own eyes? That after my long journey I'd go home just because you have a 'feeling of evil'?" scoffed the Professor.

"Of course not," said Lone Crow. "Still, it's best to be on our guard. I suggest we wait until dawn before entering the Lost City."

Lone Crow retreated to the firepit, joining with the Bororo tribesman who asked him many questions in their native tongue. Crow responded in a facsimile of their language which was far from fluent, but apparently effective enough that he was able to proficiently communicate with them

Doctor Spelling watched Crow conversing with the Bororo. "He actually has a knack for the macro-ge family of languages."

"I differ with your opinion on the classification," said Professor Splinus. "And I accede no increased modicum of intelligence to Lone Crow because of his ability to communicate with like savages. Communication between lower forms is largely a matter of instinct and body language and represents none of the finer linguistic skills which prove greater intelligence."

"He can speak English nearly as well as you," replied Doctor Spelling.

"He has mastered the rudimentary form," replied the Professor begrudgingly. "But his language is colloquial and he is incapable of expressing the more advanced learnings upon which society and culture are predicated. He falls back on theology, which is the last bastion of the ignorant."

"Perhaps," said Doctor Spelling, "Or perhaps you let your learning blind you to the spiritual or the supernatural."

"Then I am, at least, among a few of the professors at Miskatonic that understand that the research of the supernatural and occult is merely academic. Were academia to lend merit to the notion that such powers as God or Satan even exist, it would lead us into a folly of circuitous thinking."

"All I am saying is that you ought to give Crow more credit," replied Doctor Spelling, then she paused. "Have you heard the rumor that he is the one who killed Butch Cassidy?"

"Drawn between four horses and quartered; I believe that's the story that was related to me—and just as preposterous and fallacious as any other tall tale," snapped the Professor. "Even if the story were true, it hardly lends credence to the idea that Crow has greater intelligence than any others of his race."

"Apparently the Board of Directors sees something in him. They've used him to perform a number of tasks…"

"Please tell me, Doctor Spelling, that you aren't impressed by such brutal displays of machismo…"

"You're referring to the killing of a notorious outlaw…"

"Butch Cassidy certainly has attained some infamy thanks to the press trumping up his exploits."

There is a natural instinct for a female to be impressed by gladitorial feats of bravery and strength," analyzed the Doctor, "but I personally find displays of mental prowess equally arousing to the senses."

"Is that so?" asked Professor Splinus. "Perhaps we should repair to my tent to discuss our intellectual endeavors on the morrow. I do plan to heavily cite your anthropological research in my thesis. When we bring back evidences of the Lost City of da Silva Guimarães, we'll set the world afire with what we have learned about pre-history Brasil."

Doctor Spelling nodded. "I would certainly like to have a discussion about how we are going to promote our finds in a way that will best lend credence to our efforts here."

"Let me see to the security of the camp," said Professor Splinus. "These savages need very precise instruction. Left to their own devices the fire would go out and they would drink themselves into a cachaça stupor."

Professor Splinus found Lone Crow sitting by the fire, peeling some plantain that he'd plucked from a stalk on the way back from the Lost City. Before Crow could take a bite, Rapua put his hand on top of the ear.

"Don't eat it," said the Bororo headman. "It is poison unless it has undergone the rite of purification!"

"That's utter nonsense," said Professor Splinus who understood the gist of Rapua's words. "For years he's eaten food without the benefit of a purification ritual and survived."

Rapua looked at the Professor with a blank expression and Splinus realized that he had spoken in English. Only Crow could understand him.

"Yes," said Crow, "but I've always offered a prayer to the Creator to bless my food—so if Rapua wants to bless it again, in his own way, I have no objection."

"It's prepostrous to think a higher power has anything to do with the edibility of your food," said the Professor. "It's the laws of evolution that have created you from a single cell organism and that have evolved that maize into a palatable substance—but I don't suppose you would be familiar with the forefront of scientific research, such as the recent publication of Darwinian theory."

Crow's face was impassive. "I don't much care about which science my Creator used to make me, but I do understand a thing or two about natural selection."

"Indeed?" cried Professor Splinus. "You are familiar with the principle?"

"Quite," said Crow. "If I draw faster and shoot straighter than my enemy then perhaps I will live another day."

"Splendid!" said the Professor. "You do possess a rudimentary comprehension of the principle."

"As best as my meager intellect allows," replied Crow, his tone of voice giving no indication whether he was speaking facetiously.

"Then you should understand that it is merely a matter of natural selection that makes you the survivor—nothing to do with a mythical entity or higher power. There is no higher power than the laws of nature and science."

Crow gave the Professor a sidelong glance. "You have not seen the things that I have seen."

By now Rapua had summoned Tupi, one of the tribal shamans. Tupi's body was smeared in a red paste called urucum, which was mashed down from the seeds of the annatto shrub. His lower lip was pierced with a reed that projected about six inches from his chin. He gyrated his hand over the plantain and began to chant wildly, gesticulating and crying out.

Crow politely waited through the ritual and thanked Tupi before biting into the plantain.

"I feel a great evil," said Tupi. "It comes from the city below, rising with the fog."

"It is a wicked chill," said the Professor as he drew his jacket more tightly around him and addressed Crow. "I'll be retiring early. Please do not disturb me or the Doctor this evening. Make sure that you have watches set throughout the night so that we do not suffer from the depredations of any wild beasts."

Crow nodded and as the night began to fall the fog gathered again, climbing up the hillside and creeping toward the camp. The Professor looked again to the Cyclopean arches that pierced the billows of the mounting fog and watched as they turned to shadow and then were completely obscured by the thickening mists. The libidinous thrill of discovery raced through him as he thought of the ancient mysteries that he would uncover on the morrow, and then he thought of Doctor Spelling and wondered if he might be able to uncover any of her mysteries on this eve of discovery.

He rummaged through the saddlebag of one of the donkeys and uncovered two carefully packed bottles of wine from a particular Brasilian vineyard. Though their tin cups would lack the elegance of a crystal goblet, there was no reason that he and Doctor Spelling shouldn't celebrate the discovery of da Silva Guimarães's lost city.

*****

The Professor's dropped time piece read just past eleven when Doctor Spelling stumbled out of Splinus's tent, her palm still stinging from the slap she had laid across his cheek. The earth reeled beneath her, too many tin cups of wine and the heavy fog making her vision a misty haze. She clutched at the bodice of her khaki shirt where the top buttons had been torn away. Through the fog she saw a glimmering light where the campfire still burned high.

Though deep in her cups, she still recalled that her tent lay on the other side of the campfire, so she lurched toward the flickering flames only to draw up in shock when she saw the crimson-splayed bodies of the Bororo tribesmen scattered upon the earth.

A dark figure drew up through the hazy billows around the edges of the campfire. "No need to be afraid."

Doctor Spelling whirled and saw their American Indian guide emerging from the shadowed fogs. "I… I thought they were dead. I saw the red urucum and thought it was blood."

"They are only sleeping," said Crow. "I've chased away a few very large rats and a three-banded armadillo, but seen nothing else but shadows and bats… lots of bats."

"Thank goodness," said the Doctor, glancing around to see if the Professor was pursuing her. "Still, do you mind seeing me to my tent? I would feel safer."

Crow's sharp eyes seemed to discern the situation and his hand dropped to the Eagle-butted Colt that rode at his hip. "Do I need to deal with the Professor?"

Doctor Spelling paused and then it dawned on her just what Crow was suggesting. "Oh no! It didn't get so far that I need you to kill him." She glanced at the pistol. "Is it true, the story that they tell about your pistol?"

"What story is that?" asked Crow.

"That it is a holy symbol—blessed by a prophet of God."

"I don't know that it's a symbol," pondered Crow, "but it was blessed by a prophet of God."

"So it always hits whatever you aim at?"

"No, that part is up to me," said Crow.

"Then how is it different than any other gun?"

"There are some things that only bullets from a blessed gun can kill," answered the Indian.

She paused again, finding it strange that she should entrust her virtue to a red man. "Just do me a favor and make sure that he doesn't attempt to pay me a visit this evening. Once morning comes, and the Professor has sobered up, I'm sure that he'll be much safer."

"I'll let Muno know when he takes over my watch," said Crow. He escorted the Doctor to her tent and when she had fastened the latches and loaded her buffalo gun, a Remington Zouave Rifle that held one very large .58 caliber bullet, she saw his shadow drift away.

****

When morning came it was accompanied by a pounding headache and the taste of stale wine. Doctor Spelling groaned and extricated herself from her sleeping roll. If it had been another morning she would have angled for a late start on the trail, but her excitement to descend the ridge and into the Lost City overcame her desire to shut her eyes and seek the reprieve of sleep.

She found just a pair of spare buttons to partially replace the four scattered on the floor of Professor Splinus's tent and made a quick job of repairing her shirt so that it provided at least a modicum of decency—not that decency was much a consideration when traveling with a half dozen Bororo tribesmen who were all but naked. When she emerged from her tent in the morning she was accustomed to warming herself by the fire the Bororo had kept burning during the night, but this morning there was naught but smoldering ashes and a few blackened sticks that remained.

The bodies of the headman Rapua, the urucum smeared shaman Tupi, Muno and the other three tribesmen were gone, leaving only hollows in the grass where they had laid. Professor Splinus stalked about the still hazy camp, his temper foul either because of the rejection he had suffered last night or because of the morning discovery that their entire contingent of Bororo guides and porters had disappeared.

He jabbed his finger at Lone Crow. "They were your responsibility. If you had done your job they would still be here! They've packed up and left in the night because you didn't promise them a large enough share of our findings."

"Just last night you were complaining that I offered them too large a portion of our findings," said Crow without raising his voice in the slightest. "Which is it? Did I offer too much or not enough?"

That the Indian remained unaffected by his towering rage only further angered Professor Splinus. "Never mind! We're already here and the truth is that we don't need those deserters any longer. Prepare a pair of donkeys. We'll descend into the city as soon as I've eaten my morning repast—" He cut off short and glanced at Doctor Spelling, strands of her long brown hair hanging in a disheveled fashion from her loosened bun and her khaki shirt straining against mismatched buttons. "And I'll be taking it alone in my tent!"

When he was gone Crow turned to Doctor Spelling. "Did you sleep well?"

"Well enough I suppose—but I was wondering just who was going to prepare the Professor's breakfast for him?"

The slightest of smiles came to Crow's lips. "I suppose that he'll have to fend for himself this morning." He went to the smoldering fire and the smile faded.

Doctor Spelling saw his expression shift. "Is there something wrong?"

"There are tracks here among the grass. The tracks of a great dog or a wolf."

"A wolf… in Brazil? Where do the tracks go?"

"That's the thing," said Crow. "The tracks appear near the campfire and then they disappear after only a few steps."

Doctor Spelling came to the campfire and examined the tracks with her own eyes. "The tracks disappear right along with the Bororo. Do you think it could be some sort of trick? That the shaman made them to fool us?"

Crow shrugged his shoulders beneath his buckskin jacket, his long braids undulating. "Perhaps," he said, but he didn't sound convinced. "I hope that you are right."

****

They descended the ancient trail, the golden tamarins chattering in the leafy canopy above them as the fogs grew into a pea soup that was so thick they could scarcely see a dozen feet in front of themselves. Ocassionally a male tamarin would launch itself across the trail, jumping fifteen feet to another tree carrying its three-inch tall progeny on its back.

Crow watched these prodigious leaps with some wonder as he led a pair of donkeys—a duty which had devolved upon him since the departure of the Bororo tribesmen. On his previous trip into the lost city he had heard the cries of the little monkeys, but had been unable to see them because of the dense fogs. Today, the fog clung a little lower to the earth, leaving the hazy canopies just barely visible to his searching eyes.

It took two hours to descend the ridge and they did this mostly in silence, the only sound their footfalls on the cobbled road. In some spots nature had almost entirely encroached upon the ancient highway and in other spots the road heaved upward or sank into potholes, the shifting crust of the earth having taken its toll on the toil of the ancient race that once existed here in the heart of the Brazilian rain forest. Doctor Spelling spoke to the Professor only when absolutely necessary and the tone of her voice exhibited a glacial quality whenever she exchanged words with him. Still, when a trio of arches emerged from the mist—the center the greatest of the three—they could not help but break their silence.

"We're about to enter a place that most didn't even believe existed," breathed Doctor Spelling. Her voice seemed to be swallowed up by the fog.

"Notice the symbol inscribed in the keystone of the arches," pointed Professor Splinus. "It appears to be Romanic in character. Get a picture of it, Doctor Spelling."

Doctor Spelling needed no prompting. Already she had returned to one of the donkeys, pushed aside her Remington rifle and removed her photographic equipment from the saddlebag. She carefully opened the shutter two or three times at different angles to best capture the image of the three arches through the drifting mists. "This wouldn't have been possible even a year ago. I would have had to bring dark room equipment with me and develop the Daguerrotypes immediately, but with these new gelatin plates, the image stays fixed longer and I can develop them when we get back to Rio de Janeiro."

The mist was thicker here and no longer did the golden tamarinds chase them down the trail. Their chattering had ceased and the only sounds of nature were the wings of the bats that flopped through the foggy atmosphere. Though, somewhere above, the sun diffused its rays through the fog, they moved in a perpetual gloaming—passing through the portal of the lost city and into long, wide roads hemmed in by great structures with carven faces blackened by time, and with broad terraces covered with broken masonry and guarded on each corner by carven hounds, their fangs dripping with black bryophite and their eyes gouged blind by the elements.

"The hound seems to be a common motif in their architecture," commented Professor Splinus. "Perhaps some sort of totem or maybe indicative of canine worship. Doctor Spelling, would you please take photographic records of the architectural symbology demonstrated?" His voice carried through the empty city, rebounding against crumbling pillars and dilapidated walls and echoing back, hollow and strange.

Doctor Spelling shuddered at the strange timbre of the Professor's returning voice and wondered if the devil himself did not have a voice that sounded similar. She ducked her pith helmet beneath the black drape of her camera and carefully loaded another gelatin plate. After allowing Doctor Spelling the time to finish her photography, they continued down the street, emerging in a great square.

In the center of this plaza was a great black stone and at the summit of this stone stood a statue of a bearded, but bare-chested man with a broad girdle. He stood with left hand on hip and right hand outstretched and pointing toward the northern pole. Around the base of the black stone were a number of inscriptions and drawings, but much of this was obscured with moss and grime. At each corner of the plaza was an obelisk which rose toward the heavens, but in every case they showed signs of damage where the pyramidal top had been scorched or even broken asunder by lightning strikes.

It was now that Doctor Spelling became aware of the sound of hooves against the cobbles of the street. Since she knew that the pair of donkeys they had brought with them were being held by Lone Crow, she withdrew her eye from the camera's lens and her head from beneath the black drape. Moving in the mist behind Crow she saw six savages approaching and leading the remainder of their camp's donkey train. In a moment she recognized the Bororo tribesmembers who had accompanied them to the edge of the lost city and then disappeared in the night.

The headman, Rapua, called out to them in his own language. "We are sorry we are late. We saw strange things in the night fogs and became scared."

"Useless savages," said Professor Splinus in his own tongue. "Tell them to gather any interesting artifacts that might be portable."

For the moment Lone Crow ignored the Professor's demand. "Just what was it that you saw in the night?"

"Great hounds," replied the shaman, Tupi. "Their specters haunt this part of the land, and that is why this forest is taboo to the Bororo."

"Did the hounds hurt you or have they hurt others?" asked Crow.

Tupi shook his head. "They are but ghosts of greater powers hoping for release. I have performed a rite to protect against them."

Professor Splinus brushed away the dirt and moss from the engravings on the obelisk. He did not understand all that had been said, but he picked up a few of the words. "Ghost hounds?" he snorted. "What a bunch of nonsense. Some of the Brasilian tribes are known to brew psychotropics into their beverages to enhance their spiritual journeys. No doubt they were imbibing something of that ilk last night just before they had hallucinations of giant dogs. I'm sure that tonight they will be seeing pink elephants…"

"I actually saw the footprints," said Doctor Spelling, but she broke off when she saw that Professor Splinus was not listening. His attention was on the markings in the stone, which began to be revealed as he brushed away the moss and dirt with a stiff brush.

"Perhaps it would have been safer if you had stayed away from the city," Crow told the headman.

Rapua smiled broadly and held up the gold coin that Crow had found during his previous foray. "The shine of gold overcomes much fear. Tupi explained to us that if we had gold we would no longer need to raid the towns. They would just give us whatever we ask in exchange for our gold."

"The inscriptions are in Greek," said the professor who was too wrapped up in his discovery to pay attention to the conversation of the savages behind him. "And over here we again see the tetractys, the mystical symbol of ten triangles that the Pythagorean worshipers would swear their oaths by."

"What is that below the Greek?" asked Doctor Spelling. "They appear to be equations of some sort."

"I agree with your assessment," said Professor Splinus. "They are mathematical conundrums of some sort. Pythagoras was not only credited with the creation of various geometrical equations but applied mathematics to all spheres of existence—even music."

"Of course, the Pythagorean hammer theory," said Doctor Spelling, "but that's been largely discredited. It's string ratio not hammer size that produces the differentiation in tone."

"Naturally," said Professor Splinus, "but the hammer theory was just a misstep that helped him postulate the harmony of spheres which posits that all celestial bodies move in a mathematical equation."

"And that equation creates a symphony of tonal values," completed Doctor Spelling. "I've got a minor degree in music theory—even did a paper on the harmony of spheres. My Greek is rusty, Professor. How does the top line translate?"

Behind them the Bororo tribesmen were scouring the plaza, some breaking off chunks of engraved tile that might be transported in the saddlebags of the donkeys, who began sniffing the air and braying nervously.

Rapua picked up his poari, which was strung about his neck, and began to play a discordant melody in the hopes of chasing away the dark feelings that gathered in his soul. His fingers and lips seemed to move of their own accord, creating strange tunes, the likes of which he had never before played or even imagined in the most feverish of his dreams.

Doctor Spelling repeated her request, because it seemed as though Professor Splinus had been mesmerized by the music to the point of distraction. "What does the translation say?"

The Professor's tone was forced and harsh and the words seemed to rend both time and space, mingling with the eerie music of the poari to an effect that was beyond the ability of the tongue to utter. "They are lean and they are athirst!"

As these words were spoken, the overhanging fog began to churn and for a moment Doctor Spelling thought she saw a double vision of all around her, an overlapping world, that was strange and yet familiar, into which she had sudden insight. Here, horrific, shambling forms moved in a perversion of the reality just next to the one that she knew. Then lightning sprang from the pyramidal points of the four obelisks at the corners of the plaza, bathing both realities in a brilliant flash of illumination which starched her vision and seered her soul.

The air smelt of ozone and as Doctor Spelling's vision slowly repaired she felt an evil presence working upon nerves, so that fear and horror relayed through every synapse and muscle even before she saw the fiends emerging from the corners of the four obelisks. As soon as they came through, her double vision melted together into one cohesive form, but the lean hounds still remained—standing six feet tall, with great paws and slavering fangs.

Their baleful eyes burned red, as if the very fires of hell were kindled within, and their growls seemed to shake the very earth upon which they trod. Immediately, Tupi began to shake and gyrate his urucum smeared body, his voice cracked as he called out a chant of protection. Then the nearest hound leaped, its spring taking him twenty feet and his jaws snapping over Tupi's skull and shoulders with a bone crushing ferocity. Tupi's body sagged and the beast tore it asunder with a jerk of its corded neck.

The braying donkeys scattered, but the hounds were among them and the tribesmen, tearing hoof from leg and arm from body and lapping up the blood with forked tongues of blue. Lone Crow, like all the others, except for the dead shaman, had been momentarily paralyzed by the fearsome gaze of the hounds, but now his gun was out and flashing fire. The bullets punched through the side of the nearest hound and viscous blue blood gushed out upon the cobblestones. Still, with six bullets in its flank the hound stood, and diverted its attention from the grisly repast of Tupi's remains to fix its awesome gaze upon the Native American gunslinger.

This time, the dark power of its stare did not exert its hold upon Crow, who cast open the cylinder of his revolver, scattering the empty brass, tinkling across the blood-spattered cobblestones. Doctor Spelling looked to Professor Splinus for some advice, but he was fallen on the earth, with his back to the black stone—his eyes glazed and his mouth hanging wide in the face of all his unbeliefs witnessing themselves before his stunned senses.

Doctor Spelling's donkey came charging wildly past and she reached out, desperately snatching away her buffalo rifle before it ran braying into the mist, only to be pounced upon and devoured by one of the devil hounds.

"The hounds of Tindalos," muttered Professor Splinus. "It is as the Livre de Demonicis says. They are lean and they are athirst."

"What can we do?" cried Doctor Spelling, but Professor Splinus was far from regaining lucid thought, for he repeated the same three sentences over and over and they became garbled, so that the words began to tumble forth in no particular order and then even the syllables collapsed into a mash of unrecognizable sounds.

Doctor Spelling looked back to the horrific spectacle and she saw that the injured devil hound was reeling toward her. She averted her eyes so that she did not look directly into that burning, hungry gaze, and then she lifted her buffalo rifle and pulled the trigger. She fired before bracing the weapon and the heavy stock slammed into her shoulder as the rifle spewed out a .58 caliber round. Instead of puncturing the hound's body, as Lone Crow's bullets had, the lead slug ricocheted from the hound's skull and winged into the foggy thickness. The hound gave no indication of even noticing the bullet, which was a larger, and normally, more devastating round than the ones Crow had been firing from his pistol.

She hurled herself to the side as the hound leaped, and the wounded devil dog lurched into the black stone, so that the pointing figure atop began to tremble. The hound yowled—not because it was hurt by the impact with solid stone—but rather in rage, because its prey had evaded it. However, it found Professor Splinus numbed and babbling a few feet away and vented its fury upon the unfortunate professor by rending him limb from limb.

Doctor Spelling shrieked out in horror and she tried to fire her rifle again, but realized that she had already fired the one round that the single-shot muzzle-loader was capable of holding. She fumbled in her pocket to find another of the teat-fire cartridges and, sprawled on the pavings, she began to ram the cartridge down the barrel—all the while praying that the devil dog would be occupied for a few moments longer by its feasting.

Now Lone Crow's eagle-butted revolver was reloaded and he strode toward the beast, a spectral wind tugging at his buckskin jacket and pulling his braids back, so that they writhed like tangling black adders. This time he took more careful aim, placing three bullets through the side of the hound's skull. Indigo blood spattered the black stone and the hound gave out a marrow-rending howl as its spectral form withered and collapsed, dissipating until the last of its molecules evaporated on chill gusts carrying the decay of fermenting evil.

"Why... why..." stuttered the doctor. "Why do your bullets hurt the hounds and mine do nothing?"

"The flesh of the hounds is not that of mere mortals like us," said Crow. "My gun has been blessed by the power of the higher priesthood so that its bullets might sunder that flesh."

Rapua ran past Doctor Spelling and Crow, his poari dangling about his neck and a spectral hound hard on his heels. Crow snapped off three shots that blasted through the beast's cranium so that it lurched forward and slid across the dusty cobblestones, coming to rest at the foot of the black stone. Rapua climbed high upon the monument so that he clung to the figure's braced brass legs.

The hound howled and attempted to rise and Crow could see that the holes he had shot through the hound's skull were beginning to close. The gushing flow of blue plasma receded to a trickle as the wounds healed. If he didn't finish the hound quickly, the beast would rise to its feet and eat them.

Crow levered the empty brass out of his Colt and began advancing the cylinder as he pushed new cartridges into the hot pistol. The hound roared and lurched to its feet, and Crow put six more bullets into the fiend's brain from the range of a half dozen feet. A great wind howled and swept away the dessicated remains of the dog as it collapsed into cosmic dust.

The Indian looked and saw that of their party of nine only three of them remained alive. The remaining pair of devil dogs were finishing their gory meals, their hunger sated for only a few moments before they began to cast their burning gaze about the plaza, hoping to transfix fresh prey with their baleful stare.

Once again the Native American emptied his brass and began to reload. "It's taking me about twelve shots to take down just one of the hounds. If they come at us the same time, we won't survive."

"Something took over my body," panted Rapua. "I didn't know that song. An evil spirit made me play the song."

Doctor Spelling averted her eyes from the captivating gaze of the hounds and to markings on the black stone. She had difficulty understanding the Bororo dialect even when the words weren't rushed. "What's he saying?"

"Something evil forced him to play the song on the poari," translated Crow.

"And the hounds appeared immediately after the tones were played," realized Doctor Spelling. "That's it. These equations on the stone, they use the harmony of spheres theory to indicate a series of tones which unleash the hounds!"

"That's great," said Crow and he carefully aimed his freshly-loaded pistol at the forehead of the nearest hound.

Doctor Spelling seemed surprised. "That's sarcasm isn't it? All this time you were taking pokes at the Professor and me and we thought you were incapable of..."

"The inscription doesn't happen to say anything about leashing the hounds, does it?" Crow fired a pair of shots at a hound, and blood and fragments of skull erupted from the beast's forehead. It gave a baleful howl and began bounding across the plaza and toward the trio of survivors.

"Maybe if we reverse the sequence of tones…" She stretched out her hand to Rapua who was unlimbering his bow. "Give me the poari!"

The headman had no clue why the Doctor wanted or needed his feathered musical instrument, but her tone was insistent and he figured that in a few moments he would be too dead to care whether he owned a poari or not. He handed her the parrot-feathered gourd and she immediately put the reed to her lips.

As she accustomed herself to the instrument her first tones were incongruent with the pattern that she was attempting to play so she started again, accompanied by the staccato of Crow's gunfire. She didn't dare watch the hounds as they hurtled across the cobblestones, in case her fear stole her wind and she wasn't able to play the reversed sequence.

The last of the eerie notes finished a few moments after Crow's hammer fell on empty brass. The hounds rushed at them in concert and leaped for the kill. Then the landscape reeled, the vision of Doctor Spelling, Crow and Rapua splitting in twain as they momentarily viewed the physical and the spiritual worlds which existed in the same place, but on different planes. They saw ethereal hosts of the wicked dead imprisoned, gnashing their teeth and howling in misery and they saw a great black gulf over which none could pass.

The fangs of the slavering hounds snapped shut, but instead of rending the flesh of Doctor Spelling, Lone Crow, or Rapua, the hounds had already been drawn to their home plane and their emaciated bodies faded from sight as the landscape melted back to the physical plane that mortal men called their home.

Disoriented and amazed at their survival, the three explorers sank to the ground, their minds reeling as they vainly tried to comprehend the other-worldly vistas their flesh and blood eyes had witnessed. Out of habit Lone Crow numbly emptied the hot brass from his pistol and reloaded.

Rapua felt compelled to play his poari and he climbed down from his perch next to the statue and tried to pry it from the Doctor's clenching fingers. When she realized what Rapua was doing she tore the instrument away and crushed the feathered gourd beneath the heel of her boot. Immediately the compulsion left Rapua and he felt a burden lifted from his mind.

"Sorry, Rapua—but I can't have you summoning the hounds again," she said.

"Could he possibly sing the notes?" asked Crow.

Doctor Spelling took off her pith helmet, the strands of her brunette hair had broken loose from the bun and they spilled down the nape of her neck. "There's no way. Have you heard Rapua sing?"

"Unfortunately," said Crow.

"His vocal cords aren't capable of reproducing the notes no matter what force is compelling him," said the Doctor. "I think we're safe."

"I may be able to track your donkey and recover your photographic plates," said Crow. "At least, with that evidence, Professor Splinus will share in one last great accomplishment."

The Doctor shook her head. "I don't think so, Crow. This city should stay lost. When we return I'm going to tell the board at Miskatonic that our expedition was a failure—that the Lost City of da Silva Guimarães is nothing but legend, that it doesn't exist, that it never existed."

"And the silver mine that Manuscript 512 says exists less than a day from the city?"

Doctor Spelling pushed a few sweat-soaked strands of her hair away from her face. "We'll take a look, but that can't exist either when we bring back our report. If people come hunting silver they'll find the city and they'll loose the hounds—just as we did."

Crow nodded and sheathed his still-hot Colt. "I won't lie to the board, but I'll let you make the report. The Lost City remains lost."

The Shadow Walkers

The season was dry and the grass parched and brittle. Once already this season San Francisco had been cleansed by fire, but the next day the Sodom and Gommorah of the survivors had sprung from the ashes to rebuild. The California sun was sinking low in the sky, spreading its bloody rays across the horizon as Porter Rockwell and Lone Crow emerged upon the slaughter of the Tilson Shook mining camp. Rockwell wrinkled his nose at the horrible stench, shook back his long brown hair and muttered a prayer beneath his breath.

There were sixteen miners in all, their bodies strewn across the claim. Flapping black crows arose in a cloud, scared away from their feast by the presence of the two humans. The picks and shovels were broken, the thick handles snapped in half and the spades bent. The sifting screens were smashed into splinters that bristled stray wire, and the pans were scattered along the creek's edge.

Porter let out a long whistle once he had ceased praying. "What in tarnation happened here?"

Crow began to drift among the dead. "Most died of bullet wounds, but others look as though they've been killed by pick or axe."

Hefting a pick by the broken handle, Porter examined the blood stain on the point. "I reckon that this is the pick that done some of the dirty work. Any sign of this Reynolds fellow that you're looking for?"

Crow took a handful of photographs out of the pocket of his leather overcoat and compared the sepia-toned images to the faces of the dead. The rictus of a dead man's face often took on a different likeness than that of life, so he spent some time poring over the images and comparing them to the visages of the dead. Porter left the Indian to his grim work and he studied the tracks that came in and out of camp, comparing them to the boots that the miners of the Tilson Shook company wore.

"None of these dead men are Reynolds," Crow finally pronounced.

"Does Reynolds walk with a limp?" asked Porter, "because a man with a limp lit out of camp when the slaughter started." He pointed to the ribbons of a canvas tent. "He cut his way out the back and obsquatulated for parts unknown."

"Madamoiselle Reynolds did mention that he'd injured his leg in a wagon accident."

"His left leg?"

"His left leg," agreed Crow after searching his memory.

"Any other distinguishing characteristics that his old woman happened to mention?"

Crow shrugged, his long black hair laying around his shoulders. "A fondness for flapjacks and a gold fever that he couldn't shake."

"I thought you said his old woman was quite wealthy? What would prompt him to go gallivanting across the country looking for gold?"

"She's quite a beautiful woman, too," revealed Crow. "Maybe he had the wanderlust. It runs in the veins of some of us. What about your wife?"

Rockwell frowned. "She left me. I spent too much time protecting Joseph and Brigham from Boggs and his ilk. Not much fun when a governor puts out an extermination order on every Latter Day Saint in the state."

"Or when they put an extermination order on anyone whose skin is the color of red," added Crow.

"I guess we've got more in common than I might have thought," said Rockwell. "Who'd have thunk one of my closest associations would be with a redskin?"

"Or that one of mine would be a paleface," said Crow with a dry tone, that indicated there might be humor hiding beneath his words. "I think that there's a good chance Reynolds was the one who escaped. The shop-keeper we spoke with seemed very sure that Reynolds was with the Tilson Shook outfit."

"That was no shopkeeper," raged Rockwell. "That was an out and out extortionist. Did you see the prices he put on those goods? The only one getting rich around here is the ones selling supplies to the miners."

"We're in agreement there," said Crow.

"I've found two sets of tracks coming into the encampment—one from the west and one from the south," said Porter. "They're fresher than the rest, and I think they belong to whoever attacked the outfit. One set of tracks belongs to a woman."

"I've got a pair of mocassins coming in from the east," added Crow.

"You think it was an Indian?" asked Rockwell. "Five of the dead are scalped, but the other tracks were riding boots and I can see where the spurs have dragged in the earth. It's a different mark than the feet of the miners."

"I think it was one Indian with a man and a woman," considered Crow as he examined the markings in the dying light. "It's an odd fellowship, but not unheard of—after all, we're riding together. Still, there's something else that doesn't sit right about this."

"Besides the fact that they slaughtered sixteen men?"

"Doesn't it seem curious to you that not one of the attackers was killed?" asked Crow. "Look around. Most are armed with pistol, rifle, or shotgun but none of them managed to hit their attackers."

"It might not be that unlikely," judged Porter. "These are farmers, sail-ors, and city slickers that abandoned their profession to look for gold. De-spite their number, they were novices against three professional gunmen."

"But look at the placement of the shots," said Crow. "Well over half these men were shot down from behind, Porter."

Rockwell examined the grisly evidence and had to agree. "There's powder burns on the flesh and clothing. More than a few were shot down at point blank range and from behind and some were even killed with an axe! It's almost as though the miners couldn't see their attackers. I don't know how that's possible, though. Even in the middle of the night, the campfire would be more than enough to reveal an Indian, a woman with an axe, and a gunslinger gallivanting through the middle of camp. These men weren't sleeping when they was killed."

Crow's dark eyes seemed far away. "Shadow walkers," he murmured.

"Shadow what?" asked Porter.

"Shadow walkers," repeated the Native American gunfighter. "They exist in a place between death and life. They have the appearance of a ghost in the daylight, but in twilight they are merely shadows. In the dead of the night they are completely invisible to the eye. Or so I've heard."

"So you've heard?" repeated Porter. "And just where would you hear such poppycock?"

"The shamans of my tribe would repeat such stories over the campfires. I thought they were merely stories to frighten children into good behavior—or at least that's how my adoptive parents explained them to me."

"Well, after some of the strangeness we've seen I suppose I shouldn't be too quick to judge," said Porter. "Did the shamans' stories give any clue how to fight these things? I reckon we don't hold much chance against something that we can't even see."

Crow shook his head. "Guns and axe won't harm them. Our shamans said we were powerless against them—but they burned a peyote incense which they said would drive them away."

"And here I am fresh out of peyote," joked Rockwell. "I don't suppose you've been indulging…"

"Not I," said Crow. "I like to keep a clear mind so I can hear the Spirit speak. Anyhow, the peyote helped little when the Apaches attacked us and wiped out my tribe. As far as I know I'm the only survivor."

"What do the Apaches have to do with the shadow walkers?" asked Rockwell.

"There was one who led them—a great chieftain known as Red Arrow. Though they attacked in broad daylight he moved like a shadow. Though axe clove his flesh and bullets pierced his skin he did not falter. It was he that slew my parents and raised their scalps on a pole. Until that day, I didn't believe the stories of the shamans, either."

"So how do you fight something like that?" questioned Rockwell.

"Maybe nothing short of the priesthood power of a prophet can drive them into the cold earth where they belong," shrugged Lone Crow.

"Well, we may not have the power of a prophet," said Rockwell as he gestured to the elaborate grip of the revolver Crow wore at his side, "but your pistol has been blessed by one—and I've been blessed by another that if I don't cut my hair, bullet nor blade can harm me."

"Are you sure it's wise to share that? Isn't that how Samson was thrown in prison and had his eyes put out?"

"You're no Delilah, Lone Crow. Besides, I trust you to keep my secret. You know how to hobble your lip."

"At least we know that you'll live through an encounter with shadow walkers," said Crow. "Me, I've no such guarantee."

"Bullet and blade eliminates a few possibilities," mused Rockwell. "But there are a lot of other ways to die."

"It looks as though the shadow walkers took every nugget and every speck of gold dust in the camp," said Crow, examining the cut purse strings that still dangled from the belts of many of the dead.

"Tilson was in San Francisco seven days ago, hopping bars on Kearney Street—bragging to the working girls about how his mining company was 'hitting the motherlode'. That sort of talk catches the ears of folks like the Sydney Ducks. One of their nibblers heard the story from the working girl and word spread like wildfire through Sydney Town. You'll never find a more ornery group of claim jumpers and murderers collected in one spot than in Sydney Town. Still, how word got to these shadow walkers I don't know."

"They were probably hanging about in Sydney Town. Evil is drawn to evil—and even though they've suffered a half death, they have the same desires and lusts as when they were fully flesh and blood."

"I can tell you one thing," said Rockwell. "They didn't get all the gold."

"How's that?" asked Crow.

"I can see the proof in Reynold's footprints. I've seen the photographs you carry and unless Reynolds has been eating an awful lot of flapjacks since he parted ways with his beautiful wife. I'm guessing he made off with sixty or seventy pounds of gold."

Crow examined the footprints more closely in the last rays of the ruddy sun and was again impressed with Rockwell's tracking skills. "You're right. He is carrying a heavy load."

"How long do you think it's going to be before those shadow walkers count up their loot and start pondering the idea that their take didn't match up to the mother lode that Tilson was bragging about?"

"Maybe they'll think that he was exaggerating," said Crow. "It wouldn't be the first time that a man has lied to impress a pretty girl."

"He was handing out gold nuggets to the Chileno harlots," said Rockwell. "If your shadow walkers have gold fever, they'll be back to take another look around."

"Then we better find Reynolds before they do," said Crow.

In the last rays of the dying sun they mounted their horses and began following Reynolds' tracks out of the camp. Between the two of them they scarcely had to leave their horses, so sharp were their eyes. Even by the light of the moon, Crow and Rockwell were able to pick out his tracks as they traveled through scrub-covered hills. They spotted the faintest scuff, mark or bent blade of grass, and to them Reynolds' trail was as plain as if a map had been laid out for them. Reynolds was traveling on foot but though he had about twenty hours of headstart, he was carrying a heavy load.

"Looks as though he started heading back to San Francisco and then changed his mind," said Rockwell.

"A smart move," said Crow. "If someone discovered that a lone man was carrying that much gold his throat would be cut before sunrise. Just as well for me, too. The Hop Sing Tong is still looking for me. It wouldn't be wise for me to make a return appearance for some time."

Rockwell laughed. "My problem is that a handful of Missouri pukes hunting for gold over here discovered who I was. They seem to remember me shooting up a few of their wheel-horses during their mobbing days and didn't take too kindly to my presence in San Francisco."

"So that's why you had twenty men shooting at you when I found you in Sydney Town."

"I do appreciate you lending me a hand," said Rockwell. "Us brothers got to stick together. Tell me, Crow, just how does one become a shadow walker?"

"I found some manuscripts in the basement of a Massachussetts university library that talked about it."

"You can read English?" asked Rockwell.

"My step-parents were white settlers. They taught me how to read using the scriptures."

"I wish I would have paid more attention to my lessons," grumbled Rockwell, not too happy with the idea that an Indian could read English better than he could.

"Becoming a shadow walker involves the slaying of the innocent and certain symbols that must be painted and performed in blood. Then, when death would normally come, Satan's power overtakes that person and they are instead caught in a perpetual state between life and death instead of going to the spirit prison or paradise where the dead await judgment at the time of Christ's second coming."

"I heard of a Salem man named Waller who came home one evening to find that his wife, Constance, had killed his children with an axe and painted the walls in their blood. They tried three times to hang her, but she wouldn't die, so they threw her in prison. For thirteen months they gave her no food, but still she wouldn't die."

"What happened after thirteen months?" asked Crow.

"She grew so thin that she was able to slip through the bars and escape," said Rockwell. "Or so the story goes. It could be a bunch of hogwash."

The moon rose high in the sky as they pursued Reynolds deeper into the wilderness. The coyotes that ran wild through the hills sent up a chorus of howls, and Crow felt a chill crawl up his spine. He was comfortable with the sounds of the wild and though he'd faced ravenous packs of coyotes before, he knew it wasn't the coyotes' call that caused the prickle of apprehension. It was the presence of evil, and the feeling settled upon him like an oppressive weight.

He brought his gray-speckled roan up alongside Rockwell's dun stallion. "The shadow walkers are nearby," he said. "I can feel their presence."

"Reynolds isn't far off, either," said Rockwell. "The tracks are fresh and I can smell a hint of smoke on the wind."

Crow nodded. Now that Rockwell mentioned it he could smell it, too. "We'd better get to Reynolds before the shadow walkers do."

They set into a trot down the hillside, through the shadows of the valley. Here the rocky earth gave way to an undulating sea of high, brittle grass and even a child could have followed the trail plowed by Reynolds. It was midnight as they came over the rise of the next hill and saw the flicker of light from a campfire built behind the shelter of a granite boulder. A bedroll and an open mess kit lay next to a boulder, but there was no sign of the camp's resident.

"Mr. Reynolds," called Rockwell. "We come to…"

A gunshot rang out and a bullet whined past Rockwell's head.

"Get away, you fiends!" screamed Reynolds from his hiding spot behind a boulder.

"Mr. Reynolds," tried Rockwell again. "We've come to help you."

"You can't fool me," shouted Reynolds. "I saw that Indian scalp a couple of my friends!"

Crow didn't move from his horse. "We Indians all look alike to the palefaces," he muttered to Rockwell.

"You've got the wrong Indian," Rockwell replied to the hidden miner. "This is Lone Crow. Your wife, Mam'zell Reynolds, she hired him to track you down and get you home safely. She's worried that something's happened to you."

There was a moment of silence from behind the boulder. "My wife sent you?"

"She is very concerned," said Crow. "She says you have no need to prove anything to her."

"That does sound like her," admitted Reynolds. He showed himself now—a sturdy man, wearing a broad-brimmed ten-gallon hat. "Come join me around the camp fire. I thought you were somebody else."

At that moment Crow saw a shadow rise up behind Reynolds—the form of a woman bearing an axe. Without thinking, Crow drew his blessed Eagle-butted Peacemaker and fired. The .45 slug struck the shadow in the shoulder, and she let out a banshee scream and whirled away into the night.

"That gun seems to have done something," said Rockwell. "Keep it handy!"

Reynolds whirled and fired blindly into the night, emptying his .38 Smith and Wesson after the fleeing shadow. Rockwell and Crow galloped into the camp and tethered their horses, peering fruitlessly into the enveloping darkness.

"I can't see a blasted thing," said Rockwell.

"I know I must have hit her three or four times," said Reynolds, "but she never flinched. Not like when Lone Crow shot her."

"Her kind doesn't go down easily, Reynolds," said Crow.

Reynolds fumbled his revolver open and shook out six blistering-hot casings to the earth. He quickly began shoving replacement cartridges into the empty cylinders. "Call me Joshua," he said. "These shadow things came on my mining camp last night—killed everyone but me. I didn't think they could be stopped…"

"Don't get your hopes up," said Rockwell. A war whoop rang out and Rockwell pushed Reynolds down as a tomahawk whirled through the air, taking off Reynold's hat, but leaving him unscathed. A phantom came sliding through the night, a war bonnet rustling, then the flame of the campfire revealing a glimpse of war paint on naked flesh. Rockwell whirled and fired into the apparition, a pair of bullets pounding into the shadow walker's flesh. The shadow walker staggered at the impact of the bullets, but then the opened flesh closed around the wounds as if they had never been.

Rockwell felt a weight against his chest, pushing him down to the earth, and at close range the firelight illuminated the still-hazy figure of the shadow walker. He could feel the shadow walker's fetid breath upon him as a war club descended, narrowly missing his face and kicking up a spray of earth as it impacted next to his head.

Crow turned and fired at the insubstantial form that had borne Rockwell to the earth. He aimed a bit high so that he wouldn't accidentally shoot Rockwell and, owing to that, or perhaps the indistinct lines of the shadow walker in the darkness, he missed his shot. For a moment, the Indian assaulting Rockwell turned toward Lone Crow and the firelight flared to show a face that Crow had seen many years ago.

"Red Arrow!" he spat. Then the Apache chieftain was gone, into the concealment of the night.

"I know you now," came a gutteral voice, filtering from the blackness of night, heard above the rustling of the dry sea of grass. Red Arrow spoke in the Apache dialect, which was similar to the one that Crow had grown up speaking—though the low level consonants were altered so that it required a great effort for Crow to understand the words. "I scalped your parents and I'll finish my collection with your scalp."

"I know you, too—murderer!" Crow shouted back. Likely, the third shadow walker was out there somewhere waiting for an opportune time to strike. He could think of only one way to flush them out, to make them visible enough so that they stood a chance of fighting them. He plucked a flaming brand from the fire and hurled it into the dry grass. Immediately the grasses fired into a blaze.

Red Arrow laughed, his voice seemed to waft upon the leaping tongues of flame. "Some call me a murderer, but my own people—they call me a great hero. Even a legend!"

"Even a legend can die," replied Crow. He picked up another brand and hurled it, and then another, and then another. He threw these into different areas of the grass and soon guttering flame rose all about them, illuminating the hillside so that the shadows fled across its face.

Rockwell caught sight of her then, the spurred heels of her riding boots further agitating the nest as she climbed a swarming anthill to gain a temporary refuge among the flaming grasses. Perhaps it was Constance Waller, after all, the finery of her hoop soiled and torn; her extravant figure was limned in smoke and she clutched an axe, the handle of which was stained with blood and the head covered in gore. Crimson soiled the sleeve of her dress, for she clutched at her shoulder where the bullet of Crow's blessed .45 pistol had struck her.

When she realized that the firelight had revealed her position she looked upon Rockwell and spat a string of blasphemies.

"Why that was most unladylike," replied Rockwell.

Reynolds, too, had spotted the woman on her rocky perch, and he joined Rockwell as they fired a barrage of lead at the shadow walker. These bullets, fired from unhallowed barrels, did little against Waller but knock her from her perch and into the fire. This, it seemed, was enough—for Waller's ant-covered dress caught fire and her flesh burst into flame. She would have put out her own blistering flesh in the earth, but she was immersed in flame and there was no immediate recourse. So wailing and shrieking she plunged through the fires as her unnatural flesh was consumed.

"It seems we've found their weakness!" cried Rockwell.

"I've been praying that we would," answered Crow.

"You and me both," said Rockwell.

Reynolds wiped away the sweat from his brow. "You two ain't got nothing on me. I've been praying ever since I lit out from camp the night those three fiends attacked! I haven't done so much praying since—well, I've never done so much praying."

"Don't stop now," said Rockwell. "And get your gun reloaded. We may need some more firepower before this is all over."

That was when Bartholomew Black strode through the swirling smoke and into the campsite. Like his namesake he was dressed in black from boot to hatbrim, and it was only because of the raging fire he could be seen at all. The light glinted from a bandolier of .45 cartridges that stretched across his broad chest, and against the pair of six shooters thrust through his belt. He wore a great mustache that overlapped his lips, so that they could scarcely be seen moving as he spoke.

"I am Bartholomew Black and I'm here for my gold."

He needed no introduction, however, for his infamy had spread far and wide and all knew of the deeds of the cold-blooded murderer and crack-shot who had for six years scourged and terrorized the west, robbing and killing pioneers, looting stage coaches, and committing dastardly acts that could not be spoken of in mixed company. Then one day a posse had caught up with him and put four bullets in his back. When his grave was found exhumed the local constabulary thought it the work of grave robbers, but others whispered that it had been exhumed from within.

"The gold is in that rucksack by the fire," said Crow. "If you want it, go and get it."

"Not so fast," said Reynolds. "That gold belongs to me and the families of those miners that these fiends killed."

"Then maybe you'd like to gunfight Bartholomew Black over the privilege to carry the gold out of here," suggested Crow.

Reynolds blanched at the thought of shooting it out with a man who was reputed to plug a silver dollar as it was thrown into the air, and then he swallowed hard at the idea of gunfighting a man who had the capability of shrugging off bullets as if they were drops of rain on a duck's back. "No, I think not. If Mr. Black gives me his word that he'll leave us unharmed then he can walk out of here with that gold."

Bartholomew Black grinned. "I give you my word, Mr. Reynolds."

"How did you know my name?"

"I know a lot about you, Mr. Reynolds. The demon spirits whisper many things to me." He began to cross to the rucksack.

Now, Crow knew full well that the word of honor of a shadow walker could not be trusted. They existed between life and death because of the heinous acts and rituals they had committed. Whatever shred of decency they once possessed had been obliterated and forsaken by their own free will and choice. Still, he and Rockwell let Bartholomew Black cross the campsite and heave the heavy rucksack to his shoulder.

"It's been a pleasure doing business with you gentleman," said Black, and then he backed over the crest of the hill and disappeared into the wreathing smoke. The moment that he disappeared from view was the moment that Porter Rockwell stepped in front of Crow, and that was the moment that Bartholomew Black flitted back toward the camp firing his six shooters.

Rockwell groaned as a hailstorm of bullets struck him. He lurched against Crow and fell even as the Indian fired at Bartholomew Black. Crow returned only one bullet for the hailstorm of seven or eight that Black had fired from both fists. Sometimes it was more about accuracy than speed. Crow's aim might have easily been thrown off by contact with Porter Rockwell's falling body, but Crow took an extra moment and steadied his aim even as a bullet clipped the brim of his hat. The .45 caliber bullet sped from the mouth of Crow's blessed Eagle-butted Colt and punctured Bartholomew Black's heart.

Long ago that heart had ceased beating the crimson blood of mortality, but even so it still pumped the dark demonic ichor that made him a being which walked between life and death. A bullet from any other gun wouldn't have harmed the mortified organ but Black's mouth opened wide in shock and surprise as he reeled backward, then staggered to the ground.

The demonically-preserved shadow flesh of his form immediately began to decay before Crow's and Reynolds' eyes.

"Where's the other one?" asked Reynolds, his eyes trying to pierce the veil of flame and smoke. "The Indian chief?"

"Probably running off with your rucksack," grunted Rockwell as he climbed to his feet. He shook his overcoat and flattened bullets scattered from its folds.

"How did you do that?" asked Reynolds.

"It weren't my doing," said Rockwell.

"Those bullets didn't hurt you at'all?"

"I didn't say that," growled Rockwell. "It hurt like… well, I won't say, because I'm trying to control my cussing."

"Thanks for saving my life," said Crow to Rockwell. "If you wouldn't have stepped in front of those bullets…"

"What are friends for?" said Rockwell. "Besides, I knew that you was the only one here with a gun that could take Black down. I needed to give you a chance to fire it."

For a moment the wind whipped the flames into a fury and cinders fell across the campsite. The trio took refuge from the blistering heat behind the boulders until the wind shifted and carried the flame away, leaving charred fields in its wake.

"I can't thank you both enough for saving my skin," said Reynolds. "I don't know what I would have done if you two hadn't have come along."

"It weren't no accident," said Rockwell. "We were following your trail—hoping we could get to you before the shadow walkers did. It seems they have a lust for gold just as strong as any living man."

"It's just too bad that I'll be returning home empty-handed," said Reynolds. "I was hoping I could prove to my wife that I didn't need to rely on her wealth—show her that I can stand on my own."

Crow was silent for a moment, wondering if he should call Reynolds' bluff. He exchanged glances with Rockwell and the long-haired gunman revealed the faintest of grins on his soot-smudged face.

"I think you've proven that you're more than capable of standing on your own," said Crow. "Besides, you're not exactly going back to her empty-handed, now are you?"

"What do you mean?" asked Reynolds.

Rockwell gave a throaty chuckle. "We managed to follow your trail through the dark of night. Do you think that we can't see the signs?"

"Porter's the only man I've ever met, white or red, who can read sign better than I can," said Crow. "Do you think he wasn't going to notice that the earth has been disturbed by that boulder over there?"

Reynolds' adam's apple bobbed as he swallowed.

"I can see that you repacked the earth and brushed it after you dug the hole," said Rockwell. "I'm guessing that you buried your gold in that there hole and filled your rucksack with rocks."

"I didn't want to say so," admitted Reynolds, "in case the two of you got the fever and decide that my gold is worth more than the reward my wife is offering for my return."

"I don't blame you for being cautious," said Crow. "But you've got nothing to fear from us."

"If you don't mind," said Rockwell, "I may work your claim, though."

"Be my guest," said Reynolds. "I don't plan on going back."

"You may want to consider having me escort you back East," said Crow. "Once Red Arrow discovers that you've fooled him into carrying a rucksack full of rocks he'll—"

"Be mighty displeased," finished Rockwell. "He may even come looking for you."

"In that case I'd be happy to accept your offer," said Reynolds. "Besides,

I expect you'll want to be collecting that reward my wife offered."

Flame limned the hills and smoke rose up to obscure the pocked face of the gibbous moon. On the gusting wind Crow imagined he heard the sound of Red Arrow's voice, and he wondered if he would live long enough to collect that reward.

The Homunculi of Azathoth

In the depths of the Mato Grosso of the Brasilian rain forest Doctor Sylvie Spelling tore aside the flap of her tent and staggered into the misty night air, the gibbous moon casting a latticework of shadows across her body as she stumbled toward the jungle. She wore nothing but a long khaki shirt missing a few buttons and though her feet were bare she took little heed of the thorns and rock that she trod beneath her heels.

She passed the braying donkeys and a travois full of egg-shaped silver ingots, her pupils rolled back into her head so that only the whites of her eyes showed. Once she pushed a dozen feet into the jungle, she tilted back her head, her long brunette hair spilling from the loosened bun that had been drawn behind her head, and she began to sing.

The notes were odd and strangled, scarcely capable of being produced by human vocal cords, and their sequence—horrific and strange to the ear of any musician—resonated through the night, piercing both time and space, and drawing forth ancient evils from dark voids unseen by any human eye. As the blood curdling song continued, the mist began to coalesce into an amorphous bubbling blight, a monstrous shape with writhing appendages and sightless eyes. It took a shifting, mind-blasting form over the silver ingots and a reddened orifice opened up and spilled a rain of bilious dew. The donkeys shrieked in terror and bulbous growths upon the vine-like tentacles of the other-worldly fiend reached out and passed through them, turning their flesh to ash, so that their skeletons collapsed into a heap in front of the travois bearing the silver ingots.

Doctor Sylvie Spellings song was squelched as she was tackled by a man dressed in buckskin jacket, black braid trailing behind. He brought her down to the earth in a tangle of legs and she blinked, her pupils coming into view. She shook her head as she tried to focus and for an instant she took in the blasphemous, multi-limbed abomination that had taken amorphous form in the mist. Blind eyes peered from the beast, scathing the soul with dark psychic energies, and then it faded as quickly as it formed—its tenuous connection to the physical plane severed, and its energies being drawn back into the dark dimensions from whence it had been summoned.

"What was that?" gasped Doctor Spelling. "Why am I out here?"

"Something took control of you," said Crow. "And used your voice to summon that creature. There are ancient and dangerous energies that lurk here in the uncharted Amazon."

"Then wake our guide," said the doctor. "Have Rapua lead us out of here. I'm not sleeping again as long as I'm anywhere near here."

*****

Lone Crow could hear the distant gurgle of the Miskatonic River as he walked the idyllic streets of Arkham Massachussetts. Somewhere at the south end of the town, the stack of a crematorium belched black smoke, but the night air was pleasant, cool on Crow's sun-darkened skin and he took off his broad-brimmed hat so that his long black hair spilled out and his features were fully revealed. He wore a Colt pistol and an Arkansas toothpick which was nearly eighteen inches long and honed to a razor edge. Little children scurried away when they saw him striding down the avenues in his buckskin jacket, kerchief tied around his neck, and spurs clicking against the pavings at each step. Mothers cried out, and called their progeny inside the presumed safety of their homes. Little did they know, but there was nothing that could keep them safe from the doom that was descending upon Arkham.

He halted in front of a blue-painted cottage with freshly-blooming lilies growing in planter boxes that hung from the porch rail. An ivied trellis leaned up against one side of the porch, screening Crow in shadow as he climbed the steps and rapped on the front door. Warm light seeped through the gaps in the curtains and flickered through the half moon of milky glass set at eye level in the door.

Crow heard the murmur of muffled voices and then saw a flicker of movement. The door opened and a stolid, proffessorial fellow with a bristling black mustache stood in the gap. "Good evening Superint..." He broke off when he saw that the man on his doorstep was not the guest he was expecting. His eyes went wide as he took in the savage demeanor of the Indian who stood, hat in hand, the butt of a revolver, carved with the design of an eagle, jutting from a holster on his hip.

"Wha... what do you want?!"

Crow answered, his voice carrying a mid-west accent. "I'm looking for Doctor Sylvia Spelling."

The fellow's eyes narrowed. "It's Mrs. Elvin Conrad, now—and a red savage has no business with my wife, I am sure. I suggest you get out of Arkham before the constable gets a hold of you. We have little tolerance for outsiders here—especially those of your ilk."

Mr. Conrad went to slam the door shut, but it rebounded from the leather of Crow's booted foot. "I'm afraid that I must insist," said Crow. "Tell your wife that Lone Crow has come calling. I'm quite sure that she'll remember me."

"I'm quite sure that she will not!" blustered Mr. Conrad.

"Three years ago I accompanied her on an expedition into the Brasilian rain forest to find the lost city of da Silva Guimarães. Maybe she has mentioned it?"

"I'm sure that she has not," said Conrad, but his tone was less sure than just a moment before.

Crow's hand casually went to the butt of his pistol. "Go ask her. I'll wait here."

It was a few moments of heated discussion before Conrad returned to the door with a dark-haired woman wearing a form fitting bodice and a bustle skirt that was meant to produce or accentuate the appearance of an ample backside. A pair of reading glasses were perched upon the bridge of her nose and a copy of Hawthorne's The Marble Faun still clutched in her right hand. Her appearance was quite a contrast from the woman who had, alongside Crow, traipsed through the Amazonian jungle wearing khaki shorts and a pith helmet.

"Crow? Is it really you?"

"In the flesh," said Crow with the slightest of smiles.

"I didn't think I'd ever see you again… after the way we parted."

"I'd like to think we can let bygones be bygones," said Crow.

She paused for a moment, just regarding him with a quizzical expression. "Well, do come in. We have some corned beef left over from dinner—still warm, I believe. Would you like some?"

"I would love some," said Crow. "I'm famished." He shook the dust off his hat and brushed off his jacket and britches before removing his boots and entering the pleasantly appointed home.

It was apparent to Crow that Mr. Conrad still viewed him with some suspicion.

"My wife tells me that you were responsible for saving her life on at least two occasions."

"I wasn't keeping count," said Crow, "but I'll accept her reckoning as accurate."

They sat down in the drawing room, which was lit by a trio of oil lamps. The windows were left open to draw in the cooling breeze. The center wall was decorated by a tapestry woven by Brasilian indians from the fiber of the sisal plant. The other walls were occupied by bookshelves loaded with anthropology and mathematics tomes.

"Mr. Conrad," said Crow, "are you a student of mathematics?"

"A professor of mathematics at Miskatonic University," he corrected. "How did you—?"

Crow motioned to the library around them. "It was a logical guess. I knew that Mrs. Conrad's specialty was anthropology, but there were quite a few books on mathematics in your collection."

"You can read?"

Sylvie Conrad perched next to her husband on the divan and patted him on the knee. "Crow can read quite well, Elvin." Now she directed her comments to Crow. "Please forgive Elvin of his rather brusque greeting. He was raised in a family with very insular views regarding race."

"No offense taken," said Crow. "I appeared at your doorstep unannounced and I don't suppose you have too many men of my color showing at your door at dusk."

"Imagine the laugh the faculty will have, Elvin, when they find out you insulted the man who killed Butch Cassidy and you lived to tell about it."

Mr. Conrad's face tightened. "You killed Butch Cassidy?"

Crow nodded. "The method by which I dispatched him seems to vary from telling to telling, but the consensus seems to be that I did, indeed, kill him."

A young maid in a white frock came in and brought Crow a plate with corned beef and a side of collard greens. She gingerly placed it before him on the coffee table and scuttled away, casting nervous glances over her shoulder.

"I'm sure that Hepsibah has never seen an Indian before," said Mrs. Conrad. She set her book down as Crow bowed his head and offered a prayer over his meal.

"Now the meal has been twice blessed," said Mrs. Conrad when he concluded. "What is it that brings you to Arkham? Is the University planning another expedition?"

Mr. Conrad interrupted, his voice incredulous. "You've worked for the University?"

"On a few different occasions," said Crow. "They sometimes find it necessary to employ men of my unique skills."

Mr. Conrad raised his eyebrows. "Gunfighters?"

"It goes a little bit deeper than that," answered Crow. "Perhaps you aren't aware of some of the darker interests of some of Miskatonic's faculty…"

"Darker interests?" questioned Mr. Conrad. "What are you talking about?"

Mrs. Conrad let her brow furrow and her lips sank into a frown. "When I first returned from our expedition to the Mato Grosso I was obsessed with explaining what had happened to us in the lost city of da Silva Guimarães. I found that the University library possesses a great many books that delved into the darker, rarely glimpsed worlds that exist beyond the one we know. But the more I learned, the more questions I had—and those questions haunted me all my waking hours. I had the most obscene and horrifying nightmares—until I was driven to the edge of my sanity." She paused and glanced at her husband. "That's when I met Elvin. He gave me something else to focus on and pulled me out of my utter despair."

"She still has the dreams sometimes," muttered Mr. Conrad. "She speaks strange phrases or cries out in her sleep."

"Do you remember what happened that night after we found the silver mines a few miles outside the lost city?" asked Crow.

Mrs. Conrad shook her head. "I only vaguely remember finding the mines… and seeing something."

"Those silver ingots have been quite the boon to the University," said Mr. Conrad. "Superintendent Graves has found a buyer that is willing to pay top dollar for them—a German Count who finds great worth in them as artifacts."

"That's peculiar," said Crow, "because Sylvie never told the truth about where exactly we found those ingots."

Mr. Conrad opened his palms wide. "Despite the lack of provenance, he's willing to pay four times the going rate for silver bullion. I've seen the figures. They are quite impressive. Miskatonic plans to build a new wing from the proceeds of the sale."

Crow set aside his plate. "This sale must not happen. I must see Super-intendent Graves, right now."

"As far as seeing him, that shouldn't be an insurmountable problem," said Mr. Conrad. "He and his wife are scheduled to be here at any moment for a few rounds of whiskey poker. But as for dissuading him from selling the silver, I don't think you'll be able to convince him."

"Crow can be very persuasive," said Sylvia Conrad. "Just why is it that he shouldn't sell the ingots?"

"They aren't what they seem," said Crow. A rapping came from the direction of the front porch and the Indian rose to his feet, immediately striding to the front door and throwing it open.

"Why, what on earth are a pair of cowboy boots doing on your front porch?" questioned a mousy blonde that Crow presumed was Mrs. Graves. She was two decades younger than her husband, who stood wide eyed and staring at the solemn apparition of the Indian that stood before him.

Mrs. Graves' attention was still on the boots. "Why, there are even quaint little spurs mounted on the heels. Where on earth did you find this footwear?"

"They belong to me," rumbled Crow.

Mrs. Graves glanced at the source of the voice and gave out a shriek as she saw Crow filling the doorway. She staggered backward clutching her breast. "A savage! A savage!"

Superintendent Graves stood rooted to the spot, and then recognition sparked in his eyes. "Mr. Crow," he acknowledged. "I thought I made it clear that I never wanted to see you again."

"The feeling was mutual," said Crow.

"You know this barbarian?" cried Mrs. Graves.

Sylvie Conrad came up behind Crow and clutched his arm. "Not only do we know him, but he's a good friend of mine."

Mrs. Graves cast her gaze in different directions as if to ascertain whether her reality was indeed crumbling around her. "But he's an Indian!"

"I'm well aware of my heritage," said Crow, "but we have things of greater importance to discuss."

"Such as what?" asked Superintendent Graves.

"Those silver ingots that Doctor Spelling… or rather, Doctor Conrad and I brought back from Brasil. I've run across some scroll fragments—the translations of which lead me to believe that they may be vessels for the spawn of Azathoth."

"Azathoth," breathed Doctor Conrad. "The unseeing god. The blight of nethermost confusion which blasphemes and bubbles at the center of all infinity—I knew it was Azahoth that I had caught a glimpse of that night."

"Azathoth?" exclaimed Elvin Conrad. "What in the blazes are you talking about, Sylvie?"

"Azathoth, is one of the monstrous entities that exists behind the veil of reality that we know," said Superintendent Graves. "We have an extensive library at the university, and a number of volumes hint at the existence of such entities. I'm no expert, myself, but we do have some professors that are quite well-versed in the minutia of such worship beliefs. Unfortunately, the scholars that are knowledgeable in these things tend to be quite unstable and unreliable at best."

"Really!" proclaimed Mrs. Graves. "What kind of nonsense is this? Vessels for the spawn of Azathoth?" She turned to her husband. "Really, Franklin, you're not going to take this Indian seriously, are you?"

"It's a moot point," said Superintendent Graves. "Count Eicholz arrived early this evening, made payment, and took possession of the ingots. He's traveling with a pair of American henchman of rather dubious character—both armed with pistols. Gunfighters, I'd say."

The muscles in Crow's jaws worked and his brow furrowed. "Did they say which direction they were traveling?"

"No, no," replied the superintendent. "However, they did inquire about the whereabouts of a book titled the Livre de Demonicis."

"And what did you tell them?" demanded Crow.

"I happen to know that we housed one of the six known existing copies in our library at Miskatonic... but only because of a report from the head archivist which listed it as missing. So I told Count Eicholz that it had disappeared from our library. He seemed very disappointed."

"He's blind you know," interjected Mrs. Graves. "He wears dark glasses and carries a cane, but he seems to get around very well—for a blind man."

Crow breathed a sigh of relief. "It's very fortunate that Count Eicholz did not have a copy of the Livre de Demonicis. It contains certain summoning words that must be read to bring forth the spawn of Azathoth from those ingots."

Doctor Sylvie Conrad's jaw dropped. "So when I somehow summoned Azathoth it..."

"It fertilized those silver ingots," said Crow, "so that they might bring forth his children."

Superintendent Graves rubbed his chin. "Homonculi, then. Very interesting."

Mrs. Graves struck her husband on the arm. "You aren't buying into this rubbish, are you?"

"Of course not," said the Superintendent, "but I do find it a stimulating mental exercise, and I have witnessed more than a few strange things which weren't readily explainable by modern science as we know it. I do wonder where that book walked off to."

Crow turned and looked at Doctor Sylvia Conrad and raised an eyebrow.

She looked furtively to the left and right. "I have a confession to make. I have the Livre de Demonicis."

"That book is not supposed to ever leave the library," said the superintendent.

"I know it," said Sylvia Conrad. "At the time I stole it from the library, I was obsessed with finding out more about the thing that manifested in the jungle. Even when Elvin persuaded me to abandon my studies I couldn't completely let it go. Instead of returning the Livre de Demonicis to the library, I kept it hidden... in case I might someday need to resume my studies into the occult."

"Perhaps I can overlook this breach of Miskatonic University policy this once," said the superintendent, "provided that you return the book to me immediately."

"Of course," said Sylvia Conrad. She drifted into the sitting room, and crossed to the fireplace on the east wall. She set aside the hatchet and pushed away the kindling box. Beneath was a loose hearth stone and she pried this out, revealing a hollow in the stone work. Inside this, lay a book that was carefully wrapped in a sheepskin. She lifted it out, brushed away the cobwebs and handed it to the superintendent, who had followed her into the house with his wife.

"It's a good thing that you returned this. I would hate to be forced to dismiss the only female faculty member on the Eastern Seaboard."

"Is that because you'd no longer have the novelty of having a female on the staff?"

"I did stick my neck out to hire you on when our all-male faculty was almost entirely against it and I would never hear the end of it from Professor Stokely, should I be required to dismiss you."

"I'm sure he would be quite delighted to say that he told you so," commented Mr. Conrad. "He is a staunch believer that females should not be allowed in the field of scientific endeavor."

"However, I would also never hear the end of it from the rest of the faculty," said Superintendent Graves. "They've grown rather accustomed to having a beautiful woman attending their faculty meetings."

"Really!" said a dismayed Mrs. Graves to her husband. "You shouldn't say such things."

While the others were bantering, Crow crouched down at the hearth and took up the hatchet, cutting the kindling finer and building a teepee inside the fireplace over a mound of tinder.

"What are you doing?" asked Mr. Conrad. "It's already far too warm inside. The last thing we need is a fire."

Crow responded by striking a match and putting it to the tinder. He blew it into a flame and began adding larger pieces of wood, quickly building the fledgling fire into a healthy conflagration. He stood and faced the others once he was finished. "Sylvia knows what I am doing. She's the only one here, besides me, that really understands the danger."

"What in the bloody blazes is he talking about?" exclaimed Superintendent Graves.

Sylvia Conrad's dark eyes rested upon the superintendent's ruddy face and then traveled down to the book that was cradled in his arms. "I'm afraid that the Livre de Demonicis will only briefly be returned to your possession."

Mr. Conrad turned his gaze upon his wife. "What do you mean, Sylvia?"

"We must destroy the book so that it doesn't fall into the hands of Count Eicholz or his cronies. If they learn the birthing magics to bring forth the homunculi of Azathoth then…"

"Don't you think that you are taking this nonsense a bit too seriously?" questioned Mrs. Graves. "It's a book full of ancient superstitions…"

"Even if you don't believe in the dangers that book can unleash, Count Eicholz does," said Crow.

"And the University was paid quite well because of those superstitions," said Superintendent Graves. "It's a supersitious belief that I was more than happy to turn to the advantage of Miskatonic University."

"You don't understand," said Sylvie Conrad. "Count Eicholz won't accept that the Livre de Demonicis is missing. He'll track down the librarian and when she tells him of my interest in the book, Count Eicholz will come looking for me and the Livre de Demonicis."

"So give him the book," shrugged Mrs. Graves, a charming smile playing across her pleasant features. "Maybe he'll be willing to pay even more when we tell him of all the effort we went to in tracking it down."

Before the superintendent could react, Crow reached out and plucked the Livre de Demonicis from his arms and tossed it into the fire. Superintendent Graves gave out a cry and made a leap for the fireplace in order to pull the book from the flames, for indeed the book was still wrapped in sheepskin and the flames had not yet penetrated to the binding inside. Crow caught him by the back of the collar and heaved him across the room so that he flew into a cushioned chair.

"I'll have your hide for this, Crow!" blustered Superintendent Graves. "That book is worth thousands of dollars to the right collector."

Suddenly, Hepsibah stumbled into the sitting room. She coughed and blood spattered her frock and then she fell on her face, the hilt of a Bowie knife protruding from her back. Three men entered the room after her. At the center was a short man who wore dark glasses and tapped ahead of himself with a cane. He wore a brocaded jacket and silk shirt with a crimson cravat.

"Robert," he barked. "The book—grab it from the fire!"

Crow recognized the gunfighter on Count Eicholz's right as Lightning Robert Hawkins. His hair hung in long plaits with various amulets woven into the greasy strands, and his hands constantly twitched with nervous energy. Once, in El Paso, Crow had seen him gun down three gamblers and a painted lady who pulled a sawed-off scatter gun that was hidden beneath her pettycoat. The three gamblers had gone down before any of them had cleared their gunleather. The painted lady was the last one he killed. She had almost lifted the scatter gun into firing position when Lightning Robert Hawkins shot her through the heart.

Lightning Robert Hawkins was fast as a greased jaguar. He darted past Mrs. Graves and Mr. Conrad and was pulling the book from the fire before Crow could react. Hawkins jerked one end of the flaming lambskin and the Livre de Demonicis unrolled and dropped onto the hearth, still unscathed by the fire.

While Hawkins was thus engaged, Crow snatched up the hatchet and swung it at Hawkin's skull. Hawkin's jerked aside and the hatchet did naught but cut off a greasy lock of hair and a sinister amulet that was braided into it. Immediately the tremor in Hawkin's hands slowed and Crow realized that the secret to Hawkins's incredible speed was in the dark magics harnessed by those amulets. There were still a few other amulets in his hair, though, and Hawkins plucked up the warm book and darted backward before Crow could take a second swing with the hatchet.

The second gunfighter was Bishop Tarleton. Crow had never met him, but he recognized him from the descriptions he'd heard. Bishop was dressed entirely in black, from the brim of his hat to the toes of his boots. Around his neck he wore a large cross, and this was the reason that men called him Bishop. However, Crow could see now that the cross was actually inverted, and carved into its surface were symbols predating the death of Christ— antedeluvian runes from the twilight cults that worshiped fallen angels and the great, unspeakable powers that lurked behind the veil that humans called reality.

Next to Lightning Robert Hawkins, Crow wasn't even close to being the fastest gunman currently east of the Mississippi, but he still had a mean draw. Crow's eagle-butted Colt leaped into his hand as if by its own volition and spewed hot, blessed lead in the direction of his enemies. He sent two bullets hurtling toward Lightning Robert Hawkins, one at Count Eicholz as he switched targets, and the last three at Bishop Tarleton, who failed to draw his gun before the third bullet struck him mid-chest.

The effect of Crow's bullets was less than he hoped. Lightning Bob Hawkins swung around as Crow began firing and a pair of bullets punched through the thick cover of the Livre de Demonicis and lodged in the pages of the the massive tome. The single bullet that Crow fired at Count Eicholz struck his glasses, mangling them and throwing them off the German's face. With the glasses forcibly removed, the dark lenses no longer concealed the empty right socket and the strange abomination that inhabited the maimed socket of the left eye. It was a silver-skinned creature no larger than the tip of a big man's thumb, a blood-shot eye in its belly, numerous limbs that gripped the lid of the socket, and other tendrils that flailed about in obscene and horrifying fashion.

Only Bishop Tarleton went down, crashing into the wall and falling through the open front door.

"Now look what you've done!" ranted Count Eicholz, his accent thick. "You have revealed that I am the bearer of the genesis scion of Azathoth. Tremble in awe, mortals! Bow down and worship, shake in fear!"

Indeed, the horrifying sight sent Mrs. Graves reeling to her knees and the superintendent's legs lost their strength, and he scrabbled for purchase on the bookshelf, but tumbled to the ground in a cascade of scholarly treatises. Even Mr. Conrad was struck dumb, frozen into inaction. His wife, Sylvia, however, had been inured to such horrors on her journey into the Amazon and she snatched up the iron poker that leaned against the mantle. "Don't come anywhere near me, you abomination!"

Crow scattered empty brass across the wood planks of the cottage and began pushing fresh cartridges into place as he found meager cover behind the jutting mantle and stone-faced fireplace. "Get into the back room, Sylvia!"

Count Eicholz laughed, tittering and gibbering. Clearly what little sanity he had possessed had long since left him. "When I have released the hatchlings, they will overrun this entire world. Azathoth will spread his sphere of influence into the physical domain. The earth will be baptized in the blood of innocents and my name will be remembered by any unfortunate enough to still live."

Bishop Tarleton rose to his feet with a groan. He shook his coat and three flattened bullets rattled to the floor. "You can't take me down so easy, redskin."

Crow had seen such a thing before—a gunfighter named Porter Rockwell that couldn't be harmed by bullet or blade so long as his hair remained untrimmed. He couldn't be sure, but Crow suspected that it was the inverted Cross that was lending Bishop Tarleton his unholy protection—even against the supernal bullets of his own blessed pistol. Whether or not that protection extended to blades remained to be seen.

"Did you take out your own eyes?" asked Crow, hoping to buy a few more moments to finish reloading.

"Sacrifices must be made for the greater evil," cackled Count Eicholz. "To house the incarnation of Azathoth is an honor to mere mortal flesh."

"That thing is just a pale imitation of the horror that is the true form of Azathoth," said Sylvia Conrad.

Count Eicholz hissed. "You have seen him? You have witnessed with fleshly-eyes the glories of Azathoth?"

"There was no glory, just abominable chaos and madness," said Sylvia Conrad. "Just madness."

Count Eicholz took possession of the Livre de Demonicis and hoisted it with a lopsided grin. "We've got what we came for—and I thank you kindly. Now I'll be able to summon forth the birthing magics that will hatch the homunculi of Azathoth."

Mr. Conrad found his tongue. "Take the book you deformed fool, and get out of my home!"

It was natural for the human mind to seek a rational explanation when confronted with the unimaginable horrors that dwelt beyond the fragile earthly plane of existence. Mr. Conrad had found solace in the idea that the fiend that existed in the eye socket of Count Eicholz was some sort of birth defect or deformation. He still gave no credence to the dark powers that could be unleashed from the pages of the Demonicis.

Sylvia Conrad spoke to her husband as she backed toward Crow. "They can't take the book, Elvin. We can't allow it."

"What are you talking about?" spat Mr. Conrad. "Leave well enough alone. Let them have the book. It's just a few scraps of paper bound between leather. Is it worth more than our lives?"

Count Eicholz laughed. "Maybe you misunderstood me, Mr. Conrad. I said nothing about you keeping your lives. Hawkins, Tarleton! Fire the cottage. I think a funeral pyre would be an excellent way to usher in the births of the Homunculi of Azathoth!"

Lightning Bob Hawkins was still fast, even with one of the charms removed from his locks. By the time that Crow slapped the cylinder of his pistol shut and began firing, Lightning Bob had already plucked up a flaming brand from the fire, shoved Crow to the floor and was setting the Brasilian tapestry afire. Perhaps Lightning Bob Hawkins didn't realize that Crow had sheared off one of his charms or perhaps it was arrogance that prompted him to set the cottage afire first and then turn his attention to killing Crow. Even so, he had his pistol out and perforated the divan above Crow's head twice before Crow fired a bullet through his heart.

Lightning Bob Hawkins crashed against the flaming wall, the brand falling to the floor and kindling the carpet. Still, even after Crow's bullet had ruptured his heart, Lightning Bob continued to writhe and twitch, the dark energies that had amplified and pushed his nervous system to the edge of human capabilities still animating his corpse.

Bishop Tarleton fired a volley of bullets into the cottage while Count Eicholz retreated through the front door. Superintendent Graves caught a bullet in the back as he was scrambling over the top of Sylvia Conrad, who had fallen prostrate onto the floor in order to avoid being hit. He gasped and fell face forward onto the carpet, the flame creeping toward him.

Mrs. Graves crawled across the floor begging for mercy. She presented no threat to Count Eicholz or Bishop Tarleton, but Bishop Tarleton saved his last bullet for her since she was only a few feet away—the easiest of targets.

"I've got some mercy for you, darling!" Tarleton grinned, displaying a mouthful of teeth rotted and stained by chewing tobacco. He pulled the trigger and a red blossom appeared in the center of Mrs. Graves's forehead. She slumped to the floor, a crimson pool spreading across the floorboards and mingling with the disheveled blond strands of her splaying hair.

Then Bishop Tarleton ducked out the front door, passed over the trellised porch and down the stones of the walkway. Sylvie Conrad rolled the superintendent onto his side. He was still alive and he fixed his gaze upon Crow, spitting epithets through gritted teeth. "This is your fault, redskin. This is your fault!"

Elvin Conrad began to stamp out the flame on the carpet, while the bookshelf behind him turned into a raging conflagration. Crow scrambled to his feet and darted out the front door, gun in hand. If he didn't stop

Count Eicholz the whole world would burn—not just an Arkham cottage.

When he reached the front porch, Count Eicholz was climbing into a carriage and yelling at his driver. Bishop Tarleton was just a foot or two behind his boss. He whirled when he heard Crow's bare feet on the porch, drawing a second pistol that was still fully loaded. Tarleton began firing before he completed the turn and a pair of clay pots exploded, the plants they had contained toppling into the yard.

Crow's shots were not quite as hasty as Bishop Tarleton's. They peppered Tarleton and forced him backward, pinning Count Eicholz's foot between Tarleton and the carriage. Still, the bullets seemed to rebound from Tarleton's chest like popcorn from a hot skillet.

Count Eicholz, ignoring the fact that any number of those bullets might have hit him, had not Bishop Tarleton been guarding his back, swore at his henchman nonetheless. "Get off me, you oaf!"

This brief distraction gave Crow the opportunity to hurl the kindling hatchet, which he carried in his off hand. The blade whirled through the air and caught Tarleton in the face. The axe head did not rebound as the bullets, and Tarleton was nearly dead by the time that he hit the ground. It seemed that the Bishop's amulet of protection extended only to bullets and not to a well-thrown axe.

Now, the carriage was moving away, Count Eicholz still pulling himself inside, one arm clutching at the Livre de Demonicis. By the time Crow reloaded his pistol, his quarry would be halfway down the lane, so Crow thrust his pistol back into its holster and bounded from the porch, running as swiftly as his legs would carry him. The carriage driver snapped his whip, laying a stripe across the flanks of his horses and they whinnied, jolting the carriage into greater movement.

Crow was running so fast that he might lose his balance at any moment and go careening across the cobblestones. The carriage was beginning to pull away from him so he made a desperate leap for the rung at the back and caught hold of it. His bare feet scraped painfully across the cobblestones, until he jerked himself up another rung and climbed the ladder to the top of the carriage.

Gunfire erupted from within the cabin of the carriage, holes appearing in the roof and splinters flying in a haze about Crow, who danced away from the gunshots and then lost his balance and fell from the carriage. He caught himself by thrusting his left hand through the window of the carriage and hanging onto the door. Glass sliced his arm and shards tinkled to the cobblestones that sped past.

Count Eicholz, tendrils of his homonculi eye flaying wildly, approached the door as he loaded a single bullet into his Suhl pin-fire revolver. "It's the end of the road for you, Mr. Crow. The homonculi of Azathoth will be the dominant species on Earth—of that there is no doubt." He leaned closer and was about to press the barrel against Crow's forehead when Crow plunged his Arkansas toothpick through the pupil of the homunculus that dwelled in the Count's eye socket, driving the point all the way through and into the Count's brain.

The homonculus and Count Eicholz shrieked out in unison as they died. The coachmen glanced back in horror and saw his employer sprawled across the chest that lay between the bench seats, a knife jutting from his eye socket.

"Stop the coach," ordered Crow, "or I'll kill you, too!"

*****

The flame burned hot inside the Arkham Crematorium as Crow, with bandaged arm, hurled the Livre de Demonicis into the incinerator amidst the bones and ashes of Hepsibah, Mrs. Graves, Count Eicholz, Bishop Tarleton, and Lightning Bob Hawkins.

"I'll stay and help you repair your sitting room," said Crow to Sylvia Conrad, who stood next to him—her face soot-stained and her dark hair disheveled. "I know my way around a hammer."

"That will be unneccesary," replied Mr. Conrad who stood behind his wife. "I think that your presence here has caused enough trouble. To prolong your stay would only be asking for more. The residents of Arkham won't tolerate an Indian living in their midst—even if it's just for a few days. And once Superintendent Graves recovers from his wound, he'll blame you for his wife's death."

"Very well," said Crow. "I'll head west once we've finished refining the infected silver ingots." He opened the furnace door and began shoveling in heaping spadefuls of coal, stoking it to such an intensity that he could barely stand the heat. He kicked the door shut with a booted foot and backed away to the open chest of egg-shaped ingots. These, he tossed into a cast iron cauldron and, with the help of Mr. Conrad and a long pole, they placed it inside the incinerator.

Immediately the silver began to shriek and moan, and even speak in words that no human tongue was capable of uttering. The director of the crematorium shuddered, cried out and fled from the room screaming in horror. Crow and the Conrads clapped their hands over their ears to shut out the sanity-rending sounds as gestating homunculi attempted to leap from their silver shells, but were consumed within the furnace, their fledgling incarnations turned to ash.

Finally the voices ceased and nothing moved within the furnace except for the raging flame and the bubbling silver. They eased their hands from their ears and Mr. Conrad shook his head. "I admit, Crow, even after Count Eicholz and his gunmen attacked us, I thought that you were still crazy for believing this nonsense about the homunculi of Azathoth."

"What about the homunculus that lived in Count Eicholz's eye?" asked Sylvia Conrad. "Didn't that convince you?"

"I thought it was some sort of birth defect," said Mr. Conrad.

"It was just a weak shadow of what these other homunculi would have been," said Crow.

"How did you know that Azathoth had fertilized these ingots?" asked Sylvia Conrad. "Why did you come looking for me now—and not destroy these three years ago?"

"I had no idea what happened until I ran into a hermit living in the Colorado wilderness with nothing to keep him company but a pile of moldering books and some parchments, written on human skin, which he had discovered in an ancient tomb. At first I thought that he was mad—and probably he was—but as we shared a meal he began to ramble about the scion of Azathoth and how Azathoth was summoned forth by certain musical tones in places of ancient evil and would seed the purest of silver with his essence. It was then I realized just what we'd witnessed in the Amazon. He was obsessed with the idea and kept prying. It was almost as if he knew what we had seen."

"So did you tell him?" asked Sylvia Conrad.

Crow shook his head. "I didn't want to encourage him so I kept quiet."

"Is this hermit still in Colorado?" asked Mr. Conrad. "I hope you didn't mention my wife to him."

"He's still in Colorado, Mr. Conrad," replied Crow.

"How can you guarantee that?" replied Mr. Conrad. "He might have followed you to Massachusetts."

The firelight of the incinerator played across Crow's expressionless features. "When he thought I was sleeping he tried to run me through with a hot poker."

"And?"

Crow didn't answer.

Sylvia Conrad took her husband by the arm and explained. "That hermit will not be leaving Colorado anytime short of the resurrection."

The Succubus in Shotgun Ferguson

The hot Kansas wind pushed at the solitary figure that approached across the flatlands. He rode through yellow grasses which climbed high enough so that only the shoulders and head of his speckled roan pushed above the stalks. The figure wore a long duster, and a hat was pulled low over his eyes to protect them from the harshness of the sun.

To the view of the railroad enforcers, who guarded the perimeters of the Leavenworth, Pawnee and Western Railroad work camp, the new arrival appeared to be typical of any number of itinerant cowboys or gunfighters who sold their services and their guns to any who had the coin to pay. Some of the enforcers had, themselves, joined with the Leavenworth, Pawnee and Western Railroad by arriving in just such a manner as the incoming horseman.

As the rider came nearer, Bilger Doxon rose up from his spot among the grasses, his .32 Volcanic rifle trained on the newcomer, and a rebel cavalry sword strapped to his belt. "State your name and your business!"

The brim of the rider's hat kept his face obscured in shadow as he answered, his voice deep and resonant. "The name's Crow, and I'm here to pay a visit to Shotgun Ferguson."

Stanley Smith rose up on the right, about seventy yards off from the rider. He kept a single shot .52 caliber Sharps pointed at the rider, but his eyes were watering because of some grit that had blown into them. "Crow? That sounds like some kind of injun name. Are you an injun, Crow? Because we shot three of your Kickapoo braves that tried stealing our horses last night—didn't think you'd try it again in broad daylight."

A cottonwood grew up along the edge of the encampment, and three bodies hung upside down, strung up by the feet. Crow had seen the bodies two miles back, but now he could make out the face paint the dead braves wore and porcupine roaches that still clung to their skulls in death. Black crows had gathered and were pecking at the flesh. "I'm not Kickapoo, and for the safety of your encampment you should cut those men down immediately."

"They ain't men," proclaimed Bilger Doxon, his voice hard. "They're Indians."

"Yes, they're Indians and that's precisely the reason you should cut them down," replied Crow.

"You don't like it?" probed Doxon. "Well that's too darn bad. It scares the Indians from trying to steal anything else from us."

Crow's features were taciturn and he nodded. "How many guns do you have in camp?"

"That's none of your business."

"Ten," probed the Indian. "Twenty? Maybe you have fifty guns in camp?"

Doxon averted his eyes for just a moment and by the man's reaction Crow could tell that the amount fell short of even the ten that he had first mentioned. "The Kickapoo tribe that's moving through the territory is five hundred strong. That means they can probably muster a hundred warriors--maybe more. Even if all those warriors are armed just with bows and arrows, how long do you think you can hold out against them?"

This gave Doxon some pause, but his eyes hardened and he scowled. "We'll school them Indians good if they dare show their red faces around here. Now get lost before I hang you up alongside of them!"

Stanley Smith nodded his assent. "Skedaddle, redskin! We see your face around here again and we're going to blow it off."

From a group of low-lying hills about a mile off, the wind carried the cries and war whoops of the Kickapoo Indians, and Crow stifled a smile when Doxon and Smith swung away from him, gaping into the distance as if they might see the Indians that made the cries. The war whoops were too far off to indicate an immediate attack—unless they were merely a diversion for a band of warriors sneaking up from the opposite direction.

"It looks as though it's too late to cut those dead braves down," commented Crow, but Smith and Doxon scarcely heard him, so he kicked his horse and trotted into camp while the two men scryed the fields and hills for any sign of their enemies.

It wasn't hard to locate Shotgun Ferguson's tent, because Crow recognized the man's voice as Ferguson bellowed out imprecations, and a pair of Chinese laborers came scurrying out of a tent as fast their legs would carry them. They were urged to greater speed by a shotgun blast which perforated the tent flap and scathed the earth behind them. The fleeing men were so concerned about their flight that they nearly ran into Crow's horse. One ducked beneath the neck of the beast and the other scrambled beneath its belly, and then they disappeared into the maze of tents that formed the encampment of largely Chinese laborers.

Crow dismounted and tethered his horse to a pole, then continued to the tent. Seeing as Ferguson was armed and not shy about using his weapon, Crow did not go inside the tent. Instead he paused off to the side and called through the flap.

"Ferguson, is that you inside?"

"Go away!" returned the voice from within. "I ain't dead yet and until I am, you graverobbers better not lay a finger on me or any of my possessions!"

"I'm not here to rob you," said Crow. "You sent me a letter, asking for my help."

There was a long pause. "Who are you?"

"Lone Crow. I've come a long ways to see you."

"Lone Crow? Well, why didn't you say so? Come on in. You don't need no invitation. What are you waiting for?"

The Indian ducked his head and went into the tent. There he saw a tall black man laying upon a cot—and though Shotgun was large, he was not nearly so large as the last time Crow had seen him on the Barbary Coast. His massive musculature had began to wither away and his face was sunken and hollow.

"Are you ill?" asked Crow. "I can lay my hands upon you and give you a blessing of healing."

"It's not a blessing of healing that I need," said Ferguson. "It's an exorcism. I'm possessed by an evil spirit. Do you have the power to throw out demons?"

Crow raised his eyebrow slightly. "You have a demon in you?"

With the greatest of efforts, Ferguson raised himself up on one elbow. "Not at this moment, but she comes to me every night. She's stealing the life from me. Look at me! I'm wasting away—half the man I used to be."

This was certainly true, for Crow had seen Ferguson hale and full of vigor. It was true that he was a shadow of his former self. "Did you do something to anger this entity?"

Ferguson grasped the Indian's sleeve. "It's not what I did, Crow. It's what we did!"

"What do you mean, 'it's what we did?'" Crow glanced back as he heard the peppered flap of the tent rustle, and a Chinese woman wearing a wide-sleeved blouse and her long black hair pinned atop her skull entered the tent carrying a bucket of water. She regarded Crow with suspicion, but nevertheless sidled up to Ferguson and proffered him a ladle of water, which he managed to drink with some difficulty.

"Thanks, darling. I was parched." Ferguson feebly wiped his mouth with the back of his hand. "This is Mei Ling," he introduced.

Crow nodded in the Chinese woman's direction. "It's a pleasure to meet you, Miss Ling."

"Actually, it's Mei Ling Ferguson," corrected Shotgun. "We married four months ago. Before that woman started appearing in my dreams."

When Crow had first run into Ferguson it had been in the tent of the Chileno witch Buena Holguin, and Crow had been there to collect a bounty on Ferguson's head. "You're seeing the ghost of Buena Holguin in your dreams?"

"No, not that woman," croaked Ferguson. "The other one that was hunting me with her posse of Chinese immortals."

Crow's dark brown eyes narrowed. "The one that got away?"

This got Ferguson to chuckling—a taxing thing for one in his weakened condition. "You make it sound as if we were the ones doing the hunting—and not the other way around."

"True enough," admitted Crow. "We were lucky to kill four out of the five that came after us."

Ferguson made a valiant effort to push himself upright, but only partially succeeded. "Luck can only hold out for so long, and I'm afraid that mine may have run out… unless you can do something, Crow. Even if you can't, I do appreciate you coming to see me off."

Crow stripped off his buckskin duster, revealing the eagle-butted Colt .45 that rode his hip. "We don't have much time. The Kickapoo are getting restless and they'll be raiding the camp after dark."

Mei Ling's face turned stark white. "Surely the camp's enforcers can keep them at bay." The tone of her voice indicated that she was not sure of this at all.

"Not unless they've got a lot more guns in camp," said Crow. "The railroad is woefully unprepared for an Indian attack."

Crow broke out a vial of consecrated oils from his pouch. "Shotgun, do you believe in the saving power of Christ?"

Ferguson nodded. "Why, I believe that I do."

Crow dabbed some of the oils onto the crown of Ferguson's head. "This is only going to work if you have the utmost faith."

"I believe in you," said Ferguon.

"It's not me you need to believe in," said Crow. He laid his hands upon Ferguson's head and stated the authority by which he spoke, and as the words fell from his lips the shadows were driven out from the corners of the tent.

Ferguson lurched violently and gave out a bellow, and then blue smoke vomited out of his mouth. Mei Ling shrieked and lurched against the far wall of the tent, the bulging canvas threatening to unstake from the ground, and the center pole leaning. The blue smoke shifted and churned until its dense coils coalesced. The form begin to solidify in the likeness of a woman of Oriental physiognomy, with long raven tresses that swirled and writhed on a howling wind that accompanied the manifestation. This spectral wind buffeted the occupants of the tent, billowing out the canvas, the tent flap rattling like an angry snake.

"Qi Zhuo," said Crow, for he recognized the demon as one of the five immortal riders that he and Shotgun had encountered years ago on Telegraph Hill on the Barbary Coast.

"Qi Zhuo," repeated the woman with some satisfaction. "I'm pleased to see that you have not forgotten me. After all, I did swear my vengeance upon you both, Crow Shifu and Ferguson Shifu."

With the succubus out of him, Ferguson regained a small measure of his strength, and he staggered from his bed. "Shifu?"

Qi Zhuo gestured in the black man's direction. "It means instructor, for surely the both of you have taught me the foolishness of underestimating the capabilities of mortal men. Though I still burn with the desire to avenge my lost lovers, you have earned my respect."

"Respect?" roared Ferguson. "Is that why you creep into my dreams and slowly steal away my life!"

"I had to use much of my ku, my magics, to whisk myself away after our last encounter." Qi Zhuo held up a delicate hand. "When we last parted this hand was mangled flesh and bone. I needed to strengthen myself. I needed to heal. What better way than to steal the very life forces of one of those who slew the men I loved?"

"We wouldn't have killed them if they hadn't have attacked us," said Ferguson, his hand finding the shotgun that was hidden among his bed clothes.

"Leave us!" demanded Crow. "Never return haunt our sight or dreams!"

Qi Zhuo smiled a slow, scary smile and stretched her graceful limbs. "Your priesthoods may give you power over my spirit form, Crow, but thanks to Shotgun Ferguson I've gained the strength to again take physical form. Maybe you've forgotten what I can do when I've taken my corporeal form?"

At that moment Bilger Doxon and Stanley Smith entered the billowing and vibrating tent. Both carried their rifles and seemed intent on using them.

"What in tarnation is going on in here?" Bilger Doxon made the mistake of ignoring Qi Zhuo and aiming his .32 Volcanic rifle in Crow's direction. "I thought we told you to leave, injun!"

"I had business to take care of." Crow turned sideways to present a smaller target.

"Then it's going to cost you your hide!" Bilger Doxon pulled the trigger of his rifle, but Qi Zhuo was already moving with supernal speed and grace. She had Doxon's cavalry saber in her hand before he pulled the trigger, and his head was rolling from his shoulders even as a bullet sped from his rifle.

The bullet scored Crow's shirt as his hand dipped for his Eagle-butted Peacemaker. For the briefest of moments an expression of fear crossed Qi Zhuo's features, for she had seen this very gun slay some of her former companions. As Crow began to fire, she darted suddenly behind Stanley Smith, who seemed confused by the sudden turn of events. Initially, he had been intent on shooting Crow through the chest, but now he twisted his Sharps rifle in the direction of Qi Zhuo, who proved to be much faster than he thought possible.

As he twisted, he brought himself into Crow's line of fire and three bullets stitched across his chest. He pitched backward, firing his rifle into the ground. Before he struck the earth, Qi Zhuo was outside, the tent flap still whipping at her passing.

Ferguson reeled out of the tent, on unsteady feet, and saw Qi Zhuo leap like a gazelle to the top of the nearest tent, and then with a footfall that scarcely disturbed the canvas, she sprang again. Ferguson threw his shotgun to his shoulder and let loose with a hail of buckshot. However, his strength was not fully returned, and his knee buckled under him as he fired, and the blast of pellets went awry, chewing through the roof of the tent. Then Qi Zhuo was out of sight, on the ground, and flitting between the treacherous alleys between tents, avoiding peg and rope with impossible ease.

Crow had paused just long enough to pry the Sharps rifle out of Stanley Smith's still-twitching grip, for he worried that, despite having three bullet holes, there was still life in the camp enforcer. Crow emerged with the Sharps over one shoulder and the Peacemaker still in his right hand.

"Did you get her?" asked Crow.

"No, I didn't get her," fumed Ferguson. "My blinkin' knee gave out and I missed. Where were you?"

"Getting this rifle. Didn't want Smith shooting us in the backs."

Ferguson glanced down near his bare feet and noticed a severed head lying a step away. "At least we don't have to worry about Doxon shooting us in the back. I never did like that son of a…"

Mei Ling stood in the mouth of the tent. "Watch your language, Reginald."

"Yes, ma'am," replied Ferguson, with a meekness that Crow found uncharacteristic for the man he had known three years ago.

Crow raised an eyebrow. "Reginald?"

Ferguson scowled at him. "What? You think my parents named me Shotgun?"

Crow shrugged slightly. "That's what everyone calls you."

"So, we just going to sit here and let Qi Zhuo get away clean?"

"I don't think we're fast enough to stop her," said Crow. "We'd be lucky to keep up with her on horseback, and I don't think you're in any condition to chase her. Besides, I think we've got other troubles."

"Other troubles?" questioned Ferguson. "What do you…"

Ferguson ceased speaking when a volley of gunshots, accompanied by a crescendo of Kickapoo war cries, interrupted him. A Chinese man working on the rail line pitched over dead with a hammer still in his hand, and dozens of braves came rushing from the high grasses. Some were armed with rifles, and they halted to shoot at the fleeing figures of the railroad workers, even as their tribal members charged past, bearing clubs, axes and spears.

The Kickapoo fell upon any who were too slow and savagely beat them to death or sundered their skulls with the edge of a tomahawk. One trio of Kickapoo cornered a woman who cast aside her yoke and water buckets in an attempt to escape. They tore off her broad-brimmed straw hat and threw her to the ground and were about to proceed with further depredations when Crow pulled the Sharps rifle to his shoulder and put a bullet through the skull of their leader. When the other two braves saw their leader pitch forward, dead, they scrambled away from the woman, leaving her alone with her buckets.

Ferguson pulled a pair of shells out of his pocket and reloaded his double-barreled shotgun. "Where's the camp enforcers?"

Crow tossed aside the Sharps, which was a single shot rifle, and reached for the Spencer carbine on his horse. "Two of them are dead in your tent." The Spencer repeating carbine held seven shots, and from the number of braves rushing out from the grasses and into the camp, it was apparent that he was going to need every one of them ten times over.

A howling brave came rushing between tents and tripped over a peg line, landing near Crow's feet. Crow loosed the tomahawk from his belt and buried it in the back of the brave's skull before he could stand up and renew his attack. Putting his booted foot on the back of the warrior's neck, he wrenched the tomahawk loose, shook off the blood, and shoved it back into his belt.

None too soon, a couple of the camp enforcers' rifles began to cough a return fusillade. A pair of the Kickapoo warriors went flailing to the earth, but the response was feeble against such an overwhelming force. It would only be a matter of time before all resistance was swept away, and the Kickapoo slaughtered or took slaves of every man, woman, and child. With a little luck and a lot of sharp shooting, Crow thought that he and Ferguson might be able to engineer an escape with Mrs. Ferguson, but Crow hated to leave all these other innocents to die.

Though the woman with the water buckets remained unmolested for a few moments, a fresh group of braves broke through the surrounding grasses and spotted her struggling to gain her feet. She rose up, but was frozen in indecision, unable to calculate which direction was the best to run, for they all looked equally bad. The blood lust of the Kickapoo braves was upon them and they charged the woman, swinging tomahawk and club.

Crow turned his carbine in the direction of the braves, but he knew he would only be able to take down one or two of them before they reached the unfortunate woman. Before Crow could fire, Qi Zhuo darted from between tents, her dark hair streaming behind her as she moved with the speed of a fleeing gazelle. Her cavalry sword licked out again and again as she threw herself into the midst of those churning bodies, dodging club and tomahawk and leaving behind a carnage of severed limbs and disemboweled bodies.

Leaving the stunned water woman unharmed, Qi Zhuo chuckled, her laugh like the tinkling of wind chimes. She bounded back into the heart of the camp, slaying Kickapoo braves to her right and to her left.

Ferguson was bewildered. "Why is she helping us?"

Crow didn't find the time to respond. Instead he fired a pair of rounds into a brave wearing a porcupine roach who appeared between tents to his right, with tomahawk drawn back to hurl at Crow.

Ferguson spotted a painted mare running loose through the camp, spooked by the sound of gunshots and the scent of blood. He leaped forward and caught its reins, jerking it to a halt. It reared up, nearly dragging Ferguson from his feet. Using every bit of strength he could muster, he wrestled the horse into submission, the bit between the horse's teeth doing most of the work. "Come on, Mei Ling! We're riding out of here."

He put his bare right foot in the stirrup and swung his left leg over the back of the horse, then pulled his wife on behind him. With his shotgun laying on the horn of the saddle, he kicked the painted mare with his heels. "Giddy'ap, horse!"

Crow was on his horse already. From his higher vantage point, he took the time to fire his carbine at a Kickapoo brave who was about to use his club to cave in the skull of a Chinese railroad builder. Two shots took down the brave, but this aroused the attention of several of the Indian braves who did have firearms. Having a higher vantage point worked both ways, and now he was a visible target.

Shotgun Ferguson sent his horse galloping toward the edge of camp, Mei Ling clinging to him with both arms as she bounced behind. "Are you coming, Crow?"

Again, Crow hesitated, but this time it was because he saw that the water woman, confused and dazed by the events around her, was heading back into camp, where the fighting was the thickest. Once they got their hands on her, the Kickapoo would ravage, beat and murder her. Crow couldn't save everyone—that he had learned by harsh experience—but just maybe he could save this woman, so instead of following hard on the heels of Shotgun Ferguson's painted mare, he sent his roan lurching toward the woman, pausing alongside of her and offering his hand. "Jump on! You're not safe in the camp."

Crow could see the confusion in her face when she saw his dark Indian features beneath the brim of his western hat. Then she recognized him as the man who had saved her from the Kickapoo a few minutes earlier, and she took his hand. She was a petite thing and Crow nearly yanked her up and over the horse, but she caught onto his shirt and he kicked the horse into a gallop, leaning forward, and staying low in the hopes of avoiding the bullets that were beginning to whine overhead.

The Fergusons reached the grasses and plowed into them, cutting a furrow as broad as the painted mare they rode. Crow and his passenger were only moments behind, and once into the high grasses the Indian and the China girl continued to lay low upon the horse. Crow steered the roan to the right, so that it veered out of sight of the camp. Bullets whined through the yellowing stalks, chewing some of them in half as they sought out Crow and his companions, but then the Kickapoo braves were distracted by closer targets.

The grasses stretched over a series of low rolling hills, and once they reached the top of the nearest, Crow paused and wheeled his roan around so he could see the railroad encampment. Bodies lay strewn on the ground and many tents were sliced to ribbons. He could see a number of the camp's inhabitants fleeing south and even the bloodthirstiest of the Kickapoo braves had given up the chase for fear that their companions might get the lion's share of the spoils while they were gone pursuing those who had escaped. The looting had begun in earnest, and the braves were rounding up horses, smashing open chests to see what they might find, and guzzling bottles of whiskey and rum which they had discovered.

Crow's keen vision spotted a trail of severed limbs and disemboweled bodies, and his eyes followed the bodies to the south edge of the camp, where he thought he saw a lithe shape with flowing black hair leap into the grasses. Qi Zhuo moved so quickly that it was easy to attribute her presence to a rush of wind and a figment of the imagination, but Crow knew better, for often the shape moving at the corner of one's vision, or a passing shadow that flows away when one turns to regard it, was a manifestation of some presence, malign or beneficent, that man did not know or comprehend.

The China girl on the horse behind Crow began sobbing as they looked upon the camp, but he didn't have time to offer condolences or comfort, so they took to the trails, riding long and hard until their horses could scarcely put one hoof in front of the other, and the inky darkness of night made it too difficult to see the trail ahead.

They didn't suspect that the Kickapoo warriors would be chasing after them, so they chanced a small fire to keep them warm. When a coyote came sniffing around, Crow killed him with his carbine, and they made a meal out of the stringy and none-too-tasty meat.

The China girl sat glaze-eyed on a log until Mei Ling struck up a conversation with her in the Mandarin tongue, which neither Ferguson or

Crow could understand. Whatever the topic, the conversation did much to bring the girl out of her sorrow, and her fear at what the future might hold for her.

Crow and Ferguson ate in silence, until finally Ferguson could bear it no longer. "I still don't understand why Qi Zhuo came back to help us!"

"I can think of a couple possible reasons," said Crow, "but I can't read her mind."

"Why not?" said Ferguson, "you seem to know what I'm thinking half the time."

"That comes from spending a month on the road with you."

Ferguson shuddered. "I don't even want to be reminded of what we found in that sycamore grove in Ohio… or what was beneath."

Mei Ling broke off her conversation with the girl and spoke to Crow. "JinJing wants to thank you for saving her life, but she is afraid she might offend you by addressing you directly."

"Tell her that she is welcome." Crow paused as a thought struck him. "Does JinJing speak English?"

"She knows enough to get by," said Mei Ling.

Crow turned his attention to the sloe-eyed China girl. "You may speak to me whenever you wish, JinJing."

JinJing's eyes sparkled when she received this open permission to talk. It was apparent that she had many questions. "Mr. Crow, who was the woman who also saved my life? She moved like wind and struck so quick with the sword, my eyes couldn't see it."

Crow licked his fingers clean. "We don't know too much about her, JinJing. But she claims to be an immortal, and by the way she fights I'm inclined to believe her."

"She was so kind to protect me," said JinJing.

Ferguson tilted his head. "I don't know how you rate such treatment, but she's never been kind to me. First time I seen her she was ready to take me in dead or alive for a bounty on my head. Then, when things didn't work out according to her plan, she decided to take up housekeeping inside my body. I don't know how much energy she sapped out of me or how many years of my life she stole, but if Crow hadn't answered my letter she would have eventually killed me. I'm sure of it."

JinJing listened politely to Ferguson's complaints against Qi Zhuo but, by her expression, Crow didn't think that JinJing was entirely convinced of the immortal's evil and capricious nature. After all, JinJing, with her own eyes, had seen Qi Zhuo save her from those Kickapoo braves. The rest was all words.

Apparently, Mei Ling could also read what JinJing was thinking. "My husband is not lying. I was there when Crow forced Qi Zhuo from Reginald's body."

"It wasn't me," protested Crow. "It was the higher priesthood which I…"

Ferguson's mind was still back on the puzzle of the immortal. "Me, I figure that Qi Zhuo went after those braves just because she's bloodthirsty. She came back because she saw the chance to do some killing and the braves were more of a challenge than JinJing."

Crow took first watch. Clouds scudded across the face of the moon, casting shifting shadows across the land. He contemplated JinJing's beauty as she slept, and as the shadows moved across her features. Once he glanced upon her and the shadows had changed her features so that she resembled Qi Zhuo, and then the shadows fled and the resemblance was gone. Somewhere a coyote howled and Crow returned his attention to the surrounding woods. When the moon began to descend from its zenith he woke up Ferguson. "Your turn."

"Already?" groaned Ferguson. "I can't have been asleep more than ten minutes."

"It's been four hours," said Crow. "Do you need to sleep for longer?"

Ferguson pushed himself off the cold ground. "Nah, I can handle it."

Crow retired next to a log, pulling pine needles and leaves around and over him as a blanket. He had lent his bedroll to Mei Ling and JinJing. When finally he closed his eyes it didn't take more than a few moments for sleep to claim him. He awoke to the sensation of cold steel against his neck. He opened his eyes and found Qi Zhuo standing over him, her long black hair descending like a sheet. The cavalry saber that she had stolen earlier that day was at his throat.

She hissed, "Don't cry out unless you want me to kill the others. Now, sit up."

Crow struggled upright. He glanced to Ferguson, who was supposed to be on watch, and found his friend leaning against the bole of a tree, his head slumped to one side. He was in a fitful sleep which caused him to jerk and mutter.

"Don't blame him," said Qi Zhuo. "It was a simple enough thing for me to make him sleep. Even now, he dreams of me." She laughed, her voice like the tinkling of a chime. "For as long as I let him live, I'll haunt his every sleeping hour."

Crow wondered if he could get at his pistol fast enough to kill Qi Zhuo before she slit his throat. He didn't think so. "Why haven't you already killed us all? I've seen you move. You could have killed all of us before we woke."

"I'm here to even our debt," said Qi Zhuo.

"Do I owe you something?" asked Crow.

"Rather, it's what I owe you," replied the immortal

Crow shifted slightly against the log where his back rested. "I thought it was vengeance you were seeking."

Qi Zhuo bit at her lower lip. "So I was, but when I saw you risk your own self-preservation to help a little Chinese girl, I couldn't help but be moved. Once, I was mortal like you and I lived and loved, until it was all brutally snatched away. My husband was put to the sword by masterless soldiers, and my children were stolen away to be made slaves. Only I escaped out into the winter snow, crying out for the gods and begging that I might have vengeance. I would have died from the cold that night, but for the man with the iron crutch that appeared before me…

"He was the immortal Tieguai Li and he had heard my pleadings, and he offered me a bargain so that I might obtain my vengeance."

"A bargain," mused Crow. "What did you have that an immortal might want?"

Qi Zhuo regarded Crow and spread her arms as if on display. "Am I not beautiful to look upon, red man?"

"You are," admitted Crow.

"Even immortals have human needs, and at the time it seemed a small price to pay if I might assuage the ravenous hunger for revenge that I felt."

The fire burned low. A piece of cedar popped, casting a few glowing embers in the dirt beside Crow. "Was it a small price?"

Qi Zhuo shook her head. "It was a heavy price. I was still in grieving for my husband, and the demands of immortals are nigh on insatiable. But, when finally morning came he gave me a tablet from his gourd and told me that if I consumed it I would have a thousand years to exact my vengeance, if no bullet or blade ended my existence."

Still the sword blade hovered at Crow's throat, ready to slice his jugular and, even though he was reputed to be among the fastest guns west of the Mississippi, Crow did not dare make a move for his pistol, for he had seen Qi Zhuo, and she was faster yet. Crow had even seen her deflect bullets with her sword blade. "And did you take your vengeance?"

"I tracked down each and every one of those masterless soldiers who killed my husband and flayed them alive—made them suffer for what they did. They died screaming for mercy."

"And your children?"

Cinders floated into the air, crossing in front of Qi Zhuo's face, but she took no heed. "I killed the slavers to whom they had been sold, but by then my heart had grown cold and bitter, and I was no longer suitable to be a mother. Tieguai Li had given me immortality and the opportunity for vengeance, but in return he had stolen away every bit of love and compassion that ever swelled within my bosom. So, I took my children and left them at the orphanage, with a promise that I would return when they needed me most."

"And did you ever see them again?" asked Crow. He let his hand slide closer to the butt of his pistol as he shifted his weight.

Qi Zhuo laughed. "I see what you are doing, Crow. You humor my tales in the hopes that you might reach your gun. Let me reassure you that no mortal hand is fast enough to beat the tip of my sword blade."

Crow didn't respond to this jibe. "You say that Tieguai Li stole away every bit of your compassion, but I think you lie."

Qi Zhuo's beautiful face turned in a fierce scowl that revealed the ugliness beneath. "Do you dare call me a liar?"

"Did you not save JinJing from being ravished by the Kickapoo braves? You showed compassion upon her!"

Qi Zhuo's almond eyes narrowed into slits. "That wasn't compassion. It was duty. I can sense her blood running through my veins. She is my flesh and blood—perhaps a great granddaughter."

Crow turned, carefully to avoid the blade, and compared JinJing's features to Qi Zhuo's. "I thought that I had imagined the resemblance, but seeing the two of you side by side I can see it more clearly."

JinJing began to stir in her sleep, her sixth sense arousing her to the fact that eyes were upon her.

It seemed that Qi Zhuo did not want to take the risk of a reunion with her great granddaughter and so she pulled her blade away from Crow's throat. "I let you live, so that my debt to you is washed away. If I should encounter you again, I will not hesitate to slay you."

"Naturally," said Crow.

"Let me make it clear, I will seek you out and kill you! I will never forget that you and Shotgun Ferguson killed my lovers. You will pay for that. It's just a matter of time."

It was then that JinJing's eyes came open and she gasped when she saw Qi Zhuo standing near the fire, her sword blade out and still pointed in Crow's direction. At the sound, Qi Zhuo swung around with supernal swiftness, the edge of her blade whooshing through the air. Though JinJing had been grateful to be rescued by Qi Zhuo the day before, when she saw the immortal warrior standing there in the clearing with drawn blade, she thought that it was all a mistake, and that Qi Zhuo had returned to slay them all.

JinJing scrambled forward on hand and knee to grab the still-slumbering Ferguson's shotgun that rested against his leg and in the crook of his arm. She snatched this up and threw the stock of the shotgun to her shoulder.

Qi Zhuo was fast enough to have intercepted her great granddaughter and strike her down before JinJing even touched the shotgun, but she hesitated to touch her own flesh and blood and when she finally decided to flee, Crow had taken advantage of that moment of indecision and he reached for his pistol. The rasp of leather when the gun left its holster, brought Qi Zhuo spinning around, sword blade whirling in Crow's direction.

Crow fired twice, and Qi Zhuo deflected the first shot with the flat of her purloined cavalry blade. The second shot took Qi Zhuo in the shoulder and she cried out in pain—or was it anger? She drew back her blade to behead Crow, and that was when JinJing fired Ferguson's double-barreled shotgun. She unleashed both barrels at once, and though she'd never fired a shotgun or a firearm of any kind before, at such short range she managed to blow open Qi Zhuo's belly.

Qi Zhuo spun a crimson trail and then leaped, shrieking into the forest, crashing through the brush like a wounded boar, her grace and stealth gone. Mei Ling leaped to her feet and only now, the spell broken, did Shotgun Ferguson rouse from his mesmerized and fitful slumber. He gave a great snort and lurched upright, grasping for his missing shotgun.

"Where is she? Where is the witch?"

Crow gestured toward the darkling forest. "Fled into the woods with a belly full of lead."

Shotgun turned and saw JinJing holding his shotgun, black powder smoke curling out of the end of the double barrels. "She got the witch?"

JinJing's face was twisted in anguish. "After… after she saved me from those braves, I thought maybe she was a friend—but when I awoke and saw her with the sword at Crow's throat, I…"

Mei Ling put her arm around JinJing. "There… there, you did the right thing. Qi Zhuo was nothing but evil."

"Not all evil," said Crow.

Ferguson grabbed his shotgun from JinJing, cracked it open and emptied the two spent shells. He fitted two more into place and slapped the shotgun closed. "Let's go after her. I'm not letting that two-bit who…" He paused when he saw Mei Ling glaring at him. "I'm not letting that witch into my dreams again."

Crow reloaded two cartridges. "She won't get far. JinJing tore open her guts with that shotgun blast. But she'll be dangerous until she goes down."

"What do you mean she wasn't all evil?" said Mei Ling.

Crow's eyes looked to the broken brush of the forest and then to Jin-Jing. "I mean that sometimes good can come from even the most evil of people."

The Vanishing City

They'd hounded him even into Sydney Town, where the streets were splashed with filth and painted ladies beckoned from every corner. Smoke hung thick in the atmosphere, and though the air was warm the sky was leaden, sullen clouds threatening to dump their swollen bellies on the Barbary Coast.

Lone Crow swept back the edge of his duster and rested his hand on the eagle-butted Colt .45 that rode at his hip—a pistol that had been blessed by a prophet one night in the salty wastes when the dead rose from their shallow graves. He surveyed the motley assortment of rag tag bounty hunters that had been hired to find him.

In front were the Grimm brothers, Finn and Hansel, both with long thin faces and protuberant noses. Their hair hung in greasy, lank tangles and they each had a lip full of chewing tobacco. Finn held a double-barreled shotgun and Hansel a .50 caliber Sharps.

Up in the balcony of the Fancy Lady, Crow spotted Grady O'Keefe with his rifle bead pointed precisely in his direction. O'Keefe had fought in a dozen skirmishes with Indian tribes and had taken twice as many Indian scalps, with which he festooned the saddle of his horse.

Behind Crow was Six-Gun Susannah Johnson on a spotted mare, her straw-colored hair wild and frizzy from long days on the trail, and wearing a pair of well-worn britches. If not the most accurate shot, she was widely known to be the fastest gun in the west—sometimes emptying her gun before her opponent could manage a single shot. With that much lead in the air, she was bound to hit something.

Alongside of Six Gun Susannah Johnson was the Apache Wild Eagle who kept a carbine laid across the horn of his saddle. More than any of the other bounty hunters present, it was Wild Eagle that made Lone Crow's blood run cold, for it was the Apaches who had wiped out his tribe, killing every man woman and child. Only Crow had escaped.

"Now hold up there," ordered Finn. "We'd like to have a word with you."

"Is there a bounty on my head?" asked Crow.

Finn snorted. "Why yes there is. Isn't that ironic? Wasn't so long ago when it was you doing the hunting and turned me into the Loosy-ana authorities. Now I'm the one hunting you."

"As I recall you were wanted for murdering a woman."

"A whore," spat Finn. "A lousy whore and they wanted to string me up for it."

Crow's dark visage was impassive. "It doesn't appear they succeeded."

His brother Hansel spat out some tobacco juice and shrugged. "The witnesses ended up leaving town. It seems they took afright and decided that New Orleans just wasn't a safe place to be."

"They had no choice but to set me free," grinned Finn as, one-handed, he shook out a tattered page that bore a likeness of Crow and announced a thousand dollar bounty—dead or alive. "But you, on the other hand, are wanted for the murder of one Doctor Sylvia Conrad. A sad story—first she loses her husband to the plague and then she's kidnapped by a savage."

"She's not dead," said Crow.

Finn Grimm shrugged. "I don't care if she's living the high life as the Princess of Egypt or working as a fancy lady in that brothel over there. This poster says there's a thousand dollars reward and we aim to collect it. Now throw down your gun!"

To Crow it seemed he didn't have much chance of making a stand when Grady O'Keefe had a rifle bead on his head and there were four other guns pointed in his direction. Still, there might be another way out of his predicament. "By the time you divide the bounty you're only looking at two hundred dollars apiece. What if I agree to pay each of you a thousand dollars. Will you promise to go away and never bother me again?"

Wild Eagle chortled at this. "Now where's a red man going to get that kind of money in a paleface's world? Are you going to pay us in buffalo chips?"

"I'll pay you in diamonds," said Crow.

Hansel scowled. "There ain't no diamond mines in California."

In response, Crow reached into his left hand pocket and drew out a tightly-closed, fist-sized bag made from the skin of some unidentifiable reptile. He tossed it at Finn's battered boots and the Grimm brother carefully stooped and picked it up. Seeing that the rest of his posse all had their guns pointed at Crow, he leaned his shotgun against the hitching post and pried open the mouth of the bag. His jaw dropped and he dumped a pile of scintillating jewels into his palm. Greed flashed in his eyes. "Where did you get these?"

Crow raised his brow. "Do we have an agreement?"

Finn raised his palm and the glittering contents. "For these diamonds and the location of where you found them, we'll let you on your way unharmed and swear to never bother you again."

"You won't believe me," said Crow.

An avaricious grin spread across Hansel Grimm's long face. "Try us."

*****

Past the ramshackle huts of Poverty Flats and into the thick of the forests that grow dense around the base of the crystal climes of Mount Shasta, Crow left the leafy bows of his lean-to and stared out at the mountain slopes that gleamed in the rays of the gibbous moon. From the cratered top of the mountain a vapor of smoke belched from the restless innards of the dormant volcano, hazing the moon an orange-red.

Crow heard footsteps creeping up from behind. He recognized the weight and rhythm of the footfalls and only turned when he heard a feminine voice at his shoulder.

"You can't sleep, either?" Doctor Sylvia Conrad wore a khaki shirt and pants just as she had years ago when Crow had accompanied her into the heart of the Brazilian rainforest.

Crow thoughtfully observed the woman who sat down on the fallen log beside him. "No, I can't."

"It's got to be the excitement of discovery."

"Maybe that's it," said Crow, but he was pretty sure it was the close proximity to Sylvia Conrad that was making it difficult to sleep.

"Don't you think we're close?"

"I wasn't with you in Siskiyou County when you interviewed Fred Oliver," Crow reminded the doctor. "I'm only going off what you told me. Presuming Oliver told the truth, the ruins he stumbled across could be near here."

Sylvia Conrad grinned, and she looked most fetching in the moonlight. "Imagine being the first to discover a lost outpost of Lemuria.'"

"If Fred Oliver already found it, wouldn't we be the second?" asked Crow.

The doctor gave her Indian companion the side-eye. "Yes, but I'd be the first to write a scholarly paper on the subject."

"Didn't you say Mr. Oliver was planning to write something?"

She gazed out at the hazy moon. "Yes, but only after I gave him the idea. I wish I would have kept my mouth shut. His paper surely won't be as measured as mine."[2]

---

2 In 1894, Frederick Spencer Oliver finally published a book about his findings which he entitled A Dweller on Two Planets and which detailed his discoveries on Mount Shasta.

"Oliver's will be more fanciful, I'm sure," replied Crow, though he had seen many a thing that would cause people to accuse him of being fanciful or even outright insane.

"I hope to have more time to study the ruins than when we discovered the Lost City of da Silva Guimarães."

"So do I," agreed Crow, who didn't like to recall the things they had encountered in the Mato Grosso region of the Amazon Jungles.

Doctor Conrad's full lips parted as she gave a gasp, and she pointed into the forest near the base of Mount Shasta. "Crow, did you see that?"

Crow had been too busy examining the doctor's profile, but he turned his attention to the forest and saw nothing but the dark mass of trees that extended up the slope. "No, what did you see?"

A furrow creased Dr. Conrad's brow. "I saw a flash of light and for an instant I saw a great city, unlike anything I've ever seen, sitting on the slopes."

"A city?" Rather than scoff, for Crow knew Dr. Conrad to be a woman of her word, Crow looked again and in a moment he too saw a flicker of blue light in the darkness, and for an instant his eyes caught a wondrous vision of a tremendous city that contained gleaming golden turrets encrusted with diamonds, and monoliths hammered from alloys unknown to man and fashioned in some alien architecture. At first he thought it was a glimpse or a vision rewarded to them so that they might see the glories of the past, which had now been reduced to ruin, but as he gazed he thought he saw movement on the streets that were paved with red stone.

Dr. Conrad vanished from sight and then she was back from her tent with a telescope, which she carefully placed on a tripod on the crest of the hill where they camped. By the time she had finished this process, the light blinked away, leaving nothing but forest and darkness. "Where did it go?"

Crow continued to peer into the night. "I think the question is: 'where did it come from?'" He'd seen mirages in the desert wastes and he'd seen horrific mind-blasting things that he wished were mirages. To Crow's mind, this was no mirage.

Sylvia Conrad peered through the telescope, but had a hard time discerning anything among the thrusting forest of dark shapes. "Just maybe we've discovered the outpost of lost Lemuria, but there still seems to be residents. Those weren't the ruins that Frederick Oliver was describing!"

"No," agreed Crow, "but they're gone now. "Perhaps it was a vision of what once was, and we'll go down and find just the ruins of that great city."

"Have you known of people to have visions of the past and future?"

"I know one man," said Crow. "He's called a seer."

Dr. Conrad was about to inquire further, but suddenly the mysterious city once again flickered into existence, a shining beacon among the shadowing spires of the conifers. Great buttresses were built up around the encircling walls, and on those walls they could see large lumbering figures which took ungainly steps. She focused in on one of those figures and gasped. "They are half human and half beast!"

Even Crow's keen eyes could not make out such detail at this distance. "May I take a gander?"

Dr. Conrad reluctantly stepped aside, allowing Crow a moment to view the figure on the wall. The creature was over eight feet in height, with one lambent eye of crimson, and its cyclopean form was bathed in light and shadow, but gleaming so that its jagged limbs appeared to be formed from some living metal capable of movement. The hands of the fiend were like blocks of stone, with each finger thick as cordwood. On one wrist a long spike grew. Then, as this demonic creature moved along the wall, the light shifted and he saw that encased within this metallic body was the figure of a slender woman dressed in a glittering bodice that resembled a shirt of chain mail. Her thin limbs were strapped into each respective arm and leg, so that they moved with each step of the massive metal feet and with each swing of those mammoth arms.

Now, Crow could see pistons and machinery working in those limbs that reminded him of a steam locomotive. The extreme thinness of the woman made her strange to look upon, though her facial features were not unattractive. Her alienness was accentuated by the emerald tone of her exposed skin, and the long dark hair which spilled around her face and shoulders, reflecting purple highlights. From this distance he could not tell whether the woman and the framework around her were permanently melded into some unholy mating of man and machine, or if she was merely piloting the contraption like an engineer might guide a steam engine.

Crow stepped aside so that Dr. Conrad could see what he had. "There's a woman inside the beast!"

Dr. Conrad squinted through the telescope. "Is she actually part of the machine?"

Crow had seen some strange things in his day. "It may be possible."

Dr. Conrad threw her backpack on and when she had finished tightening the straps she slung her .58 caliber buffalo rifle over her right shoulder. "You think that they're friendly?"

"I wouldn't count on it."

Dr. Conrad started down the hillside, heading down the trail that went through the intervening forest and to the slopes of Mount Shasta where the gleaming city had appeared. "I guess there's only one way to find out."

Of course, Crow wasn't going to let Dr. Conrad traipse into the dark of the woods by herself, so he took a bearing on the highest spire of the alien city, which seemed to flicker and jump before his vision and then he pursued the voluptuous shadow of the anthropologist into the all-consuming blackness of night.

As they descended the hill and into the forest, they lost sight of the city, and whether it had disappeared again or still remained on the slopes of Mount Shasta they could not say. For some time they traveled in silence, and Crow let Dr. Conrad lead the way until he noticed that she was straying from the course."

"We're off the track," he said. "Shift your course to the right."

"How can you tell?"

Crow pointed to a towering fir with a branch bent by the wind to a peculiar angle. "When I took a sighting at the top of the hill that tree was directly between us and the city, but now we're drifting to the north."

Dr. Conrad knew better than to argue with Crow's tracking know-how and she immediately adjusted her course to set them back on track toward the mysterious city. Now, she followed Crow's lean figure through the brush. He was sure-footed even in the darkness and every step was carefully placed so as to avoid an excess of noise—surely this was the practice of a seasoned hunter and tracker. Her own passage through the nettles and shrubs of the undergrowth was less subtle and more than once a twig snapped underfoot or she stumbled and fell. Each time, Crow halted and extended a hand to help her to her feet.

"Maybe you should just stand right beside me, so that if I start to stumble I can grab on to you," she murmured.

"The overhead branches block out much of the moonlight," said Crow. "It's difficult to find your footing."

Despite the darkness, Crow seemed to be sure of his heading and finally they emerged into a clearing on the mountain slopes. Crow halted. He could feel an electricity in the air and the same scent of ozone that tainted the atmosphere after a lightning strike. In the light of the moon he could see the stumps of the trees that had once stood in this spot. Instead of being sawed off a couple of feet from the ground, these stumps were level with the earth and were cut so their surface was as smooth as glass—no sign of axe or saw upon the rings.

Though Crow stood at the edge of the clearing, reluctant to venture any further because of the wrongness of what he witnessed within, Dr. Conrad moved into the deforested area, kneeling down and noting how the roughness of the earth had been smoothed, as if it had been tamped down by a giant foot that was hundreds of feet long and nearly as wide. The branches of the trees surrounding the clearing seem to have been lopped off as smoothly as the stumps, however there was no sign of broken or cut branches on the ground. They were gone, just as the city was gone.

"Is this the right place?" she asked. "Where did the city go?"

A humming began to build at the outside edges of Crow's hearing and static electricity made the hair on Crow's arms began to rise. He looked at Dr. Conrad and noticed that her dark hair was forming a wreath about her head which rose and twisted like a nest of vipers on Medusa's scalp.

"Sylvia!" Crow reached out to her and caught her by the forearm. He yanked hard, jerking her off her feet, and pulling her, tumbling, into the curiously-trimmed brush outside of the clearing.

She struggled to her knees, straightening the rifle slung across her shoulder. "Why did you do…"

Dr. Conrad ceased speaking as the hum grew louder and louder, drowning out her words. Electricity snapped and popped, chains of it skipping along the earth and catching brush afire, then there was a great flash of light and in the formerly vacant clearing a great city sprang into existence. Right in front of their eyes, as solid as the sheer sides of Mount Shasta, appeared a great wall of curious workmanship. It was hewn from an unearthly red stone and joined with mortar which was mixed with crushed diamonds. Curious symbols, unreadable to Crow or Dr. Conrad were hewn into the face. Some of these symbols had been obliterated, and all that was left were smoking scorch marks that blackened and pitted the stone.

"I saw what happened to the trees which had been in the spot where the city appeared," said Crow, "and I wondered if we would be sliced away, too, if the city…"

"…should reappear," finished Dr. Conrad. She raised her chin and sent her gaze upward, but she was so close to the wall that she could see nothing of the mechanical guards she had seen before.

Crow caught Dr. Conrad's sleeve and motioned to the north. "There is a gate through the wall in this direction."

She looked and saw an arch about ten feet in height, which opened in the red rock of the wall. It appeared just wide enough for two people to pass abreast. With Crow following closely behind, she moved along the wall and as she came to the gate she fell back with a gasp. Crow was only a stride behind her and he saw the same thing as the doctor of anthropology. The slender woman they had spied atop the wall was standing in the open gate. Her flesh was indeed emerald in hue, where it emerged from her glittering cuirass, and jet black hair with a hint of violet fell in a tangle around her shoulders, but more startling than viewing her at a distance was the morass of machinery in which she was encased. Great pistons churned, mimicking every move of her musculature so that the framework provided her locomotion. Cords of thick cable bunched along the arms and legs, imitating, if not in function, the form of a human's musculature—but in a way that seemed disproportional and obscene to the uninitiated eye.

The great spike mounted on the left arm spun and whirled like the auger of a woodworker, accompanied by a high-pitched buzzing that sounded like a hive of angry wasps. The emerald-skinned woman swept this spike forward, stopping it only a hair's breadth from Doctor Conrad's throat.

Crow's hand slapped leather and just as he was about to pull the trigger of his eagle-butted Colt .45 the emerald woman spoke, but the syllables clamored harshly and alien against their ears and they did not comprehend a thing she uttered. Apparently, she saw the uncomprehending expression upon Dr. Conrad's face, and she pressed a glowing toggle within the great mechanisms that encased her hand and suddenly her voice registered in their minds, and not on their auditory senses as before. "Do you understand the words that I now speak?" intoned the voice. Though it was understandable, the accent was strange to Crow and the tonal qualities more resonant and inculcating, as if the words were seeping into the fiber of his being.

"We do," answered Dr. Conrad, who was quite pleased to be speaking instead of having her neck drilled through. "I am Dr. Sylvia Conrad and this is my companion Lone Crow."

"Was it you who were observing from the ridge before the last jump?" asked the woman from her nest of cables and machinery. The movement of her lips didn't quite match the words that formed in their heads.

"It was," said Dr. Conrad.

The features of the emerald woman took on a disdainful expression. "Surely, you knew that it would be dangerous to approach the city. Why did you allow your male companion to descend with you? Are men so commonplace that without thought you lead them into danger?"

Many women would have blanched in fear of the strange spectre of a creature that was both woman and machine, but to Dr. Conrad it posed a myriad of questions. "There are as many men as there are women here. Is your society any different?"

The emerald woman looked at her with an expression of amazement. "In our land there is only one man for every ten women." She glanced aside to see that Crow was still leveling his pistol at her chest. "Tell your man to put away his gun. I see that you mean no harm. Your primitive weaponry would do me no hurt, anyhow."

"Remove the horn from her throat," demanded Crow, "and I will put away my pistol."

The emerald woman scowled. "I am not in the habit of taking orders from men."

"I swear that Crow will not fire his gun. Please remove the horn," pleaded Dr. Conrad.

The emerald woman seemed appeased by the fact that it was a woman making the request. She pulled back the spinning horn, and it suddenly ceased whirling. Crow lowered his pistol and dropped it into the leather of his holster.

"My name is Ralyia," spoke the emerald woman. "I am a Lemurian by birth."

"Are you flesh or machine?" asked Dr. Conrad, and Crow kept his silence because it was clear to him that he was not welcome in the conversation. He looked past Ralyia and into the byzantine depths of the shining city, where he saw a maze of highways that were occupied by vehicles which moved independently like locomotives, but without rails. Bridges connected brightly-lit towers which were encrusted with sparkling diamonds, and he could see other beings of flesh and mechanics moving through tunnels and across impossibly smooth roadways. A great horn periodically sounded, though there were no buglers in evidence.

"I am flesh," said Ralyia, "but the gravitational pull of my own planet is much lighter than Earth's and in order to move more freely on your planet we wear exoskeletons that amplify our movement."

"So it's true," breathed Dr. Conrad, voicing her suspicions. "You are not of this earth!"

"We come from the fourth planet from your sun," confirmed Ralyia, "where it is much easier to move abroad."

"Why do you come to Earth, and how do you bring this whole city with you?"

"We have mastered the use of the temporal vortex which allows us to bridge both time and space, but the energy requirements are enormous." As Ralyia spoke there was a low hum that began to build until it seemed to vibrate through every fiber of Crow's being. Ralyia's expression grew grave. "The Lemurites are being beset by our enemies and the very face of Mars is being laid waste. Even our strongholds in the depths of the earth are being utterly destroyed. Our only hope of escape was to bring an outpost of Lemuria off-world, but the bombs of the enemy disrupted our access to the vortex and now we are caught in a temporal loop—flashing from time to time, stopping for only a few minutes before being sucked to another place in your history or even your future."

Amazement shone in Dr. Conrad's face. Crow had seen that expression before when the thrill of discovery was upon her. "That would be amazing just to get a glimpse of the past or even the future!"

Ralyia shifted in her saddle. "It's more worrisome than amazing for my people. We can never return to Mars and the strain of jumping between times causes much stress on our bodies, which are not accustomed to the heavy pull of your planet. Our scientists are working desperately to stop the leaps, but our mechanically-aided bodies are not sufficiently nimble nor small enough to perform the necessary work to repair the temporal engines. We need a sufficiently intelligent native of Earth to aid us, so that our outpost can settle into a single chronology."

Dr. Conrad shot a glance at Crow then spoke to Ralyia. "I'll do it."

Relief flooded the alien woman's features. "We will be most appreciative, but I must warn you that we may never recover the ability to restore you to your proper time frame."

"I understand," said Dr. Conrad.

Crow began to object, but Dr. Conrad drew near to him and put a finger to his lips. "I know you feel something for me, Crow and I want you to know that I feel something for you, too—but in this world a red man and a white woman could never find happiness. Society wouldn't let us. If I go with the Lemurians, I'll be able to study a culture unlike any I ever dreamed existed. This is the answer to all my prayers and aspirations—almost."

"Come quickly," said Ralyia. "The closer you are to the edge of the vortex, the more danger there is of disruption."

Then Sylvia Conrad kissed Crow for long moments that echoed into infinity, and Crow found himself speechless as she slipped away and through the veil of energy that surrounded the last outpost of Lemuria.

Strings of lightning leaped from the building energy field, hopping along the ground. The air crackled with static. Crow fell back as the city grew blinding with an effulgent light that seemed to radiate from the very bricks and stones that composed it. He threw his arm over his face to protect his sight and then a bolt of rampant energy picked him up and flung him through the brush.

The blinding light faded, leaving the overarching darkness of the star-speckled firmament. The shining city was gone, leaving nothing but an empty clearing that sparkled with shiny stones which had broken loose from the Lemurian wall. Ozone vapor drifted like wraiths. No! There lay scattered bits of machinery and a sundered body. Heart in his throat, Crow ran to the figure and found that it was not, as he feared, the body of Dr. Sylvia Conrad. It was Ralyia. Her emerald flesh had been torn from her exoskeleton, parts of which lay scattered and smoking in the scorched earth.

She spoke a last few words as she lay dying, her damaged translation device sputtering so that there were halts and delays in her speech. "Dr. Conrad escaped to the inner city to help the technopriests fix the temporal engines. I was standing too close to the edge of the vortex. It reached out and grabbed me." She clutched Crow's forearm. "I know the sacrifice you made by letting her go. I would bequeath you with some things before I go. I understand that these stones are of some value on your planet. They are merely shiny baubles on Mars—as plentiful as pebbles on the shores of our great canals."

Ralyia dropped a pouch into Crow's palm and when he later opened it he found it full of cut diamonds—some small as pebbles and others as large as cat's-eye shooter marbles that he had seen children use in street games.

*****

Crow finished his story. "And that is how I came into the possession of those diamonds."

Finn Grimm levered back the hammers of his double-barreled shotgun. "That's the biggest load of hogwash that I've ever heard."

"I think the diamonds speak for themselves," said Crow. "And there are more that were left behind when the city disappeared. They litter the burnt earth where the city once stood."

Six-Gun Susannah Johnson pushed back a wild lock of straw-colored hair. "Why didn't you gather them? I would have stayed until every last one of those diamonds was plucked out of the ground!"

"I couldn't stand the solitude any longer," said Crow. "My own thoughts were too loud and I needed the diversion of humanity."

"Solitude?" mused Wild Eagle as he studied Crow's features. He twitched in his saddle. "You wouldn't happen to be a member of the Kohanis Tribe, because I heard tell that one or two might have escaped when we found them wandering through our territory? Those shellfish eaters should have known better than to come inland into Apache lands."

For many years Crow had wondered what he would do if he should find another who was responsible for slaughtering his people and making him a lone outcast in the world, but in perusing the scriptures he had been struck by one verse in particular, so instead of letting anger flood him he unconsciously spoke the words. "Vengeance is mine saith the Lord."

"So you are one of them." Wild Eagle laughed incredulously. "Instead of trying to scalp me you quote white man's scripture? You are nothing but a cowardly white man wearing red skin."

"At least I am not a murderer," said Crow, "who cut babies from the bowers and dashed them upon the stones."

Wild Eagle leaned forward in his saddle with a sick smile spreading his lips. "I've done worse than that, Crow. Perhaps you'd like me to describe how Chief Red Arrow killed your m…"

Crow interrupted Wild Eagle before he could speak further. "You have my diamonds and I have kept my part of the bargain. I told you where I found them. Now let me pass."

Six-Gun Susannah Johnson shrugged. "So what if his story sounds crazy? We've got the diamonds. A bargain's a bargain."

Wild Eagle's face contorted with rage. He found it unacceptable that he had been unable to taunt a reaction out of Crow. "That's not good enough! I say we take the diamonds and the bounty."

Finn Grimm dropped the bag of diamonds into his pocket, the aim of his shotgun momentarily wavering. "I agree. Kill the loco Indian!"

Before Finn Grimm finished speaking, Crow moved forward with lightning speed. Sharp shooter Grady O'Keefe pulled the trigger of his rifle from the safety of a nearby balcony. If he had been firing at Crow's body he would have hit, but he had been aiming at the Indian's temple and the bullet whined past, kicking up a plume of dust.

Crow brushed the twin barrels of Finn's shotgun aside even as the long-faced bounty hunter pulled the trigger. Double barrels of shot blasted into the chest of Six-Gun Susannah's horse. The spotted mare shrieked and reared up before crumpling to the ground, hooves flailing. Six-Gun Susannah Johnson had her pistol out and was firing even as she flew through the air, but her aim went awry, spattering the siding of the nearby cantina. So quick was she on the trigger, that she emptied her pistol of all six shots before she hit the hard-packed road, where she lay stunned.

Crow spun behind Finn Grimm, arm around the bounty hunter's throat even as his right hand unsheathed an eighteen-inch blade that folks affectionately referred to as an Arkansas toothpick. He plunged this into Finn's side and the bounty hunter's struggles ceased. His knees buckled and his weight sagged so that he lurched away from Crow, leaving the Indian unshielded from the gunfire of the other bounty hunters.

Before Finn Grimm hit the ground Crow hurled his Arkansas tooth-pick. It flipped end over end and took Wild Eagle through the throat, so that the point emerged, crimson, near his spine. Wild Eagle fired his carbine as he pitched from his horse and the bullet pounded into Crow's chest.

Crow staggered backward. He did not fall, but the bullet slowed his draw. Hansel Grimm shouted out in anguish as he saw his brother fall and he pumped a .50 caliber round into Crow's side, spinning him around in the dust of the street, so that Crow faced Hansel. Grady O'Keefe fired another round into Crow's chest, but, miraculously, the Indian still stood.

Finally, Crow unholstered his eagle-butted Colt .45. His first shot took Hansel Grimm between the eyes. He shifted his aim higher, two shots splintering the balustrade behind which the sharpshooter hid. The third shot took Grady O'Keefe just beneath the left clavicle, and the fourth shot nicked the sniper's heart.

Of the five bounty hunters that had attacked Crow, only one of them was not dead or dying, but Six-Gun Susannah Johnson still lay gasping for air on the street, clutching her empty six-shooter. Crow unbuttoned his shirt and examined the spots where the trio of bullets had struck him. A glimmer of sunlight slipped through the swollen clouds that obscured Sydney Town and glinted against a marvelous coat of finely wrought mesh that had not been formed by earthly forges. There was scarcely a mark where the bullets had hit, and even the .50 caliber slug of Hansel Grimm's Sharps rifle had merely flattened one of the links.

Satisfied that he had escaped with only a few bruises, Crow approached Six-Gun Susannah Johnson. He had one bullet left in the cylinder of his Colt.

She looked up and saw Crow standing over her, the gaping barrel of his gun pointed at her head, and she saw the shining coat of unearthly armor that he wore beneath his unbuttoned shirt. "You were telling the truth," she gasped. "That armor belonged to the green-skinned woman!"

"It was the other thing that she bequeathed to me," said Crow. "Besides the diamonds."

Six-Gun Susannah Johnson managed a harsh laugh. "I thought your story had the ring of truth. Now shoot me and be done with it."

Crow made a quick decision and holstered his gun. Instead of shooting Susannah Johnson he proffered his hand to help her up from the earth. "I won't shoot you. You were the only one who would have kept their word. That shows some honor—something that is rarely found among thieves... or bounty hunters."

Susannah Johnson regarded Crow with suspicion and then finally reached up to take Crow's proffered hand. He pulled her to her feet, and for a moment she bent over, resting her hands upon her knees, wild hair hiding her features as she regained the last of her breath. "Well, it looks as though I'll be going home horseless, and empty-handed, but at least I've got my life."

"Share a sarsaparilla with me and I won't send you home empty-handed," said Crow as he recovered the bag of diamonds from Finn Grimm's belt. "You'll have a horse beneath you and a pair of diamonds in your purse."

Susannah Johnson stood upright and pushed her empty revolver into its holster. "You sure know how to sweet talk a gal. I suppose I can manage a sarsaparilla, though I am accustomed to much stronger drink. What makes you think that I won't shoot you when given the chance and collect that bounty?"

Crow retrieved his Arkansas toothpick from the bloody throat where it jutted and wiped the blade clean on Wild Eagle's dusty trail garb. Though he had been willing to relegate vengeance to the Lord, God had for some reason allowed him to take a hand in it. "Give me your word that you won't, Susannah."

Susannah Johnson's lips quirked in an odd sort of smile. "You have my word, Crow. Now, buy me that sarsaprilla and tell where I can get me one of those chainmail shirts that you're wearing."

*****

That night in the shabbily furnished hotel room of the Raven's Roost, Crow laid aside the shirt of armor on the arm of a roughly-hewn chair. When he awoke the shirt was gone. He still had the painful bruises to show where he had been shot, so his first thought was that Six-Gun Susannah Johnson had crept into his room, stolen the shirt while he slept and made for parts unknown. But when she rapped upon his door and called out to him that grub was on, he noticed some scorch marks where the shirt had rested. Just maybe the Lemurians had settled their city into a single time and decided that they should leave no evidence of their passing but the moldering and decayed ruins of their great city which would be discovered by explorers thousands of years later.

Old Mother Hennessy

Deep in the Colorado wilderness, Six-Gun Susannah Johnson felt an eerie foreboding in the form of a chill that crawled up the back of her neck. She stopped in mid-tread, something crunching beneath her booted foot. Her hair was an untamed mass of corkscrew curls, mats, and fly-away strands, which played about her flannel-covered shoulders as she glanced back at the taciturn Indian who followed her, dressed in the clothing of a cowboy, a pistol jutting at his right hip, a tomahawk thrust through his belt on the left hip, and a short-barreled carbine rifle slung over his shoulder.

"What did I just step on, Crow?"

Susannah wasn't much for wearing corsets or bustles and Lone Crow let his eyes wander down the straining seams of the worn and stained denim of her trousers to the scarred leather of her boots, which was wearing thin since the Hennessy Brothers' ambush had killed their horses. "It appears we've stumbled upon some sort of graveyard."

The gunwoman moved her boot and saw the hollow eyes of a skull, now missing a few more teeth, staring vacantly up at her. "Are we on some sacred Indian land? Because I feel something here." Susannah thought she saw something out of the corner of her eye and she whirled, her gun snapping into her hand with an uncanny speed that few alive could match, but when she looked for something to shoot, she could see nothing but the encroaching wilderness.

Crow crouched, making no comment on his companion's quick draw. Experience had made him more aware of the influence of the supernatural, and he knew what Susannah was feeling. He could hear them in his head, the voices of the wronged crying out from the dead, yearning for vengeance. Crow brushed away the earth from another bone that was close to the surface. "I don't think so. This is Ute territory and they bury their dead stretched full out beneath a bed of rock—usually they burn the dwelling and belongings of the deceased to make sure that the ghost of the dead does not linger on Earth."

Susannah looked closer and saw numerous bones thrusting up from the weedy loam. "The dead here seem to have been thrown into some sort of mass grave, without any care how they were buried. Some aren't even completely buried at all."

Crow found a mouldering pouch and dumped its contents on the ground. "The possessions of the dead seem to have been buried with them—except for any sort of valuables. They seem to have been removed."

Susannah began to calculate how many dead lay in this graveyard. "Was it some sort of disease that kilt them? Malaria or smallpox?"

Crow found the top of a skull and pried it free from the loam. He held it aloft so that Susannah could see the four bullet holes that punctured the bone. "More likely it was cold-blooded murder."

"I think we're getting closer to the Hennessy Brothers," breathed Susannah.

With some reverence, Crow placed the skull upon the earth and picked up a damp card from the belongings he had emptied upon the ground. "This is a card of business with George McKee's name upon it. He and his wife Vanetta went missing when they took the Butterfield Overland from Atchison."

"Along with the entire stagecoach and three other passengers," said Susannah. "Trapper Olsen told us that the Hennessy Brothers haunted these parts. You think that they're responsible for the missing stage, too?"

"Four bank robberies and seven dead, four kidnapped" recited Crow. "I don't think they'd have any compunction about a few more murders on their consciences." He found the stub of smoked cigar and lifted it, passing it beneath his nostrils. "Seems that our gravedigger has a penchant for cigars."

A few moments more of digging and Crow found Vanetta McKee buried next to her husband, her dress soiled, her scalp and hair missing, as well as her heart. Further digging uncovered more bodies, few with more just a thin layer of dirt over them. Apparently, whoever had dumped the bodies hadn't been much interested in giving them a proper burial, and cared little whether the wild animals got to them.

Susannah grinned, her teeth white against sun-darkened lips, but her smile was forced and had no humor. "Now that we found the Hennessy burial ground, do you think you can pick up the trail of the Hennessy Brothers, Crow? The word is that they're momma's boys and that old mother Hennessy is the one that plans their robberies for them. She's a fat old hag who sits in her shack counting her loot and figuring out who they'll steal from next."

"Some of this earth is freshly turned," said Crow, "which means that they've recently added bodies. The rains haven't been heavy, so I think there's a good chance I can find some markings." He pointed across the graveyard. "Check under that leaf over there."

Susannah raised an eyebrow and glanced at her Indian companion through a squinted eye of hazel. "I'll eat my hat if there's a marking underneath that leaf." She stepped over and flipped the oak leaf over, finding a boot print beneath. She muttered an imprecation beneath her breath, and Crow spoke from behind her.

"I hope you have enough salt for that hat."

"How did you know?"

"The ground's marshy over here and I saw several broken blades of grass that indicated something had passed this way."

Susannah rose, the top of her head coming to Crow's shoulder. "I should know better than to second guess your tracking."

"The print's about two days old," said Crow. "It looks like the tracks head up the slope and toward that ridge."

They struck out, climbing the slope and gradually the plaintive cries in Crow's head subsided. As they put some distance between themselves and the graveyard, Six-Gun Susannah Johnson began to breathe more easily, and the goosebumps on her arms sank into her golden, sun-darkened skin. Crow pointed out a number of prints to Susannah. He read smudges in the earth as plainly as a professor could read print upon the page, and even pointed out where moss had been brushed from tree trunks as the man who had passed that way had used the trunks to aid his climb. At the top of the ridge they encountered a dirt path rutted by wagon wheels.

"He stopped his cart here," said Crow, "and threw bodies down the slope. He collected them at the bottom and dragged them into the grave-yard."

"You said that the Utes burned the belongings of the dead so the spirits wouldn't return. Is there something about people's stuff that keeps them attached to the earth?"

"Sometimes a person becomes so attached to their belongings that they don't want to let go of them," said Crow. "It may take their spirit awhile to realize that they can't take those possessions with them."

"What about vengeance? Do you think a spirit might stick around until it sees justice served?"

"It's been known to happen," said Crow.

"You don't say much about it, but I know you've seen some strange things, Crow. Have you ever seen a ghost come back for vengeance?"

"No," said Crow. "Not in the way that you mean."

They begin to follow the rutted trail up the meandering road. "So what have you seen, darling? You know, I've seen some strange things, too."

"The world is full of strange things," said Crow, and a faint smile played across his lips. "Who would have ever thought they might see an Indian and a white girl traipsing around together?"

Susannah wrinkled her nose and laughed. "And bounty hunting, no less! Those Hennessy Brothers won't know what hit them. I'll save one of them for you. I am the fastest draw, after all."

Few would dare impugn the speed of Crow's draw to his face, but the

Indian seemed to take no offense. "The fastest draw west of the Mississippi, I've heard people say—but you'd best steady your aim. The fastest draw doesn't win the gunfight, but the better shot does."

Susannah squawked in indignation. "Are you implying that I can't hit my target?"

"I'm not implying it," said Crow. "I'm saying it."

"You would do well to remember that I've killed four men in fair fights."

"I'm alive right now because you couldn't hit me," Crow reminded Susannah.

"Well, that was different," scowled Susannah. "No one could kill you that day. Not even the ones that did hit you." She shrugged. "Besides, I'm glad I missed. Maybe, it was just that I didn't want to hit you."

"Maybe," said Crow. "That must have been it."

They continued up the trail and through dales and across creeks where Crow kept a sharp eye out for any sign of an ambush. He had no indication that the Hennessy Brothers might be suspecting a visit from either him or Six-Gun Susannah Johnson, but sometimes means both mundane or strange were employed to warn the hunted that justice was on their trail.

The trail of the horse drawn cart led through a gulley and Crow put out his left arm to keep Susannah from passing through the tree-framed entrance into the rocky ditch that still-trickled with a bit of moisture, despite the mid-summer heat that had reduced the flow.

"What is it?" murmured Susannah.

"I smell tobacco smoke."

Susannah lifted her nose and caught a hint of the sickly sweet scent of burning tobacco wafting on the breeze. "Good thing we're downwind."

As she spoke, the wind shifted and carried the scent in some other direction. Susannah glanced at Crow, her left cheek crinkling as the corner of her lip rose in a wry smile. "Let me borrow your carbine. I'll keep them distracted and you can circle around behind them."

Crow unslung his Winchester .44 and handed the carbine to Susannah. "You've got thirteen rounds." He melted into the surrounding woods as Susannah took up position behind the gnarled tree at the entrance to the gully. She fired a round toward a rock on top of the sloping earth walls and sent a bullet whining away. "Come on out, you lily-livered cowards! If you throw down your weapons and come along without a fight, I promise I won't kill you."

Her response was a volley of bullets which chewed the bark on the twisted pine behind which she stood. She couldn't help but laugh when she saw a quartet of smoke puffs rising from various positions upon the ridges on either side of the gully. Crow would see the rising gunsmoke and know where to find the ambushers. "The Hennessy Brothers?" she taunted from behind the tree. "You shoot like you're the Hennessy Sisters! I've seen bordellos full of calico queens that have better aim than you soft-horns."

Susannah kept up a verbal volley of insults and haranguing while Crow crept through the woods, emerging through a stand of stunted pines and up the rocky slope. He could see a pair of riflemen prone upon the ridge, their attention fixed on Susannah, who occasionally fired a bullet in their direction to punctuate her defamations of their characters. Between this and their own gunfire they didn't hear Crow climbing the slope behind them until he was a dozen feet away.

Kyle Hennessy glanced over his shoulder and saw the taciturn Indian standing behind him, a .45 Peacemaker in his fist.

"Drop your guns," warned Crow.

Kyle Hennessy hadn't been born with much sense, nor had he learned any in his twenty-seven years on planet Earth. He swung his rifle around in a ponderous arc that gave Crow plenty of time to put a pair of bullets into Kyle's heart.

Beside Kyle, Cromwell Hennessy couldn't help but notice his brother's sudden movement and he endeavored to use his brother's demise to give him a moment to fire off a round at the Indian. He flipped over and brought his rifle to bear just in time to catch a bullet beneath his chin. The bullet traveled into his brain and lodged against the interior of his skull.

Though only Crow's head and shoulders were visible to Kenneth and Stanforth, who held positions on the opposite ridge over the gulley, they didn't fail to notice what was happening to their brothers and immediately shifted their aim from the well-concealed Six-Gun Susannah to the black-haired Indian in cowboy attire.

Kenneth's first shot took Crow's hat off, and sent it careening down the slope. Crow threw himself down and avoided a volley of bullets that came his direction, slicing over his head. That was when Susannah came sauntering into the gulley firing Crow's carbine from the curve of her denim-clad hip. There was only a fraction of a second between each shot, just long enough for her to lever another round into the barrel so she could pull the trigger. She fired insanely fast, but the shots were entirely inaccurate, spattering the slopes and ridgeline with a volley of bullets.

No one could predict where the next bullet would strike and so Kenneth and Stanforth Hennessy danced down the ridge as bullets whined and ricocheted around them. Stanforth was a big bear of a man and seeing him pirouette and prance to cover might have been a rather humorous sight if it wasn't for the deadliness of the situation.

No sooner had the Hennessy Brothers found some safety in the cover of chunks of rock growing with stunted shrubs, then Susannah emptied the last round from Crow's carbine. This left her in a particularly dire strait. She was in the center of the gulley with an empty carbine, and a particularly easy target for anyone who might be able to draw a bead upon her.

Though Stanforth and Kenneth Hennessy were fully aware that the wild-haired woman gunfighter had ceased firing, they weren't anxious to climb back to the ridgeline in case the Indian on the opposite ridge was waiting for them, or in the case that Susannah was carrying another weapon beside the carbine. Indeed, she possessed a holstered .44 revolver—wearing it on the same hip from which she had been firing the carbine.

Stanforth Hennessy had no inclination to expose himself to any more gunfire. He wiped his bristling mustache with the back of one palm and then reached into the pouch on his belt for a match. He struck it on the stone behind which he crouched and lit a stick of dynamite, watching the flame eat the fuse away for just a moment, so that when it landed the unfortunate recipient of the sputtering gift would have little time to react before it exploded.

Kenneth Hennessy giggled like a schoolgirl as he watched the fuse burn down. When he spoke, his voice was incongruously high-pitched, a contrast to his stubble-cheeked appearance. He handed his brother a small cloth bag with an open mouth. "Give them the old Hennessy Special."

Stanforth shoved the stick of dynamite into the bag. This was a favorite tactic that the Hennessy Brothers used to clear out banks. They would thrust a stick of dynamite into a bag of nails, tie the mouth and light the fuse, creating a makeshift bomb that would throw nail shrapnel in all directions. They would lob this through the window of the bank they were robbing and rush in during the ensuing chaos—killing survivors and cleaning every paper and silver dollar out of the safes.

Stanforth sent the bag of nails, with the sputtering stick of dynamite inside, lofting into the air.

Crow saw the bag fly from behind the concealment of the opposite ridge and without conscious thought he tracked its flight and began firing. Three times he struck the bag, slightly altering its trajectory. The impacting bullets caused the makeshift bomb to fall short of the gulley, and it landed near the top of the ridge, then exploded casting nails in all directions.

One nail sliced the cartilege of Crow's ear, and a half dozen impacted in the dirt around him. In the gulley below, Susannah stood unscathed, eight-penny nails flying over her tousled head.

In his eagerness to see the bloody results of the bomb, Kenneth Hennessy had begun to scramble toward the top of the ridge. When the bag fell short, he suddenly found that he was in all too close of a position to witness the carnage firsthand. Eight-penny nails bit through his clothing and his face. Blinded, he went to his knees, his hands feeling the wetness of his own blood as he vainly tried to stanch the flow from the carnage of his mutilated features.

"Stanforth!" he cried out. "Stanforth, get me to my horse. Put me on my horse and lead me back to the house."

Kenneth's brother Stanforth, however, was nothing if not pragmatic. He saw that two of his brothers were dead, and that Kenneth was severely wounded. He realized that precious moments, which might be better used toward making his own escape, might be lost by helping his wounded brother—who likely would never recover and be a hindrance and a burden for the foreseeable future.

Stanforth retreated to his dappled stallion and swung into the saddle. He paused just long enough to swivel and put a bullet into the skull of his brother's horse so that neither the Indian or the woman gunfighter could easily pursue him. The horse gave a short shriek, reared upon its hind legs and then collapsed, throwing up a cloud of dust.

Stanforth dug his heels into the flanks of his stallion, and it started into a gallop that took him away from the site of the ambush gone awry. The plaintive cries of his brother echoed in his ears as he fled.

Susannah scrambled up the wall of the gulley, and at the sound of her booted foot tread in the gravel, Kenneth Hennessy pulled his bloodied hands away from the mangled ruins of his face and drew his pistol. Before he could fire, Six-Gun Susannah Johnson slapped leather, drew and fired, fanning the hammer of her .44 as she pulled the trigger.

Only one of the six bullets actually hit Kenneth Hennessy. But it caught him through the top of the skull and he toppled slowly backward, his gun dangling impotently from slack fingers.

Amazingly, Kenneth Hennessy was still conscious when Susannah Johnson reached him, putting her boot on his wrist, then reaching down and prying the unfired pistol from his fingers.

Kenneth Hennessy's gaze was bleary and unfocused. "You kilt me…"

Susannah checked Hennessy's pistol and found that it still contained two rounds. "How does it feel to be killed by a woman, Kenneth?"

"You know my name," he groaned. "Mother was right. You're here to collect the bounty that Denver sheriff put on our heads."

"People have a tendency to get angry when a bunch of scum of the earth ride into town, killing, maiming, and kidnapping innocent women and children. They don't mind putting up what little money they have left in order to see some justice done."

"How much?" asked Hennessy. Fluid was leaking from the bullet hole in his skull.

"Five hundred dollars each. By my calculations Crow and I have earned fifteen hundred dollars this afternoon, but I would have killed you for free. That's how much I loathe you."

Kenneth Hennessy seemed to have lost his vision, for now he stared into the brightness of the falling sun. "Mother will get you. She can talk to the dead. I'll warn her that you're coming…"

With those last few words garbled out from his uncooperative throat and tongue, Kenneth Hennessy gave up the ghost and slumped lifeless in the dust.

Crow came up alongside of Susannah. "He say anything important?"

Susannah tipped up the brim of her hat, with the barrel of Kenneth Hennessy's revolver. "Why, he complimented me on my fine shooting. It only took me one shot, you know."

Crow glanced at Susannah's holstered .44 and noted that the chambers of the cylinder were empty. "You mean, of the six shots you fired it took only the one that hit to kill him?"

Susannah cocked her head to one side. "Isn't that what I said?"

Crow marked the dust lingering in the air and the hoof marks of Stanforth Hennessy's horse. "Not precisely."

"Kenneth did say that his mother can speak with the dead and that now that he's joining them he'll be warning his mother that we're coming."

"I'm sure that Stanforth will be warning his mother as well. There will be no need for her to speak with the dead."

"It seems strange that a bunch of full grown men should be such momma's boys," mused Susannah.

"You already said she's the brains behind the operation."

Susannah kicked some dirt on Kenneth Hennessy's corpse. "Well, having met the Hennessy Brothers in person I can say that I give some credence to the theory. There didn't seem to be more than the intelligence of a prairie dog spread between the four of them."

"Sheriff Adler thought enough of the rumors to put a five hundred dollar bounty on her head as well."

"Dead or alive?" asked Susannah.

"He wasn't picky," said Crow.

Susannah frowned. "A woman that birthed four such sad excuses for men, it might be better if she were brought in dead than alive."

Crow strode to Kenneth Hennessy's still-twitching horse and opened the saddle bag. He found some hardtack, a trail-stained map, a worn deck of cards, and a bible from which half the pages had been torn—apparently used as rolling papers, because Crow found a cigarette rolled with a page from the book of Daniel inside a pouch of dried tobacco.

Susannah reloaded her pistol. "We'd better hurry. We won't catch Stanforth on foot, but we don't want to give him time to set up an ambush either."

Crow spread out the map and jabbed a finger at a spot marked in black ink. "No need to follow his tracks. This map shows a couple of different routes we can take."

Susannah arched an eyebrow. "You know where he's going?"

"Back to old mother Hennessy's house, I'm guessing, and there's no need to go on foot. There's a pair of horses tethered on the other side of the gulley."

"Why didn't you tell me? My boot leather has about worn through since the Hennessy Brothers kilt our horses in that Gold Fork ambush." Susannah slugged Crow in the arm and Crow absorbed the punishment without expression.

The sun sank and the waning moon rose as they steered Kyle and Cromwell Hennessy's horses down crooked paths, across meandering streams and up steep and winding trails formed by the Utes who had inhabited this ancient land long before Columbus had ever set foot on the American continents.

Overshadowing trees spread their branches in a smothering canopy that blocked all but a few faint glimmerings of the stars and moon. Crow and Six-Gun Susannah were cloaked in shadow as they proceeded, their pace scarcely a crawl so they would not tumble into a hidden precipice or gulch.

Susannah coaxed her horse alongside of Crow's. She had to pull on the reins as her mount attempted to bite the ear of the other horse. The horses that had belonged to the Hennessy Brothers were as mean and foul tempered as their owners had been "I feel like there's a hundred pair of eyes watching us. I've got goosebumps on my goosebumps—like I did in the graveyard we found."

"It's restless spirits," said Crow. "I hear their voices. They want us to be their instruments of vengeance against their killers."

"The Hennessy Brothers? We've killed three of them. What more do they want?"

"They want Stanforth to join his brothers. They want Mother Hennessy, too."

"We're working on it. Can't they leave us alone? I'm not much interested in riding with ghosts—whether they're friendly or not. Can you make them go away?"

"There are ways for a holder of the priesthood to cast away evil spirits in the name of Christ, but these spirits aren't evil. They linger here, hoping to see justice done."

"Don't they know that justice is a rare thing in this world?"

Crow made no comment. Susannah's statement was true enough. The world was full of injustice and perhaps the scales wouldn't be fully balanced until judgment day.

How Crow managed to guide them to a vale where the candle light of a small shack glimmered in the endless umbra of night, Susannah could not say, but there they were on the crest of the hill, leafy bowers whispering overhead and their horses nickering and shifting restlessly beneath them.

"The horses recognize their home," said Susannah. "Any sign of Stanforth?"

"There," said Crow, "nearing the shack."

Susannah looked and saw shadows shifting, a great black shape that resolved itself into the form of a horse, and a slightly smaller shape that resolved itself into the bear-like figure of Stanforth Hennessy, illumined in the candle light as he tethered his steed. She handed Crow his carbine. "I reloaded it."

Crow took the short-barreled rifle and threw it to his shoulder, but the shot was long, the path was dark, and by the time he had sighted in, Stanforth disappeared into the interior of the shack.

"You could have made that shot," teased Susannah. "You can shoot a flying bag of nails out of the air with a pistol, you ought to be able to hit a big man like Stanforth at three hundred yards with a carbine."

"It's a long shot for the carbine," said Crow. His voice betrayed no sign of being irked by Susannah's needling and his face was cloaked in shadow. "I didn't want to miss the shot and warn them we are here."

"I'm just saying that I would have taken the shot," replied Susannah.

"Yet, you handed me the carbine."

"It's your carbine, darling. I was just borrowing it."

They slipped from their saddles and tethered the horses in a copse of trees on the ridge, then crept down the scrub-covered slope toward the shack. Someone drew a drape across the milky panes of glass, and the yellow light that seeped through the window was reduced to the faintest outline. So, by starlight, Crow and Susannah navigated the treacherous slope, and drew near to the shack.

"I'll distract them," whispered Susannah. "You burst in through the back door."

"Let me check and make sure there is a back door first," suggested Crow. He could hear the voices of the dead strong in his ears now—a cacophony that would have driven most men insane, if they did not understand the dead souls were merely thirsty for vengeance.

Susannah shivered and cast a glance over her shoulders. "They're still watching us, aren't they? I mean, the dead we found in that graveyard are watching us…"

"They are," said Crow. "I can still hear their voices."

"Tell them to shut up and leave us alone," said Susannah, "or we'll climb right back up that slope and leave Stanforth and his momma alive and well."

The spirits must have heard Susannah, because immediately the voices calling out in Crow's head died to a murmur. Susannah breathed a sigh of relief and the ice cold fingers that climbed her spine faded to a moderate chill.

"That actually seems to have helped," said Crow.

"Good, now maybe we can do our job."

"I'll be right back," said Crow. "Don't go anywhere."

"I'll be right here waiting for you, darling."

Crow's lean form faded into the night, and he circled around the back of the shack. Here, he found that the shack abutted a great ravine which he had not earlier been able to divine in the cloak of darkness. A wagon trail was cut into the edge of the ravine and wound into its abyssal depths. The stench of death was lifted from below, carried on the slightest of breezes. Indeed, there was a back door to the shack and it was slightly ajar, as if someone had already slipped out the back but not latched the door for fear the sound of the latch might carry in the night. That meant that Stanforth might already be creeping around front. Was it possible that Crow and Stanforth had passed right by each other, just a few paces away in the darkness? Crow judged it unlikely, but perhaps Stanforth had circled around the other direction.

Crow heard a rapid stacatto of gunshots and he recognized the boom of Susannah's .44 mingled among them. Instead of circling around the hut, Crow decided upon the more direct option. He bounded up the steps of the shack and burst through the back door, making a beeline for the front door. The stench inside the shack was palpable, and though Crow did not slacken his pace he couldn't but help to notice the implements of dark magic that marred the interior: an altar to the demonic Beezulbub over which hung an inverted cross, and then there were the gnawed and rotted hearts which moldered in a silver chalice marked with evil symbology meant to summon the dark powers that inhabited the tractless voids of otherly worlds and dimensions. Scalps, trophies of sacrificed women, festooned the rafters of the shack, drawing flies with their charnel reek, and long tresses hanging down, brushed at Crow and blocked his vision.

Crow ducked low and that was when a shotgun blast lit up the interior of the shack, then extinguished the dripping tapers that lit the interior. Crow felt hot fragments of lead burning in his shoulder and he went down, knocking over a table, and striking his skull. Something scattered across him, pasteboards of some sort. He reached for his pistol, but the blow to his skull had him addled. Instead he found one of the pasteboards, his gun hand closing about it.

Before Crow could recover his senses he heard the sound of a shotgun being reloaded, and then one of the tapers flickered again into life, revealing the features of a dark-haired woman with silken skin as pale as the face of the moon. Though she was beautiful, there was something malign in her features, the pinched nose and the dead eyes which betrayed no hint of humanity, only evil intentions. She held the reloaded shotgun so that it was trained on Crow's recumbent form. She pursed her lips and blew, and as the wind passed those crimson-painted lips all the candles within the shack lit, shedding their wavering flame upon the grisly trophies and demonic symbology that lay upon the altar and was painted in blood upon the walls.

"You've been a lot of trouble for me," said the woman. "You and that harlot killed three of my sons."

A sharp pain zig-zagged through Crow's skull. "Your sons?"

A slow smile spread across the woman's face—supercillious and mocking. "Just how old do you think that I am, red man?"

To Crow, the woman appeared to be no more than twenty years of age—perhaps younger, but he had difficulty judging such things. He found that appearances could often be deceiving. Normally, he was not inclined to indulge in small talk with a stranger, but given the gaping maw of the shotgun that faced him, he thought that some conversaton might buy him a few moments. "Your face and figure are young, but your eyes have seen much."

"Very good, red man. I'm Lilith Hennessy, matron of the Hennessy clan."

"You're not as I heard you described," said Crow.

This seemed to have touched a nerve, for the corner of her mouth twitched downward into a momentary scowl. "Oh, and just how was it that you heard me described?"

"Does it matter?" hedged Crow. "Obviously the descriptions were wrong."

Lilith Hennessy's voice became sharp. "Tell me. What do they say?"

"They spin rumors of a fat old hag that directs the thievery and murders of her sons," answered Crow. "But such does not seem to be the case. How is it that you have borne four sons, the oldest of at least thirty-five years, and you seem to be just half of that age?"

"It's a gift from my master for my devoted service," answered Lilith Hennessy.

Boot steps sounded on the front porch and the bear-like Stanforth Hennessy entered with Susannah slung over his right shoulder.

"Ah, my stalwart son returns bearing a plaything for our rituals. I trust that you are unharmed?"

Stanforth grinned. "The charms you gave me protected me. She fired six bullets, but not a single one struck me."

Crow refrained from commenting that this was not unusual for Susannah to miss her target. She was so fast on the trigger that she often began firing the moment her pistol cleared leather.

Susannah was draped over Stanforth's shoulder, her torso and mass of tangled hair hanging down. She wasn't moving.

"You didn't kill her, did you?" asked Lilith. "Because I do need her alive for the ritual."

"I gave her a backhand," said Stanforth. "It was just a love tap."

"You've broken necks with that backhand before," said Lilith, her voice hard. "Remember that banker in Des Moines?"

Stanforth's laugh was rough and deep. "He flopped around like a fish out of water before he died."

"Dump the woman on the floor and remove this Indian's weapons. He's coming to his senses and he's as dangerous as he looks."

"Let me wring his neck, Mother. He killed Cromwell and Kyle. He was the one that did it."

"No," warned Lilith. "This one has an uncanny vitality. I can use that to sustain my own strength and youth, draw upon it as I have drawn on the life of the others that you have brought to me."

Stanforth none too-gently dumped Susannah on the floor, her head thumping against the uneven boards.

The big bear of a man paused only long enough to plant a lingering kiss on his mother's lips and then he moved toward Crow. The moment that he interposed himself between Crow and his mother's shotgun was when the Indian gunfighter made his move. He was quick on the draw, but Stanforth Hennessy was quicker than he looked. The bigger man lurched forward and wrapped a huge mitt around Crow's wrist, forcing the gun backward.

Though outmatched in size and strength, Crow possessed a wiry power in his frame and resisted the elemental force that was Stanforth Hennessy. Crow attempted to twist away his gun, and bring it into play, but his attempts were to no avail. His wrist was being bent back and Stanforth threatened to snap the bone at any moment. Crow fired a shot that pierced one of the hanging scalps and lodged in the beam of the ceiling. The shot had been fired as more of a distraction than with the hopes of actually hitting Stanforth. Still, the muzzle flash momentarily blinded the Hennessy brother and though he did not release his grip on Crow's wrist, Crow was able to reach down and pull loose his tomahawk—a gift from the Indian Chieftain Onahuk, after he had saved his daughter from being devoured by the beasts in the labyrinths beneath Chichen Iza—and he plunged the blade into Stanforth's side.

Stanforth was saved by the wood grips on the butt of his pistol, which jutted up to take the brunt of the blow. Even as the Indian rose up to his feet, Stanforth cast the gunfighter across the room. At the same time he tore the blessed pistol out of Crow's hand, so that it pin-wheeled over the floor.

Lilith Hennessy gave out a delighted shriek and reached for the pistol. When her slender hand closed upon it her shriek was that of pain, and she let go of the pistol as if it were the handle of a hot frying pan. She abandoned her shotgun and clutched at her palm. "The pistol—it's a holy relic!"

"Blessed by a prophet," grunted Crow as he climbed back to his feet, still holding his tomahawk in his left hand.

Lilith Hennessy grinned. "No blessing of a prophet will save you now, red man." She reached up for a lever. "You'll join the others and be carted to the graveyard when we're finished with your gunfighter gal friend."

Susannah was stirring slightly now on the floor, but Crow was only minimally aware of this. The voices that had followed him since the graveyard were screaming in his mind. "Step away!" they cried. "You're standing in danger," they screamed out a disjointed chorus.

Crow heeded the warning of the ghostly choir and he leaped just as Lilith Hennessy pulled the lever, releasing a trap door over which he stood. His booted feet scarcely found purchase on solid floor boards before he launched his tomahawk at Stanforth Hennessy, who barreled toward him, intent on pushing Crow into the open hatch, so that he would fall forty feet into the blood and brain-spattered cart that stood in the ancient cavern below. This was how the Hennessy Clan disposed of the bodies after they dragged them here to be sacrificed in heinous rituals to the dark demon Beezelbub.

The tomahawk revolved once and then buried in Stanforth Hennessy's skull. As the bear of a man pitched forward, tumbling through the open hatch, Lilith Hennessy gave a shriek of pain and horror as her son and lover met his demise. "By Beezelbub, my master, and the eternal youth he bestowed upon me, I swear that you'll suffer for that!"

She continued to shriek, and as her voice raised in pitch the flame on the candles grew in strength and in fury, until sheets of fire swept through the air, propelled toward Crow by the motion of Lilith's hand, buffeting him with heat that singed the ends of his raven hair, and crisped his duster, so that smoke rose from the cloth, and it threatened to combust. Crow fell back from the raging firestorm, his stumbling steps carrying him back, toward the open hatch through which Stanforth Hennessy had pitched headlong. Blinded by the flame, he fell through the hole, just as Susannah rose from the uneven floorboards and picked up Crow's eagle-butted .45 Colt.

Unlike Lilith Hennessy, who had recoiled in pain, Susannah was able to hold the revolver without discomfort and in a flash of speed for which she was so well known, she was pulling the trigger and fanning the hammer. Lilith Hennessy's back was to her, arms outstretched, her dark hair streaming as torrents of flame rushed past her, chasing Crow into the hatch, and kindling glowing embers on the floorboards of the shack. The grisly trophies of many sacrifices burst into flame, scalps charring and hair shriveling.

At this range, Six-Gun Susannah could hardly miss, and at least two of her five shots bit into the witch's back, one of them sundering her heart. Blood blossomed on Lilith Hennessy's back, and her legs became unstrung as her ruptured heart ceased to pump blood. She tumbled to the floor, her dark hair splaying about her, and instantly the fire storm ceased, the candle flames returning to their natural state and the floorboards and scalps still smoldering.

A bruise was forming on Susannah's cheek where Stanforth Hennessy had struck her, and she groggily lurched to her feet, Crow's empty six-gun in her hand. "Crow!" She lurched over to the hatch and looked down.

She saw Stanforth Hennessy's body broken across the sideboard of the cart below, but she did not immediately see Crow amidst the haze of smoke.

She cried out in joy as the haze drifted away and she realized that Crow was hanging from the lip of the open trap door. With the greatest of efforts he heaved himself onto the floorboards and coughed out a wreath of smoke. He noticed the body of Lilith Hennessy lying a few feet away, and he knew that Susannah had done the deed. "You're resilient. I was worried that Stanforth's backhand might have knocked you out for the rest of the night."

Susannah snorted. "My ex-husband used to give me beatings ten times worse than that—until I decided that I'd had enough. Stanforth's backhand was easy enough to shake off."

"Just in time to save my skin," said Crow.

"Well, you're too good a man to leave to the mercies of a woman like Lilith Hennessy." Susannah held out her arm. "My goosebumps have disappeared. Are the ghosts gone?"

Crow nodded. "The voices in my head have disappeared. The blood of the innocent is no longer crying out for vengeance."

Susannah rolled Lilith Hennessy over with her foot. "She's still beautiful... even with a bullet in her heart."

"Perhaps on the outside," replied Crow, "but how many innocents did she put to death in order to maintain her outer beauty, while her inside self was black and shriveled?"

"There's something lyrical about that, Crow. Maybe your true calling is a poet."

"I doubt the poems of an Indian would sell well in a white man's world."

Susannah picked up a bag of coin that was marked with the seal of the Denver Savings and Loan. "We won't need to depend upon your writings to feed us. There's plenty here—even if we return it to the bank there should be a sizeable reward."

"Twenty percent," said Crow, "plus five hundred dollars for each of the

Hennessys. Maybe a poet's life is the life for me."

"Maybe I could be a poet's wife," suggested Six-Gun Susannah Johnson.

"Could you give up whiskey and cards?" asked Crow.

Susannah narrowed her left eye and raised her right brow, indicating that such a prospect was of a dubious likelihood. "I like my whiskey and cards."

They left the Hennessy homestead in flames as they rode away, leading a train of horses liberated from the Hennessy stables. The bodies of Lilith and Stanforth Hennessy were bound across two of the mounts, and they would retrieve the bodies of the three remaining Hennessy Brothers before they returned to Denver to collect their reward. As they slipped into the night, the embers of the burning shack trailing into the night sky, the ghosts of the vengeful dead fled to the spirit realms which awaited their too-long lingering souls.

The Steam Devil

They followed the Southern Kansas railway deep into the Western District of Arkansas, through Chickasaw territory. Usually, deputy US Marshal Bass Reeves would have seen some sign of the Chickasaw by now, but the tortured and rugged lands were strangely barren of life. The motley procession of horsemen that he led halted at the top of a ridge, and their eyes followed the rail track down the slope and into the valley, where steam engine and box cars lay in a jumbled accordion of wreckage.

Bodies lay amid the debris and some outside the perimeter of the wreck, where they had dragged themselves only to die of their wounds and to be picked over by the predators. Even now, vultures pecked at the bones, except where a pack of wolves had staked claim to the carrion.

Lone Crow unlimbered his carbine and fired a shot that killed the largest of the wolves and sent the others scampering for the rocky forest. "That should keep them at bay for a while."

Reeves spoke from beneath a massive mustache that flowed to the edges of his jaw. "Nice shooting, Crow. It could draw attention from the Chickasaw, though, if any happen to be in the area."

"I thought you were on good terms with the Chickasaw," questioned Pinkerton agent, Washburn Bickers. "After all, that's why we hired you."

"No one asked me if I was on good terms with the Chickasaw," said Reeves.

"So you're not?"

"For the most part I am," replied Reeves, "but there are a few malcontents who would just as soon skin me alive and hang me up for the crows as talk to me."

"The only good Indian is a dead one," said Bickers.

Lone Crow, himself an Indian, raised an eyebrow at this as he loaded a replacement cartridge into his carbine. He found it wise to always keep his firearms fully loaded. "Why are they malcontent?"

"The train hit some of their cattle and the rail boss refused to reimburse the tribe for the loss—claimed that it was the tribe's responsibility to keep their cattle off the railway. Anyway, one of their medicine men, Angry Wolf, has riled up the some of the young braves and taken them on the warpath for retribution."

"So much for 'good terms' with the Chickasaws," grumbled Bickers.

"At least you're getting your money's worth with Crow's shooting," said Reeves.

Washburn Bickers scoffed. "The redskin was shooting at a sitting target. I'd like to see him hit a running wolf." He shifted impatiently in his saddle and looked down the line of pack horses. "Where's that Irish whore? She needs to take some pictures from the ridge, before we go down. Daylight's wasting…"

Reeves slipped from the back of his big black roan and put his broad brimmed hat on the horn of the empty saddle. "Get off your horse, Agent Bickers."

Bickers scowled. "Why?"

"The last four days we've been traveling I've heard you refer to Crow as a redskin, me as a darkie and a nigger, and Pulaski as a Pollock. We've all been very patient, but I won't stand for you calling Miss Seagraves a whore. Now come down here and defend yourself."

Bickers surveyed the rangy black US Marshal, who stood well over six feet. "Don't you dare lay a hand on me. Remember who's paying you a bonus if you recover the missing cargo. If you so much as touch me you won't see a red penny! Right, Crow?"

Crow's face was laconic as he turned. "I think I speak for both myself and Mr. Reeves when I say that we can survive just fine without any of your Pinkerton money. I suggest you apologize to Miss Seagraves immediately, or I'll second Mr. Reeves' challenge—except I prefer knives over fists."

Bickers couldn't help but remember the foot-long Bowie knife that he had seen Crow use to skin hares for their dinner. "Fine," he blustered. "Since we're running out of daylight, I will apologize, but we'll take this up again later when we have more time."

"I've got plenty of time," said Reeves, flexing his hands into fists. "You're the one that's in the all-fired hurry."

A slender red-haired woman of seventeen years of age came into view, mounting the ridge on the seat of a buckboard wagon that contained her photographic equipment and chemicals. She wore an incongruous belt just above the bustle of her dress, to which was strapped a long-barreled .38 revolver.

Crow couldn't help but feel a disturbing sense of loss whenever he gazed upon her.

"Miss Seagraves," said Bickers as she came within earshot. "I do apologize for my impatience in awaiting your arrival."

"I wasn't aware you were impatient," said Miss Seagraves. "So no harm done."

Reeves cleared his throat.

"Ahem… I may have wrongfully impugned your character in my impatience," said Bickers. "For that I do apologize."

Miss Seagraves narrowed her eyes. "Really? Just what was it you may have said, Mr. Bickers?"

"It does not bear repeating," said Bickers. "I do hope you'll forgive me and take a few shots of the train wreck."

Seagraves pushed her bonnet up and her mouth fell open as she surveyed the devastation and death below. For the moment, any insult that Bickers had offered up out of her presence was lost from her mind. "I'll set up my camera and prepare a plate in the wagon."

"How long will it take?" asked Bickers. "Twilight is upon us and we need daylight to search the wreckage."

"It will take quite some time," said Seagraves. "Photography is not an instantaneous creation. I suggest you go down and begin your search for that missing strongbox. My wagon will be within your sight at all times, and I'm perfectly capable of taking care of myself. If I have need of any help I'll fire my hog leg into the air to get your attention."

"Fine," said Bickers. "Pulaski, get your flea-bitten nag over here and let's take a look for the express car. It's got to be somewhere in that jumble."

Pulaski lifted up the brim of his woolsey, revealing a young face with uneven patches of whiskers.

"Yes, sir." He kicked his nag toward the crest of the hill and followed Seagraves over the rise, then descended toward the awesome destruction below.

Reeves and Crow lingered for a moment while Miss Seagraves carefully set up the tripod for her camera.

"What do you think of her?" asked Reeves, his head nodding toward the red-headed photographer.

"She's a plucky girl," said Crow. "That and the red hair remind me of my wife."

Reeves raised an eyebrow. "You're married to an Irish woman?"

"Was," said Crow. "She's passed on now."

"I'm sorry," said Reeves.

"So am I."

Crow's face was impassive, but Reeves thought he saw a deep anguish lurking behind those brown eyes, so the black marshal changed the subject. "There's something here that doesn't feel right. It seems like we're being watched, but not quite the same..."

"I feel it," said Crow. "It's the presence of a dark force. It permeates everything around it."

"A dark force?" questioned Reeves. "Something besides the fact that we're standing over a bone orchard?"

"Pinkerton didn't hunt me down in the Dakotas and offer me a thousand dollars because they needed my tracking skills to follow a train track to a derailed train," said Crow. "Detective Bickers could have done that all on his lonesome."

"A thousand dollars?"

Crow nodded. "Makes you wonder, right?"

"Durn right it makes me wonder," rumbled Reeves. "It makes me wonder why I didn't demand more money."

"Probably figured you as an easy mark since this is your territory and you'd be investigating anyway," said Crow.

"Yeah, I probably would have come out here for free," grumbled Reeves. "So, tell me, Crow, what is it that makes you so durned special that they'd pay you a thousand cartwheels to come out here?"

"I have a reputation for being experienced in the supernatural," said Crow.

"Like ghosts and goblins and that sort of stuff?"

"Sometimes," said Crow.

Reeves wasn't quite sure what to make of this. "I saw some spook lights one night as I was riding the trail."

"Whatever you do, stay on the trail," advised Crow.

"Well, naturally," shrugged Reeves. "I'm not fool enough to go chasing phantom lights through the marshes."

Miss Seagraves returned from the back of her wagon carrying the bulky apparatus of the camera.

Crow gently slapped his horse with the reins. "That makes one of us using the brains God gifted us with."

When they reached the wreckage the stench of death rolled upon them. They found Bickers and Pulaski at the express car, which lay on its side, both ends crushed inward. Reeves didn't dismount, but instead continued through the wreckage toward the rail line. Bickers and Pulaski were attempting to pry open the side door with a crowbar, but were having not the slightest bit of success.

Pulaski took off his woolsey hat and rolled up his sleeves, already he was breaking a sweat. "I think it's locked from the inside."

"You really think so, you stupid clod? Now bend your back into it or I'll send you packing without your pay."

Crow clambered onto the wreckage of an adjacent car, then down the other side where he could not be seen by the others. "Who did you say the stupid clod was, Bickers?"

"What's it to you, savage?"

Crow didn't respond and Bickers began swearing at Pulaski, urging him to greater and greater efforts of futility, which did little more than bend the edges of the door panel, inextricably jammed shut as it was.

"Come on, Pollock. I'm not paying you to twiddle your thumbs!"

There was a heavy thump at Bickers feet and the Pinkerton detective looked down to see a strong box which Crow had thrown to the ground.

"Is that what you're looking for, Bickers?" There was a tear in Crow's buckskin jacket, where there had been none before.

Bickers' jaw dropped open. "Where did you get that?"

"Inside the express car."

"How did you get inside?"

"Does it matter?" asked Crow.

"The head office told me that you could do magic," said the Pinkerton, "but I didn't believe them until now."

Crow didn't bother to disillusion Bickers about his magical abilities and explain that a portion of the car's roof had been peeled away during the derailment. "What's inside the strongbox that you're so anxious to recover?"

"About forty thousand dollars worth of gold from the California fields."

"No more lies, Bickers," said Crow. "I just picked up that strongbox. It's not heavy enough to hold that much gold."

Bickers didn't deny that he had lied. "It's none of your business, redskin. Whatever is inside belongs to a client of Pinkerton's and we are being paid very well to retrieve it from the wreckage."

"Whatever is inside of that strongbox is evil," said Crow.

Bickers snorted. "Superstitious savage, an inanimate object can't be evil."

"Who said the object was inanimate?" Crow drew his eagle-butted Colt .45 revolver, which had been blessed by a prophet in the salty wastelands one night when the dead came to life.

"What are you doing?!" demanded Bickers.

"I'm blowing the lock off that strongbox so we can take a look inside and see just what we're dealing with."

"Don't!" Bickers moved to interpose himself between the box and Crow's gun. "You might damage the object."

Crow's finger eased off the trigger. "You almost got yourself shot, Pinkerton man. Is what's inside that box more valuable than your life?"

"It may well be," said Bickers. "I know for sure it's worth more than your useless hide! If you'll give me a little space I can get the strong box open without damaging the box or its contents."

Bickers withdrew a set of picks, and in less than two minutes he had the padlock of the strongbox unlocked.

Now Reeves returned from an exploration further along the rail line and observed as the Pinkerton agent finished picking the lock. "You're a man of hidden talents, Bickers."

"Pinkerton agents are recruited because of their useful skills," said Bickers. "I assume you discovered something, or you wouldn't be back here pestering me. What did you find?"

"A portion of the rail was removed. That's what caused the accident."

Bickers undid the hasp of the strong box. "How was the rail removed?"

"Someone roped a railroad tie to a tree, then felled it—yanked the tie and the rail out of place."

Bickers paused for a moment, ready to lift the lid of the strong box. "Who?"

"Judging by the broken axe haft stamped with the mark of the La Roux Brothers, I'd say that it was somebody who passed through New Orleans and took the occasion to purchase some tools. The tracks indicate boot styles that are more particular to the cobblers in Boston, though. These weren't Indians or country folk that did the deed."

Bickers hissed. "Alain LeFleur comes out of New Orleans."

Reeves climbed off his black stallion and tethered it to the wreckage of a freight car. "Who is this LeFleur?"

Crow responded without any change in his expression. "He's renowned in certain circles as a powerful necromancer."

"Is that some sort of magician?" asked Reeves.

"It's a branch of magic that deals specifically with the dead—drawing up their souls in séances, harnessing the powers of the deceased, and sometimes even raising the dead."

"Like Christ resurrecting Lazurus?" asked Pulaski.

Crow frowned. "Nothing like that. Usually these dead are bodies animated by Satanic spirits."

Bickers choked out a laugh. "Nothing but myths and tall tales. However, LeFleur keeps some very bad company and has been linked to a string of murders—been tried on two or three of them, but the jury always finds him innocent."

"So why would this Alain LaFleur derail the train?" asked Reeves.

"I didn't say he would," replied Bickers.

Reeves' face became hard as stone beneath his great flowing mustache. "Don't play games with me, Bickers. As soon as I mentioned New Orleans you immediately identified Alain LaFleur, and I want to know why."

Bickers' lips pressed together and anger glinted in his visage. He was used to putting others on the spot and didn't much like the tables being turned, especially by one he viewed as his inferior. "Because he offered my client a large sum for the item in this box, and when my client refused the offer, Lafleur became irate and made threats."

"Your story doesn't hold water," said Crow. "If LaFleur caused the train wreck why isn't he already long gone with that strong box? Tell me, just who is your client?"

"I can't divulge that," said Bickers. "I'm afraid that's confidential."

"Pinkerton didn't hire me to play nursemaid, Bickers. I'm here to provide expertise in supernatural matters. Now, give me a name!"

Bickers' visage twisted in outrage that any man, let alone an Indian, would dare talk to him with such impudence, but before he could retort, Bass Reeves interrupted. "Maybe LaFleur didn't get a chance to collect the strongbox."

A pair of wolves had crept back from the edge of the forest and they had hold of a corpse dressed in a black suit, which was feathered with a couple of arrows. Crow threw his carbine to his shoulder, sighted along the barrel, exhaled, and squeezed the trigger. One of the wolves lurched, took three steps and then swayed to the ground. The other wolf whimpered and disappeared among the wreckage.

Pulaski grinned. "Apparently the wolves didn't get the message the first time."

"They are unusually bold," said Reeves. "Hunger will do that, but these wolves look particularly well fed."

Crow started toward the black-clad corpse and the still writhing wolf that lay beside it. "There may be some other reason behind their boldness."

Reeves strode alongside of Crow. "You think it has something to do with the shaman Angry Wolf?"

Crow didn't immediately answer. Instead, he turned back toward the Pinkerton agent. "Bickers, don't open that chest until I get back."

"Maybe you're forgetting who's in charge here," replied Bickers.

"You don't fully comprehend what we may be dealing with. Now leave the chest shut until we return!"

As they drew nearer the body, the wounded wolf lurched to its feet and lunged toward Crow. Reeves slapped at the leather of his holster and fired his .45, putting a bullet through the wolf's skull before it could reach the Indian.

"Didn't you see that wolf coming at you?"

Crow's mind seemed to be in an entirely different world. "There's something wrong here and I'm not quite reckoning what it is."

"Durn right. We've got a derailed train, dead bodies, wolves, a mystery strongbox," he motioned toward the arrows protruding from the body that was clad all in black, from cravat and silken chemise to trousers and boots, "and we've got rogue Chickasaws. I recognize that arrow construction. I'd say we're between the bull and the barbed wire."

"It's none of that," said Crow. "Something's been making me uncomfortable since the beginning of our journey." He observed the body and rolled it over so that he could see the face. "Without a doubt, that's the necromancer Alain LaFleur. That scar on his cheek was caused by a summoning gone awry."

Behind a toppled car, which lay broken in the gouged earth, they saw two more bodies bristling with arrows. One was a woman with dishwater blonde hair. She wore a soiled dress and even in the repose of death her aquiline features were quite beautiful. A four-barreled Lancaster pepperbox pistol was still clutched in her hand and the disarray of her hemline revealed a knife that was strapped to her thigh.

"This is Pepperbox Sally," said Reeves. "She's wanted for seven murders—mostly male clients. There's a five hundred dollar bounty on her head."

"You think the Chickasaw will be wanting to collect?" asked Crow.

Reeves chuckled. "If they knew about it..."

"I recognize the other fellow," said Crow as he crouched over the body. "This is Spades Henderson. See that scar on his palm? I put a bullet through his hand in New Orleans one night, when he tried to ambush me in the mausoleums."

"What were you doing in the graveyard?"

Crow hesitated.

"Long story?"

"Not so long as it is painful." Crow rose to his feet, a breeze fluttered his long raven hair.

"You told me that Miss Seagraves reminded you of your wife. Could be why you're feeling out of sorts?"

Crow started as the pieces suddenly fit together for him. He glanced toward the brow of the hill and saw the tripod and camera, but there was no sign of Miss Seagraves. "That's it! Miss Seagraves is not who she seems to be. Her likeness to my wife, Abigail, was done on purpose to mask the fact that I was traveling with an old enemy."

"What old enemy is that?"

"The Aryan Society. I've been a hindrance to their plans before." Crow began to sprint back toward the strongbox. As he drew closer, he could see that Bickers had not heeded his warning. The strong box was open and Marvin Pulaski was standing over it, goggling at the bundles of cash within. It was not the cash, however, that Bickers was interested in. He held something in his hand, which he was unwrapping from the cloth around it. He threw back the covering folds and revealed a piece of polished jade set in the middle of a golden amulet, marked by archaic sigils of some alien language. This was the Eye of Ulutoth and now that it was fully revealed and pulled from the strong box, which was lined with verdigris tainted copper that tended to mute the evil emanations of the alien artifact, Crow could feel horror and despair washing over him—engulfing him like the waves of an ocean.

Crow had thought the Eye of Ulutoth permanently lost beneath the cold waters of Lake Bennett in the Alaskan wilderness, but here it was in the midst of a train wreck in Arkansas Territory.

"Put that back in the box!" bellowed Crow.

Bickers turned to him, with the slightest of smiles upon his face. "What's wrong, Crow? I'm merely examining the merchandise we recovered. I'm sure that our employer will be most pleased when we return this lump of jade and gold to her." He held it up and it caught the dying rays of the sun. "Despite it's value, it's quite a hideous thing, don't you think?"

Crow caught a glimpse of flowing red hair as a slender figure darted out from behind a wrecked boxcar and toward Bickers. The Indian reached for his Colt, but before he pulled the trigger Kelly Seagraves, or the woman who was masquerading as Kelly Seagraves, plunged the knife into Bickers' kidney. She withdrew the blade and bloody droplets spattered on the surface of the polished jade eye, where they sizzled and then were drunk in so that the emerald surface of the eye became veined with crimson.

Bickers staggered and Seagraves kicked him down, plunging her blood-wetted knife into this belly and pushing the amulet into the crimson and bile that welled up from the wound.

Now things changed quickly in a way that was baffling to the finite human mind. The image of Kelly Seagraves stripped away as if it were a thin veneer, revealing a woman with thin lips and wild hair the color of freshly turned New Mexico tilth. A variety of arcane amulets and charms hung around her slender neck and thin wrists. This was Carina Crawley, agent of Blavatsky's Aryan Society, a splinter faction of the Theosophic group who sought the dark powers of the occult.

Crawley turned her malevolent gaze upon the Indian. "Surprised to see me, Crow?"

"You've been right under my nose for the last four days," said Crow. "And it took me until just a moment ago to smell out the stench of your sorceries."

Crawley smiled, but there was no humor in her grin. "A nice touch, using the subtle likeness of your wife, don't you think, Crow? It was enough to throw you off your game for days."

Bickers groaned and heaved, but he was dying—his strength failing—and unable to escape Crawley's grasp.

Crawley twisted the knife and released a fresh gout of crimson. "Bickers' blood isn't exactly as pure as I would have it, but the blood of the truly innocent is difficult to find—except in children, and none seem to be available at the moment. Nonetheless, it will serve to draw in the powers from the dark dimensions from which the Eye of Ulutoth came."

Even as she spoke these words, dark shapes flitted across the landscape and somber clouds scudded across the sky, driven by unnatural winds. Pulaski drew back with a cry as a menacing black shape crossed his path.

Reeves forced himself forward through the buffeting winds, and he saw Crawley crouched over Bickers, hand upon the dagger which she had thrust into the Pinkerton Agent's belly. The US Marshal drew his pistol and fired twice, bullets that would have unerringly found her skull if not for the dark magics that protected her. The bullets burst into dust before they reached the sorceress, and the motes were cast away on the winds.

Crawley laughed. "I've spent years researching incantations that will protect my flesh against the bullets of even Crow's sanctified pistol. If I can find protections against the blessing of a prophet, do you think that a simple piece of lead can hurt me?"

Reeves snarled from beneath his impressive mustache as strange, unnameable shapes crawled across the landscape and shadowed terrors emerged from the cold bowels of the earth. "What in the blazes is going on here, Crow?"

"Blood feeds the amulet and gives it the power to draw forth malicious powers from other existences."

"So, that was what was in the strong box?"

Crow nodded. "I thought it was lost at the bottom of a lake in Alaska."

Crawley thrust the amulet deep into the wound and it drank up Bickers' blood voraciously. "Did you think the power of dowsing beyond my capabilities, Crow? I broke away the ice and dove naked into those frigid waters until finally I had my prize."

"So why put the Eye of Ulutoth on the train?"

"The ignorant gold hunters of Lake Bennet saw me coming out of the ice and thought I was a witch—hung me. I had to dig my way out of a frozen grave and make my way back to civilization where I could recoup my strength and hire an agent to recover the Eye of Ulutoth from the sheriff's vault. That went well enough. Unfortunately, the train was waylaid by Lafleur, who insisted on sticking his nose into my business." She turned her eyes upon Crow. "But you wouldn't know anything about sticking your nose into other people's business, would you Crow?"

Crow pulled back the hammer of his pistol. "You seem to be misremembering the facts."

Neither Reeves nor Crow was ready to give up, and together they emptied their pistols, but the results were the same—a fine powder of lead that was whipped away on the howling winds.

Reeves glanced at Crow and shrugged his broad shoulders. "It was worth a try."

Crow lurched toward Crawley, the winds and sinister shadows conspiring against him. Arcane words and sinister syllables memorized from forbidden texts dropped from Crawley's thin lips, and the dark shapes crawled into the wreckage of the train, which began to creak and groan, shifting shape and form.

Crow managed to push through the winds and for a moment he laid a hand upon Crawley's sleeve. He reached for his Bowie knife and was about to plunge it through her black, shriveled heart when a great metallic claw plucked him into the air, so that his Bowie knife merely cut away a lock of Crawley's hair.

Crow's carbine fell to the ground as he jerked, flailing into the sky. Crawley laughed maniacally as she saw the monstrous thing her magics had created.

Reeves gaped as a great, creaking fiend formed from the ruined jumble of the derailed train, pulled together in a haphazard shape that formed monstrous limbs which plowed the earth with ponderous step.

The shadow shapes of demons drawn from nether dimensions by the Eye of Ulutoth flitted through the gritty winds and took refuge inside the corporeal form of the fiendish conglomeration, giving it motion and horrifying life. At its heart was the smashed steam engine. Its furnace glowed with ruddy light and great gouts of steam blew through vents so that the beast seemed to breathe out smoke at every orifice.

It was in the grasp of this incomprehensible mixture of demon and machine that Crow found himself, and he struggled against the metallic claws that pinioned him ever tighter, threatening to rend him asunder if he could not break free.

Crawley widened the wound and her blade found Bickers' still-beating heart. She extinguished the last flickers of Bickers' life, and the Eye of Ulutoth greedily drank up every drop of the Pinkerton Agent's blood. As his blood ran dry, Crawley's eyes fixed upon Marvin Pulaski who, hoping to escape notice of the demonic fiend, huddled behind a great clot of earth, which had been thrown up by the steam devil as it gathered its form. Pulaski had tried to avoid catching the attention of the brown-haired witch as well, but as soon as their eyes met he found that he could not turn away. Even his instinctual self-preservation could not break the powerful spell which Crawley cast. She beckoned to him and Pulaski found that he could not resist the call of the deadly beauty. His limbs began to move of their own accord, and he rose, drawing nearer to the witch, who readied her blade for yet another victim.

Reeves reached for the rifle on his horse, but he found that the tether had been broken as the steam devil had formed, and the horse had bolted in terror. Then Reeves spied Crow's carbine on the ground where it had fallen when the steam devil had snatched Crow up. Reeves dove for it and aimed for the steam engine at the core of the beast, firing round after round into its glowing center. The bullets whined or ricocheted away, and though some of them penetrated into the furnace heart of the fiend, they seemed to have no effect whatsoever.

The vice of metal continued to tighten around Crow's body and he jammed his Bowie knife between the two pincers, buying him a few more moments of life. Through the haze of earth and twigs carried on the unnatural winds, and piercing the billowing steam, Crow could see Pulaski as he was inexorably drawn toward Crawley, who awaited him with the same blade she had used to kill Bickers. Even with his life hanging in the balance, threatened to be snuffed out once the Bowie gave way, Crow noticed that the blade was dry of blood. Every droplet had been sucked into the jade of the voracious amulet. It occurred to Crow that, if it was blood that was giving the power to draw in the dark forces from otherworldly dimensions, maybe if the amulet were deprived of additional blood, Crawley would no longer be able to animate the steam train with the devils from beyond. She was a powerful sorcerer, but this was beyond anything that Crow had ever seen her do.

"Bass!" shouted Crow. "Get the amulet!"

The winds whipped at Reeves as he levered an empty shell out his pistol's cylinder and shoved a fresh cartridge into its place. He adjusted his aim as the cyclone-like air currents tore at his arm. Over his head, the demonic conglomeration of train cars spouted steam, emitting a whistling moan as it brought up a great foot of iron with the intention of smashing it down atop the US Marshal. Reeves stood his ground and fired.

As intended, his bullet clipped the Eye of Ulutoth—and though few witches were known for their honesty, Crawley had inadvertently given Reeves the target he should aim for when she had announced that it was her flesh that was fortified against bullets. The Eye of Ulutoth spun from her grip and fell to the wind-ravaged earth.

Great clots of sod whipped past Reeves as he hurled himself to one side, and then the foot of the steam devil impacted into the earth. Surely, it would have crushed Reeves to a pulp if he had moved a fraction of a second later. The US Marshal found himself sprawled next to the foot which was formed from parts of a boxcar, and without hesitating, he climbed up a malformed ladder that still clung to the side, figuring that the devil would be unable to crush him beneath its foot if he was clinging to the top of it.

From this perch he could see Crawley scrambling across the earth and reaching out to regain the amulet, her hair whipping in the storm. Reeves didn't have time to load another round into his empty pistol, but he did have a five-shot Remington Elliot pistol hidden beneath his jacket. This was a petite .22 caliber gun that was short-barreled and easy to conceal, but it was designed for a smaller hand than Reeves', and he could barely thrust his index finger through the ring that served as the trigger. The other draw-back was the poor accuracy of the pistol, which was primarily intended for use at point blank range.

For this reason, it took Reeves three shots to find his range. The first two shots turned into powder against Crawley's shoulder and the third hit the amulet, so that it leaped forward, through the wind-blown sward, keeping out of Crawley's reach. The witch scuttled after the escaping Eye of Ulutoth, but with his last two remaining shots Reeves managed to strike the amulet in mid-hop and push it even further away.

The foot of the steam devil rose up and vibrated wildly, as if it were at-tempting to shake Reeves loose. The US Marshal clung to the bent ladder with all his strength and skill. He had ridden a few uncooperative horses in his day, so though his teeth jarred together, he managed to stay onboard the steam devil; but with his pistols empty there was no longer a way for him to keep the Eye of Ulutoth out of Crawley's hands.

Overhead, Crow managed to wriggle out of his buckskin jacket and from the pincer-like grip of the steam devil. Just as he slipped free, bal-ancing atop those jagged pincers, the tip of his Bowie knife broke off and the vibrating blade sprang from the spot where Crow had jammed it. The pincers lurched beneath Crow's feet and, as he fell, he plucked the broken blade out the air by its hilt. He slitted his eyes against the airborne grit as he plunged toward Carina Crawley.

The witch reached out and grabbed hold of the Eye of Ulutoth and drew the .38 pistol riding her hip. Then Crow struck her, driving the broken blade into her back, through her black heart, and out the front. She spasmodically jerked the trigger of the pistol, and it fired twice into the storm-whipped skies. Her blood gushed out of the wound and vomited from between her lips, drenching the eye of Ulutoth.

It sucked up the crimson fluids, and as soon as it had tasted of Crawley's tainted blood, the winds began to subside, for the Eye of Ulutoth gained power only from innocent blood, and where there was utter and wholly evil it could not feed. The steam devil creaked to a halt, the fiery light of the coal engine dying and the hideous shadow shapes fleeing their mechanical corpus for more hospitable dimensions.

Crawley blinked, her long lashes sweeping away tears of pain and frustration.

"You think you've won, Crow?" gasped Crawley. "I've made obscene pacts with unimagined devils—sold my body and soul. I'll not be so easily vanquished." With that her body stiffened, her eyes closed, and a last rattle of breath gurgled from her throat. Still, she clutched the Eye of Ulutoth in her hand, and Crow could feel the evil emanating from the blood-veined jade at its center.

With the demons fled, the steam devil came to a creaking halt in midstride, and then its unbalanced weight began to wobble. Reeves threw himself from the foot of the mechanical monstrosity and then the unholy conglomeration of engine and cars gave one last moaning whistle and toppled forward. The earth shook as it struck, and the cars burst apart from their cursed melding. Reeves pushed himself to his feet and straightened his hat. Pulaski was crouched in the grass, his eyes glazed and uncomprehending of the horrific things he had seen.

Reeves came up alongside of him and shook him by the shoulder. "Snap out of it, son. It's all over."

Pulaski's gaze regained some semblance of sanity, but there was still a wild look in his eye. "None of that could have happened. It couldn't have. I'm out of my head. I'm out of my head."

Reeves gave a rumbling chuckle. "Then I must be out of my head, too, Marvin."

"What was it and why did it happen?" shuddered Pulaski.

Reeves had witnessed many horrors, most of man's making. "Sometimes, for sanity's sake, it's best not to ask why. Just know that it is, and keep on moving."

Crow could not shake the Eye of Ulutoth from Crawley's death grip and so, with his tomahawk he hewed off her hand at the wrist—for he dared not touch a thing so evil as the Eye of Ulutoth, lest it infect him with its insidious poison. Reeves tried six bullets to destroy the eye, but the amulet remained unscratched and still clutched in the witch's severed hand.

When the medicine man, Angry Wolf, arrived, flanked by two great black wolves and six fiery young braves on painted horseback, Pulaski was attempting to smash the amulet with a sledge hammer drawn from the photographer's cart. He gave it six great strikes, but nary a scratch showed on the jade and nary a fleck of gold had flaked from the setting.

Angry Wolf took one look at the amulet and the pulped hand which would not relinquish its hold upon the evil object, and he shouted excited orders to his braves. They immediately retreated, riding over the brow of the hill, pausing only to rifle the unattended cart and steal the horses still harnessed to it.

Finally, they were urged on to haste by the frantic gesticulations of Angy Wolf.

Pulaski wiped the sweat from his brow. "That's the second time today I thought I was a dead man."

"They didn't much like the sight of that amulet," observed Reeves. "I may have to go after Angry Wolf later—if he continues to insist on causing trouble."

The final brave threw a flaming brand into the cart and the photography chemicals went up in a blaze that engulfed the canvas covering and threw up a pall of black smoke.

Crow watched the leaping flames. "I'm not a gambling man, but I would bet that Angry Wolf isn't going to reform his ways anytime soon."

"There's something that I don't understand," said Marvin. "I was soft on Kelly when she was but fourteen and me fifteen. Was she really a witch the whole time?"

Crow took out an empty burlap bag and opened up the mouth. "You knew Kelly Seagraves when you were younger?"

"Her father and her moved into town six years ago and she took over his business when he died of the consumption."

Crow scooped up the mangled hand and Eye of Ulutoth and then knotted the bag. "Crawley must have chosen her because of her unfortunate likeness to my deceased wife. There's a small chance that Miss Seagraves is still alive, tied up in her home."

Reeves hollered for his horse and it obediently came out of the woods at the sound of his master's voice. "We best ride fast so she doesn't starve to death while we're on the trail."

Crow tossed the bag into the strongbox, where the copper lining would reduce the emanations of evil, and slammed the lid shut. "I agree, but I don't want you to get your hopes up. Crawley had no qualms about shedding innocent blood." He locked the box. "I'll catch up with you."

Reeves mounted his black horse. "Where are you going to be, Crow?"

"Right here. A witch's bones—especially a witch like Crawley—should be burnt in order to ensure that she doesn't come back."

Pulaski crawled into his saddle. "What about Bickers?"

"I'll bury him," said Crow. "He wasn't a pleasant man, but I figure he deserves to be planted in the earth."

"And the Eye of Ulutoth?" asked Reeves. "How will you dispose of that?"

"Apparently the icy depths of an Alaskan lake is not enough," pondered Crow. "How deep does the ocean go?"

The Eye Of Ulutoth

Chapter 1: Shootout in Puntarenas

Ox carts of sun-dried coffee beans were still arriving from the Costa Rican highlands when Lone Crow, searching among the sprawl of weathered masts and creaking ships moored along the uneven docks and quays, found the wide-waisted steamship. The crewmen viewed the Indian with suspicion, but they were too busy helping the longshoremen load crates of coffee beans, to harass the newcomer who was dressed in the garb of an American cowboy. The .45 eagle-butted Peacemaker riding on his hip might have also been a deterrent.

A western wind was picking up, blowing thick clouds over the Pacific Ocean and toward the port of Puntarenas where the barge Amente el Diablo was docked. The scent of tar was strong in Crow's nostrils, mingling with the salty tang of the sea, as he mounted the gangplank. The waves became capped with white and Crow found Captain Gutteriez swearing up a Spanish blue-streak at the inauspicious weather.

"Captain Gutteriez?" inquired Crow.

The Captain, a squat man with a bristling beard, and the scar from a gaffing hook over his left brow, broke off from profaning the names of a long string of saints, and peered curiously at the strange man who had accosted him. "What do you want?"

"I understand that you're taking a load of beans north to San Francisco?"

"What's it to you?" growled the Captain.

The Indian's face showed little reaction to the captain's hostility. "I'd like to purchase passage."

"And who are you?" grunted Captain Gutteriez, somewhat mollified that this might mean a few added coins in his pocket.

"I'm called Lone Crow."

Captain Gutteriez spotted the pistol now. "Can you use that thing?"

"So I'm told," replied Crow.

"If the gunmen I hired don't show up before we set sail you can save your dinero and earn your passage. Sometimes we have trouble with piratas coming out from the coast and attacking the barge. The Amente el Diablo is not very swift, and it helps to have a few pistoleros aboard to discourage the piratas."

"I understand there are some very deep ocean trenches not far from the coast," said Crow.

"Too deep to measure with a weighted sounding line," said Captain Gutteriez. "Some say there's a trench in the Pacific that goes miles deep, but I don't see how they could know. What's it to you?"

"I would like to dispose of something," said Crow.

The Captain scowled. "As long as it's not a body, I don't care and I don't want to know. Talk to my first mate, Nemesio, he'll show you your quarters. It's not much more than a broom closet."

"It will be sufficient," said Crow.

The boom of gunshots and the clip of horses' hooves on cobblestone streets brought their attention to the quays and the low-lying thatched huts that formed the town of Puntarenas. Then a knot of riders appeared, chasing a lone horseman, or so it seemed to be at first glance, but though the foremost rider was wearing a straw-brimmed hat, poncho, and denim trousers, to Crow's keen eyes the form of the rider was decidedly feminine.

The Captain observed the horsemen that were trailing behind. "I do believe that those are my pistoleros. You may have to pay your passage after all."

The rider on the lead horse plucked a pistol out of her belt and, without looking, fired over her shoulder, emptying the six shooter with wild abandon. One of the bullets took a pistolero in the center of his sternum, knocking him clean off his horse.

"I do believe that there's a job opening," said Crow. "And I do believe I recognize that style of shooting."

"He's an amazing shot—to kill a man backward over his head while riding a horse."

"He is a she," said Crow, and he didn't bother to point out that it had clearly been a lucky shot.

The Captain was incredulous. "A woman can shoot a gun like that?"

"She's also one of the fastest draws that I've ever seen," said Crow.

"Really." The Captain stroked his beard as if in deep contemplation.

"I'll get my rucksack," said Crow, and he started down the gangplank, reached the hitching post where he had tied his horse. He unscabbarded a Belgian Tersen percussion rifle. He threw it to his shoulder, and sighted. It was a difficult shot, because the lead rider was in the way, and the chasing pistoleros were bouncing up and down on their galloping horses, so that for a moment Crow had a line of sight on them and the next moment he did not. The pistoleros were blazing away at the lead rider, but from their unsteady perches had not been able to connect. Crow went for the easier target, and shot the horse from beneath the lead pistolero, and the other horses went down in a tangle of stirrup, flesh, and flailing hooves as they stumbled over the first. Two of the pistoleros at the rear, managed to rein their horses to a stop, and Crow cleared the chamber and pushed in another cartridge. He sent a shot whizzing by the ear of one of the still-mounted pistoleros, and the pair of them decided to scatter for less dangerous streets.

Crow reloaded the single shot rifle as the lead rider galloped past him on the quay, giving him a sidelong glance. "Gracias, senor!"

"De nada," said Crow.

The rider sent her horse galloping up the gangplank. "Time to set sail, Captain! Right this minute! Ahora mismo!"

Captain Gutteriez clearly did not like to be told what to do, especially by a woman, and he happened to have witnessed this wild pistolera empty her guns, so he supposed she was defenseless. "Throw her off my ship!"

Immediately five of the Captain's marinero crewmen leaped forward and grasped the woman by the arms and legs and began to carry her toward the edge of the ship. She writhed and struggled, but she was outnumbered and she was about to be heaved over the side, when Crow stepped into their way and pulled off the pistolera's sombrero. The wild blonde hair that had been tucked beneath spilled out in curly torrents, and some of the marineros gave way, loosing the limbs of the pistolera, because they had not realized they had been restraining a woman.

"Senorita pistolera!" cried one of them. "It is her!"

"I don't care who it is," said Gutteriez. "No one rides their horse onto my ship and demands I set sail, whether I was ready to set sail or not!"

Chapter 2: The Eye in the Chest

"Captain," said Crow. "I do apologize for the temerity of my partner. If you allow her to earn her passage, I can't promise she'll be on her best behavior, but she'll be an invaluable gun to have on board, should we run into trouble."

"Trouble!" cried Captain Gutteriez. "She is trouble! Why would I want to invite trouble aboard my ship!"

Senorita Pistolera reached into her pouch and counted out some silver coins. "Here's ten pieces of silver. When we reach San Francisco, I'll pay you another ten—and should we run into any bad hombres I'll lend a hand."

This seemed to satisfy the Captain. "Fine," he grumbled, "but if you cause any trouble, I'll have you pitched overboard for the sharks!"

"Understood, Captain," replied Senorita Pistolera.

The marineros backed off now, for apparently the woman gunfighter had made some reputation for herself while in Costa Rica. As soon as they went back to their duties, throwing off the mooring lines, the woman launched herself into the arms of the Indian and planted a big kiss on his lips. "Crow! With all the people shooting at me, I didn't recognize you at first. Are you a sight for sore eyes! What brings you to Costa Rica?"

Crow seemed surprised by the sudden kiss, but he didn't object to this show of affection. "Six-Gun Susannah Johnson, it seems that our paths are destined to cross over and over again."

"Until we get it right," said Susannah. "I knew you couldn't stay away for long!"

Crow licked his lips, tasting the residue of alcohol. "You've been drinking. And it seems you've earned a new nickname for yourself here in Costa Rica, Senorita Pistolera."

"Six-Gun doesn't roll off the tongue so well in Spanish, and I had just a nip of tequila, to be sociable while I played a few hands of poker."

"And you've been gambling," added Crow. "It seems to me that this was why we parted ways in the first place."

"What's the harm of one drink and a friendly game of poker?" said Senorita Pistolera.

"You tell me," said Crow. "How did you come to have a pack of angry pistoleros chasing you?"

Susannah Johnson waved her hand in a dismissive gesture. "Ah, they were just sore that they were losing their dinero to a gringo woman. They decided they wanted their money back, and since I won it fair and square, I wasn't going to let no cheating jugadoro take what was rightfully mine!"

Crow nodded. "Has it ever occurred to you that you could avoid all this trouble if you cut a wide swath away from taverns and cards?"

"Only when you tell me so, Crow!"

"So what brings you to Costa Rica, Susannah?"

She cast a sidelong glance at the Indian and bit at her upper lip in a fetching sort of way. "I might ask you the same thing."

"You might," agreed Crow, "but I asked first."

Steam and coal smoke billowed from the stacks of the barge as it moved out of the bay. Some of the disgruntled pistoleros managed to extricate themselves from their fallen horses and began firing a barrage of lead at the retreating Amente el Diablo. One round managed to clip the rail next to Susannah and she shook her fist toward the diminishing quay. "Watch where you're shooting, hombre, and you might actually hit something."

"You're giving shooting advice, now?" asked Crow, for though Susannah was actually one of the fastest draws he had ever seen, she wasn't very accurate—and this was fortunate for him, because the first time they had met she had tried to kill him.

"I'm not so bad a shot now, Crow. All that time you spent showing me how to aim paid off in spades, and occasionally I'll get in a lucky shot, too—like that pistolero I took off his horse, while firing over my shoulder."

"Don't tell the captain it was a lucky hit," said Crow. "He was mighty impressed. That shot might have been the only reason he relented and let you stay aboard the ship."

Susannah smiled. "Actually, it was me thinking about you that brought me to Costa Rica. I remember sitting around the fire roasting rabbit and you telling me about Costa Rica, the warm breezes, and how the fruit would fall off the tree."

"And?"

"And Costa Rica is everything you said, but without you here to share it with me, I found myself at loose ends and got myself into trouble."

The shots of the pistoleros were falling short now, flecking the storm-tossed waves.

"Trouble seems to have a way of finding you," observed Crow. "Or is it that you have a way of finding trouble?"

"A little of both," admitted Susannah. "Perhaps if I gave up drinking and gambling?"

"That's what I keep saying," said Crow.

"You know the other reason I hopped a steamer to Costa Rica?" asked Susannah.

Crow nodded slightly. "Yes."

Susannah didn't seem to acknowledge this admission and continued on as if the Indian had told her he didn't have the slightest of ideas. "It was a sheriff in San Francisco. He couldn't keep his hands off me and I told him I'd shoot his fingers off if he touched me again. Apparently, he took that as a challenge, and so I shot off his little finger."

"You have improved your shooting," commented Crow as he watched the shrinking shoreline, and the wind-bent palms along the frothing shore. The steamer rocked and heaved as it labored over and through the waves.

"The sheriff took it personal and rounded up a posse and came after me. I decided it would be a good time to hightail it for Costa Rica." Susannah sighed. "I suppose the sheriff will be waiting for me when we sail into San Francisco."

"No, he won't," said Crow.

Susannah furrowed her brow. "How do you mean?"

"Sheriff Tarrant is dead."

"And his posse?"

"A bunch of deputized cutthroats and murderers, most of them former convicts from Sydney Town," said Crow. "They're dead, too."

"What happened to them?"

Crow shouldered his rifle and then his rucksack. "When I came into San Francisco, I heard that he'd tried to take liberties with you and shared a few words with him."

"Just words?"

"Then I shared a few bullets with him… and his posse," concluded Crow.

"All by yourself?"

"You think I'm crazy?" said Crow. "There were twelve of them."

"So you put together a posse of your own?"

Crow headed toward his quarters, and let out a short laugh. "Nah. You think anyone's going to join a posse that an Indian's putting together? I had Rockwell pitch in and give me a hand."

"Porter Rockwell?"

"He's handy in a gunfight and we brothers stick together." Crow opened up the door to his narrow berth. It contained a double bunk, but it was scarcely more than the closet that Captain Gutteriez had described. Crow laid out his rifle on the top bunk, next to his rucksack, because there certainly wasn't any space to put them on the floor. "You better talk to the captain and find out where he can put you up."

"Still protecting my virtue, eh Crow? Because I've proven I can protect my virtue, just fine."

"Best for me not to have such temptation in so close a proximity," replied the Indian.

Susannah grinned. "Why, Mr. Crow, I do believe that you're flattering me!"

"No flattery necessary," said Crow. "You're at least a five horse woman."

Captain Gutteriez found an equally diminutive compartment for Susannah on the opposite side of the steamer and managed to find a spot for her horse in the hold, between secured crates of coffee beans. He handed Susannah a shovel. "I'm not asking my marineros to clean up after your horse. You clean up after her, or I'll have el chef make a stew of her for dinner."

Susannah narrowed her right eye and turned down the same corner of her mouth as she took the shovel. "Not Molly, he won't. I can take care of my own horse. I've shoveled plenty of manure in my time."

"The next port we stop at is in Honduras. You'll need to go ashore and buy some feed. I'm not paying to feed you and the horse."

Beard bristling, the captain departed the hold and left Susannah alone with a couple of the crewmen who were checking over the cargo and making sure that everything was secure. Already, the waters were choppy and it wouldn't do to have loose barrels and crates of beans running rampant when they hit rough seas. Susannah removed the saddlebags from her horse and leisurely brushed Molly down until her coat was smooth and the mane untangled. Here, Susannah's wild demeanor softened and she seemed at peace.

She heard Crow's voice behind her. "You always were good with horses."

"Her name is Molly. Were you spying on me, Crow?"

"Just coming down to tell you that grub will be on in a few minutes."

"I've been thinking, Crow."

Crow scratched the horse's nose and presented him with an oblong water apple from a bag he had brought aboard. "And?"

She detached one of her saddlebags and handed it to Crow. "Get rid of these for me. I'm done with them."

Crow set the saddlebag on a crate and untied the leather laces. He pushed back the leather flap and saw a half dozen bottles of Costa Rican brewed guaro that were packed with straw. "You sure about this?"

"Throw 'em overboard," said Susannah. "They aren't doing me any good."

Crow closed up the bag.

"You know the real reason I came to Costa Rica, Crow?"

Crow regarded her evenly, with his dark brown eyes. "What was that?"

"I was looking for you."

The ship rocked beneath Crow's feet. "You thought I was in Costa Rica?"

Susannah's long lashes fluttered behind a screen of stray, straw-colored locks. "I ran into Jake Higgins and he told me you were already headed here."

"You just ran into him?"

"I went looking for him," corrected Susannah."

"I told Higgins I was planning on going to Costa Rica, but I had a few things to take care of first."

"Like Tarrant and his posse?"

"That was just one of the things," said Crow. "Apparently, you beat me here. What else did Higgins tell you?"

"He said that you were looking for something… and trying to get rid of something, but he was pretty vague and I couldn't pry much else out of him. Not that I had much time to try. His wife didn't much approve of me, and saw that my welcome was short-lived."

Crow smiled faintly. "Henny can be a bit abrupt. She tolerates me for only short periods of time, and then lets it be known that my welcome is worn out."

"She approves even less of women gunfighters than Indian gunfighters. My welcome was so short-lived that it died before birth." Six-Gun Susannah Johnson paused. "So, did you find what you were looking for, Crow?"

Crow took off his hat, revealing the glossy black hair beneath. "Yes, but it wasn't all that it was rumored to be."

Jealousy sparked in Susannah's eyes. "What did she look like?"

Crow played along. "Short, sturdy... with a hammer head that was forged from the metal of a fallen asteroid. It was rumored to be able to destroy artifacts of evil with just one blow, but when I struck the Eye of Ulutoth the hammer head shattered into a thousand shards. I thought that I could destroy it, but perhaps the best that I can do is lose it before it tastes human blood again."

"What is this Eye of Ulutoth?"

"Something evil I discovered in Alaska. I thought I'd seen the last of it, but it showed up again in the Oklahoma Territories, and I needed to figure out a way to dispose of it."

"So you still have this Eye of Ulutoth?"

Crow grabbed up Susannah's saddlebag of guaro and replaced his hat. "It's in my cabin."

"Is it safe to leave it alone?"

"Probably not." Crow turned to leave. "But I can't stand to be near it. The copper lining of the box that I keep it in reduces its evil emanations, but doesn't completely block them. The longer I am in the presence of the Eye of Ulutoth the deeper I fall into darkness and despair. I can't do it much longer."

"What can the Eye of Ulutoth do?" asked Susannah.

"It can summon dark entities from otherworldly dimensions," said Crow.

Susannah appeared dubious. "I've seen some strange things with you, Crow. I won't deny that, but perhaps the rumors of what this Eye of Ulutoth can do are just rumors, like the rumors about this hammer that was supposed to be able to destroy anything."

"They're not rumors," said Crow. "I've seen the Eye of Ulutoth work, and it's nearly destroyed me. Its mere presence has an evil influence upon men, and if it drinks of human blood it brings forth shadow creatures from dark dimensions that we don't know."

"Is it like a real eye?" asked Susannah.

"It's a jade amulet," Crow started up the stairs to the deck.

Susannah patted Molly goodbye and followed the Indian. "So, what are you going to do with it?"

"Throw it in the Pacific Trench, and perhaps, miles deep in the ocean, it won't be able to harm anyone again."

"Show the Eye to me," urged Susannah.

Crow reached the top of the step, and fat rain drops splattered against the brim of his hat. The storm was beginning to take hold. "It's too dangerous to take it out of the box. You'll be fully exposed to its power."

"I can take it." Susannah replaced her sombrero and followed Crow onto the deck.

"And I'll be exposed to its full power," Crow reminded her. "I've been in it presence for many months now. After all this time, my strength has been weakened, and I might not be able to fight its influence."

"Influence? What does it want you to do, Crow?"

"It wants me to slit my own throat, so it can drink my blood."

"Piratas!" came the cries of a marinero from the deck. "The Captain wants you on deck immediately!"

Chapter 3: The Doomed Thief

The full force of the gale was upon the steamer, and the wind gusted black coal smoke and steam down to the decks of the Amente el Diablo, into the eyes of Crow, Six-Gun Susannah Johnson, and the marineros that were battening down the hatches. Blinking away the sting of smoke from his eyes, Crow peered into the stormy horizon, and on the frothing white waves, he saw a two-masted schooner emerge from behind a nearby island. Shifting its sails, they bellied full of wind, and the schooner cut a direct path toward the struggling steamer. From the main mast a flag bearing the mark of a skull whipped in the wind.

Susannah saw the ship, too. "It looks as though we're about to earn our passage to San Francisco."

Amidst the wind-whipped spume, Crow could see armed figures crowding the deck of the pirate schooner. "I'll head to my cabin and get my rifle.

They still had a few minutes before the pirate ship bridged the gap between it and the steamer, so Susannah followed Crow to his cabin. "You don't happen to have a second rifle lying around, do you? All I've got are pistols."

Crow adjusted his stance as the ship heaved and threaded the narrow walk toward his cabin. "How many pistols do you have?"

"Three," responded Susannah. She lifted up her tunic to reveal a pistol tucked into the front of her pants, in addition to the pistol on each hip.

"Good girl," said Crow. "Maybe we can discourage the pirates from boarding."

Crow reached his cabin and noticed that the door was not completely latched. He was quite sure that he had locked it before seeking out Susannah in the hold.

"Get a pistol ready," said Crow in a low voice. "I think that I may have a visitor."

"So soon?" asked Susannah, who didn't bother to unholster her pistol because, after all, she was one of the fastest draws in the West, and in the world for that matter, and could have her pistol ready in a split second. "I didn't think that we'd been here long enough to have any callers."

Crow responded by throwing open the door. Inside, they could see the back of one of Captain Gutteriez's marineros hunched over a small chest. Apparently, he had prised it open, for a pry bar lay on the floor of the narrow cabin next to him. The marinero was reaching in to seize the contents of the box, but when he heard Crow open the door he snatched up the pry bar and whirled. In one hand he held the Eye of Ulutoth, made from a curious jade of the darkest green, and set in a peculiar gold, marked with alien symbols. No longer contained in the copper box, Crow could feel the unleashed evil emanating from the Eye, and the radiations of its abject darkness were so palpable that they beat against him, forcing him to take a step backward.

Still, Crow knew that this was by no means the worst that the Eye of Ulutoth was capable of. If it tasted of blood, dark forces from the nether-worlds were unbound and released upon the earth. Innocent blood had the most powerful effect upon the Eye, but blood from anyone, except the most entirely irreedemable would work. For this reason, when the mari-nero lurched toward him with pry bar in hand, Crow hesitated. Six-Gun Susannah Johnson was not, however, known for her hesitation, and though she could feel the hatred and enmity radiating from the daemoniac amulet she did not understand its malevolent properties. She was lightning on her draw, and as she had told Crow earlier, she had indeed improved her aim. In the close quarters of the cabin she could not miss, and she put three bullets, the sound of their firing nearly lost in the howl of storm wind, into the marinero's chest before he could reach Crow with the downward swing of the pry bar, which clattered against the door frame.

The marinero fell face forward upon the floor, the Eye of Ulutoth be-neath him. Immediately, Crow crouched down and tried to heave the dead marinero off of the Eye of Ulutoth, but the room was so narrow that there was nowhere to roll the body.

Johnson leaned next to the door frame and blew the black powder smoke from the barrel of her gun. "What are you doing?"

"The Eye!" answered Crow. "It feeds upon blood!"

Johnson spun her six-shooter back into its holster and then thrust her hand beneath the marinero that Crow was lifting, as if to pluck out the Eye of Ulutoth. Already, blood was pooling beneath the dead Costa Rican.

"No!" cried Crow. "Don't touch the Eye. It has the power to take over your actions."

Johnson's lips turned in a scowl, but nevertheless she pulled her hand back. "You think that I'm so weak-spirited that one touch of some piece of costume jewelry is going to turn me into a raving lunatic?"

"Perhaps not." Crow lifted the body and dragged it out onto the deck of the ship, where he let it fall. "But I can certainly feel the influence of the Eye, and it wasn't even necessary for me to touch it."

Johnson gestured toward the dead marinero. "How did the sailor even know that you had it?"

Crow frowned when he saw the Eye of Ulutoth sitting in a puddle of the marinero's blood. The jade pulsed an aura that seemed to gobble up the surrounding light, even as it voraciously sucked in the blood, devouring every droplet so that the boards of the cabin's floor were dry—not even stained by the blood. "Even in its copper-lined box the Eye had the power to call out to him. Probably, he was a thief by habit, and so the Eye had only to exert a little of its influence."

Johnson had ridden strange trails and seen many wondrous things before she had come into Crow's company and so when she saw the mystifying sight of the amulet absorbing the blood of the marinero she had shot, she was not awestruck or dumbfounded. Instead, she pursed her lips and furrowed her brow. "Maybe you were overly worried, Crow. The amulet is an evil thing, for sure, but the taste of blood doesn't seem to have wrought any dire events."

Crow was perplexed, for the last time he had seen the Eye of Ulutoth drink blood, he had witnessed loathsome shadows and dire spectres as they were unleashed upon the earth. "I hope you're right."

"Still," conceded Johnson, "that amulet is a disgusting thing. I can feel the evil rolling off of it. You say that you tried this mystical hammer on it and it broke the hammer?"

"Yes," said Crow.

"Holy water?"

"I've no faith in it," said Crow.

"How about that consecrated oil I've seen you use to cast out devils and heal the sick ?"

Crow paused, for he had not considered the use of the holy oil upon an inanimate object. He withdrew a small metal vial from a pouch on his belt and unstoppered it. He bent over the eye to administer the oil and he felt utter desolation and bleak despair sweep over him, as the Eye of Ulutoth turned the focus of its unmitigated power against him. Under the overbearing sway of such influence Crow felt the desire to end his life, to hurl himself into the jaws of the raging sea and drown in its fathomless depths. But calling upon the Lord, he felt the fog of doom lift from him, enough that he was able to pour out the contents of the vial upon the dark jade of the Eye of Ulutoth.

The consecrated oil sizzled upon the surface of the amulet, pitting the jade and the tentacle-like filaments that stretched out from the setting, and in his head Crow heard the Eye of Ulutoth voice a shrill, mind-blasting scream, the power of which threw him out the door of the cabin, past Six-Gun Susannah Johnson's denim-clad thighs. He came to an abrupt stop against the rail of the Amente el Diablo.

For a moment Crow blacked out and when his consciousness returned, the beautiful Six-Gun Susannah Johnson was leaning over him, the locks of her wild blonde hair tickling his face.

"Crow, speak to me!"

"Am I in heaven?" muttered Crow.

"No," said Johnson. "Because it's doubtful that I'd be there. Too much drinking, gambling, and shooting."

Crow's senses were blunted by the outburst from the Eye of Ulutoth and the piercing scream still rang inside of his head. He continued to feel the evil influence of the Eye, and so he staggered to his feet, using the rail to pull himself to a standing position. In his hand he still clutched the vial, so he stoppered it to preserve the last few precious drops of consecrated oil within. Like acid, the holy oil continued to work upon the jade face of the Eye of Ulutoth, eating away at the evil concentrated within. Crow could hear the pain and fear of the Eye as it called out to the sinister shadow entities that dwelt in the planes and worlds adjacent to the one that he and

Six-Gun Susannah Johnson knew.

"Ulutoth ascends," spoke a voice in an alien tongue. "Ulutoth ascends."

Chapter 4: Riders of the Storm

Crow stepped over the Eye of Ulutoth and retrieved the copper-lined chest. He used this to scoop up the amulet, so that his flesh never came into contact with the evil artifact. The hasp and lock were broken now and so he withdrew his Bowie knife and cut a length of rope which he used to encircle the chest three times and then he cinched it tight with a knot. The sinister and alien voices inside his head muted, and Crow took the chest to the rail of the Amente el Diablo.

At the rail, he paused for a moment, poised to hurl the chest, and the Eye of Ulutoth which it contained, into the depths of the ocean and the miles deep Pacific Trench which furrowed the floor of the sea. The voice continued in his head, both alien and loathsome. "Ulutoth ascends. Ulutoth ascends." This voice was not originating from the Eye of Ulutoth, but rather it was serving as some sort of conduit for the voice. Even now, the Eye of Ulutoth exerted all its efforts upon Crow, restraining his mind and limbs so that his fingers were fixed tightly around the box—so tightly that he could not relinquish his grip upon its battered panels.

Johnson stood a half step behind him, her brow creased with concern. "What's wrong, Crow? Just throw it in!"

Crow was so much under the influence of the Eye that he could scarcely form the answering words. "I… I can't. I… can't move."

Johnson blinked once, and then she stepped forward and shoved the box from Crow's grip. It struck the rail and cartwheeled into the spume-capped waves, then sank beneath. "There. That wasn't so hard."

"Thank you," said Crow. He watched the waves for long moments just to make sure that the chest was gone, and wasn't by some mystical means going to rise again to the surface. Out of the presence of the Eye, which had been serving as a mystical conduit, the overwhelming voice that had resounded within his mind was reduced to a distant whisper. "All its energies were focused on me, leaving you free to act."

"Easy as pie," said Johnson. "Now we can concentrate on our other problem."

Crow followed her gaze across the stormy ocean and saw the two-masted pirate schooner was closing the gap between them. The deck was crowded by men of many nations, who had put aside their differences in the name of plunder, but mostly they were Costa Rican sailors who had grown discontent with their lot in life and decided that pirating offered a quicker, easier way to support themselves, as well as their drinking and carousing habits. They were a rowdy and dissolute lot, prone to temper and fits of violence, and they clamored at the rail of their ship, eager for a chance to let blood and for the first pick of the loot. A few of them began firing at the Amente el Diablo, but the range was too great for their pistols, and the bullets fell into the sea, far short of their target.

Though he was exhausted from his months-long battle of wills with the Eye of Ulutoth, Crow forced himself to the rail, unlimbered his Belgian Tersen rifle and laid it on the rail to steady his aim. The problem with using the rail was that it rolled along with the ship, so Crow had to time the rise and the fall of the Amente el Diablo. Meanwhile, the pirate craft was lurching on waves of its own, so it made for very difficult shooting—not to mention the fact that they were at the extreme range of the Belgian rifle. Crow's first shot went high and sent a haze of splinters flying from the mast.

Instead of frightening the rum-soused crew of the pirate ship, the fact that Crow had missed his shot seemed to encourage them to wild revelry, for they hooted, hollered and jeered, shaking their fists at the Amente el Diablo while reeling off creative and far-fetched curses.

Johnson observed the reaction of the pirate crew, her wild blonde hair blowing in long tangles behind her. "Is it time for a show of force?"

Crow cleared the empty shell and chambered another. "Not yet. Our show of force will be more effective if we actually do damage. If you start firing now we'll just be wasting ammunition and shooting into the sea. Let the pirates do that."

As if to illustrate, the pirate crew let off a volley of gunfire that succeeded in pocking the waves with lead, but still came a good hundred yards short of reaching the Amente el Diablo and its crew. Crow took careful aim at a pirate with an eye patch. He rode out the waves as the pirate schooner drew closer and closer, then, between heartbeats, he squeezed the trigger of his rifle. It was sheer luck that the bullet punched through the eye patch and buried itself in the brain of the pirate, for Crow had been aiming for the chest. Still, as the pirate pitched backward, the other pirates ceased reloading their firearms and gave way, crying out in awe and fear when they saw where the bullet had struck.

Crow was chambering a new cartridge when he saw the tumult aboard the pirate ship. He cast a sidelong glance at his wild-haired partner. "Now might be the time to inspire a little fear, Susannah. Aim high, they're still at extreme pistol range."

Six-Gun Susannah Johnson went for the guns riding the swell of her hips. In the blink of an eye she emptied them into the air. The guns spun back into their holsters, and before another second passed she retrieved her third pistol from the waist of her trousers, and put six more bullets into the air. None of these shots were carefully aimed, but in a matter of a few seconds she, alone, had put eighteen bullets into the air, and they came down in a hailstorm upon the deck of the pirate schooner, some ricocheting from iron cleats, other bullets cutting through the rigging, and others splintering the decking. In this onslaught, two pirates fell: one from a ricocheting bullet that caught him between the ribs, and another from a bullet that dropped through his forehead.

One saw-toothed pirate leaped to the bowsprit of the schooner as it cut through the waves, casting up spray. He raised a cutlass, pointed it at the Amente el Diablo and shouted to the crew. "Board her and cut the throats of every man, woman, and child!"

Crow put a bullet through that pirate's chest and he fell, his foot tangling in the rigging, so that he dangled from the same bowsprit he had stood upon moments before.

Johnson reloaded her pistols from the bandolier that she wore over her shoulder. "Nice shooting, Crow."

Crow pulled back the bolt of his Tersen rifle and sent a hot piece of brass spinning across the deck. "Not so bad, yourself, Susannah."

Johnson smiled. "Why, I do believe that was a compliment—and this from the man who once told me that I would never be able to hit the broad side of a barn!"

"I was frustrated," admitted Crow. "It seemed as though you were never going to get the hang of it."

Unfortunately, the pirate crew was lean and hungry and they were not so easily deterred by the casualties of four of their men. A hollow-cheeked pirate with a sombrero tied to his head cried out as the schooner neared the Amente el Diablo. "More loot for the rest of us!"

"Oh," said Susannah. "I see how it's going to be."

Captain Gutteriez was at the helm, his beard flecked with spume as he wrestled with the wheel of his ship. He yelled back to the furnace room for more steam, but the marineros shoveling the coal were already working as fast as they could, stripped to the waist and ruddy light glistening off their sweat-sheened torsos. It was a futile effort trying to keep the lumbering steamship ahead of the swift schooner and despite Gutteriez's expert captainship there was nothing he could do except buy a few more moments. Once he realized that the race had been lost, he cried out to his marineros to arm themselves. They did this with great alacrity, snatching up gaffing hooks, harpoons and axes, but the only firearms among them belonged to the captain and the first mate, and at least half the pirates seemed to have a pistol of some sort, even if it was merely a muzzle-loaded flintlock that used ball and powder instead of a cartridge.

Bullets began to fly thick across the deck of the Amente el Diablo, but most of the crew found some sort of cover to keep them from being hit as the pirates strafed the ship with wild and undisciplined fire that sent bullets ricocheting from iron fittings, chewing up the deck, and even putting a hole through Captain Gutteriez's hat. The Captain ducked low behind the wheel and returned a pair of shots into the crew of pirates on the deck of the schooner, dropping at least one of the the motley horde. The first mate,

Nemesio, fired a couple of shots that went low, splintering the strakes of the schooner. Crow took a pirate through the throat with a bullet from his Belgian rifle and he loaded a fresh round as the bowsprit of the schooner pulled up alongside of the Amente El Diablo.

The hollow-cheeked pirate pushed back his great sombrero so that it rested on his back, still tied about his neck, and then leaped from the bowsprit, which still dangled with the body of his compatriot in crime. Grappling hooks snaked out from the schooner and caught on the rails of the Amente el Diablo, and the ships were drawn together. Then the pirates came swarming over, howling and cursing, and thirsty for blood.

Chapter 5: Ulutoth Arises

The butt of Crow's peacemaker was ivory, carved with an eagle—the symbol of freedom. It had been a gift from the famous Mexican pistolero Isidro Acevedo after they had fought against each other and then side by side against the ghouls that rose from the crypts one steamy night in New Orleans long ago. On another night, when the dead rose from the salty wastes in the Utah deserts, that same pistol had been blessed by a prophet of God, so that its bullets would pierce the flesh of fiends and beasts, be they from hell or the outer dimensions. The pistol held no special power against mankind, other than the alchemy of gunpowder and lead, which was a sorcery wielded by gunslingers and pistoleros at every corner of the habitable continents. So when Crow fired the loaded cartridge from his Belgian Rifle and killed a pirate that rampaged down the deck toward him, axe raised, he set aside the rifle and his pistol leaped into his hand nearly as quickly as Six-Gun Susannah Johnson could draw hers.

Johnson finished loading the last of her three pistols. "They take so long to load, but only seconds to shoot."

"Take your time firing," advised Crow as he stooped and retrieved the axe from the still-trembling fingers of the pirate he had shot. In his youth he had been trained in the use of the tomahawk, and though this was a poor substitute, it would do. "There are plenty of targets. Make your bullets count."

"Don't you worry about that, Crow." Her answer was flippant, but as they walked side by side, she chose her targets with deliberate care—not firing wildly, as she was prone to do. As a result, there was less shock and awe to her presence, but she killed or felled a pirate with nearly every one of her first six shots. Crow did the same, but then the thick of the battle swirled upon them and Susannah drew out both her remaining pistols and began firing with abandon at every pirate target within sight. There was no opportunity for Crow to reload his pistol, so he shoved it back into its holster and hewed about himself with the axe, laying bone bare, hewing through skull, and cleaving faces to the teeth. It was unclear whether he or Six-Gun Susannah Johnson was the most savage of the Amente el Diablo's defenders, but they fought with such fury that even the bloodthirsty pirates gave way, falling back from the two of them.

Johnson shoved her last pistol back into the waist of her trousers and hissed as the hot barrel burned her skin. She snatched up a harpoon from the dying hands of a marinero and made a menacing thrust toward the nearest pirate, who scrambled backward to avoid the already bloodied point. Crow snapped the axe to a halt and sent blood spattering from its edge.

The captain was still alive, reloading his pistol with shaking fingers while his first mate, dying at his feet, clutched at the spokes of the helm's wheel.

"You two are devils," spat Captain Gutteriez. "You brought doom upon my ship the moment you set foot upon the deck!"

Johnson frowned, her eyes still fixed upon the pirates who were milling upon the perimeter of the deck, deciding their next move. "What are you talking about, Captain?"

The Captain loaded another round. "You chased away the pistoleros that I hired and took their place and you brought something evil aboard. I didn't feel it at first, but as we sailed farther out to sea I could feel it more and more, weighing me down. I should have hurled you both into the ocean the moment I first laid eyes upon the two of you!"

Johnson's lips formed a hot retort. "If it wasn't for me and Crow those pirates would already have your ship and your guts would be spilled on the deck. Don't blame these pirates on me and Crow. We're saving your worthless hide!"

The hollow-eyed pirate with the sombero slung across his back began whipping his pirates into a fervor, urging them to make a concerted rush to overtake the last few defenders of the ship. "Kill the Indian, the woman and the captain, and the spine of the marineros will melt like butter in the sun. They will surrender the ship and its cargo to us and we'll live like kings!"

Crow figured that the pirate's estimation was accurate enough. The marineros were ready to surrender or to throw themselves into the raging seas. However, the pirates had lost many men and he figured they were just as close to abandoning their designs upon the Amente el Diablo as the marineros were to surrendering to the pirates. They just needed a little more incentive to make the right decision. He cocked back his arm and snapped it forward, letting the axe fly from his hand. The blade struck the sombrero-wearing pirate in the center of the forehead, and he lurched backward in a crimson fog of his own blood.

The pirates moaned and howled, and they began to flee the deck of the Amente el Diablo for that of their own schooner. To urge them to greater speed, Johnson sprinted forward and thrust a harpoon into the backside of one of the pirates, who slipped from his perch on the railing and fell between the ships, taking the harpoon with him. He might have had difficulty sitting down for the rest of his life, but it was mercifully short, for the storm waves pushed the hulls of the two ships together, grinding him between.

Crow drew his Bowie knife and began cutting the grappling lines so the two ships could part ways. One pirate couldn't resist the temptation to swing a gaffing hook at him, and Crow sent him reeling away minus one hand. Then the wind and waves sent the two ships spinning away from each other. Immediately, Crow and Johnson fell to reloading their pistols, just in case the pirate ship should return or in case there were a few healthy and hearty pirates still hidden aboard the Amente el Diablo. The marineros sent up a cheer to the heavens when they saw the pirate schooner being carried away by the storm winds, but their joy was short-lived for they had many wounded and dead among them.

Captain Gutteriez ordered a pair of men to begin dumping the bodies of the pirates overboard, and this they did, whether the pirates were dead or whether they still lived. It didn't take long for the sharks to smell the blood in the water, and soon their fins cut the stormy surface, and they devoured the dead and the still living, alike. As Johnson and Crow finished a sweep of the ship looking for any hiding pirates, and finding only a dying Portuguese marauder with a bullet in his lung, Crow's head began to throb and he leaned against the rail.

Johnson put a hand upon his shoulder. "Not feeling too chipper?"

At first, Crow chalked it up to the adrenaline and exertions of battle, but gradually the throbbing drumbeat became a voice that redounded in his consciousness. "Ulutoth ascends. Ulutoth ascends. Ulutoth ascends."

Crow gripped his raven hair and felt as though he should tear it out by the roots, if only it would end the voice in his head. "It's wormed its way into my mind," he gasped. "Something is coming!"

"What's coming, Crow?"

"Ulutoth. Ulutoth is coming, and he won't get out of my head!" Crow went down to his knee, the intruding voice in his head drowning out all his other thoughts.

Johnson knelt down beside him. "What can I do, Crow? What can I do?"

"Pray," choked out Crow, who felt as helpless as a kitten in the mouth of the wolf. "Pray, to drive out the voices!"

The only time, since her youth, that Susannah Johnson had prayed was fire side over their meals, when she and Crow had traveled together, so the words didn't come easily to her, but Crow's tongue was bound up by the pain and the insanity of the fiendish presence in his mind, and so he could not be the one to voice the plaintive cries to the heavens. "Our Father which art in heaven," began Johnson, "hallowed be thy name. Please release Crow from the grip of whatever it is that fevers his mind. He's my only friend and I need him here. And please forgive us for all the blood we shed. We only did it in defense of good people. In Jesus name. Amen."

The prayer said, Crow felt strength flow through his limbs, and though the voice of Ulutoth still echoed in his brain, it was diminished just enough so that he could struggle to his feet. As he did this, he looked out upon the rain-pocked swells, and saw the waters displace and move in a heaving motion, such as the way the ocean moved when a whale was about to surface, but this thing was far larger than a whale… or even twenty whales. Crow and Johnson gaped as the sea opened up wide beneath the fleeing pirate schooner, and a titanic beak encrusted with barnacles and draped with seaweed emerged, catching the hull of the pirate ship. Great spiked tentacles lashed the already stormy surface of the sea, whipping it to a frothing frenzy. Peculiar polyps, which blossomed with flagellated petals, pushed through the waves and stood erect, undulating and rotating as if listening or moving like speaking lips, and emitting shrill sounds that were not meant to be heard by the human ear, but rather transmitted to some sixth sense.

The crew of the Amente el Diablo heard this mind-blasting shriek and they went to their knees, clutching their skulls in agony. Captain Gutteriez staggered toward the rail, his eyes glazed, and clutching his pistol, but unable to use it against the unfathomable thing that had appeared from the ocean's depths.

Chapter 6: Hooves and Guaro

Crow had seen mind-wrenching things before, but nothing of this magnitude. Still, to Crow, the horror of the unknown, and the months of mind-bending torture had been worse, but now that the entity which had been speaking to him through the Eye of Ulutoth had revealed itself, it was almost a relief. Here was the thing that had been haunting his dreams, coloring his world gray, poisoning his mind, and pulling him into a morass of self-loathing and despair. Still, now that it was here, how was he going to fight it?

As if to demonstrate the utter futility of the task before him, the great beak clenched, cracking open the hull of the schooner as if it were the shell of a nut, and the rough seas poured in, even as pirates fell shrieking from the shattered plankings. Some fell directly into the maw and down the gullet of Ulutoth and others thrashed about in the sea until they were impaled by the spiked tentacles and then drawn toward the beak, where they were shaken loose and dropped into the waiting mouth.

Johnson's eyes went wide and her jaw dropped. "What is that thing and where did it come from?"

"I think it's Ulutoth," said Crow. "And I think I played right into its hands."

"Or tentacles," observed Johnson. "What do you mean?"

"I mean, it played on my desire to get rid of the Eye of Ulutoth—to put it out of the reach of bad men who would use it for evil purposes."

For a moment, Johnson observed the horrific creature as it chewed up the debris of the pirate ship, snapping the main sail into three sections and devouring the sail and the pirates who still clung desperately to the rigging. "You did the right thing, Crow. That Eye is something that should never have existed upon this earth."

"I did the right thing, but I did it at the wrong place," said Crow. "Ulutoth has been here dormant for aeons, lying at the bottom of the Pacific Ocean. I thought I was successfully resisting the influence of the Eye of Ulutoth, but it turns out it wasn't my idea to drop the Eye into the trench at the bottom of the Pacific. I could have dropped it into the ocean anywhere in the world, but the Eye wanted me to bring it here, near to where Ulutoth lay buried—near enough so that when the Eye tasted blood it would awake Ulutoth, itself, instead of bringing forth other forces."

"But how could Ulutoth have arranged for me to shoot someone?"

"Ulutoth's influence is greater or more easily asserted over those who are dishonest or evil."

The wind gusted Susannah's tangled mane over her face, hiding her expression of displeasure. "What are you saying, Crow?"

"I'm saying that it didn't take much effort for the Eye to plant the suggestion in that one marinero's mind that there might be something worth stealing in my cabin. And it took just a little more effort to persuade him to pick up that pry bar and attack us."

Johnson pushed the hair back from her face, and now her scowl of displeasure was because of her own actions and not what she thought Crow might be suggesting. "And I did what I do best. I reacted—didn't think through the consequences."

Crow watched Ulutoth's beak destroy the rest of the schooner. "You couldn't have known."

"But you did," said Johnson, in a tone that suggested she was still chastising herself for her rash actions.

"Remember," said Crow, "I'm the one that got fooled into bringing the Eye out here in the first place."

This seemed to cheer up Johnson, and she laughed. "Hah! You did, at that!"

The captain took slow steps toward the edge of his ship, his eyes still blank and staring. Johnson turned around and slapped him hard across the face. "Captain! Get a grip on yourself, and order your men to stoke the engines. We need to put some distance between ourselves and this thing!"

Already, overwhelmed by the impossibility of such a creature existing, two of the marineros had gone stark, raving mad. Gibbering strange consonants and impossible combinations of vowels, they hurled themselves into warm seas and were sucked in by one of the multitude of whirlpools that had been caused by Ulutoth's rising. Captain Gutteriez, despite his somewhat ornery nature, was a good man and Johnson's slap brought some sense into his addled mind. He realized that if he didn't take some action, his ship and the entirety of his crew would be lost to this gargantuan monster. He went in among his crew, shaking them one by one and ordering them back to work. The minds of some of his marineros were irrevocably shattered by the appearance of Ulutoth and yet others had been broken by the alien clamor of sound and fury that unhinged their sanity. Some he was able to rouse from their soporific stupor, and once roused, it wasn't difficult to incite fear enough to urge them to the greatest of efforts in trying to get the Amente el Diablo moving away from the monstrosity which had destroyed the pirate's schooner.

Between the deaths and injuries caused by the pirates and those marineros who were struck deaf, dumb, or insane, the Amente el Diablo was manned by a skeleton crew now. Just a third of the crew was functioning, while others lay dying and yet more were gibbering strange visions which their shattered minds had revealed to them. Even the remaining marineros were on the verge of breaking, throwing down their coal shovels, and fleeing. It was only by Captain Gutteriez's constant encouragement that the furnaces remained stoked and that the Amente el Diablo had enough steam to push through the high seas and tear itself out of the grasp of the swirling whirpools which threatened to drag down and subsume the freighter.

Lightning forked through the storm-lashed sky, followed by a boom which thundered across the waters. The Amente el Diablo was putting some distance between itself and Ulutoth, but Crow knew that this was only because the creature was thoroughly engrossed in disposing of the pirate schooner and its crew. Crow feared that once that task was finished Ulutoth would not yet be satiated—if it could ever truly be satiated—and would turn its unwelcome attentions to the Amente el Diablo. He sincerely doubted that the steam ship would be capable of outrunning Ulutoth, at even double its top speed.

Johnson leaned on the rail, heedless of the elements which beat against her, and unable to tear her eyes away from the ghastly thing that was so large its slightest movement stirred the surface of the Pacific ocean. "What does that thing want?"

Still, Crow could hear the weird ululations of the beast echoing in his mind. "It hungers. It has no other aim but to destroy and to devour."

They were far enough away now that Crow began to have a sliver of hope that perhaps Ulutoth might leave them unmolested, but this faint suggestion of hope was quickly dashed as Ulutoth finished its repast of the pirate ship and the seas began to churn as its spiked tentacles and gelatinous bulk began to undulate in concert, pushing Ulutoth in the direction of the fleeing Amente el Diablo.

Johnson snatched up Crow's Tersen rifle. "It's coming for us."

Crow didn't say anything as Johnson plucked a round from his bandolier and loaded the rifle. She aimed as Ulutoth drew nearer and, when she fired, her aim was true and struck a portion of its bulk as it surged above the waters. The bullet, however, seemed to have no effect whatsoever on the monstrous fiend and it continued to move through the ocean swells, the great ears on its polyps moving and rotating.

"Nothing," said Johnson. "It didn't even notice. What about your blessed pistol?"

"The range is too far," said Crow.

Johnson fished another rifle round out of Crow's bandolier. "Do you have any of that consecrated oil left?"

"Not much," said Crow, but he understood what Johnson was getting at and handed her the vial of consecrated oil.

She carefully shook one drop out to the edge of the vial and then dipped the tip of the cartridge in it, before loading the rifle. Johnson aimed and fired and this time the bullet tipped with consecrated oil took the ear off a polyp. Immediately a wave of dark psychic energy rolled across them, the shrieking ululations driving Johnson back from the rail so that she fell to the ground.

Crow went down to one knee. "You hurt it, Susannah." He could see how fast Ulutoth was gaining upon the steamship, the seas mounting up before it, so quickly it came. "Hand me one of your pistols."

Johnson handed Crow her pistol. He popped open the cylinder and, holding the already loaded cartridges in place with his palm, carefully dripped a trace of the consecrated oil on the tip of each of them. Once this was completed he snapped the cylinder shut and handed the pistol back to Johnson. "Make these count. That's the last of my oil."

"Can you get more?"

"I can consecrate more if I find some olive oil."

"Good luck finding any aboard the Amente el Diablo," muttered

Johnson, and she gratefully accepted the pistol.

The steamship heaved and rolled as the waves threatened to capsize her. Captain Gutteriez lashed himself to the wheel and he turned to see the monstrous spottled bulk of Ulutoth rising up behind his ship, spiked tentacles thrashing the air, and its titanic beak snapping. The grotesque and alien sight of the sentient polyps that were attached to such a creature were enough to ruin the mind of most men, but Gutteriez was determined to die valiantly. He emptied his pistol into the great bulk of the towering fiend, but his bullets were simply absorbed into the gelatinous flesh of Ulutoth's corporeal form.

A tentacle snaked out and crushed Captain Gutteriez, pinning his pulped form beneath, and shattering the planks of the decking. Simultaneously, Crow and Johnson began firing—Crow his blessed eagle-butted Peacemaker and Johnson the pistol that contained bullets that were annointed with consecrated oil. These bullets tore into Ulutoth's gelatinous flesh, but were not so easily absorbed as were Captain Gutteriez's bullets. Again, Ulutoth psychically shrieked, and the breath was driven out of Crow's and Johnson's lungs. Ulutoth's tentacles flailed crazily now, knocking off pieces of ship and unlucky marineros. Ulutoth was hurt badly enough that its attacks were no longer aimed or directed, but just random thrashing prompted by searing pain.

Susannah Johnson raised herself up on one elbow, still gasping. "We hurt it bad, Crow."

Crow pulled himself up and put his back to the wall of the cabin. He dumped the empty brass of his revolver upon the deck and began reloading with .45 rounds. Yes, they had hurt Ulutoth, but had they hurt him enough? It didn't seem that Ulutoth had any parts that were particularly vulnerable or that would cause incapacitation if hit. A spiked tentacle caved in the wall over his head, but instead of striking out with his Bowie knife, Crow chose to finish loading his pistol. Thus far, only his blessed Peacemaker and bullets painted with consecrated oil had proven to have any effect upon the monstrosity.

Now, the bulk of Ulutoth's body was hidden again beneath the waves, though tentacles rose above the water in half a hundred different spots, as well as the sensory polyps which waggled and waved as it took in psychic, auditory and visual signals. Crow figured that if he could destroy each of these he might be able to effectively reduce Ulutoth to blindness, dumbness, and deafness, but there were far too many to maim with the six bullets in his revolver, and after his pistol was emptied, Crow didn't think that he would have the opportunity to reload again. He'd likely be dead.

"Susannah! Go grab your saddlebag full of guaro. It's still in my cabin."

"I've quit," shouted Johnson over the roar of the ocean. "Remember? Besides, it's hardly the time for a drink."

"It's precisely the time," said Crow. "But we're not going to be the ones drinking."

Johnson managed to find her footing on the heaving deck, and she stumbled toward the cabin. "Whatever you say, Crow. I'll be right back."

True to her word, Johnson was back in a few moments, dragging the heavy saddlebag of guaro bottles along with her. While she was gone, Crow kept busy by tearing strips of clothing from the dead. He uncorked the first bottle and began shoving one of these strips inside. "Do the same with every bottle."

The sea shifted and swirled, violently rocking the Amente el Diablo, while Crow and Johnson prepared each bottle of the high-powered Costa Rican liqueur with a wick soaked in guaro. While Johnson finished the last of the bottles, Crow struck a match and began to light the wicks one by one. One of the lit bottles tipped over and went rolling over the side, splitting open on Ulutoth's great beak as it opened up to swallow the Amente el Diablo. Flame spilled down the chitin of the beak, and then Crow and Johnson began hurling the flaming bottles of guaro into the gaping maw of the creature. They disappeared down Ulutoth's dark gullet, some breaking open so that flashes of flame were visible, but the sea poured in, quickly extinguishing the flames.

Johnson grabbed the rail of the tilting steamship, feeling a tinge of regret at the waste of all that good guaro. "I don't think it even noticed that."

Crow's dark hair flailed about his shoulders as he reached for his pistol.

"I guess that it was too much to hope for, that a creature that could stand the cold and pressure at the bottom of the sea might be effected by a little flame."

"It's about to get a belly full of it anyhow," pointed out Johnson. "The boiler of this ship ought to give it a little indigestion."

"Not if I can help it." Crow climbed the tilting rail, with his eagle-butted Peacemaker firmly gripped in his right hand, and the salty wind whipping his buckskin jacket. "This gun's all we've got left that can cause it pain. Maybe I can dissuade it from swallowing the ship."

Immediately, Johnson could see that Crow intended to leap into the great beak and fire his gun into Ulutoth's guts—from the inside. She heard the clip of hooves coming up from the hold and realized that her horse had managed to chew loose from her tether. "Crow. You do know that I love you, right?"

Crow paused in his precarious position, perched at the top of the rail. "I know it. It's just that…"

"It's just that I've got a few bad habits that don't make me good marriage material," finished Johnson. "I know that, Crow, but you should know I'm willing to give up more than just drinking and gambling for you."

Crow coiled his legs beneath him, preparing to leap. "Maybe we'll get another chance in the next life."

Six-Gun Susannah Johnson gave a shrill whistle and her horse came running across the deck. Crow was distracted by Molly for just the smallest of moments and then he leaped, but in that moment of distraction Johnson reached out and grabbed the tail of Crow's buckskin jacket, pulling hard so that Crow not only failed to complete his leap, but his head clipped the rail of the ship, and he came tumbling down on the deck, stunned and bleeding.

Johnson leaned over Crow and kissed him on the lips, even while she pried loose his blessed Peacemaker. "Love you, Crow. See you in that resurrection that you're always talking about—and take good care of Molly for me." She ran up the side of the rail and with a rebel yell she leaped out over the gaping beak of Ulutoth, and not until she was deep in its gullet did she begin to fire Crow's peacemaker, the holy bullets burning tunnels through the guts of the monstrosity. The holy bullets pained Ulutoth far more than the frigid depths of sea or the chill outer voids of damned dimensions, or even the gouting flames of the dying suns on the outer rim of the decaying universe, and it gave out a shriek which froze the marrow of all aboard the Amente el Diablo, and slew thousands of fish that swam in the Pacific Ocean, so that they turned belly up and floated to the rain-pocked surface.

Severely wounded, the fiendish monstrosity known as Ulutoth which had breached the earthly plane from distant dimensions, rolled over in the ocean and slowly sank, Six-Gun Susannah Johnson digesting in his belly, retreating into the caliginous depths of the Pacific Trench, where no light of the sun could penetrate, and where it could lie dormant for centuries more, healing and dreaming, exerting its poisonous influence over the people of the earth, until that distant day when once again it would be summoned forth to reap a harvest of blood and destruction.

Receive a free ebook of your choice! Sign up for Joel Jenkins' newsletter at JoelJenkins.net and receive occasional emails with information about his latest books and bargains. Also, choose a free Kindle book or ebook!

About Joel Jenkins:

Joel Jenkins lives in the heron-haunted shadows of the Rainier Mountains, and finds the perpetual twilight conducive to writing. He is the former front-man for several obscure rock bands and once impersonated a ghost.

Books from Pulpwork Press Authors:

<u>Joel Jenkins</u>

Dire Planet Series:
Dire Planet
Exiles of the Dire Planet
Into the Dire Planet
Strange Gods of the Dire Planet
Lost Tribes of the Dire Planet

Tales from the City of Bathos Series:
Escape from Devil's Head
Through the Groaning Earth

The Gantlet Brother Series:
The Nuclear Suitcase
The Gantlet Brothers Greatest Hits
The Gantlet Brothers: Sold Out

Damage Incorporated Series:
The Sea Witch
The Sun Stealer

Denbrook Supernatural:
Devil Take the Hindmost

Children's Books:
The Pirates of Mirror Land

Arthurian Fantasy:
Island of Lost Souls

Collections:
Weird Worlds of Joel Jenkins
Weird Worlds of Joel Jenkins 2

Biography:
One Foot in My Grave

The Greattrix Chronicles:
Skull Crusher

Lone Crow:
The Coming of Crow

Barclay Salvage
Off Season
One for the Dark and Shadowed Sky

Derrick Ferguson
Dillon Series:
Dillon and the Golden Bell
Four Bullets for Dillon
Dillon and the Pirates of Xonira
Dillon and the Voice of Odin
Young Dillon in the Halls of Shamballah
The Vril Agenda (with Josh Reynolds)

Joshua Reynolds
Dracula Lives!
The Vril Agenda (with Derrick Ferguson)

Russell Anderson, Jr
How the West was Weird
How the West was Weird 2
How the West was Weird 3
How the West was Weird: Campfire Tales
Myth World

Coming in 2015
The Specialists (Sly Gantlet & Dillon) by Joel Jenkins & Derrick Ferguson

For more information on these and other titles or for online ordering visit us at PulpWork.Com or find our titles at Amazon, and BarnesandNoble. com

Printed in Great Britain
by Amazon